TALKING TO GHOSTS

Hervé Le Corre

TALKING TO GHOSTS

Translated from the French by
Frank Wynne

MACLEHOSE PRESS
QUERCUS · LONDON

First published in the French language as *Les Coeurs déchiquetés*
by Éditions Payot & Rivages, Paris, 2009

First published in Great Britain in 2014 by

MacLehose Press
an imprint of Quercus
55 Baker Street
7th Floor, South Block
London W1U 8EW

This book is supported by the Institut français (Royaume-Uni)
as part of the Burgess programme

A CIP catalogue record for this book is available
from the British Library.

ISBN (HB) 978 0 85705 206 3
ISBN (TPB) 978 0 85705 207 0
ISBN (Ebook) 978 1 78087 304 6

10   9   8   7   6   5   4   3   2   1

Designed and typeset in 11/15pt Minion by Jouve (UK), Milton Keynes
Printed and bound in Great Britain by Clays Ltd, St Ives plc

TRANSLATOR'S NOTE

The judicial system in France is fundamentally different to that in the United Kingdom and the U.S.A. Rather than the adversarial system, where police investigate, and the role of the courts is to act as an impartial referee between prosecution and defence, in the French inquisitorial system the judiciary work with the police on the investigation, appointing an independent *juge d'instruction* entitled to question witnesses, interrogate suspects, and oversee the police investigation, gathering evidence, whether incriminating or otherwise. If there is sufficient evidence, the case is referred to the *procureur* – the public prosecutor who decides whether to bring charges. The *juge d'instruction* plays no role in the eventual trial and is prohibited from adjudicating future cases involving the same defendant.

The French have two national police forces: the *police nationale* (formerly called the *Sûreté*), a civilian police force with jurisdiction in cities and large urban areas, and the *gendarmerie nationale,* a branch of the French Armed Forces, responsible both for public safety and for policing the towns with populations of less than 20,000. Since the *gendarmerie* rarely has the resources to conduct complex investigations, the *police nationale* maintains regional criminal investigations services (*police judiciaire*) analogous to the British C.I.D.; they also oversee armed response units (*R.A.I.D.*).

GLOSSARY

Brigade anti-criminalité – equivalent to the U.K. Homicide and Serious Crime Squad, the *brigade* handles murders, kidnappings and assassinations.

Brigade des mineurs – the police department dealing with young offenders and young victims of crime.

Brigadier – the rank in the *gendarmerie* equivalent to Sergeant.

Commandant – the rank equivalent to Detective Chief Inspector (U.K.).

Commissaire divisionnaire – the rank equivalent to Chief Superintendent (U.K.)/Police Chief (U.S.), though comprising both an administrative and an investigative role.

C.R.S. (*Compagnie républicaine de sécurité*) – the French riot police infamous for their uncompromising methods.

D.D.A.S.S. (*Direction départementale des affaires sanitaires et sociales*) – the equivalent of the U.K. Department for Work and Pensions.

D.S.T. (*Direction de la surveillance du territoire*) – the French equivalent of the old UK Border Agency, or of the Department of Homeland Security in the U.S.A.

G.I.G.N. (*Groupe d'intervention de la Gendarmerie nationale*) – a special operations unit of the French Armed Forces, which forms part of the *gendarmerie nationale*, and is trained to perform counter-terrorist and hostage-rescue missions in France.

Identité judiciare – the forensics department of the *police nationale*.

Juge d'instruction – the rank of "investigating judge", a role somewhat similar to that of an American District Attorney. He or she is addressed as *monsieur* or *madame le juge*.

Maréchal des logis chef – the rank in the *gendarmerie* roughly equivalent to that of Staff Sergeant.

Procureur – the title comparable to Crown Prosecutor in the U.K. He or she is addressed as *magistrat*.

R.A.I.D. (*Recherche, Assistance, Intervention, Dissuasion*) – the special operations tactical unit of the *police nationale*.

R.G. (*Direction centrale des renseignements généraux*) – the French Intelligence Service.

S.A.M.U. (*Service d'aide medicale urgente*) – the French ambulance service.

The ravaged hearts that talk to ghosts
Leo Ferré

But I have wept too much, it's true! The Dawns are heart-rending.
Every moon appals and every sun is bitter:
Acrid love has swelled me with heady torpors.
Let my keel split! Let me founder in the sea!
Arthur Rimbaud, "The Drunken Boat"

Often in the morning at about 11.15 he would park his car near the school, on the far side of the street, since from there he had a better view of the deserted playground with its chestnut trees and the classroom windows on the first floor. He could make out brightly coloured cut-out figures stuck to the windows, Christmas trees, animals and little men. Sometimes he would catch a glimpse of the teacher, or a child's hand going up, and then his heart would pound, he would feel a dry bitterness in his throat, he would swallow hard and force himself to blink, his eyelids stinging from staring for so long.

The first floor had four classrooms, but it was in the one with the fantastical menagerie galloping across its windows that Pablo had sat. Third desk, middle row, in the CM1 classroom. It was a nice room, its walls papered with children's drawings, modern art posters, maps and photographs from all over the world, forming a sort of encyclopaedic fresco around the children.

One of Pablo's drawings was pinned up on the back wall. He had seen it when he came into the classroom, afterwards. Pablo was always drawing. People said he was gifted. Painted on a square sheet of paper a metre across, you could easily see that it was a safari scene with lions, elephants, giraffes and antelopes . . . Two 4 x 4s were hurtling through the yellow grass in the middle of the painting; a huge blue rhinoceros was overturning a third vehicle with its horn, tossing its occupants into the air, spreadeagled like little frogs. He had immediately gone closer to appreciate the details, and couldn't help smiling because the boy had given each of the hunters a particular expression – happy, terrified or gormless – and drawn beautiful eyes for the animals, some gentle, some savage.

He had smiled, then turned around to dry his eyes and stifle the sobs racking his chest. The following day the teacher had come to his house and handed him the drawing, rolled up like a parchment and tied with a red ribbon. He and Ana had managed to smile that evening as they pored over the painting spread out on the coffee table in the sitting room. They had run their fingers gently over the colours their son had painted, sometimes with bold, determined brushstrokes, sometimes with painstaking care to capture a zebra's stripes, for example, or give a hunter a strange hat with a blue feather. Afterwards they had fallen asleep on the sofa, exhausted by tears and helpless attempts to comfort each other. Waking in the dead of night, they had slipped into bed but been unable to get back to sleep, both isolated by exhaustion.

At 11.30 the gates would open, and the children who didn't take lunch in the canteen would start to trickle out. Parents would be waiting for them, mothers mostly, some of whom took charge of a whole brood of kids and slowly walked away surrounded by skipping or whining midgets. There were some men waiting, too, for the most part those practising the art of being a grandfather. Frozen, his hands clamped to the steering wheel, the man in the car would watch all this. Lying next to him on the passenger seat, hidden beneath a navy blue cloth, he had placed a 9mm pistol with a 15-round magazine, the first round already engaged in the barrel.

He kept a keen eye on the children who were unaccompanied by an adult as they walked away from the school. In his mind he urged them to hurry up, to run home while he studied the passers-by – there were few – and the cars that had to slow for the speed bump. He was tense, ready to jump from his own car, weapon in hand, and press the muzzle to the forehead of any guy he saw acting suspiciously around one of the kids, or to open fire on any car that stopped next to a child.

And then, when nothing happened, he drove off again, baffled with rage and grief, and headed back to work where he forced himself to deal with the violence of others which was everywhere, engulfing him, terrifying him, seeping unstoppably into his mind and pooling in the innermost recesses of his brain, adding to his inconsolable grief; nothing, it seemed, could staunch the flow of calls to the switchboard and the station, or all the screams, the blood, the contusions and the deaths those calls announced, all this endless misery, and it seemed to him that he could smell the rank sweat of a grubby, sick society the moment he set foot in the brand-new police station that backed on to the Chartreuse cemetery, a pompous white fortress where dark destinies were played out, tragedies enacted without footlights or curtain. It did not stick in his throat like the prison smell of men and burnt fat, no, it was more subtle, more insidious, filling his head until it nearly split.

The man's name was Pierre Vilar. His son Pablo didn't like having lunch in the canteen so as soon as he and Ana had decided that he was old enough – being almost ten – safely to walk the 400 metres from school to the house, they'd given in to him. A neighbour, Madame Lucien, looked after him and made his lunch. Pablo loved Madame Lucien and probably loved her boxer dog, Billy, even more. She would often go and fetch Pablo, when it rained, for instance. Sometimes Vilar or Ana would arrange to pick him up. It was seldom that the boy had to make the journey alone.

On 20 March 2000, a Tuesday, Vilar had been supposed to collect him, but he had been held up at the station and then there had been the accident on the boulevard: a fender-bender, one person slightly injured, he'd found out later, the sort of traffic jam you've forgotten about come evening. Vilar had pulled up outside the school at 11.38.

When he rang the doorbell at Madame Lucien's and saw her face grow pale and her eyes widen with the question that exploded in her head at the same instant as in his – "Pablo's not with you?" – he started to run towards the school following the same route he had taught Pablo twenty times over, but he did not find him in the street or at the school where there was a remote chance he could have been kept back for some minor misdemeanour or injury. He was clutching at straws, really, so as not to sink into panic, but even then he realised, he knew, in spite of the investigation that was immediately launched, an investigation that went on all day, went on for days, for weeks, without turning up anything despite the huge resources and dedication the police put into the search for a fellow officer's son. He knew. But because people may know something and still not believe it, it felt as though the ground opened up beneath his feet that day, a yawning chasm that threatened to swallow him, and he was standing on a bridge of ice above it, sometimes drawn to the abyss.

Pablo had vanished on the corner of a street where a car had turned, a car with metallic paint, grey maybe, or green, or sky-blue, a Peugeot, or maybe a Citroën, driven by a man – on this last point the four witnesses agreed.

After that, Pierre and Ana forgot what it meant to sleep, to eat, to smile, to love each other. At night they collapsed onto the mattress and sank into a mindless stupor from which they awoke exhausted and with aching heads. They shovelled food into their stomachs and digested it. Their faces became cardboard masks, animated by involuntary, polite, expected expressions, and then gradually etched with deep wrinkles like shifting fault lines.

They no longer thought to look at each other, to whisper pointless tender words, to reassure each other even though they did not believe in reassurance, to lie to themselves just for the pleasure of tasting the lie's illusory flavour, delicious and deceptive like the taste of an acid drop, merely so they could stay upright a little longer. They no longer touched, no longer knew the taste of each other's tears on their faces, forgot to hug each other to stifle their sobs and calm them.

They could not find each other, because Pablo had not been found.

Vilar got into the habit of going back to the school, as soon as he could, in the irrational hope of surprising the kidnapper, of seeing him, seeing his face appear on the street or in a car. He will come. He will be there, hunched in his car seat, and when the kids come out he will start the car and he will waylay one of them. He will do it again. And I will be there.

He knew this vision was lunatic, it was madness. It was his job to know. He knew how much his obsession was damaging him too, felt himself cracking a little more every time, felt his strength being sapped. But on the rare occasions when he found the willpower to give up his stake-out he felt a deep, all-pervading, exhausting pain, an aching absence that overwhelmed him, a pain he sometimes wanted to dig out of his body with a knife. He tried to talk about it to those around him, but he saw that he frightened people, saw them back away too, from this contagious evil that might rouse the fears coiled in the back of their minds like hibernating snakes.

Two years later, during a difficult arrest, he opened fire on a suspect. The bullet lodged between two vertebrae. It was successfully removed, and the victim benefited by having his case dismissed and being awarded six months in a nursing home. The internal investigation proved beyond doubt that the shooting was not justified by any mitigating circumstance, by imminent threat or legitimate self-defence. The policeman's nerve had probably failed him. Vilar admitted that the guy, a stocky thug with a long rap sheet who was known always to carry a weapon and shoot at the first sign of trouble, and was suspected of having gunned down two security guards and a policeman, wasn't worth the bullet he'd taken. The policeman's grave error was solemnly condemned but the inquiry was unwilling to punish him further, given the tragedy he had lived through, was living through still, if he could be said to be living. He was compulsorily referred to a psychiatrist, but after several sessions the two men acknowledged that nothing could be said or done that would make it possible for him to accept the unacceptable, to ease this bereavement without there being found a body. They parted courteously, each thanking the other for what little they had learned.

Vilar swore to himself that he would never again carry a gun on duty, in spite of the regulations.

Except when he came to park outside Pablo's school and stalk shadows.

1

Victor plunged into the darkness of the shuttered house, struggling to close the door behind him as though repelling some intruder trying to force his way across the overheated threshold. When he had finally managed to shut out the blinding sunlight, he sighed with relief. He slipped off his little red rucksack, the straps pulling at the neck of his T-shirt, baring a thin, tanned shoulder that he quickly covered up again. Without bending to untie the laces, he kicked off his trainers and smelled his bare, sweating feet. The cold tiles made his toes curl. He walked gingerly, leaving a trail of damp footprints that instantly faded, heading for the kitchen which reeked of stale tobacco smoke and bleach. Dust swirled in two shafts of sunlight streaming through the venetian blinds. He trailed his hand through the warm gold dust, sowing silent, microscopic confusion. In the fridge he found a can of cold cola and opened it, closing his eyes at the hiss of carbon dioxide, drinking in long gulps, leaning back against a cupboard, then screwing his face up and burping suddenly. He stepped back into the hall which ran the length of the house connecting the two small gardens. He noticed that the door to his mother's room was ajar. That meant she was alone, and he called out to her as he approached.

His dull, muffled voice met with a smothering silence that absorbed it like water. She must be asleep. She often took a nap in the heat of the day when she was at home. He pushed open the door and at first could see nothing in the dim light that came through the closed shutters. He could smell nothing but a musky odour of sweat mingled with lily of

7

the valley perfume. He saw the rumpled bed, the sheets and blankets piled on the mattress. He saw the torn curtain hanging by just two or three rings from the rod. He saw the panties on the floor, the small television upended.

And, sticking out from the other side of the bed, his mother's bare feet. He felt a stabbing pain and something inside him shrivelled and ran dry instead of bleeding out. It was not his heart or his brain, but something deep and vital, some secret life force unknown to science. He took another step and saw her lying on her back, completely naked, one arm lying across her stomach, a silver ring glittering on the slim fingers that rested on the curve of her hip. He called to her again softly, but she did not answer, and he moved closer the better to see her now that his eyes had adjusted to the darkness.

He knelt down.

Her face had a blueish tinge, the whole right-hand side swollen from temple to jawbone. Her cheek was cut and puffy, one eye swollen shut and almost black. Her brow bone had been shattered, and the blood that had trickled down was drying on her jaw, around her ear, on her neck. Blood had clotted in her ear, hardening to form an ugly black scab. There was blood on the pillowcase and on the sheets. Her lips were swollen and slashed and hung open to reveal her tongue poking through shattered teeth.

Victor searched in this ruined visage for his mother's face, but he recognised only her left eye, the long curling lashes, the pupil cloudy and unmoving, staring but now sightless.

He could barely bring himself to look at her body, which was a constellation of bruises. On her breasts, on her ribs. One leg was black from knee to groin.

He got to his feet again and stood there for a few seconds, hands clasped behind his neck. Now and then he could hear a car passing in the street, and the silence that followed was all the more devastating. He crouched down, grasped his mother's body under the armpits and lifted her, staggering back with the weight and bumping into the wall behind him. He stayed leaning against it to catch his breath and summoned all his strength. He adjusted his grip and the mutilated head lolled against his arm and in that moment he almost screamed, but gritted his teeth and shed silent tears as, step by step, he dragged the body to the bed, her heels scraping across the carpet with a dull rasp. He grunted and grimaced from the effort and from grief, then finally felt the edge of the mattress against his legs and collapsed onto it, the body falling on top of him, his dead mother's head between his thighs; he wriggled out, contorting himself so that he could pull the legs onto the bed, then, finally, got to his feet again and pulled her arms, managing to lay her out more or less naturally and prop a pillow under her head.

He tried to catch his breath, his heart pounding, sweat dripping from his chin, and took deep breaths, bent double, his hands on his legs, a trickle of snot hanging from his nose because every breath came out as a sob.

He stood up straight, wiped his mouth and chin with the back of his hand and drew a sheet over his mother who now looked as though she were asleep, then wiped the sweat from his neck, leaned over the body and stroked this mother's face; he pressed his fingertips to her eyelids but could not bring himself to close them because there was a fixedness in her stare that he could not comprehend, so he traced a finger over her battered lips, over her teeth, then, holding his breath, he gently kissed her forehead. He stepped back from the bed and stood for a moment, arms dangling by his sides in the middle of the room, listening to the buzzing of an invisible fly. Standing stock-still, his mouth open, he tried to take a deep breath, struggling to swell his scrawny chest.

A car passing outside made him start and shook him from his trance. He went and sat on the swivel stool in front of the dressing table, stared at the lifeless body, the glistening eyes, then turned to look in the mirror, hoping to see his mother's image come alive again. He stared at the dressing table, cluttered with women's things, perfumed and gleaming: brushes, bottles, tubes, expensive-looking packages, jewellery that glittered like gold. He pressed his palms to his cheeks,

9

pulled his eyelids downwards, distorting his face, in an effort to make it seem grotesque or monstrous. Gurning into the mirror, he seemed ageless. Already too old, or forever trapped in this day, imprisoned in this grim moment. He took the rings lying on the dressing table and slipped them on his fingers, stretching his hand out to admire the effect, but the half-light of the room dulled any sparkle so he took them off, having to tug at the ones that were too tight. Then he trailed his fingers over the pots of creams, the lipsticks, brought the soft make-up brushes to his face and the feeling – like small docile animals – made him shudder. He sat for a long time staring at this collection of beauty products, carefully, painstakingly going through the vanity cases and soundlessly replacing everything, spraying perfumes at the mirror which mingled in the sultry heat to form a mist of heady scents.

He opened drawers, rummaging in them at random, aimlessly taking out brushes, combs, tweezers, hair slides, a whole paraphernalia, then sat for several minutes absorbed in untangling the hair caught in them and winding it gently around his fingers, then unwinding it and trying to shake it off, but the auburn threads clung to his damp skin and for a moment he struggled in silence, almost breathless from the effort. Eventually he rubbed his hands vigorously and went on exploring the contents of the drawers. He unearthed a tube of tablets and made out the words "DO NOT EXCEED THE PRESCRIBED DOSE" in red letters, and slipped the tube into his pocket.

He spun around to face the empty darkness, almost falling off the stool as he did so. He stared at the body laid on the bed, lying tangled and bloody in the pale sheets. He got up and ran to the kitchen, filled a large glass with water, and in three goes gulped down the tablets in the tube, shaking his flushed face after each swallow. Then he closed the windows and shutters tight, shot home the bolts, ripped the phone out of the wall and, putting a pillow under his head, he lay on the floor next to the bed in the place where he had found her. He reached up, slid a hand under the sheet and clasped his mother's hand. He quickly drifted into unconsciousness, a sick feeling in the pit of his stomach, and did not feel the blowflies that landed on his skin, rubbing their front legs together and flying off again, heavy and buzzing, towards what really attracted them.

*

A face loomed over him, shining with sweat, eyes wide, the nose and mouth covered with a white mask. Someone slapped his cheeks, he heard voices, then saw the faces around him, all wearing masks, and imagined he was in hospital on an operating table. The voices were muffled, indistinct, and the faces of these people circled around, a languid merry-go-round with him floating at the centre, weightless and unreal. He closed his eyes again, but a blue dazzle played on his closed eyelids, a lightning flash that burned into his brain. A hoarse cry brought him round and he saw the sunlight spilling over the bright white ceiling, on which amorphous shadows danced.

The man was still bent over him, raising his eyelids to inspect the pupils. He shone the harsh beam of a tiny flashlight into his eyes. "He's coming round," a voice said. Victor tried to turn his head, but immediately felt a cold stiffness in his neck, and the merry-go-round of shadowy figures whirled before his eyes. He felt a blood-pressure cuff press against his skin, to be almost immediately removed again. He felt someone grab him under the armpits and watched as the room righted itself, everything suddenly stopped spinning, and the scene froze into a tableau, men peered down at him in pity or in shock, and he looked from face to face at their masks and their huge eyes all turned on him, seeming to hold him upright like invisible poles held out to a drowning man. He heard a voice whisper in his ear, asking if he was alright, if everything was alright, but he didn't know what to say because in that moment he was not sure he would ever again be able to speak to anyone, would ever be able to utter anything other than a groan or a wail. But the voice was insistent, and a face surged up from behind him, moving into his field of vision, and then he turned his head, or rather bowed it, and managed to shrug.

The memories flooded back just as the stench of decomposition reached his nerve endings, as one by one they reawakened, and he stumbled hesitantly towards the bed hidden behind three men in surgical masks, wearing latex rubber gloves and white overalls. He stumbled and had to stop, and felt hands at his sides ready to hold him upright. Bewildered he stared down at the tube from the drip attached to his arm, then walked one, two, three steps, seeming to defy the bustling officers who had not moved. Once more a brutal silence fell over the room, the only sounds were ragged breaths and coughs, and as a car passed in a deafening roar that streamed through the window half open against the heat of the day, the boy lurched forward and fell at the foot of the bed on which lay a woman he no longer recognised, her skin mottled and blue, her face swollen, her lips curled into a rictus of horror, as though aware of what she had become. He had fallen on his knees and now raised himself to the height of the mattress, staring directly between the slightly parted legs, leaning against the foot of the bed, and his stomach lurched uselessly, unable to vomit up this dread which would be forever lodged inside him like some bird of prey. The men pulled him back, advising him to come away, but he struggled, grabbing the sheets so tightly they had to prise his fingers open one by one and drag him from the room in a soft murmur of soothing words and reassurances until, as he reached the front doorstep bathed in sunlight, he passed out, scratching his arms on the climbing rose.

*

Everything was white. The ceiling, the walls. A woman in a white coat was staring at him, her hands in her pockets. She smiled and told him he had been asleep for two days, that he was much better now, then she asked if he needed anything. When he said nothing, she came over and sat on the bed, listened to his chest, tested his reflexes with a small round hammer. The boy simply lay there, watching her perform these tests, and his eyes betrayed nothing, they simply shimmered, wide-eyed, taking in everything that he covered up in unfathomable depths. The woman got to her feet and looked down at him for a few seconds, still smiling, until he turned away, looking out of the window where the tips of poplar trees glinted in the sun.

"There's someone who wants to talk to you. He's with the police. He wants to ask you some questions about what happened. Is that O.K.?"

Since he remained silent, the woman turned and signalled to someone to come in. A man stepped into the room and said hello, but the boy did not react. Victor looked him up and down, not daring to meet the policeman's curious or astonished gaze. He had dark hair and was wearing a black sweatshirt, a jacket and light trousers. He quickly settled himself in a heavy chrome and faux-leather chair that scraped the floor unpleasantly.

The boy ignored him, allowing his gaze to wander to a corner of the room, as though he were looking for dust.

"Victor? Can we talk for a bit? I'm Commandant Vilar. I'm here to find out who . . ."

He trailed off as the boy looked up at him, his eyes black and glistening, blinking more quickly now.

"Can we talk? Is that O.K.?"

The boy nodded, then started to rub the scratches on his arm from the rose bush, idly ripping off the tiny scabs with his fingernails.

At first the policeman said nothing: he simply looked at the boy who was studying him out of the corner of an eye. They could hear a muted hum of activity from the hospital, a creak of doors, muffled shouts, laughter too, sudden bursts of women's laughter that quickly died away into a grave chorus of deep voices. From his jacket pocket the man took a small notebook and a ballpoint that he clicked. Then, in a low, sometimes hesitant voice, he explained that he needed to find out more about his mother so that he could catch the person who had done this to her (this was how he put it, as though he were talking about a mugging, unable to bring himself to mention death, to mention the stench or the horror they had stumbled into two days before, choking back the urge to retch, swallowing their bile), maybe it was someone who knew her, someone the boy had met, or overheard, someone whose name might be familiar. He asked the boy to rack his brains, to go through every face, every name, anything the dead woman might have said, they really needed his help, he was their main witness, it was important that he make an effort, even if it wasn't easy. He repeated his questions, rephrased them, weighing them down with superfluous words and convoluted phrases, interwoven with unspoken warnings, coughs and conciliatory gestures. Victor watched the man's hands, like strange animals, puppets vainly waved about in order to distract him, but when at last the policeman fell silent, slightly out of breath, the boy said nothing, only let this invisible clock, humid and halting, mark out the time.

So the policeman reeled off the questions once more, in a low voice rephrasing them, leaning over the boy like a priest taking confession.

A quarter of an hour later the doctor came back, still smiling, and found herself mired in this oppressive rhythm of murmured questions that went unanswered, and that was more uncomfortable than if no-one had spoken at all. After a short while, in the same low voice, she suggested to the policeman that he stop the questioning now because the boy was tired. Reluctantly, Vilar got to his feet and said goodbye. He held out his hand to Victor and, lifting a skinny arm, the boy shook it, his hand as limp as a spray of withered flowers.

2

The body lay huddled at the foot of a wall, the head resting on an arm, as though asleep. It had fallen in front of a sex shop whose brash neon colours turned the faces all around into shifting, sickly masks. The dead man had his back to the police, to the onlookers, to the cars that passed, slowing in the glare of the strobing blue lights, to the pool of blood trickling across the sloping pavement into the gutter which reflected the seedy, squalid lighting. The body had not yet been covered and, under the jacket and the rucked up T-shirt, the pale skin of the man's lower back was visible. On the far side of the street passers-by hurrying towards the nearby train station lugging heavy bags and suitcases craned their heads, hoping for a glimpse of something in the scrum of police cars and the uniformed officers patrolling the crime scene.

Vilar pulled on a pair of latex gloves and crouched down in order to make out the man's features, examine the wounds and determine cause of death. He noted a shallow gash below the right ear a few millimetres wide, which had not bled significantly. Lifting away the front of the stained denim jacket, he could see only a black Johnny Hallyday T-shirt, slashed in three places across the chest and soaked in blood that had already begun to clot. There was a stab wound to the left of the sternum. Vilar moved a latex-gloved finger tentatively over the gash, then withdrew it with a sigh.

The face was that of a man of maybe twenty-five. Short dark brown hair. Three days' stubble. Delicate features. As he always did when he examined a body, Vilar watched intently for several seconds – motionless, holding his breath – for some shudder that might indicate that the victim was not quite dead, that there was yet something to be done, but of course nothing happened. Once again he cursed the illogical stubbornness that made him reject the evidence of his own eyes, the refusal to accept the inevitable that, some years earlier in a morgue, had made him scream at the pathologist to stop just as he was about to make an incision because he thought he noticed the pale fingers trembling on the stainless steel table. The pathologist had not seemed surprised and – out of kindness or pity – had smiled and explained that it sometimes happened to him too.

Vilar was the sort of man who did not resign himself to death, who felt that it could be conquered, could be eliminated. By force of will, through memory, or by summoning ghosts.

"Kevin Labrousse, born 8 July, 1979 in Villeneuve-sur-Lot," a voice above his head said.

An officer from the *brigade anti-criminalité* who had been first on the scene was waving a wallet and a plastic I.D. card.

"Someone found it on the street, not far away. There's some cash, forty euros, and a couple of photos, social security card, bank card, that kind of thing. We had a scout about for the knife, but we didn't find anything."

Vilar stared at the photograph the *brigadier* was holding, but the face smiling defiantly into the camera, chin slightly raised, no longer resembled the dead man. He gently pushed the hand away, got to his feet and took a small plastic bag from his pocket, into which the officer dropped the victim's effects.

"There was someone with him, wasn't there?"

"Some friend from work. He's in shock. Over there in the ambulance."

Vilar peeled off his gloves and walked over to the ambulance. He looked around for his partner, Laurent Pradeau, and saw him questioning a weeping girl. Two forensics officers from *l'Identité judiciaire* appeared, weighed down by their cases. As they shook hands, Vilar

16

racked his brain to remember their names. He had worked with them before, particularly on the Dejean case in which a girl had been doused in petrol and burned alive right outside her house, by an ex-boyfriend who couldn't bear the fact he had been dumped. Vilar could still picture the girl's body slumped against a metal door, half her face bloated and contorted, the other half charred to the bone. He felt a chill run down his spine. He remembered the arrest, too, remembered hurtling down the stairs, gun in hand, chasing a lunatic with a sword. In the lobby of the building, the ex-boyfriend tripped over a pushchair and lay, still struggling, arms flailing, spewing obscenities about the dead girl; it had taken two or three well-placed kicks to persuade him to shut up and be still. Vilar had pistol-whipped him, breaking his nose, and would have pounded his skull against the floor if the other officers had not pulled him off. Vilar could still picture the suspect sprawled on the ground, his face covered in blood, sobbing convulsively like a small child. Even now he could felt a twinge of anger, felt his heart beat a little faster at the memory of that arsehole wallowing in self pity while a team of firemen gritted their teeth as they carried away the charred body of his girlfriend. He remembered the details so clearly, it was almost physically painful: the sweltering heat of that early June morning, the exact address where it had happened and yet the names of the two forensics officers at the scene were buried in some remote corner of his brain. It didn't matter. Vilar handed the evidence bag to the younger of the two officers, who slipped the dead man's possessions into his case and asked what the story was.

Vilar sighed.

"Knife attack. Multiple stab wounds. The guy probably died instantly, or pretty much. Heart or artery. I'm going to question the victim's friend. The scene is contaminated, there's been people trampling all over it; the only thing I can say for definite is that the body hasn't been moved."

"Right, no surprise there. Assaults on a public roads are always shit. It's not like we're going to take samples of tarmac."

Vilar left them to deal with the body, climbed into the ambulance and asked the paramedic comforting the witness to leave them. The man climbed down without a word and lit a cigarette. The dead man's friend, who was still shivering spasmodically, had been wrapped in one of those foil survival blankets that shimmer in the midst of a catastrophe like a silver gown at a society ball. The man was about fifty with grey, receding hair cropped close. His shirt and trousers were smeared with blood. The man's broad shoulders, stocky build and thick neck reminded Vilar of a rugby forward. He wondered just how tall the man was.

"Commandant Vilar. I just have a few questions. Would that be O.K.?"

The man nodded. He still had not looked up. Pradeau, who had followed Vilar into the ambulance, produced a wallet with a sigh. His face was drawn, his eyelids heavy. Vilar tried to meet his gaze, to see how he was holding up, but Pradeau managed to avoid him.

"His papers," Pradeau said, nodding towards the man. "There were two guys and a girl. We've got their descriptions. The guy with the knife was tall, skinhead, earring, wearing combat trousers. The other guy . . ."

"What did the girl look like?" Vilar said, turning towards the witness who was shivering where he sat.

"Short, skinny, dyed red hair, wearing a black leather miniskirt and a chunky pair of Nikes."

"Are you sure of the brand?"

The man shook his head, screwed up his face.

"Um . . . no, what I meant was big trainers, you know? With those thick soles."

"What did she do?"

"She tried to intervene, tried to calm them down, told her mates to quit it, said they were off their faces. She ran off when things got out of hand. She was long gone by the time they left, just after . . ." He fell silent and bit his lower lip. His eyes filled with tears, which he wiped away with the back of his hand.

Pradeau patted the man on the shoulder, shooting Vilar a look that might have been exhaustion or impatience, then quickly looked down at his pad, several pages of which were covered with scribbled notes.

"That confirms the witness statement I've got here: a girl coming out of the station heading to school, she saw the whole thing, though at first she didn't realise what was happening. The other witnesses showed up a few minutes later when the victim was on the ground, all they saw was the two guys running away. We've got cars patrolling between here, Les Capucins and La Victoire, I radioed in a rough description."

Vilar nodded. Pradeau added that Darien, the deputy *procureur*, had just shown up and was dealing with the girl. Vilar scarcely heard, focused as he was on the man huddled beneath his foil blanket, slowly rolling between his hands the tissue he had used to wipe his eyes. He let it fall at his feet, then touched his neck gingerly with his fingertips as though afraid he had broken or dislocated something. Vilar leaned towards him.

According to his papers his name was Michel Vanini, born 1961 in Sainte-Livrade. Married with two daughters aged twenty-four and seventeen.

In a weary voice, hoarse from tiredness and probably too much drinking and smoking, Vanini explained that four of them had gone out on the town to celebrate the end of a job laying cables in the Quartier du Lac. He was the foreman. They had been supposed to head back to Agen that day, but had ended up partying at a club called the Black Jack until getting on for 3 a.m. After they left the club, the two others had gone home to bed but he and the dead man, Kevin, had decided party a little longer since this was Kevin's stag night, he was supposed to be marrying a girl called Vanessa; Vanini was distraught at the thought of how she would react. Vilar tried to distract him, asking where they had gone after the club. Vanini said they had been to a peepshow – not the one the victim had been killed outside, but one a bit further down the street on the corner of the cours de la Marne, they had only gone in for a laugh, you know, nothing sleazy, they had been working their arses off for two weeks straight, with no time off to go home to kiss the wife and kids, nothing but a breather on Sundays, but it had meant a lot of overtime and besides it was not as though they had a choice – their boss had been clear that they either took the job or they found work elsewhere, so yeah, they'd gone to chill out, there was no harm in that.

The guy seemed to regain his confidence as he confided this, he looked up now, giving Vilar a defiant look that said hard-working labourers had a right to some downtime and searching the policeman's vague, distant expression for that shrug of approval and support that men reserve for that kind of boys' night out, probably thinking, *Hey, you know what it's like, it's O.K. to look as long as you don't touch*, and the man, who a moment earlier had been devastated by his friend's death, ventured a smile, and his heavyset rugby player's frame relaxed.

Vilar was tempted to ask whether the girl was pretty, what she had looked like, what she had done, whether Vanini thought she was younger or older than his own daughter and – while they were on the subject – whether he was planning to visit the peepshow next time he was in Bordeaux. He pictured the woman behind a pane of glass on that cramped, grubby podium and wondered whether she was Romanian, Bulgarian, Ukrainian, whether by now she was sleeping, exhausted, on some filthy mattress while her pimp and the peepshow owner divvied up the cash, or whether she was already round at her dealer's, offering her services to save on the price of a fix.

This ordinary, decent labourer and his friend considered the city at night to be one big playground, they probably knew nothing – or chose to know nothing – about the sufferings of the woman they were leering at, just as, in their exhausted state, they did not expect to run into some idiot off his face on drink or drugs, ready to plunge a knife into the heart of the first passing stranger who refused to give him what he wanted because, in that moment, he could not defer gratification even by a second and, in a fit of blind rage, would stab this stranger he suddenly thought of as his enemy. To Vanini, their night on the town was like a visit to the zoo, but the cages were open, and having been terrified that he might not make it out alive, he was now convinced the worst was over.

Vilar wanted to take him down a peg or two. The man squirmed in his seat, perhaps eager to have done with all these pointless questions.

"Tell me exactly how it happened."

"How what happened?"

"What do you think? You think I'm looking for a detailed description of the arse of some girl at a peepshow? You don't think there's something more significant that's happened since?"

Vilar had raised his voice. Vanini took the words like a slap in the face, slumping back against the seat, his shoulders hunched.

They had been coming out of a bar, having had one for the road before going home to hit the sack. They heard a voice behind them asking for a cigarette, and, turning around, they found themselves face to face with two young guys and a girl who was totally off her face, hardly able to stand on her skinny legs in her huge trainers. After that everything was a blur. Kevin rummages through his pockets for a pack of cigarettes, the little wiry guy snatches the pack and helps himself, Kevin gets angry and tries to grab the cigarettes back, then the guy headbutts Kevin and that's when it all kicks off.

There's a fight, the girl screams, then suddenly a knife appears. The little guy lunges like it's a sword, then waves the knife around as Kevin stumbles back against the sex-shop window, clutching his chest, blood seeping between his fingers, and then he slumps slowly to the ground and the wiry little guy is still calling him a bastard and a fucker, still waving the knife, while the tall guy tries to drag him off, saying they can't hang around, that he's killed him.

Then his best friend is whimpering in his arms, the blood keeps pumping, he cannot staunch the flow, then suddenly the body feels so heavy he has to lay him down, let him go.

Vanini quietly began to cry, his face distorted by grief, he gave a sharp, muted wail and his broad shoulders shook with sobs.

Pradeau leaned towards Vilar, waiting until the man calmed down so that he could say something. With a nod, he confirmed that the story tallied with the other witness statements, then asked Vilar to come with him.

"We've pretty much tracked them down," he said. "All three are regulars in the local bars. They're always hanging around the area. Tonight they were out playing the slots and getting hammered. The two guys are Jonathan and Cédric, the girl's name is Coralie. They've got a place somewhere between Les Capucins and Saint-Michel. They were spotted coming out of a bar just behind the station. They're not criminal masterminds, just three drunken arseholes who butcher some guy who happens to be walking on the wrong side of the street. . . 'on the wild side', like the man says."

Vilar looked at him blankly.

"For fuck's sake, you've heard of Lou Reed haven't you? 'Walk on the Wild Side'? It's a song. It's on 'Transformer'."

Since he knew Pradeau was quite capable of reeling off the name of the bassist and the sound engineer, and possibly even reciting the "special thanks" in the sleeve notes, Vilar raised a hand to interrupt him.

"O.K., fine. So what about you? How are you holding up? You don't look too hot."

"You and me both, if it comes to that. I haven't been getting much sleep lately."

"You need to get laid once in a while."

"I try my best, but it's not much fun out on your own, you know?"

"I know. Anyway, while we're waiting for Blue Velvet to re-form, why don't you get on with taking statements from the man and the girl. Where is she, anyway?"

Pradeau jerked his chin in her general direction.

"Over by the fire engine. She's a minor, we're looking for her parents. I didn't know you knew the classics."

"If it's trickled down to you . . ."

Vilar trailed off and looked at his watch. Not far from them, an ambulance started up and pulled away. The two technicians from *l'Identité judiciaire* were stowing their gear into a van.

"I'll leave the rest to you. I need to get back to the murder over in

Bacalan. I suspect it's going to be a lot more complicated than these three cowardly fuckwits who we'll probably have tracked down by tomorrow. Give it a couple of days, and we'll have them banged up. We've got all the information we need, it should be pretty straightforward."

"How's the boy?" Pradeau said.

Vilar shrugged.

"O.K., I think. Physically, at least . . ."

"Shit, a kid lying in a coma next to the rotting corpse of his mother . . . I can't get it out of my head. It's not as if we're not used to wading through sordid, pathetic shit, but a case like that, it's sad. It's really scraping the bottom of the cesspit."

Vilar shrugged again. He stared at the Saint-Jean station buildings in the distance and mused about all the people waiting for a train or for someone to arrive. That simple world of reunions and clear-cut destinations. Those quiet, joyful moments.

"What does it matter what we think? Like you said, we're just here to bail out the shit. So I try not to think about whether or not a case is sad. But you're wrong, there's no bottom to this cesspit. You can always dig deeper."

He gave Pradeau's arm a friendly thump and forced himself to smile, then walked back to his car. He noticed that they were taking away the body, now hardly more than a shapeless mound in the regulation body bag, and he looked away, fumbling in his pockets for his keys.

Before driving off, he sat for a moment, hands on the steering wheel amid the muffled clamour from outside. In the rear-view mirror he watched the procession of police officers and emergency vehicles moving off. Car doors slamming, men shaking hands or giving curt salutes. He had a metallic taste in his mouth – iron, maybe, or copper – and under his tongue he produced a little saliva which he swallowed with difficulty. Just as he pulled away the sun appeared above a rooftop, dazzling him, and he blindly groped for his sunglasses, then remembered he had left them back at the station with his cigarettes.

He turned onto the cours de la Marne, his eyes smarting, squinting against the white light that flooded the city. He thought again about the boy, Victor, lying mute in that hospital ward, about the viscous silence that oozed from him, that invisible tar in which, in spite of his best efforts, he had become bogged down. And immediately an image of Pablo came to him and Vilar glanced in the rear-view mirror, hoping to catch a glimpse of his son's face. It was something he used to do, and he would feel stupidly happy seeing his son's little face, grave or curious, intent on his Game Boy or staring at the passers-by and the scenery, and Vilar closed his eyes and felt a painful shudder around his heart because there was no-one in the mirror, nothing but the blinding rays of the sun on the stream of cars.

"Pablo." He spoke the name aloud as though it were a fact, or a report. Or some magical incantation. And though nothing appeared still he savoured the sound in his mouth like cool water, even if, as he drove on, it could do nothing to quench the acrid burning lump in his throat, the dull pain that crept into his jaw.

When he climbed out of the car, his back and neck stiff, he could still feel the weight of his son on his back and he reached behind him to touch his neck, slippery with sweat, hoping to brush the boy's fingers clinging there. In the lift he ran into one of the drug squad officers, Bachir, a tall thin guy with stooped shoulders, who leaned heavily against the side of the lift, rubbing his eyes with the back of a hand in the manner of a sleepy child. In a weary voice he asked how Vilar was, but he did not listen for the reply. Eyes half closed, dead on his feet, he was already standing in front of the doors, ready to step out as soon as the lift stopped.

Vilar knew by the smell of perfume in his office that Capitaine Marianne Daras, his team leader, had been looking for him, leaving this faint scent in the air and, on his desk, a fluorescent green Post-it note on a blue file, asking him to call her. *I got the autopsy report for you. Nothing new. You'll see. We've got some information on the victim too that I think warrants further investigation. We need to focus on the neighbours.*

Vilar sat down heavily and opened the file, rummaged in the drawer

How could a teenager, in this day and age, resist the magnetic pull of the great wide world? Or was the elderly neighbour lying?

Vilar shook his head, sighed. He turned the pages of the file without reading them. This reality was clearly more complicated, more personal. More violent, perhaps. Both of the women in this family were dead; he would have to make do with father and son. An imperfect, pagan Trinity in which death was the Holy Spirit.

He closed the file, got to his feet and went to get a telephone directory. He dialled the number for S.A.N.I., rummaging in his desk for cigarettes. A voice answered. Vilar gave his name and rank, explained what he wanted, and was transferred to some middle-manager who sounded excited to be talking to the police. The man said he could be free that afternoon, but Vilar insisted that they meet as soon as possible. He would be there around 11.30 a.m. That gave him an hour to get there. After he hung up, he called Daras, got her answerphone and left a brief message explaining what he planned to do.

In the corridor he bumped into Pradeau on his way to prepare for the interviews in the stabbing incident. The key witnesses were scheduled to make statements that afternoon. One of the attackers had already been identified as Jonathan Caussade, who had a rap sheet for minor drugs offences and assault with a knife. Bingo.

"He lives with his mother in Cenon. I've got a plain-clothes unit keeping tabs on him. Should we bring him in, or wait until we can collar all three?"

Pradeau was talking quickly, gesticulating, sweating. Vilar tried to focus on the question. His first thought was to say he didn't give a toss, but he was backed into a corner, Pradeau was staring at him, waiting for a response. Vilar sighed.

"I don't know . . . Maybe wait until the two guys are together. Apparently they're inseparable. You can pick the girl up later, wear her down. Charge her with failing to report a crime – that should put the wind up her. Ask Daras what she thinks, it's her call."

"Pull in both guys at once? Things might get a bit lairy."

Vilar tried to think of something to say, his brain humming with an inchoate tension that felt like grief. He pictured the photograph of Nadia, remembered the smell of the body. He felt something well in his chest. He struggled for a little breath to say:

"Maybe, but it buys us time and it simplifies things. This way we don't have to stress over it. We build a watertight case and we bang them up, that makes things easier for the *procureur*'s office. You go in mob-handed and take them down, job done."

Pradeau nodded and stood aside. Vilar heard him ask how the Bacalan case was going and he shrugged.

As he was pulling out of the car park, his mobile rang. Awkwardly, he turned onto the boulevard, trying to extract the phone from his jacket pocket and change gears in the heavy, fast-moving traffic, the fumes thick and rank in the sweltering heat.

"Hey, it's Morvan." The voice on the other end was distorted by heavy static.

Vilar's heart leapt. He told Morvan that the line was bad, that he was driving.

"Listen, my battery's about to die . . . Shit! Can you hear me?"

"Yeah, but—"

"Don't worry. Give me a call tonight at my place, I've got—"

The line went dead. Behind him, someone leaned on their horn. Vilar had slowed to a crawl; he saw a shadowy figure behind a steering wheel throw up his hands, but did not have the energy to give him the finger. A bit further on, he wound down the window, stuck the blue light on the roof, turned on the siren and floored the accelerator. He could feel a knot in his stomach as he headed towards Bruges and the S.A.N.I. office, oblivious to the traffic left in the wake of the siren's wail.

3

During the four days he was in hospital, Victor slept a great deal. Most of the time he lay on his belly, his face pressed into his pillow to muffle his sobs, sometimes his body was wracked with little spasms, like dogs when they sleep. He was stripped to the waist, and his back glistened with sweat, even at night when the sweltering heat of the day was tempered by a cool breeze. Sometimes when he woke, he looked around him, and each time he struggled to work out where he was, to identify the nurses and doctors who were forever popping in on one pretext or another, chattering brightly, bustling around him, their actions precise or offhand. Victor did not acknowledge their presence.

Commandant Vilar came to see him every day, and would settle himself in a heavy vinyl chair, a notebook in his lap. Victor watched him in silence, more thoughtfully, perhaps, as the visits dragged on, listening as the policeman gently asked him to describe everything he could remember so that they could arrest the man who had killed his mother, so they could stop him doing it again, so they could punish him, do you understand, Victor? One day he even used the word "retribution", and the boy looked at him intently, his black eyes glittering more than usual as Vilar explained the word and then talked about justice, about sentencing, about prison. Maybe you saw him hanging around – maybe you didn't realise you'd seen him, obviously, because if we always knew what was going to happen . . . Maybe your mother mentioned him, do you remember? When she went out to work nights, and she left you alone, did anyone babysit you? Maybe she had a boyfriend? Was he blond, or tall, or fat or dark-haired with brown eyes? Maybe he had a limp or wore glasses. Vilar went on talking to himself, trotting out his theories, a rogues' gallery he repeated each day, each time embroidering a little more, with each visit the monologue grew like some fantastical tree that every night sprouted new branches. But after a while the boy would turn and stare at the poplar trees, swayed by the breeze so that they disappeared from view, letting the policeman's theories founder under the weight of his silence.

Then Vilar asked an almost pointless question whose answer he felt he already knew:

"Where was she when you found her? Was it you who put her on the bed?"

Finally the boy looked him in the eye. For a long time, without blinking, mouth half open. He nodded almost imperceptibly.

"Why?"

"So she'd be more comfortable."

Victor's voice guttered out in a hoarse croak that brought tears to his eyes.

"That's good," Vilar said. "You did good."

Some nights the staff heard the boy's screams and found him huddled at the foot of the bed, his eyes wide with terror, sometimes they found him roaming the corridors, the needle from the I.V. drip still embedded in his arm. He would mumble incoherently, talking to the walls, to the air, to the darkness that was mapped out with night lights. They would lead him back to his room, try to reassure him, fuss over him for a while, cooling his fevered brow with cold compresses. Once they arranged a visit from a psychiatrist, who managed to elicit no response from Victor beyond the blank, weary gaze he turned on everything, the trembling lips wet with spit. The psychiatrist suggested he draw some pictures, but the pen just sat there, clutched in the boy's lifeless fingers. Afraid he might have fits, the doctors prescribed sedatives. Finally, they decided there was nothing more they could do for him.

The morning the nurse told him he was being discharged, that the police inspector was coming to fetch him, Victor got up without being asked, washed himself and even splashed on some cologne they didn't realise he had brought with him. Afterwards he sat on his bed and waited, ignoring the little boy in the next bed who kept asking where he was going, whether his parents were coming to collect him.

"Hey, what kind of car your parents got? My dad's got a Merc. Well, actually, he's my stepdad."

Tethered to a drip, the kid squirmed in his bed like a cat slowly strangling itself. He had a split lip and several missing teeth and so could not speak clearly.

"I gotta cranium trauma thing, but it's not serious, the doctor said. Soon as it's cured I'm going home, I got rabbits to take care of. I'm not letting them bastards keep me in here. Hey, you listening?"

Victor turned and looked at the little kid in his great big bed, at the shifting shapes beneath the sheets as his limbs twitched endlessly. The boy stared back at him, head tilted because one of his eyes was red and swollen shut, ringed with blue-grey bruises. The bruising made him look like a little old man. At that moment Vilar arrived, and Victor walked over to the kid and held out his hand. The astonished boy shook it, his mouth half open and twisted.

"Don't take it anymore," Victor said softly.

"It's only 'cos I do dumb things," the kid said. "Maman says I need to learn to behave, but I can't help it."

Victor turned suddenly on his heel and left the boy with his hand in mid-air, his good eye spinning in its socket trying to follow him. As Vilar opened the door for them to leave, they heard the kid's faint voice behind them:

"My name's David. David Boulet."

He said something else, but by then they were out in the corridor and Victor, three metres in front of Vilar, was walking too quickly to hear.

In the car park the sun was waiting for them, and Victor squinted and looked down to avoid the blinding glare from the windscreens. As soon as the policeman opened the car door, the boy jumped in and curled up on the passenger seat. As Vilar reversed, Victor stretched out his hand towards the blue police light sitting on the dashboard.

"Can we turn it on?"

"So you can talk now? Well, that's something."

"So, can we?"

"Do you know where we're going?"

Victor started looking at the car parked next to them.

"You've probably got a good idea, haven't you?" Vilar said. "When someone dies, something has to be done with the body, right? Your mother had funeral insurance. Did you know that? Did she ever mention it?"

The boy shook his head. His face was impassive, the deadbolt of his eyebrows drawn into a frown.

"We're going to the church, Victor. Your mother wanted to be cremated."

They drove in silence though the sweltering city, bleached almost white in the sun. Victor screwed up his eyes so much that he had to close them for minutes at a time, or shield them with his hand.

There were only three cars outside the crematorium, even counting the gleaming hearse, and aside from two undertakers there was no-one in the chapel except a stocky man with cropped grey hair who rushed to greet Victor and Vilar, holding out a fat stubby hand. His name was Bernard, he was the social worker who would be looking after Victor from now on.

The coffin began to roll towards the furnace and the boy got up to touch the wooden box as it stopped, stroking the pale wood while his lips mouthed words no-one else could hear, then the coffin juddered again and Victor let it glide beneath his hand and disappear behind the navy blue curtains. He did not take his eyes off those curtains during the cremation, but stood motionless, ramrod straight. From time to time he swayed a little and Vilar felt the urge to jump forward and support him. An hour later, one of the crematorium staff appeared, carrying an urn, and turned to the policeman and the social worker, uncertain who should take it. Vilar jerked his chin towards the boy.

The undertaker hesitated, then handed Victor his mother's ashes. The boy placed the urn on his knees, letting his hands trace the curved surface: it was hot. He hugged it to him and began to cry quietly, his sobs echoing in the huge, bare, empty chapel.

After a moment the social worker came over and said it was time to go, that there was no point in staying. Victor asked what time it was, and when the man said "nearly twelve", he glanced around him in surprise, his eyes puffy, then got up, clutching the urn to his chest, and followed the social worker. In the car park Vilar handed the boy a card on which he scribbled something.

"That's my name and a number where you can reach me if ever you need to talk. If I'm not there, leave a message. Call me, and I'll be there. I won't let you down, have you got that? In a few days you'll have to appear in front of a judge who will talk to you about what happens next, about where you'll be living. Everyone will look out for you."

Victor took the card and studied it, then turned and looked at the policeman, who was standing to attention. He carefully folded the card and slipped it into his pocket.

*

It was a long single-storey building ringed with flowerbeds and shrubs, set in a small park full of mature trees. Bernard told Victor to take the red sports bag which was packed with some of the things that officers had collected from his house. The boy hunkered down in the middle of the car park and, creating a sort of nest among his clothes, he carefully slipped the urn into the bag.

"I don't know exactly what's in there," Bernard said. "But in a couple of days we can go back and pick up the rest."

The boy picked up the bag, one side of it bulging from the urn, and slung it over his shoulder, waiting for Bernard to lock the car. The social worker led him into a lobby and went to the caretaker's office to pick up a key.

"I'll show you to your room, and afterwards I'll give you the guided tour. You'll see. It's not so bad here."

Victor bowed his head, then, hearing the front door creak, he turned to look. A man carrying a satchel appeared, framed in the rectangle of golden light. Victor watched as he disappeared down a dark corridor. Bernard tried to take his bag, but the boy refused, gripping the handles, staring blankly at the floor. The social worker turned away with a sigh and walked on ahead down the corridor.

He walked purposefully, rolling his broad shoulders, his thick arms hanging away from his body as though preparing to fend off a rugby tackle. The boy walked behind, staring at the man's broad back, his short neck. Bernard seemed both heavy and agile, swift and powerful. He made Victor think of a boxer. The wooden floor creaked or groaned, and every step they took seemed to stir up the smell of floor polish.

They went into a cramped little room furnished with a bed with a whitewood frame and a red chair and a table. A built-in wardrobe was fitted with shelves papered with blue plastic. The wallpaper was beige with square patches that seemed less faded, peppered with holes from thumbtacks and drawing pins. The social worker gestured to him to put the bag on the bed.

"There you go. This is your new home. They'll be serving lunch soon."

Victor sat down next to the bag. A bedspring creaked. He set the urn on the bedside table and pressed his hands flat against the mauve bedspread. Through the open window he could hear excited bursts of birdsong that seemed to come from the mass of trees he could see. He craned his neck and could make out berries at the top of a cherry tree glistening in the sun. Everything shimmered in the sunlight, quivered with the sounds of shouting and laughter, the rumble of traffic from the avenue or the bypass nearby. Bernard asked if he was hungry. The boy immediately got to his feet and followed him. Before he left the room, he put the urn in the wardrobe, which he carefully closed. Bernard said that as long as he kept his key with him at all times, his belongings would be quite safe. After lunch, he would have time to get himself sorted. As they walked down the corridor, Bernard showed him where the showers and the toilets were.

They heard the tinkle of cutlery, a clamour of voices and scattered laughter. The large dining hall was equipped with tables that seated four. The posters on the walls were cheery, sun-drenched wildlife scenes of placid animals. Victor's attention was caught by two lions, their eyes shining, staring straight into the lens, and he slowed down to have a closer look.

"This is Victor," Bernard said in a loud voice, briefly interrupting the various conversations. "He's just got here, so I'm counting on all of you to help him settle in."

There was a burst of laughter. Victor saw a skinny boy sniggering. He had thick brown curls falling over of his face and was staring down at his plate. There were about twenty kids, most of them bent over their plates, absentmindedly scraping the floor with the soles of their shoes. There were only eight or nine girls who clustered together at two tables, chatting quietly, with a seriousness that was obvious from their broad sweeping gestures and the attentive way they listened. Some had finished eating but had stayed behind to chat. Victor was seated at a table with two younger children whose feet barely reached the tiled floor and who watched indifferently as he sat down. From a corner of the dining room, two men and a woman were keeping an eye on things, and after Bernard had wished him *bon appétit*, he went over to join them, sitting at right angles to Victor.

A woman immediately appeared and gave Victor his lunch. He thanked her with a nod.

He ate. He did not know if he felt hungry. He did not look at anything or anyone. His gaze flitted around the room like a tired, heavy bird, seeing nothing. He sopped up the sauce from his plate with a piece of bread and then passed the time by drumming softly on the table with his fork. The two boys at his table struggled to cut the meat from the bone on their chops, then cut away the fat which they pushed to the edge of their plates, making identical piles. Every now and then a pea would roll off onto the tablecloth, and they would pop it into their mouths with an irritated look. They often did exactly the same thing at the same time, or almost, it was as if they were playing some sort of silent, intuitive game, where the goal was to mimic each other. They didn't speak, but gave each other knowing or quizzical looks, and giggled noiselessly.

Victor, who finished before them, watched as they smeared *fromage blanc* around their mouths. Both boys had small, dark eyes, almost devoid of eyelashes, which gave them a sly and slightly stupid expression. They were obviously brothers, one was blond, the other had jet black hair that glinted blue under the strip lights. It was hard to tell which was younger. Maybe they were twins. The dark-haired boy regularly poked out a long, pointed tongue and licked around his mouth. His constant snuffling screwed up one side of his face. The blond boy, who had close-cropped hair and a long scar running across his scalp, often froze with his spoon in mid-air for several seconds, glanced vacantly at what was going on around him, then went back to noisily shovelling his dessert into his mouth so fast he almost bit his fingers.

Gradually the children got up and left the room in twos and threes, stacking their plates on a trolley as they went. After a while Victor found himself sitting alone at his table: at some signal known only to them, the two boys had jumped up from their chairs in perfect unison and cautiously walked away, carrying their plates and their glasses in front of them like holy relics. Then, like the others, they too disappeared through a doorway from which Victor could hear shouts and laughs, fists banging on walls and the scrape of tables or chairs. Soon he heard the voice of a television presenter, intercut with snatches of music, applause and adverts. Standing in the corner, the social workers were smoking and talking in low voices. From time to time they laughed, covering their mouths as though they were shy. Victor noticed that apart from him there was only one boy still at his table: the tall boy who had giggled earlier when Victor arrived, and was now bent double. He looked as if he was asleep, his head resting on his folded arms. Or maybe he was crying, because every now and then his body shook.

Victor got down and stacked his plate and cutlery on the trolley. His fork fell on the floor, and the noise made the three adults turn and stare. They did not take their eyes off him until he had left the room.

Four boys were playing table football, cheered on by two more who promised they were going to thrash the winners. The game was tense, the players punctuating their furious wrist flicks with muttered obscenities directed at nothing and no-one in particular.

Victor stepped closer and watched the game for a few minutes. The ball flew off the table and bounced at his feet. He caught it as it bounced and gently tossed it back to one of the players, but the boy did not thank him, in fact he did not seem to notice the newcomer standing silently a few feet away. Other boys were watching the television, sometimes mocking the adverts that all seemed to feature beautiful women, fast cars, and jewels in sumptuous settings. Victor wandered away from the table football and slowly walked around the room. The two brothers were staring spellbound at the television, though they were sitting some way back, lolling in armchairs, methodically picking their noses, rolling the snot into little balls and flicking it into the distance. The dark-haired brother was still regularly poking out his tongue as if, like a snake, he could use it to sense the universe of smells around him. The boys' restless feet were constantly scuffing the floor, twitching or quivering convulsively in a continuous fidgeting that spread to every part of their bodies except their round, staring eyes, which remained glued to the television in the distance.

Victor turned away, walked over to the window and stood there. He watched a group of sparrows squabbling over food on the lawn beneath a big oak tree. They hopped about, pecked at each other, and flew up suddenly into the dark leaves, only to drop down heavily onto the other birds. All around the light was blinding and brutal, from the metallic glare of the sky to the short grass that was yellowing in patches, and everything seemed transfixed by the stultifying heat. Even Victor did not move, he stood stock-still as beads of sweat began to trickle down his face and onto his neck. He did nothing to wipe them away, even though he found the warm tickling sensation uncomfortable, and then his eyesight misted, his eyelids twitched feverishly and suddenly snapped shut, as he slumped to the floor and started to vomit, eyes closed, clutching his stomach, breathless and seized by convulsions.

*

He was woken by an angry blackbird, slicing across the rectangle of the open window with a dark caw. Or perhaps it was the cold contact of the stethoscope against his skin. A man with a worried look was sounding the depths of his body. He gave a smile when he saw the boy open his eyes. He inflated the blood-pressure cuff and checked the dial, intent on the sounds that only he could hear. He told Victor everything was fine, and smiled again. It was just an after-effect, he said, and stood up, his face suddenly disappearing from view. Victor blinked in surprise. The doctor said he was going to give him an injection to help him relax, and asked if that was O.K. The boy's eyelashes fluttered and, unblinking, he watched the needle slide into a vein in his arm and the plunger of the syringe slowly being depressed.

When someone came to fetch him for dinner, he was roused from the half-sleep he had been drifting in all afternoon, twisting and turning on the sheet that stuck to his clammy body. He wondered what time it was, but his watch was sitting on a shelf and he did not dare ask this man who was trying to persuade him to come and eat something. Victor refused to go downstairs, his only response was to turn away, curl up into a ball and pull the sheet over his head. He stayed for some time beneath this pale blue shroud, in the hush of his faint breathing, aware of the dim glow that seeped through the fabric, looking at his fingers, wriggling these tame, secret creatures, his lips moving, mouthing words with a faint hiss of saliva creating a confused counterpoint to the birdsong that came in random bursts from outside. Then he shifted in the bed, sat up and looked around, eyes puffy with sleep, at the peaceful haven of his room. He reached out, pulled his backpack towards him and began to make an inventory. Apart from a few clothes, the police had packed a little Walkman that had belonged to his mother, and a handful of cassettes by old-fashioned singers. He rummaged for his MP3 player but could not find it, so picked up the Walkman again, examining it from every angle. He ran his finger over the buttons, then pressed EJECT and extracted the cassette, which he also examined, turning it over and over, probably because it had no label. He reloaded it into the little red player, put on the earphones, and pressed PLAY.

Nothing happened. He shook the device, took out the tape, reinserted it and closed his eyes. Still there was no music, the tape did not move. He opened his eyes and noticed the battery compartment was empty. He poked a finger in to be sure, then tossed the Walkman onto the bed, leapt to his feet and paced the room, his hands in his pockets, his shoulders hunched, then stood at the window and stared out at the heat haze that stained the sky with a sickly grey-green veil, even as the patches of shadow spreading at the foot of the walls announced that night was drawing in. In the distance he could hear the low roar of the motorway. The warm air quivered with the metallic breath of the city.

*

Victor stood for a long time, finding it now possible to remain utterly still but for the deep and steady rise and fall of his breath, the quivering of his eyelids that made his face seem alive, and the anxious curiosity of his eyes searching out everything there was to see: there was not much, trees, birds, a few insects, buzzing specks against the evening light.

A loud crash from the corridor behind him made him start. It sounded like someone banging on his door. He went to open it and peered into the dark, empty hallway. He could hear muffled laughter from behind a door beneath which a band of light flickered with shadows. The cold wooden floor creaked with every step. On his right he could see a bright room and the faint sound of water dripping. Warily he stepped inside, as though walking into a trap tiled in white and blue. He walked past a line of washbasins, peered into the shower cubicles, the toilets, then locked himself into a cubicle to pee. As he was doing up his flies the door of the next cubicle slammed shut, he heard a sigh of relief and a series of intimate splashes and almost immediately the foul stench reached him. The toilet flushed. The door banged so hard that it shook the thin partitions separating the cubicles. As the stranger left the bathroom he burped and started to whistle a shrill, unfamiliar tune, then there was the squeak of hinges and the click of a latch. Victor waited until everything was silent; only then did he emerge and creep back to his room, terrified that one of the other doors might open, distracted by the snatches of music that faded away and died in the twilight.

He lay on the bed again, staring at the ceiling, watching as night drew in, darkening the pale rectangle of sky he could see through the window. The room around him was sketched in mauve and grey with patches of blue shadow in the corners. He laid a hand on his chest and felt his heart beat, and in his head he felt the same dull throb, buzzing like an insect. He did not see the darkness finally take hold, because by then he was snuggled up with his mother, naked and warm as she stroked his hair, whispering softly to him – *my little boy, my darling* – sweet nothings scarcely louder than a breath and planting kisses all over his face. He let himself melt into this dark embrace, pressed his body and his face into the soft mattress, groaning, shifting listlessly, suddenly overcome with suffocating sleep.

Then he fell. A short, brutal jolt that woke him with a start. He found himself on his back, his arms flung wide, his legs tangled in the sheets, gasping with terror. He shook the hem of his T-shirt to dry the sweat from his skin, kicked out to free his legs, and opened his eyes onto the darkness. When he felt calm again he got up, walked over to the window, and pressed his face against it. A rustling silence. The day's clamour all but gone. A perfumed coolness rose from the grounds. A steady breeze, calm and gentle. The mute breath of hidden flowers. A faint shushing of leaves broke the silence. He looked at the sky, trying to make out the stars as they glided towards the west. He hoped there might be a comet, hoped he might see the moon, but could make out nothing save the perpetual pulse that seemed to keep everything alive. He shivered suddenly. He had been taught that the universe was cold and utterly black, streaked with ancient light and rocks no-one had thrown. He dismissed this paradox, which was too difficult for him to resolve, and with clumsy, groggy hands undressed and went back to bed, quickly slipping back into restless sleep.

4

Questioning the staff at S.A.N.I., Vilar discovered that Nadia's co-worker – and probably her friend – was a woman named Sandra de Melo: the pair had been hired at about the same time and had been assigned to work on the same team. The executives and the line managers he interviewed talked about the staff as if they were interchangeable, as though they were pack animals, and it took considerable effort to get any personal information about the young woman who had been working for their company for almost four years. Some fell silent the moment they heard that Nadia had been murdered, while others seemed more than happy to be "helping the police with their inquiries". Vilar had a nagging suspicion that some of them imagined themselves playing a role in a crime novel. It hardly mattered since the management, in spite of all its talk of proper procedures, could barely disguise its disdain for "human resources" – despite having been given an award by the Chamber of Commerce the previous year. One interesting fact did emerge – Nadia only worked part-time, and her shifts were irregular.

The rumour that the two women had been friends came from the team leader responsible for training them when they joined. The man had nothing but praise for their work, and stressed what a pleasure it had been to work with two beautiful, sexy women. Vilar had loathed the man's knowing smiles and his studied pauses, the tacit male bond this moron thought he had established between them.

Sandra de Melo lived out in the *banlieue* sandwiched between the motorway and the train tracks in a forbidding tower block on a bleak housing estate that some architect had tried to jazz up with wrought-iron balconies painted in garish colours. A boy leaning in the doorway barely moved to let Vilar pass. Another was leaning against a window crazed with cracks, and a third was sitting smoking on the stairs next to the lifts. The air reeked of dope. As he reached the middle of the lobby the policeman felt their eyes boring into him, but he ignored them as he tried to make out the illegible labels on a bank of mailboxes, some of them padlocked – those that still had a metal door to protect their post.

"You looking for someone?" a voice said behind him.

S. de Melo. Apartment 317. The mailbox was stuffed with junk mail.

"I'm talking to this fucker, you'd think he'd fucking answer?"

Vilar felt an electrical charge trill through his shoulder blades and spread up into his neck making his hair stand on end. He turned towards the boy who had spoken, the one still standing by the door.

"It's O.K., I've found her. Didn't want to tax your brain."

He forced himself to smile. The boy kept his hands in the pockets of his white shell suit. He was probably about sixteen or seventeen, like his mates. The one sitting on the stairs dropped his joint and stubbed it out with his trainer, his head lowered, observing Vilar from under his baseball cap.

"It can be pretty dangerous here, *m'sieur*," the boy said, leaning against the window. "On the stairs and that. Even in the lift, when it's working. There's thugs here who get a kick out of scaring people."

The other two nodded in agreement, mocking Vilar, waiting for him to react.

"It's pretty scary," Vilar said, rolling his eyes as if he meant it, taking in the walls tagged with graffiti. "You guys must be really brave to hang out here, what with it being so dangerous."

"Yeah, it's not safe," said the boy who had been smoking the joint. "But the Feds never come here, the fuckers."

"There's never a policeman around when you need one," Vilar said, nodding. "Why don't you give them a call?"

All three burst out laughing.

"Guy's a comedian."

"Don't got their number," the guy in the white hoodie said.

"Well then, our hands are tied," Vilar said.

He took a few steps towards the stairs. It felt hard to breathe, as though he were trekking high up in the mountains. He tried to catch his breath, only to feel a painful, familiar weight pressing on his chest.

"Hey, mister comedian, you wouldn't be busting our balls there, would you?"

Vilar turned to the guy in the shell suit, who was standing in the middle of the hall, his legs apart, gesturing defiantly. The dope smoker had also jumped to his feet and was standing on the bottom step. The third youth was still leaning against the window, his head back, watching carefully between half-closed lids.

Vilar looked from one to the other, sizing them up rapidly, mustering every ounce of willpower not to lay into them. He would have enjoyed it too much; he would have done his utmost to really hurt them. His muscles crackled with undirected electricity; his heart was thumping in his throat. He could feel his arms tensing at the thought of the pounding he would give them. He heaved a sigh.

"You'd have to have some balls for me to bust them," he said at last.

He strode towards the lift. The smoker had lit a cigarette and was looking him up and down, his face screwed up, fag drooping from the corner of his mouth.

Vilar turned instead to the stairs. The boy there put out an arm to block his path, looming so close that Vilar could smell the dope on his clothes.

"Give me a break. I'm tired."

He said it in a low voice, a lump in his throat, struggling to swallow the anger he could feel welling in him. The boy stepped aside and Vilar slowly started up the stairs, finally exhaling the stifling air trapped in his chest. When he reached the next floor, he stopped and looked along the grey corridor, blood pounding in his ears, distorting the silence.

The door was opened straight away. Sandra de Melo was a small, pretty woman with bronzed skin and large, dark, expressive eyes. When he showed her his warrant card she nodded and smiled, explaining that Monsieur Dumas, her boss, had called to say he was coming. She led him down a corridor laid with wood-effect vinyl. The brown striped wallpaper that made him think of a mattress. A vacuum cleaner spilled its brushes and nozzles in the doorway to the living room, and the woman pushed them aside with her foot and told Vilar to sit where he liked as she tidied the magazines on a coffee table. He sat down on a leatherette sofa that creaked under his weight. Sandra took a seat opposite and lit a cigarette. She took a deep drag, her eyes half closed. She seemed nervous or tired, and was doing her best to hide it with lively gestures and the youthful smile that softened her features.

"I was doing some cleaning, just for a change . . . You timed it perfectly, I was just going to take a break. Do you fancy coffee? I've just made some."

Vilar nodded, and she got up eagerly. As he listened to her bustling about in the kitchen, he looked around at the mismatched furniture and the widescreen television on mute, showing some American sitcom. As she came back with a tray with two cups, a cafetière and a porcelain sugar bowl, he thought he could hear a steady pounding on the wall. A soft hammering, rhythmic, muffled. Someone was hitting the wall. A neighbour, probably. Vilar had grown up in this kind of building, the constant noise from the neighbours, shouting, doors banging, televisions blaring late at night.

They drank their coffee without saying much. Vilar said it was good, and added that he knew people who could not make a decent cup of coffee, something he considered a serious failing. Sandra smiled, fluttering her eyelashes. The pounding on the wall, which had stopped for a moment, started up again.

"Sorry," Sandra said, "I'll be back."

Her face had suddenly tensed, she looked older, and Vilar heard her sigh wearily as she got to her feet.

He could hear her talking in the next room. She obviously had a child. Too young to go to school. Or sick, maybe. He got up, wandered over to the window and stared out at the grim geometry of the tower blocks, the dreary rows of windows with their tiny balconies, almost all sprouting satellite dishes, all interchangeable even though the buildings had recently been repainted in pastel colours, with garishly coloured tubes and pipes designed to cheer up the entrances. Vilar suddenly thought of the Red Hand Gang, the three dim-witted nineteen-year-olds who had left two dead at a bank in Avignon. They had been caught because they stopped at a petrol station to try to wash the red ink off their hands after the dye pack exploded when they opened the booby-trapped strongboxes. They had burst into tears as they were handcuffed, snivelling about how they had only carried guns to scare people, how they never wanted any of this to happen, never wanted anyone to get killed – nor, obviously, to be arrested, something that had apparently brought their whole world crashing down around them. Did the architects of these hovels, and those who commissioned them, weep when they drove past them now? Or had they washed their well-manicured hands of them?

Sandra reappeared after a few minutes, holding the hand of a little boy who looked a lot like her, thin, almost scrawny, teetering on spindly legs. His dark eyes darted here and there without looking at anything, he blinked constantly, dazzled perhaps by the brightness of the room. Behind him he dragged a clown puppet.

"Meet José."

Vilar said hello and waved, but the boy stared down at the grinning face of the clown.

"José," his mother said. "See that man? He's a policeman, just like in the movies. An inspector, you know what that means? He arrests robbers and murderers. José, are you listening?"

The boy glanced up at her, then collapsed on the floor, a ragdoll clutching a puppet, as through his muscles had suddenly given out. He landed gently and lay there on the carpet, staring up at Vilar.

"Are you going to stay there? You don't want to come with me? What about him?" Vilar pointed to the clown. "What's his name?"

"That's Toto. He takes him everywhere. It was the first thing he ever really noticed. One day I was holding him in my arms and he started covering Toto in kisses, and I was just relieved that for once he wasn't screaming and struggling. If he had kissed me, I couldn't have been happier."

She blew José a kiss then sat down again opposite Vilar. She poured more coffee. Her hands trembled.

"I'm sorry about this. We missed the taxi this morning, so I have to look after him today, they weren't able to send another. And since I'm on my own . . . I'm sorry. I'm wasting your time."

"Don't worry, it's no problem."

She turned towards the boy and waved and smiled at him and still he lay on his side, his cheek resting on the clown's head, staring up at the policeman.

"Especially as you've come to talk about Nadia, the poor thing."

"It's me who's come at a bad time. I hoped to talk to her family and friends at the funeral, but no-one came, so I've been forced to come bothering people at home to ask them questions. Did you know Nadia well?"

"We got on O.K., but I wouldn't say I knew her well. We had coffee sometimes, talked about our sons, about our problems . . . I wanted to come to the burial, sorry, I mean . . . she was cremated, wasn't she? But I didn't have the strength. I'm not good with that sort of thing."

"No-one's good with that sort of thing."

The woman sighed. She seemed to be thinking, searching for words.

"I can't stop thinking about Victor, the poor kid, he's all alone now."

"Doesn't he still have a grandfather? Nadia's father."

Sandra shook her head.

"I don't think she'd seen him in years. He lives somewhere near Aix-en-Provence, I think. That's if he's still alive . . ."

"What do you mean?"

"Nothing, I mean . . . He might be dead, I don't know, she burned her bridges long ago. I don't think she really saw him after she ran away from home in her teens. Can I ask you something?"

She did not give Vilar time to reply.

"How did she die? What did he do to her?"

"Do you really want to know?"

Sandra blushed a bit, but held his gaze.

"Yes. It's important to know if she suffered. We might not have been close, but we talked a lot, we talked about our troubles, she'd come round to mine for dinner or we'd go to hers. Victor and José got on well. So yes, I really want to know whether they hurt her, even if I know it doesn't change anything."

Her eyes were glistening. She poured herself another coffee, her movements halting, almost trembling.

"She was beaten and then strangled."

Sandra de Melo nodded, sitting motionless, staring down at the cup in her hand. Vilar allowed her time to collect her thoughts, to imagine what Nadia must have suffered in her dying moments. When she raised her cup and sipped her coffee, he said gently:

"A minute ago you said something about her running away from home . . . Can you tell me a bit more about that?"

Sandra hesitated. She turned towards her son, who was crawling slowly towards the table, clutching his puppet.

"Yeah. She told me she left home when she was sixteen, that that's when her life went all to hell. Before that, things had been going really well, she was good at school. A bit like me, I did O.K. at school, I actually liked it. I even managed to get my *baccalauréat*. Anyway, long story short . . . She'd been really close to her mother – I think she was a teacher."

"Her mother committed suicide, didn't she? Was that after Nadia left home? Because you said she ran away, but it sounds like she was really leaving for good. You said yourself, 'she left home'."

"I don't know. I couldn't ask her. If I so much as mentioned her mother she'd end up crying. But her father, I don't know, it was like she hated him."

Here was something interesting. The father was the only surviving member of the nuclear family. His daughter runs away, his wife commits suicide, and there he is, alone. What sort of state must he have been in? How does someone survive something like that? In his

49

notebook, Vilar scrawled half a dozen circles around the word "father".
Nadia would have been a minor at the time. There would have been a
missing person's report. There might still be something on file.

"You've no idea what her problem with her father was?"

Sandra only pursed her lips to say she did not know. She glanced at
her son, who was under the table now, curled up on his side with his
back to them.

"He'll go to sleep and later I'll have a hell of a job getting him out
from under there. He's getting so big and heavy. And if I wake him
sometimes he'll throw a tantrum and I don't know how to calm him."

Vilar looked at the child curled under the table, like a little animal.
When Pablo was learning to walk, he had loved to hide under tables
and stretch his hand out to touch people's feet as they passed and, if
they bent down, Pablo would laugh and scuttle away between the legs
of a chair as though this were a dark forest. If someone made as if to
catch him, he would scream "Wolf! Wolf!", pretending to be scared but
then suddenly he was no longer pretending and he would snuggle in
your arms, hot, panting. Vilar noticed that the young woman was waiting, holding the coffee pot.

"He's calm for the moment. Would you like more coffee?"

Vilar almost asked who was calm, struggled to come back to the present. He held out his cup, mumbling an apology. Painfully he swallowed
a scalding mouthful, though the smell of the coffee did him good.

"I'm terrified of what will happen when he grows up," Sandra
said. He—'

"Never say that."

He had spoken sharply. The woman froze, the cup pressed to her
lips. She bowed her head.

"I . . . I didn't mean . . . Well, I'm sure you know that kids like this
grow up, but they'll never really be adults."

Vilar got to his feet and walked to the window, staring out without
seeing. The light hurt his eyes. He had to take a breath before he could
speak again. He turned back to the woman.

"I'm sorry. I have . . . I *had* a son, and I . . ."

He sat down again, shook his head.

"I won't keep you much longer. Just a couple more questions and I'll leave you to take care of him. Let's see . . ."

He consulted his notes. Bit by bit, he managed to marshal his thoughts.

"You said that Nadia's life went to hell when she ran away. Did something happen?"

Sandra hesitated. She seemed unsure for a second, then sighed.

"I suppose I should tell you, in case it might help to . . . It was something Nadia didn't really talk about, or she'd make, like, some vague reference to it, but, bottom line: she was raped by these guys and after they forced her to become a prostitute."

She rattled it off in a single breath, desperate to unburden herself.

"This was in Marseille?"

"I don't know. I suppose."

"Did she give it up?"

Sandra stiffened, as though the question were inappropriate.

"Of course she did . . . She was raising a kid, she had a job . . ."

"She was only part-time from what S.A.N.I. told me. A few night shifts."

"Yeah, I know, and that doesn't mean she worked every night . . ." the woman snapped back.

She frowned and bit her lower lip.

Vilar leaned towards her.

"Tell me a bit more about that."

"I've let her down. I can't keep my mouth shut. I'm hopeless. Nadia's dead and here I am trash-talking her."

Sandra buried her face in her hands.

"You haven't let anyone down. All we're trying to do is catch the guy who killed her, the man who beat her and strangled her. Anything that will help us do that can't hurt the memory of your friend. Besides, we already know that what she made at S.A.N.I. wasn't enough to cover her expenses. She had to pay the rent, the car, the bills, so she had to be getting the money from somewhere. And we know she didn't have another job, so if you rule out a lottery win, it's not hard to work out where she got the cash. According to her neighbours she left for work almost every night at around the same time. Where did she go when she wasn't cleaning offices for S.A.N.I.? Right now, anything seems possible, so if you don't tell us, we're likely to suspect Nadia of anything and everything. Now that *would* be letting her down."

Sandra stared intently at Vilar, winding a lock of hair around a finger.

"She had a boyfriend."

Vilar shuddered.

"What boyfriend?"

"I don't know. She mentioned this guy called Thierry, that's all I know. She saw him a lot, but, him being married . . . Well, he threw his money around, at least that's what she told me. He said he wanted to help her, to get her out of here. He had money, he was the boss apparently, the C.E.O. or whatever . . . She ran into him one night. He was there when she showed up to clean his office. Scared the hell out of her when she saw him because she wasn't expecting anyone to be there at that time of night, so anyway he apologised, offered her a drink, and one thing led to another . . . I told her I thought she was pushing it but she said she needed to make ends meet, that the ends justified the means. That was Nadia's motto. She used to say that she wanted her son to get on in life."

She took out another cigarette and lit it. Her hands were trembling again, and she could not bring herself to look at Vilar.

"You ever see him, this man?"

"Once, from a distance. He was driving a Mercedes. He was waiting for her outside the office. He had dark hair, I think, and he wore sunglasses."

Vilar shook his head.

"Well that's a big help. What kind of Mercedes?"

"I don't know. I don't know much about cars. A sports car, you know, a two-door saloon. Black, I think. Yeah, black."

Vilar was thinking, he had something now, a lead, maybe even a suspect: a spurned, upstanding citizen gets angry, lashes out and kills, he smashes his little toy and with it any vague impulse to be a Good Samaritan; or maybe the girl was blackmailing our upstanding citizen in which case he's hardly likely to risk his perfect family and his social status for some fantasy, for some sleazy little affair that's supposed to end with him saving her? A perfect crime? People think they can pull it off. They think that if they leave no prints, they can disappear for good, the way a child who covers his eyes thinks no-one can see him.

By tomorrow, this Thierry would be spilling his guts, snivelling about how his life was ruined, about his poor children, and his wife who would curse the son of a bitch for generations to come. After he confessed he would have all the time in the world to re-edit his movie, to put the finishing touches to a script in which the bad guy never gets caught, not because he is not guilty, but because he is clever.

Vilar played out this scenario in his mind, then decided it was drivel. Sandra de Melo had turned her attention back to her son, who was awake now. He was gently wriggling his legs, and Vilar could tell he was playing with the clown, whispering to it. The officer got to his feet, thanked Sandra for what she had told him, and thanked her again for her coffee.

She walked him to the door and, as he passed the boy, the policeman crouched down to say goodbye and was surprised to see José roll over and stare at him with his big, vacant eyes.

Down in the lobby, he was relieved to find that the three sentries had given up their duty. The smell of dope still hung in the air, like an invisible marker of their territory. As he walked back to his car he spotted them at the far end of the tower block, glaring at him defiantly. One of them gave him the finger and shouted something Vilar couldn't make out. Vilar simply shrugged.

As he drove away from the estate, he called Ana. She picked up almost immediately. She had just got in from work and was exhausted, it had been a tough day and there was a month to go before her holidays. Vilar could hear the tension and tiredness in her voice.

"Can I call round? I won't stay long."

She didn't answer straight away.

"I mean, if you're on your own."

"I'm pretty much always on my own. Where are you right now?"

"Pessac. I've been on the go all day. There was a stabbing near the train station this morning around breakfast time."

"I heard it on the midday news. People are insane . . . Come round, I'll be here."

With that she hung up and Vilar, as he always did, found the silence, like a thick curtain between them, unbearable.

She smiled as she opened the door and gave him a quick peck on the lips, her fingers cool and soft against his neck. Vilar ran his hand over her hip, but she slipped away, turning and shaking out her mane of black hair.

"Sorry about earlier. I was shattered. But I feel better now I've taken a shower."

As she walked down the hall ahead of him, she tried to pile her hair up into a sort of chignon, taking a large red slide from the hall stand and clipping it to the top of her head. She was wearing white cotton capri pants and a black spaghetti strap blouse. She moved clumsily, tottering in a pair of ancient leather mules. He liked to watch her from behind. Those hurried, flirtatious movements; that hesitant way she walked. That grace. He wanted her to turn so he could take her in his arms, tell her how beautiful she was. He felt the urge to say soppy, sentimental things. She led him into the living room, sat down on the sofa and immediately got up again and offered him a drink. Vilar shook his head. She shrugged, pouring herself a bourbon, and announcing that she was having one even if he wasn't.

She did her best to appear cheerful, but Vilar knew that dark look she sometimes got, those fine wrinkles under her eyes.

She sat down, took a swig from her drink, and screwed up her face.

"What are you doing drinking that? I didn't have you down as a bourbon drinker."

"I had a lousy day," she said. "Desperate measures for desperate times. We had to find urgent foster care for two kids whose parents took off to Metz last week and left them with a fridge full of frozen ready meals. A boy and a girl, six and eight. Apparently they weren't allowed to go with their parents because they hadn't worked hard enough at school this year. The neighbours heard them knocking on the door and called the police. Three days we've been working on this, and today was the case conference with the parents, so you can imagine: screaming, sobbing, even threats. Hang on a minute, I'm going to get something to nibble on."

"Why Metz? What the fuck were they doing there?"

"No idea," she said from the kitchen. "Something about an aunt being ill, or dying. Two years ago they won a holiday in Martinique and pulled the same stunt, apparently. Between them they've got a mental age of twelve."

She came back with a bowl filled with olives. Vilar tucked in. He realised he was hungry. He wanted a drink, but he didn't dare go back on his earlier refusal.

"When are you off on holiday?"

Vilar made a vague gesture.

"I pencilled in three weeks in late August, early September, but I'm not sure . . . the idea of going on my own . . . What about you?"

"Some friends are renting a place in Tuscany and asked me to go with them, that way we'd share the costs. You can just imagine the price of a villa there . . . I'm going for two weeks at the end of July. You remember Suzanne and Samuel? And there's another couple, but I haven't met them.

"Sounds good," he said.

He almost mentioned the holiday they had taken near San Gimignano, before they married, before Pablo was born. Before . . . He could still picture the Italian countryside, the way it had shimmered in the May sunlight, and could not remember ever having felt such harmony. He swallowed hard, feeling his throat tighten again.

"Are you O.K., Pierre?" Ana was looking at him anxiously. "You look all . . . I don't know what."

"It's nothing, I . . . Sometimes I get like this. I find myself upset over something trivial. Don't worry, I'll be fine. It's probably because I feel happy, being here with you. Sorry . . ."

She put down her glass. For a moment he thought she might come over and sit next to him. He wanted to put his arms around her, to feel her arms around him, but he knew that she would not, that it was too much for her to bear. They sat for a moment, gazing at each other with mournful affection. Then Vilar slumped back against the sofa.

"I had a call from Morvan."

Ana shook her head.

"Don't, Pierre. Please . . . I told you before, I . . ."

"He only ever calls if he's got a new lead," Vilar went on, as though he had not heard. "It's usually something worth checking out."

"Pierre . . ."

"He's never given up on the investigation. He's been working on the case full time since he retired from the force. He's still got his police contacts, he's managed to gather a lot of information. And these days he doesn't have to go cap in hand to his superior officers. In the year he's been working as a freelance investigator, he's already managed to solve one case."

Ana had murmured something inaudible and buried her face in her hands. Now she looked up, leaned towards Vilar, and stared into his eyes.

"Pablo's dead," she said softly. "Just like those kids Morvan found."

"How do you know? Have you seen his body? What would you know about it?"

The words used up what little oxygen he had. He felt as though he might faint and forced himself to take a deep breath.

"I just *know*, I can feel it in every fibre of my being, Pierre. I'm the one who carried him for nine months, so I know, something deep inside me knows that he's dead."

As she stared at him, her eyes filled with tears.

"Bullshit," Vilar said. "This whole maternal instinct thing is bullshit. Jesus Christ, Ana, we can't just give up. I refuse to accept that Pablo is dead until I've got proof, until . . ."

He trailed off, suddenly overwhelmed as the chilling image of a child's body lying in a ditch popped into his head. He squeezed his eyes shut, unable to breathe.

"I just can't give up," he managed to say. "I'll find him . . . Even if only so that I can mourn him."

"But you're mourning already."

"No. That's just it. I haven't cried for him. I choke and splutter, but the tears never come. It's like an endless nightmare . . . I . . . I don't even know whether it's rage or grief. There are times I feel like killing some-one, times I feel like dying myself, it amounts to the same thing. It's worse than grief."

Ana huddled into a ball and stared at the far end of the room, biting her lip, her cheeks wet with tears.

"Don't you understand?" he went on. "Searching for Pablo is the only thing that keeps me alive . . . I need to know how . . . I need to know what happened, what they did to him."

Ana shuddered. "Stop, please . . . I'm begging you . . ."

Vilar despised himself for daring to mention such a thing. They were both condemned to live the same nightmare, each of them alone, each in their own way marshalling every ounce of strength to fight against it. Vilar got to his feet and stood forlornly for a moment. Ana stared up at him, her eyes shining.

"I should go. I'm so sorry. Every time we meet up, we hurt each other all over again."

He tried to smile and stretched out his hand, and she brushed it with her fingertips.

In the car the heat of the day lingered, muggy and oppressive in spite of the gathering dusk. Vilar rolled down all the windows but still he could not feel even the slightest coolness as he sped through the narrow streets and plunged into the dark, airless car park of his apartment building. He called Morvan and left a message on his answerphone, then stood in the spray of a shower so cold it left him gasping, until finally his body relaxed to become a leaden, shapeless mass barely capable of movement. Later he dozed off in front of the television, a half-eaten sandwich in his hand, dreaming fitfully.

5

Someone was knocking. Someone was calling his name. He wondered where he was. The diamond of sunlight on the bed shifted as the boy's legs twitched. He could hear Bernard, the social worker, asking if he could come in. A great weight seemed to press him down on the mattress, and his voice died in his throat before he could say a word. When he did not answer, the man turned his key in the lock. Victor sat up suddenly, blinking into the harsh, blazing sunlight.

"You should have closed the shutters."

Bernard went over to the window, stared out, then turned back to Victor.

"It's breakfast time. You hungry? We let you sleep in a bit. Did you see? The weather's lovely."

Out in the hallway and again on the stairs Bernard patted him on the shoulder, telling him everything would be fine. He asked Victor why he didn't want to talk. Victor shrugged and stepped into the dining room which was bright and already uncomfortably hot, and sat down in front of a white bowl that cast a soft halo of light on the table. Bernard poured him some hot chocolate and the boy thanked him in a faint voice still thick with sleep. He ate heartily while Bernard sipped a cup of coffee, glancing at him anxiously from time to time. The boy avoided his gaze, staring at a hunk of bread, at the bottom of his bowl or at the far wall where there was a huge poster of a pride of lions being pestered by their cubs.

"Pretty hot," Bernard said. "And it's only the middle of June."

Victor turned to the window. Behind the lowered blinds the sun was gathering all its dazzling power.

"We're meeting with a judge this morning," Bernard said. "A children's judge."

Victor looked up at him in surprise.

"Don't panic, it's not what you think. She needs to think about your situation and decide what to do for the best. You can't stay here forever, I mean, it's not exactly much fun, is it? And since you don't have any family to look after you, she'll have to settle you with people who will be your new family. She'll talk to you about what you want, what you'd like, alright? She'll ask you questions, so you have to try and answer. Is that O.K.?"

On the poster one of the lion cubs was nipping at his mother's back and she let him, her big jaws gaping, her eyes closed. The boy finished his bowl of chocolate and started to gather the breadcrumbs into small piles.

"Victor, did you hear what I said?"

"Yes," the boy said in a whisper.

Bernard smiled. He rarely smiled, so when he did he looked like a completely different person.

"See? We're making progress."

Victor looked down at his feet. He wiggled his toes in his slippers for a minute, long enough for the social worker to get to his feet and clear away their bowls and their cutlery. He asked Victor to help by carrying the bread basket and the pot of jam, which the boy did straight away, and they went and stacked everything on the trolley at the end of the room.

Victor took a long shower, pushing his face into the powerful, cold spray, then scrubbed his body until patches of his skin were red raw. He sniffed his clothes before putting them back on, then brushed his shock of black hair back in front of a small mirror hanging on a wardrobe door. When he came down to the lobby, Bernard told him he looked very smart and said all the girls at his school must fancy him. Victor shrugged and followed him outside and over to a red car, squinting into the sun. They set off immediately.

*

The town flashed past. He watched the stream of buildings, shop windows, passers-by whisked out of his field of vision as they sped by. Bernard was talking about the judge again, using simple words that made everything sound complicated, so Victor stopped listening. At some point, while they were stopped at a red light, Victor asked if he could turn on the radio. A drawling voice immediately filled the car; the song was something about a fisherman's cabin, and the social worker whistled along until the signal faded into static as the car turned into an underground car park opposite the soaring columns of the courthouse. Victor glanced around at the vast empty car park, divided up by concrete pillars and banks of strip lights. From time to time he could hear a squeal of tyres or the sound of a car door slamming, but it was impossible to tell where it came from, since there was not a living soul in sight and the few cars there looked as though they had been abandoned.

They were asked to sit on a bench in a long hall lit by tall, grubby windows through which he could see pigeons launching themselves into the blue sky. The social worker tried to reassure him, telling him the lady judge was very nice, that she was caring and kind, that Victor could ask her anything he liked. The boy simply nodded, staring down at the chequerboard of black and white tiles. He only looked up when a teenage boy came and sat opposite with his police escort, a huge, fat man in a pale blue shirt stretched to bursting over his pot belly. They were handcuffed together, their hands flat on the bench, seemingly indifferent to the short chain connecting them.

A few people passed while they sat waiting: a lawyer, two policemen, harried clerks carrying piles of case files, and each time Victor would stare into their faces, trying to interpret their worried or tired expressions, then watch until they disappeared through a door or into the stairwell. He was vaguely intrigued by these people, but spent much of his time trying to guess from which side of the lofty window the next pigeon would appear. When they were finally called, Victor tried again to catch the teenager's eye, but the boy, his face now almost on his knees, was slowly scratching his cropped hair, apparently oblivious to what was going on around him, he looked like a meditating penitent on the verge of withdrawing into himself completely.

The judge, a young woman in a red jacket and a black blouse, was by turns solemn and smiling. She jotted constantly in her notebook without ever taking her eyes off Victor, who wondered how she could write without looking at the page. Whenever he tried, his writing scuttered all over the place, heedless of lines and margins. The judge wrote even during the silences, of which there were many, when all that could be heard was the rasp of pen on paper, the sound of breathing, and the creak of the woman's joints every time she moved. Perhaps she was taking notes about the silence or about the unseasonal heat stealing through the half-open window that made their faces shine. Victor answered her questions only with a "yes" or a "no", the rest of the time he simply stared into the judge's eyes, his mouth half open, his bottom lip glistening with saliva. At the end of a particular silence that seemed longer than the others, the judge asked whether he enjoyed school, mentioning his good grades and the positive assessments of his teachers. Victor nodded and immediately thought about his friends, about Mourad, about Camille who sat in front of him in class, flicking her blonde plaits under his nose, Camille who had once kissed him on the lips, teasing him with the pointed tip of her tongue. He remembered the brightness of the art room when, bent over a big sheet of paper, he carefully drew a line in Indian ink, remembered break times last winter and the talk about whether or not it would snow. He thought back to those days that now seemed idyllic, and realised he could not remember them all. He wished he had a photographic memory so that he could call them up at will and replay them like a D.V.D., because suddenly there were too many things he could not remember, and he had the agonising feeling that his life was full of holes, that he had only lived those scant few things he could remember, as though the rest of the time he had been asleep, unconscious, or dead.

The judge talked about a foster family in the country, about the fresh air, about how kind they were, and Victor had to brush aside his meagre memories to focus on her words, which seemed to buzz around his ears like flies threatening to land on him, the same flies he had seen swarm into his mother's bedroom.

"A family with children your own age, you'll be able to play in the woods and the fields, the sea isn't far, you'll be able to go to the beach every day, you'll see, Victor, life goes on and I'll help you, we'll all help, me, your guardian *ad litem*, that's what we call the social worker looking after your case, do you understand? If you have any problems you can call me, but I don't think you'll need to, usually everything works out just fine, these families are used to looking after children like you who need help to get a new start in life. Did you know that little by little you can create a new family? Do you think you'd like that?"

Silence returned, more sticky and oppressive than ever. The boy felt all eyes staring at him, so he scratched the back of his hand with a fingernail, hunching his head into his shoulders, and desperately tried to think of something to say the way he did when a teacher suddenly sprang a question on him in class, finally filling his lungs and whispering:

"In the country?"

"Don't you like the countryside?" Bernard said.

Victor shrugged. *The countryside*, he repeated to himself again, as the hearing drew to a close. Everyone stood up and the judge patted him on the head and solemnly shook his hand. "Come on, Victor, you're a brave boy, you're almost a man. And we all have to be brave, don't you think?" She turned to the social worker. "It should take about eight to ten days, things aren't too busy just now, so the placement should come through quickly. I'll have a word with Monsieur Castet at the D.D.A.S.S."

"Did you hear that, Victor? You won't have to stay at the children's home for long. Did you hear what *madame la juge* said?"

Victor nodded and stepped out into the hallway while the judge and the social worker murmured something he made no attempt to hear. He looked along the benches, hoping to see the teenage prisoner and the fat policeman, but the hall was deserted and the deep silence was broken only by the creak of distant doors.

*

He spent the afternoon aboard the *Nautilus* with Professor Aronnax, watching hundreds of fish swim past the vast picture window of the submarine. Sitting in a deckchair under a large oak tree, he listened to the melancholy of Captain Nemo's organ-playing. More than once he set down his copy of *Twenty Thousand Leagues Under the Sea* to watch the birds flitting among the shadows of the trees or to doze for a while. Time passed quickly. Without quite knowing why, he was waiting for nightfall, perhaps because it meant a relief from the heat. He thought about his mother. Over and over he pictured her, terrified that he might not be able to remember what she looked like, leafing through memories that were clear and sharp as photographs, but sometimes the pages of this mental photo album were too heavy, they refused to turn or became muddled and the images were incomprehensible. When he did manage to isolate a clean, clear and luminous image that showed the softness of her look, the glint of sunlight on her hair, the strange sad smile she sometimes had when she looked at him, he replayed it over and over, studying every detail, storing it carefully in a corner of his brain, the way he might have learnt by heart a poem.

He allowed the evening to slip by, watching the frantic activities of the other children out of the corner of his eye. The two brothers were constantly together, each mimicking the other's actions to the point where, without a word, they would simultaneously turn and focus on the same point with the same flutter of their eyelids, which could as easily signify boredom as fear. At some point, in a perfectly synchron-ised action, they got to their feet and, with small, quick steps, walked towards the stairs leading to the bedrooms. The older children spent the evening gathered around the table football, but this time Victor kept his distance, happy just to watch their wild gestures, to listen to the dull thwacks and obscenities that were a raucous running com-mentary on the fiercely contested games.

Bernard and another social worker came and sat next to the boy and asked him how he was doing, and he said, "Fine, I'm fine," but when Bernard wanted to know how he felt about the hearing Victor stared at him so intently, his eyes glistening with sadness and confusion, that

Bernard had to turn away. The other social worker, Farid, suggested a game of table tennis, "a quiet game, just the two of us," but Victor shook his head, staring down, and the three of them sat motionless in this pocket of silence, the adults staring at the boy who sat, curled up, his head in his hands. After a while Victor said quietly that he was going to bed, the two men wished him goodnight, and he rushed off.

He took the urn containing his mother's ashes from the wardrobe and sat on the bed, cradling it, running his hand over the smooth surface that glowed red in the evening light. For some minutes, he stared sightlessly into some dark corner of the room, then he began to weep silently, his body wracked by sobs, his forehead pressed to the lid of the urn, sniffling and murmuring inarticulately as those who have a god do when they pray.

Shortly before 10.00 p.m. the other children came upstairs, there were doors slammed, muffled noises, pounding on the walls, pipes rumbling. Shouts, laughter and curses erupted in the corridor. The noise brought Victor to his feet again and he stood in the middle of the room, listening to the uproar, anxious and wary. He stared in alarm as his door shuddered from the racket outside, petrified lest someone come in and steal what little he had salvaged from this tragedy.

But no-one was interested in Victor's pitiful belongings or his relics, and he was not called on to protect them. After a while, the commotion faded and he could hear only hushed voices, creaking doors, the throbbing bass of some unrecognisable piece of music, and within an hour everything had fallen silent and the night, with its rustling of trees, its rumble of cars and honking trucks on the motorway, had prevailed. For a long time Victor listened in the darkness to the obdurate, varied life of the city, all the while staring at the shelf where he had placed the urn, watching it intermittently flicker with a crimson glow, or rather a radiance, since no light could cling to its metallic surface.

*

He had no idea what time it was, but he knew this was the moment. He had been half asleep, but now he got up, and in three steps he was at the window. He leaned across the sill and, gripping with his hands, swung himself out until he found himself hanging by his arms, then he let go, dropping the three metres to the ground. He rolled as he landed on the lawn and stayed for a moment on all fours, feeling the soft grass against the palms of his hands. He looked back at the building, studying the shadowy windows. Nothing moved. He ran through the darkness along the line of trees towards the fence and scaled it effortlessly. He started walking northwards. Towards home. When he came to the first streetlamps he tugged vainly at the collar of his jacket, trying to hide his face. He took only dimly lit streets, running past houses slumbering in small gardens where now and then a dog rushed up, barking at him and baring its teeth through the wire fence. Then, suddenly fearless, he dashed across broad avenues, bent double as though dodging sniper fire. He could easily have encountered a police car, but he saw none. Above a billboard he saw the time: 1.30 a.m. The city was deserted, the only noise now was a low murmur, the gentle breathing of a monster at rest.

It took him almost two hours to reach home. As he cut through the dockland area known as Les Bassins à flot, he got scared. Water swirled in the darkness, gurgling like a hungry mouth, and he had a fleeting image of some terrifying slimy creature. Sweat ran down his back in ticklish rivulets and he rubbed the back of his T-shirt with his fingertips. Passing the old submarine base and turning onto the rue Blanqui he felt the urge to run, to sprint the last few hundred metres, but his legs stubbornly refused to obey him and he trudged along the streets where he had spent his childhood, glancing anxiously about him like a wanted fugitive. He kept a watch on the sky, for at any moment, he knew, the treacherous blue of dawn might appear, rousing innocent sleepers.

He stopped at the corner of his road, suddenly breathless. He could see his house, and the dark blinds of Madame Huvenne's house next door, could picture her tossing and turning in her bed, her legs crippled with rheumatism. A jumbled crowd of memories teemed in his mind.

For the first time, he pictured his life in the past tense.

He scrambled over the gate, just as he had whenever he forgot his keys, jumped down into the garden, panting, scratching himself on the perfumed rose bushes, those familiar hydras that bent their many heads towards him, walked around the house and stood under the silk tree, breathing in the smell of the long grass. He tried to calm the beating of his heart, breathing deeply through his mouth, then fumbled under a flower pot, found a bunch of keys and, ripping away the police tape, managed to open one the French windows. He stood on the threshold, panting. The smell of death still hung in the darkness, a fetid spectre that forced the boy back outside, where he bent double, his stomach heaving, retching up bilious gobs of phlegm.

Steeling himself, Victor stepped into the house, throwing the French doors wide and waving his hands, which did nothing to dispel this thing that still haunted the place, that gnawed at his stomach, crushing his lungs in its loathsome invisible hands. Turning on the light, he walked more confidently into the hallway, stepped into the kitchen and opened the drawer next to the sink, searching methodically until he found a packet of batteries which he stuffed into his jacket pocket. He looked around at the familiar décor, the cupboards with their crooked doors, the potted plant by the window drooping for lack of water. He stepped closer to the large calendar of film posters that was still showing "Les Enfants du Paradis" and studied the dreamy expression of Arletty and, behind her, the faces of Jean-Louis Barrault and Pierre Brasseur leading the jubilant crowds on the boulevard du Crime. He knew nothing about these actors, or about the film, but was surprised to see the name of Jacques Prévert in the credits. He lifted the page to see what film had been chosen for July: it was "The Asphalt Jungle". In the foreground he saw Sterling Hayden, worried, tense, half swallowed by the darkness. He knew nothing about this film either. He unhooked the calendar and laid it on the counter next to the draining board, where two plates and two glasses had long ago finished drying, the last that they had used. He picked up the glasses, held them up to the light, trying to make out a lipstick smear, some trace his mother might have left when she last had a drink. But there was nothing, the curved glass was immaculately, devastatingly transparent.

He went up to his bedroom, running his fingertips over random objects, uncertain what to do. He sat in front of his computer and was about to turn it on to read his email, then decided against it and sat staring at his faint reflection in the black screen. None of it mattered anymore. All the hours he had spent playing in fantastical familiar universes, with their rules and their strange creatures, their vicious and preposterous battles, all the time he had spent flying around only to find himself, with a sigh of relief, on the edge of an accursed forest or on some battlefield where he was to wage war against some enemy, all the while sending instant messages to other players, mocking or berating some prince of darkness – it all seemed so remote now, it was in the past, a crumpled memory, a scrap of paper to be tossed away, a vanished childhood.

Slowly he got up and went over to the bookcase to look at a photograph taken the previous winter: snuggled together on the sofa, he and his mother were staring solemnly into the lens. The resemblance between them was striking: they had the same big, dark eyes and thick lashes, the same black hair, their mouths were the same shape. They might have been mistaken for brother and sister, something she often joked about until one day when he had asked her if it was possible for him to be both her brother and her son. She had gazed at him for a long time, then shook her head, shrugging as though to shake off a spider's web, then with a cheery smile said don't be ridiculous, just think about it for a second, you silly goose! "That really would be the last straw," she added. She planted a loud kiss right on his ear and he shook his head, laughing, to banish the ringing noise.

He took the photograph from its frame and slipped it into his backpack, then rummaged through another drawer for more fresh batteries for the Walkman and a few cassettes that she had given him that he never listened to, some pens and a new exercise book; from his bedside table he picked up a knife she had given him a year ago, running his finger over the embossed Laguiole logo, a copper bee, examining the sharp blade in the lamplight. He sat on his bed for a long time staring at the wall above the shelves of school textbooks, plastered with posters of football players, musicians or singers, and the big poster for "Lord of the Rings", a film he had seen in April. He studied every inch of these few square metres where his past life was frozen in time. He let himself slip into the confusion of memories that came unbidden. Sensations and precise images flooded back, he was powerless to stop them. He would have liked to cry, to hack up this bitter sadness lodged in his throat. He wanted to sleep here, in his own bed, one last time. To pretend. To wake to the promise of the dawn glow, to lie in bed a little longer, watching sunlight move across the shutters. To hope that maybe the bedroom door would open: 'You not up yet? Have you seen the time?" He could hear his mother's sing-song voice and remembered the pleasurable laziness that made him turn over in bed and go straight back to sleep, and the memory of this ghostly pleasure made him shudder.

He stripped off the bedspread and curled up, his cheek pressed against the coolness of the pillow, turned off the light and lay in the dark listening to the silence, expecting a whispered voice, a rustle of fabric, expecting a miracle, staring wide-eyed into the darkness where even now that miracle seemed to be stirring.

It had probably been a dream. Nothing had happened. He was lying on his bed surrounded by the familiar outlines of his room, utterly at ease in this familiar space. He didn't know where his dreams began or ended. He felt he was hovering on the brink of an extraordinary event.

He scrambled from the bed and stood in the boundless silence. A shiver ran down his back.

"Manou?"

His voice sounded strange, hoarse, a whisper. It may not even have stirred the air. The air around him felt thick and heavy.

And yet there came an answer. A sound like a throat being cleared. Almost a cough. He stood motionless and listened. He called his mother's name again, softly, as though talking to someone who might be asleep. A low moaning sound filled the air. A soft, almost imperceptible groan. He did not dare to breathe.

Then suddenly he smelled tobacco smoke.

He pushed open the bedroom door and glanced down the hall. The kitchen light was on. Someone was smoking. He did not know whether or not he should be afraid. Brushing his fingertips along the wall, he groped his way through the semi-darkness towards the orange light.

She was sitting with one elbow propped on the table, staring at the window as she exhaled a plume of smoke, she looked thoughtful, her head tilted back. She was wearing cream cotton trousers and a baggy black T-shirt. A packet of cigarettes lay beside the ashtray, a small blue lighter standing next to it.

Victor had seen her like this dozens of times, sitting in precisely this position, smoking in silence; she never heard him approach, never turned until he was standing in the doorway, when she would turn and smile to hide the sadness that tugged the corners of her lips into a bitter crease. He did not speak now, but made the most of this daydream so that he could study her. As always, he found her beautiful, in this moment perhaps more beautiful than ever.

She reached out a hand to tap the ash off her cigarette into the ashtray and shook her black hair.

"Manou?"

She did not react. She just ran her hand through her hair and down her neck, lifting the dark mane that shimmered with blue.

"Maman? Is that you?"

Victor waved his hand to attract her attention, and suddenly everything faded and darkness enveloped him, forcing him back against the wall. He slumped there for a moment. With a groan, he forced himself to stand up straight and, flicking the light on, he stepped into the kitchen.

He walked around the table, eyes filled with tears, and stood on the very spot where, a moment earlier, he had seen her. He pulled out the chair, ran his hand over the seat, looked around for the ashtray and saw it lying upside down on the draining board. He spun around, then sat where she had been, adopting the same pose, staring out of the window, one elbow propped on the table, hoping that by some magic of this place, this pose, his mother's body would materialise in this very spot, on him or within him. He waited, breathless, tears pouring from his eyes and snot running from his nose. "Come," he tried to whisper, "come, Manou," but no sound came but trickles of grief and desperate sobs.

After a while he got up and looked around again. He put his head under the cold tap, drinking in long gulps. Dripping wet, he reluctantly returned to his room and found his backpack into which he slipped some books – *I Am Legend, The Mysterious Island, Moby Dick* – and his MP3 player. Then, checking that he had everything he needed, he glanced around the room one last time, and carefully closed the door.

Investigating the other rooms, he was surprised that the police investigations had not created more of a mess. A few cupboard doors or drawers stood open, their contents spilling out, but it was nothing like what he had seen on television or in movies. On the large sideboard in the living room he searched in vain for the photo album that was a record of his life, of both their lives over the past thirteen years: the police must have taken it away, and he fleetingly wondered what they might want with pictures of babies or toddlers in pushchairs, children swimming or playing ball. He had to make do with three or four framed photographs of his mother, alone or with him, taking them from their frames which he replaced – gaping, empty windows – exactly where he had found them.

He did not go into the room where she had been killed. He stood in the doorway, paralysed by this solid block of darkness, so compact that the light from the hallway seemed unable to pierce it. The smell seemed stronger here, so much so that he stepped back, suddenly terrified of this malevolent place, and retreated down the hallway as far as the door, open onto the cool of the night, though he could not feel a breath of wind against his neck. His mind was filled with grisly images, and suddenly the familiar creak of the beams and the walls, the woodwork and floors, seemed evidence of some secret, ominous presence in the house. He found himself out in the garden, gasping for breath, staring back at the doorway into the brightly lit hall, from which no ghost appeared, though a swarm of moths had already begun to flutter in. He turned off the light and closed the French windows, leaning his full weight on the door while he turned the lock, as though on the other side evil forces were trying to push their way out so they could seize him, then, slipping the now useless keys into his pocket, he ran out into the street.

*

Victor spent all of the following day listening to his mother's cassettes on the Walkman, using the batteries he had brought from home. Apart from meal times he stayed in his room or went out and sat on the grass beneath the oak tree, and read a hundred pages of *The Mysterious Island*. In the afternoon four girls came out with a C.D. player, sitting or lying on towels and passing around headphones so they could listen to songs they knew by heart, singing along to the choruses, humming the sentimental lyrics, nodding their heads. They bickered over which singer should make it through to the next round of some television programme they watched religiously. Victor observed them out of the corner of his eye, feigning indifference whenever one of them turned his way, but soon they were all staring at him, giggling and whispering things that made them burst out laughing, and he felt himself start to blush and began to sweat even more, unable to concentrate on his book.

He pretended to be interested in the football match that a dozen or so boys were playing a little further off, raising a huge cloud of dust. They yelled for the ball, swore at each other, and crowed over every goal scored. They were the same yells, the same insults as when they played table football, but choked now with exhaustion and aggravated by the heat. They often fell, especially the smaller boys who were knocked to the ground by the bigger players, and it looked more like some kind of primitive battle, a confusing jousting match where almost anything was permitted and the survival of the fittest was the only rule.

The roaring of the boys, the singing and laughing of the girls, this constant reminder that life went on, gradually faded, and Victor, leaning back against the deckchair's rough canvas, spent a long time staring up into the oak leaves, glittering here and there with scraps of light. From time to time he was blinded by a shaft of sunlight, and, closing his eyes, would see a glowing red wound, watch it slowly close and grow black, leaving only darkness and a shower of stars dancing before his eyes. Then he would go back to watching, disturbed now and then by a gust of warm air, until finally he dozed off.

He woke to find himself alone, with birds waging war in the branches above and the light, which had paled to yellow, now spread at his feet. He struggled out of the deckchair and looked around. Traces of dust still hung over the deserted football pitch. He imagined himself the sole survivor of an apocalypse, which sleep had allowed him to come through unscathed, and took a few steps, tasting the illusory power of this solitude. A wasp buzzed around his face and he lashed out and saw it fall to the ground, where he crushed it with the toe of his espadrille. He picked up his book and walked towards the building, its windows and shutters closed now to try to maintain some semblance of coolness inside. He was sweating, his T-shirt was stuck to his skin and he tugged at it, shaking the hem to dry the sweat that trickled from creases and crevices where it had collected. It would probably be cooler inside. He longed for shade, for darkness. He also longed to take a shower and thought of the cold showers he used to take at home all the time, and how he used to run out into the garden afterwards without bothering to towel himself dry, just to feel the cool air wash over him for a few minutes. He dismissed the idea as he thought of the only options now open to him: those cold, tiled cubicles that constantly rang with the voices, groans and whistles of other boys.

He took the stairs three at a time and shut himself in the dim light of his bedroom, and as he turned the key into the lock the door creaked on its hinges and the boy's heart stopped as he peered into the darkness, trying to make out who was moving about in the room.

He saw a stooped form sitting on the bed, saw the open urn sitting on his lap, saw the hand hastily withdraw.

"Put it down."

"What is it?" the boy said.

His name was Nicolas. He was tall and thin, his arms and legs were solid muscle, with long hands that lashed out and punched at random. Victor had seen him keeping watch at night over the table football. His eyes gleamed faintly in the darkness, broken only by a vertical strip of light between the closed shutters. His eyes were very pale, huge, wide with surprise or perhaps fear. He was much taller and stronger than Victor, but he stared at him anxiously, without the slightest expression of defiance, perhaps because he sensed this was something he could not understand. He put the lid back on the urn, hugging it to him, and wiped first one hand and then the other on his shorts to get rid of whatever had stuck to them with sweat.

"Down," Victor said.

No air seemed to come from his throat. He took two steps and knocked over the other boy, just as he set the crimson urn down next to him on the bed. The intruder's head hit the wall at the foot of the bed and he fell on his back, his arms and legs thrashing, and, feet together, Victor jumped on his stomach so that the boy could not even scream, his breathing coming in short, ragged gasps. Victor clamped his hands around the boy's neck, his fingers squeezing the carotid artery like a vice, felt the boy's hands gripping his wrists, still covered with a film of his mother's ashes, and he focused his whole weight on his fingertips that gripped the boy's throat. In that moment he could have dug straight through the skin, into the very pulse of the blood that he could feel pounding frantically beneath his fingernails, and he brought his mouth close to the boy's face, already bloated by suffocation, feeing a sudden urge to gnaw off a hunk of flesh and spit it back in his face, but, as he was about to bite down, as his lips brushed the cheek just below the right eye, he felt someone yank him back and instinctively Victor grabbed a big hank of dark hair so as he toppled onto his back he pulled the boy's crimson face towards him, the eyes bulging, staring and so swollen with terror they looked as though they might pop like the corks from a wineskin. Victor wriggled away from the hands gripping him, managing to headbutt the apoplectic face in front of him. The boy let out a groan and fell backwards, blood spurting from his nose or his mouth, and Victor pounded his head against the wall, the dull thuds setting off panicked cries from behind him. He felt an arm around his throat cutting off his breathing and he let go as voices screamed at him, *Stop, Calm down, Are you crazy or something? What the fuck has got into you? Stop that right now.*

The bodies of the two boys were disentangled, one convulsed with pain and fear, the other paralysed with rage, a mute statue of fury, all muscle and nerves.

Victor was pushed to one side and rolled against the wardrobe door where he curled into a ball, hands on his head, fingers gripping the hank of hair that he had ripped out. He heard the other boy panting and coughing, snivelling and sobbing like a child. He closed his eyes, turning his back on the cacophony of voices murmuring vague, useless, anxious or reassuring platitudes that drowned out the moans of the boy who for some reason they were now calling Thomas.

Someone leaned over his shoulder and said that they would have to have words about this later, that it was a serious matter, and then the noise abruptly faded, and the silence was so dense he could hear his heart pounding with hatred, wracking his whole chest. He lay curled up on the carpet for a long time, maybe an hour, moving only to stretch a hand out and pull the upturned urn towards to him, hugging it to his neck. Fragments of memory came to him: images, a few happy feelings. He heard voices echoing within him, dominated by his mother's: the tone of the voices was so clear, so precise in their inflections that for a moment he thought that they were in this very room talking to him, he felt almost sure that if he turned he would see all these strangers whispering into his ear with that kindness that made him smile in spite of himself, so he did not turn around, he clung to this pleasure like a child slowly unwrapping a present, savouring the moment when it will finally appear.

He must have been dreaming. He remembered a film he had seen once in which unearthly voices heralded the appearance of mournful ghosts who demanded that the survivor exact revenge for the agonies they had endured. He wondered whether his dead mother might not be calling to him from the beyond and at first the thought frightened him, though later it reassured him since it was so easy to respond to her request. But Victor did not believe in the afterlife, he did not believe in salvation, and so he turned back to the empty room, shrugging off the idea. All that remained of the living, he was convinced, was contained in the urn that he now opened to study the grey ash so recently profaned, and he began to cry, his tears falling into the vessel, leaving darker spots, a fine drizzle on parched soil.

That evening he found himself alone at dinner. The two brothers had initially walked towards his table but changed their mind and sat some distance away, staring at him gravely, holding their forks aloft, before starting to eat with the same mechanical gestures. The conversations seemed less raucous. The girls seemed quieter than usual, and Victor caught them looking at him and turning away as soon as he looked back, but they did not laugh, they only talked in low voices.

Victor got up to stack his plate and his cutlery on the trolley and headed into the T.V. lounge where the sound of the set drowned out the voices of the younger kids who had raced to play table football before the older boys chased them away, as they always did. The boy called Nicolas was nowhere to be seen. Victor sat on a red sofa near the open window, through which a warm breeze blew, stretching his legs out, staring out at the dark green shadows of the grounds framed against the grey-green sky, marked by high clouds that perhaps heralded a storm. He was not looking for anything, was not thinking about anything, or maybe he was thinking so many impossible things that it amounted to the same thing. He strained to isolate the muffled roar of cars on the motorway from the muddle of sound.

The following day Victor was summoned to the director's office, with Bernard and Farid, to be questioned about the incident the night before. The director ran a worried hand over his close-cropped grey hair. He demonstrated his irritation at Victor's frequent silences and his mumbled, often unintelligible answers, by taking deep breaths, his nostrils flared, his beady eyes staring from behind his thick glasses before sinking back heavily into his armchair.

Head bowed, glancing up surreptitiously at the men, Victor explained through clenched teeth that it had been the other boy's fault for touching ... He could not bring himself to name the object, alluding to it with faltering words and silences.

The three adults explained to him that such violence could not be tolerated, that it was no way to settle a disagreement. Naturally they understood that he had experienced a terrible tragedy; what had happened to his mother was appalling, it was shocking, but it was no excuse. He was an intelligent young man, surely he could understand that if he were to perpetuate the sort of violence his mother had suffered, there would be no end to it. They explained the concept of a vicious cycle. They patiently took it in turns, speaking in the same placid tone, despite the different timbres of their voices, but their words, which were intended to placate, became a garbled murmur, fraying like a piece of fabric against a blade as they began to grope for something new to say, for anything to say, and finally, faced with the boy's obdurate muteness, they trailed off into silence.

That night, when it got dark, he listened to some rap on his MP3 player, lying on the bed and staring out of the open window. He grew tired of the swaggering proclamations of the ghetto and grabbed his mother's Walkman and slotted in one of the cassettes the police had randomly packed, on which she had recorded a few of the old-fashioned, elegiac singers she would hum along to, suddenly dreamy and sad whenever she heard them on the radio.

When these songs from the past had died away, he noticed that a still, deep silence had settled all around him, and the moment was so tender that he suddenly found himself wishing that day would never dawn again.

6

Vilar slept through the night only to be woken, sweating, heart hammering, by a nightmare, the same nightmare he always had: someone was ringing his doorbell and he ran to open it, but his legs refused to respond, he could see the dark door at the far end of the hall, quivering from the intense ringing, he choked with fear at the thought of what would happen, panting as he tried in vain to run, and then suddenly he would find himself on the threshold, the door would open, and a sobbing man would place Pablo's lifeless body in his arms and vanish into thin air, and Vilar would hear himself crying out as he hugged his dead son close, but when he finally looked down the face was not that of his son, the features faded, became blurred, anonymous, though in his mind he knew that it was Pablo, *my son, my son, Ana, come quick, help me*, but Ana did not come because the nightmare always stopped on that moment of utter isolation, that dizzying drifting through space, that howl as white-hot metal seared the terrible truth into his brain: Pablo is dead, Pablo is dead.

Vilar wiped away the tears streaking his face with the back of his hand and glanced at the clock radio. He waited for his pounding heart to be still, trying, as he always did, to picture the face of the man from the nightmare, who vanished as he howled with grief, a face that seemed ordinary, familiar, a mask at once recognisable and impossible to make out. But the pale screen of the ceiling remained blank as the morning light slowly crept over it, stealing through chinks in the shutters.

He got up. He did what people usually do in the morning, he did it unthinkingly, motivated only by the need to get moving, to get through another day. He wondered when these "heart-rending dawns" would end, tried to remember where that phrase came from, a poem maybe, something he had studied in some other life. Not his early-morning life, jolting and creaking like some rickety train along a disused railway line. Sometimes he reached for the communication cord, the emergency button that would stop the train, but could never quite bring himself to press it.

Courage or cowardice? He had weighed these words, measured their elusiveness, endlessly rehashed this fruitless argument. In the end he had decided to act according to his preference, or his utter lack of preference. To act on instinct.

He basked in the sun out on the balcony that morning, sitting on a plastic chair, sipping a cup of coffee. He listened to the birds trilling and rustling the leaves of the trees in the park. The heat was sufficiently mild that he closed his eyes and surrendered to it. The moment was sufficient unto itself: it evoked no past, aroused no feeling of nostalgia, and the longer he could drag it out the longer he could stave off the future.

The phone rang. Vilar felt himself rudely torn from this luminous interlude. Stepping back into the dark apartment, he could hear nothing but a faint buzzing.

"It's Daras. We've tracked down the three people involved in the train station stabbing. They're at 25 rue des Douves. We're meeting up outside the police station at Les Capucins. Half an hour. Get your arse in gear."

He felt a tingle beneath his skin. That nervous electricity, those galvanic shocks that shot down to his fingertips. He stood motionless, staring at the telephone, savouring this feeling, his eyes closed, massaging his temples with his fingertips, then he managed to get ready within five minutes. His movements felt easy, lithe, confident. He turned away from the window and all its pointless light.

The police station at Les Capucins, next to the covered market, looked like a matchbox laid on its side. A squat, narrow, brown building, it was singularly ugly, the windows conspicuously barred.

As he drew up beside the cars already parked there, Vilar imagined the possibility of the three duty officers having to withstand a siege some night, remembering a film he had seen years ago, John Carpenter's "Assault on Precinct 13", because the station's layout and its surroundings lent themselves to that sort of sordid, violent scenario. The first man he saw as he got out of his car was taking a pump-action shotgun from the boot of a Peugeot and checking that it was loaded. His name was Garcia, and he wore a bulletproof vest. Vilar abandoned any attempt to consult his increasingly selective memory for the man's first name – Didier, Denis? Or maybe Gérard? What did it matter, he thought, and shook Garcia's hand.

"Is it war? Have they found Bin Laden?"

Garcia screwed up his mouth.

"Is that supposed to be funny?"

Ever since the destruction of New York's Twin Towers, Garcia had made a personal crusade of tracking down terrorists. He saw himself as a soldier in the war between good and evil, between Western values and barbaric obscurantism. His voice took on a tragic quality whenever the subject was mentioned: Western civilisation was at stake, and he was not about to allow people to joke about such things. Rumour had it he had applied for a transfer to the intelligence services, the R.G. or the D.S.T., so that he could join the grown-up version of hide-and-seek, and jokers would ask him when he planned to take the entrance exam for the C.I.A. Vilar laid a hand on his shoulder.

"Relax, pal, and take it easy on the ammo."

He spotted Daras talking on her car phone and walked over. She hung up and flashed him a half-smile.

"Glad you could make it. Hope I didn't get you out of bed?"

"No. I was drinking coffee on my balcony, listening to the birds singing, that kind of shit. It was really sunny."

She looked at him suspiciously. Unconvinced.

"Marianne, I was having a moment, O.K.? I was almost happy."

A police radio crackled in her pocket. She brought it to her ear and listened, nodding.

"Game on."

They piled into two cars. Daras, Vilar and a lieutenant from Galand's squad in a clapped-out 306, the others in a brand-new Renault estate. It took only a few seconds to arrive in front of 25 rue des Douves. Two cars from the G.I.G.N. Special Ops unit pulled up at the same time and officers in combat gear jumped out: some took up positions with backs flat against the front of the building, others crouching in the hallway, waiting for orders.

As he got out of the car, Vilar noticed that the street was cordoned off at both ends and swarming with officers. Pradeau appeared out of nowhere, carrying a gun.

"One of the guys has a record for aggravated assault and possession of a firearm," he said. "It was Daras who insisted we come tooled up. You're not carrying?"

Vilar pushed back the flap of his jacket.

"No, I've got nothing. Just this. At least this way people will know who I am."

He took a police armband from his pocket and slipped it over the sleeve of his jacket.

The apartment was on the first floor. They plunged into the dark hallway, Daras leading the way, as usual. Two men in helmets carrying a battering ram ran past her, and everyone else moved away from the entrance and out of the line of fire. The apartment door splintered like a Chinese paper screen and Garcia disappeared inside, waving his gun, kicking over furniture and roaring "Police!" The others following him spread out through a dark flat, stumbling over the junk strewn across the floor: chairs, clothes, glasses, bottles. The place reeked of dope and stale sweat, of mildew and smelly feet. A voice shouted "Light!", someone threw open a shutter with a loud bang, and sunlight flooded into a living room looking like a rubbish tip, piled with pizza boxes, Chinese takeaway boxes, beer cans, and empty wine bottles. The ashtrays were overflowing with cigarette butts and the remains of spliffs. Hunkering down amid the chaos, an officer started to make an inventory.

They found the three suspects in the bedrooms, in bed – alone or accompanied – together with two others. They identified the girl who had been spotted at the crime scene by her short orange hair. When they asked her to stand up, the hulking skinhead she was snuggled up to hurled himself at the two policemen trying to prise them apart, and the ensuing tussle amid the sweaty sheets was swiftly concluded by a rifle butt to the recalcitrant thug's face. The girl yelled something about making a formal complaint about police brutality, and one of the officers mockingly suggested she might like to get some clothes on first. Hands cuffed behind his back, her self-appointed bodyguard was left sprawled naked on the bed; someone would see to his bloody, broken nose later.

The two male suspects offered no resistance. The girl found in the bed of Jonathan Caussade, the man suspected of stabbing Kevin Labrousse, was a bottle blonde, something that was immediately apparent when she leapt out of bed, fighting mad, calling the policeman who told her not to move a "fucking cunt" and hoarsely spewing a torrent of abuse until Daras told her to shut her hole and instructed her to be taken out into the corridor and cuffed to a cast-iron radiator. Caussade simply fell back on the pillow, his palms turned towards the ceiling.

The last suspect burst into in tears and, lying flat on his stomach, his face buried in the pillow, the barrel of a gun pressed to the back of his neck, he sobbed that he hadn't done nothing, that it was all Jonathan's fault, that he'd tried to calm him down, that Carole would corroborate his story. Without even being asked, he gave them his name: Marc Chauvin, nicknamed Marco.

"You got a record?" Pradeau said.

"Yeah, had a bit of a run-in with the drugs squad, but I'm done with that shit now."

"You can tell us all about it later," Pradeau said. "Now shift your arse and get some clothes on. And don't try anything stupid."

The guy nodded, staring fearfully at the gun pointed at him, and, snuffling, started picking up the clothes scattered around the bed.

A team of officers turned out the wardrobes, turned over the mattresses, raising clouds of dust that made everyone choke, so they opened the other windows and sunlight flooded in, thick with specks of powdered gold.

Vilar was rummaging through an old sideboard when he suddenly stopped and listened.

"Quiet, everyone!"

Garcia, who was holding a bag of grass, stared at him in surprise. Loud voices still came from the bedrooms.

"Everybody! Shut the fuck up!"

A child was crying. Vilar turned pale and stepped away from the sideboard, listening for the kid's sobs in the sudden silence. They had searched all the rooms. The sound was not coming from the apartment.

"It's coming from across the hall, from the flat opposite," someone said. "Someone's banging on a door, or a wall."

Vilar stepped out onto the landing and went over to the closed door, pressed down on the handle and was surprised to find it unlocked.

The sobbing was louder now. It was coming from behind one of the two doors he could just make out in the darkness. He pushed the door to his right: it was a kitchen, but the chaos and the filth were such that it was a moment before he could take it in, he had never seen the like of it before. The smell, which he had not noticed at first, almost made him retreat. The sickly, almost sweet stench caught in his throat, making his gorge rise. The smell of rotting meat and rotting vegetables. A dozen bloated bin bags were piled up under the window; one had burst and was oozing a thick, brownish liquid like toffee. There was washing-up piled in the sink, on the gas cooker and on the kitchen table, one small corner of which remained relatively clear and was set with a bowl, a packet of biscuits and box of sugar. Before he closed the door, he heard the *brigadier* push open the front door and cough, offering to open a window to air the place.

The living room at the end of the corridor was in darkness. Vilar groped for a switch, turned on the light, and noticed three or four large boxes containing televisions, stacked in a corner right behind the T.V., and various other boxes that looked to contain computers and D.V.D. players. On a sideboard, in a red frame, was a photograph of the girl with orange hair, cradling a baby. At the far end of the room was a Marilyn Manson poster, pinned to a black door. Vilar stepped around the battered leather sofa, passed the coffee table, on which were two beer cans and a nearly empty gin bottle. He was surprised at how tidy this room was compared to the general squalor.

The black door was locked. He looked around for a key but found nothing. The crying stopped as soon as he rattled the doorknob.

"Don't be frightened, we're coming to find you."

He wanted to break the door down, but he was afraid he might scare the child on the other side. A noise behind him made him start. Turning around, he saw Daras standing in the middle of the living room sniffing the neck of the gin bottle.

"What the hell are you up to? Where is this kid?"

He did not answer, he simply strode past past her and crossed the landing to the flat opposite.

The girl with orange hair was sitting facing Garcia, who was taking notes.

"Name's Carole Picard. She's twenty-four."

Vilar grabbed the girl by the scruff of her T-shirt and pulled her to her feet. She screamed and called him a fat fucker. He dragged her into the narrow hallway. Her hands were still cuffed behind her back. She tripped on an empty bottle and she fell to her knees, crying out in pain and shock, but Vilar did not turn around, did not let go. He hauled her across the landing, kicking and screaming. Daras blocked his path.

"Jesus, Pierre. Take it easy!"

Vilar looked her in the eyes, but did not see her.

"Let me deal with this. Don't bust my balls, Marianne. There's a kid all alone in that room."

She stood aside to let him pass, still dragging the girl who had managed to scrabble to her feet.

"Open it," he said as they stood in front of the door.

She twisted her hands behind her back.

"And how exactly am I supposed to do that?"

He uncuffed her and told her to make it quick. He watched as she shifted a pile of magazines and retrieved a Yale key.

Together they stepped into the murky room, lit only by a small bedside lamp with a shade decorated with cartoon characters. An acrid smell filled the air. He saw a potty beside the bed.

And on the bed, hugging her knees, sat a dark-haired girl, about five years old, maybe six. Her black hair fell across her face and her eyes shone in the half-light. She stared at the two grown-ups curiously, without apparent fear. Snot had dried on her upper lip, and her eyes were wet with tears.

"It's O.K.," the girl with orange hair said. "Maman is here. It's all fine, sweetheart."

The girl got off the bed and trotted over to her mother and allowed herself to be picked up, made a fuss of, closing her eyes, a vague smile on her lips. Vilar looked away as they kissed and cuddled. Then the girl broke off and put the child down.

"Are you hungry? Maman will make you breakfast."

"Are you taking the piss?" Vilar said.

Carole Picard turned as though she had forgotten he was there.

"Are you taking the piss?" he said again, his voice choking at the back of his throat. "I don't think you have quite understood the situation, mademoiselle."

He managed get the words out, but the effort left him breathless, almost trembling with rage.

The girl drew herself up to her full height, she looked defiant.

"Are you going to stop me making breakfast for my kid? Is that it? What right have you got? Is there a law against a mother giving her daughter something to eat?"

She didn't see Vilar's hand coming. He grabbed her under the chin and slammed her against the wall, banging her head.

"Now listen, you little slag: you better calm down, and quick, because you're about to make me seriously angry. You leave this little girl alone, locked in a room with a potty, while you go and get off your head in the flat next door, and to listen to you, you'd think you were the perfect mother! Are you planning to make breakfast sitting on a bin bag in that shit-tip of a kitchen? And all the hi-fi gear next door, I suppose that's her Christmas present? Don't take me for a mug, or I swear I'll deck you. The way I see it, the only reason you gave birth to this kid was to be rid of the weight, and you've treated her like an animal ever since."

He said all this in a low growl, his hand still squeezing her neck, oblivious to the fact the young woman was having difficulty breathing. The little girl rushed to her mother, hugging her legs, wailing with terror.

Vilar felt hands on his shoulders, on his arms, pulling him away, forcing him to let go, he heard voices, among them Daras' telling him to cool it, not to manhandle a witness. He took a few steps back, out of breath, and roughly shook off the hands of the others still holding him. Daras handcuffed Carole again and she was led away by two officers.

"Michel! Call the *procureur*'s office and the *brigade des mineurs*. Tell them you're bringing in a child. And get me a car."

She pulled up a chair and sat down close to the little girl who was still standing, petrified and silent, in the middle of the room amid the forest of legs of the motionless and now silent police officers.

"We'll look after you. Your maman has to come with us so we can ask her some questions. What's your name?"

The little girl looked at the gun one of the policemen was still holding.

"Could you give us some space, please?" Daras said quietly to the policeman, jerking her chin towards his weapon.

The man left without a word. Daras brushed a lock of hair from the girl's face.

"What's your name, sweetie?"

"Manon."

"And how old are you, Manon?"

"I'm five."

A female officer came in, taking off her cap.

"I can take care of her, if you like. We've got a free car. They'll give her something to eat back at the station. I've worked with them before."

Daras started to explain to the little girl what was going to happen. Vilar left the room, his head buzzing and filled with cotton wool. He crossed the landing and went back into the living room where his colleagues were collecting the spoils of their search: fifty grams of weed, a dozen rocks of crack, two hunting knives and an Astra revolver with no ammunition. The five suspects were sitting on the sofa, they did not move, did not speak to each other, did not look at anything, seemingly indifferent to what was going on around them. Only Carole Picard looked up and shot at Vilar a look filled with hatred to which he responded with a shrug.

He found himself suddenly useless and drained. He went out onto the landing and started down the stairs, dazzled by the solid slab of sunlight carved by the door onto the street.

"Pierre!"

Daras' voice. Vilar kept walking, squinting as he came into the harsh sunlight. It was almost 11.00 a.m. He fumbled in his pockets for cigarettes, but he had left them at home. He saw a *gendarme* standing nearby light up and was going over to bum one when Daras' voice caught up with him.

"Here," she said, holding out a pack of cigarettes.

She was smoking herself. He was surprised, and gave her an ironic smile.

"You've started again?"

"Too right. Bought them last night. I'm allowing myself a cancer break."

"Not a bad idea. That way you get used to the beast and you won't be so shaken when it shows up."

"Yeah, and then what? Shit . . ."

They smoked in silence. Daras calmly turned her face towards the sun.

"Is that it, then? Have you calmed down?"

"Yeah, I'm fine. You should have let me put the fear of God into that bitch. Maybe she might start to understand."

"You understand everything, do you?"

Vilar shook his head, flicked his cigarette into the distance.

"What about the kid she kept locked up, do you think she understands? What are we supposed to tell her?"

"Her mother . . ."

"Mother? I'm not sure the word really applies."

Daras blew the smoke far out in front of her and looked him in the eye.

"As I was saying, the mother said that one of the guys had a thing about the kid, which is why she kept her locked up while . . ."

"While she was getting her leg over in the neighbours' apartment. Model fucking parent. Why don't we give her a medal?"

Daras looked around and sighed, tight-lipped. The muscles in her cheeks twitched.

"I never said she was a model parent, I'm not stupid. But she's still the girl's mother, and I don't suppose she got to be a mother all by herself. Did you stop to think about the father?"

She was standing close to Vilar, talking into his face. He stared back defiantly.

"She told us everything, because she's terrified of her child being taken into care. The father was her boyfriend at university. She wasn't exactly an innocent, a bit of a rock chick, and the guy was immature. When he found out she was pregnant, he was thrilled. Refused to let her have an abortion, threatened to leave her if she did. She believed him, she kept the baby. The little fucker showed up to the maternity ward just once. She never saw him again. He went back to his parents in Brive. A practising Catholic, with a degree in politics and a clean-cut image. He'll probably be a cabinet minister before he's thirty. After he left, the girl fell out with her parents and she had a tough time bringing up her kid. That's the story. I'm not sure your macho morality lessons are appropriate."

Vilar shook his head.

"The kid was locked up all by herself. She was scared stiff. There's no excuse for that."

"I'm not making excuses. I'm just telling you how it is. We're police officers, not judges. Especially not in cases like this. We collared three fuckwits who stabbed and killed a random stranger. That's what we're paid for. But when it comes to her child, it's not my job to judge that girl – and it's not yours."

Vilar was about to say something, but Daras put a hand on his arm:

"You have to stop losing it every time you come across some kid who's had a tough life, otherwise one of these days you won't be able to do your job at all."

An officer came over and said they were taking the suspects down to the station. Daras checked her watch, swore under her breath, she had a ton of paperwork to get through that would probably keep them busy well into the evening.

Minutes later the police cars that had cordoned off the street since dawn had disappeared. Two officers stayed to keep an eye on the forensics team as they gathered up the evidence.

Caussade quickly confessed to the stabbing, but justified his actions because the victim, Kevin Labrousse, had been slow to give him a cigarette. Besides, he said, he had been up all night drinking. When asked if he had been aware that his actions might have fatal consequences, Caussade did not seem to understand the question, and when Pradeau, who was leading the interrogation, rephrased it, he sighed peevishly and said he had no idea.

Caussade's answers were an object lesson in studied weariness. All these questions "were making his head spin", he said. It was not his doing, he said, it was "fate". At this, Pradeau kicked the chair out from under him.

"You're the one who murdered him," he yelled, "not 'fate'!"

"Yeah, yeah, alright, fine!" Caussade grumbled. "No need to get all worked up, it's not going to bring the guy back. It's not like I wanted to kill him, I couldn't give a fuck about him. Look, I was off my face, it just happened. Too late to fix it now."

Carole Picard and Marc Chauvin claimed that there was nothing they could have done, that it all happened so quickly, and when asked why they did not report Caussade – who, after all, had killed a man who had never done him any harm – they both insisted it was a matter of loyalty – one of the few values they clung to – and besides, they said, they didn't grass. Chauvin was panicked about the possible repercussions, but a man's death barely seemed to touch him, it was something remote, abstract, it was meaningless. Like something in a video game. Neither expressed remorse or even a whit of compassion.

The *procureur* was kept regularly informed, and towards 11.00 p.m. the three accused were taken to the cells to appear before the court first thing in the morning.

The officers quickly headed towards the underground car park, each of them finally alone but done in. Engines roared into life, tyres squealed, and a procession of vehicles sped up the exit ramp, like gangsters making a getaway.

The first thing Vilar did when he got home was turn on his computer. Morvan had sent him an email an hour earlier: they needed to meet up, he had something to show Vilar, he could not talk on the phone. "It's not exactly a lead, Pierre, don't get your hopes up, but it's interesting, we need to talk," the former *gendarme* had written. Vilar sat for a long time staring at the two-line message on the screen, as though somehow more information would appear by magic. He felt as though he were on a slow merry-go-round watching familiar faces flash past, a dizzy feeling keeping him rooted to his seat.

Not a lead, no. The best Vilar could hope for was a snake-infested field of brambles, and maybe a few old footprints, all but worn away.

*

The following morning at 7.30 a.m. he called at the home of Thierry Lataste, the man in the Mercedes who had been dating Nadia Fournier when she died. Posh area, nice, two-storey middle-class house, a pretty wife called Mireille who could not hide her panic when he showed his warrant card and asked to speak to her husband. Without even asking what it was about, she stepped aside to let him in. Lataste appeared from the kitchen, holding a large mug and wearing a pale suit over a bottle-green polo shirt. He was about to leave for work, he said.

"Well, then, you'll need to call and tell them you'll be late."

"Would you mind telling me just exactly what . . ."

Lataste had said the words a little too brashly, setting his cup down with a faint clink on a glass table and stepping forward in the hope of intimidating this interloper. Vilar sized him up: early forties, not bad-looking, and, as the head of a property advisory office, probably used to being obeyed, even feared, but now, behind the arrogant facade, he looked nervous. He glanced furtively at his wife who stood, frozen, leaning against the banister, staring at Vilar as though an exterminating angel had come to call.

"I believe you knew Nadia Fournier?"

Lataste shook his head.

"She worked for S.A.N.I., the industrial cleaners. You know them?"

Lataste again glanced at his wife who was staring at him intently, willing him to answer but terrified of what he might say.

"Ah yes, I do vaguely recall someone of that name. A dark-haired girl. We sometimes ran into each other if I was working late. And?"

"Perhaps you might prefer to . . ."

"No, no, we can talk here . . . There's not much to tell anyway, I have nothing to hide."

Mireille Lataste suddenly seemed to emerge from her daze and took a few steps up the stairs. From the floor above came the sound of children chattering.

"I'll leave you to it," she said weakly. "You can tell me about it later. I'd rather give you some time to think about your version of events, it might make it a little less hard on me."

Vilar wanted to hurt them, and he did not wait for the woman to reach the top of the stairs before saying, "You know Nadia is dead?"

Lataste's wife stopped, but did not turn.

"How would I know that?"

"It was in the papers, it made the local news."

"I don't take much interest in the local news. I never read the paper."

"You've got a short memory," his wife interrupted. "We were watching T.V. together the other night, you got home early for once. They even showed her picture. A pretty girl, as I remember. I made a point of mentioning it."

She came back downstairs and planted herself directly in front of her husband.

"Why are you lying?"

"I don't think there's much point me staying," Vilar said. "I'm not going to get any straight answers."

Lataste stepped towards Vilar.

"What do you mean? Go ahead, ask your questions and let's get this over with, I haven't got all day."

"I've got all day, and all night too if you're going to lie to me. It's up to you. But since we got off to a bad start, maybe it's better if you come down and explain it to me at the station, where we can write up a formal statement. But let's be clear: a young woman has been murdered. Now you don't seem to care too much about that, which is a little strange since you knew her pretty well to judge by the witness statements we have . . . If I were in your shoes, I wouldn't be so arrogant and dismissive. But that's up to you. Now, we can do this the easy way or keep up the cocky attitude and I'll call for backup, have you dragged out of here and personally call the *procureur*'s office to inform them that you made false statements."

Madame Lataste turned and ran up the stairs, a door slammed, and the children's chatter trailed off.

Vilar had taken out his mobile and was about to call Pradeau, who was probably transferring the three suspects in the stabbing case to court.

"No, that's O.K., I'll come with you," Lataste said, patting his pockets to make sure he had his wallet, mobile, whatever.

Before he followed Vilar, Lataste stood for a moment staring up at the landing, now utterly silent. He hunched his shoulders as though about to step out into the rain, muttered, "Let's go," and slammed the door behind him.

When Vilar explained why he had decided to bring Lataste in, Daras insisted on conducting the interview. She sensed that that man was more likely to respond to a woman, which would save them time. They left Lataste to sit and stew for a quarter of an hour while they had coffee and talked about how good it would be to get a week away from all this bullshit.

Daras went through Lataste's I.D. papers, then laid a picture of Nadia Fournier on the desk in front of him, followed by several photographs taken at the crime scene. Vilar was sitting at the computer, taking down the statement.

"Can you confirm that we are talking about the same person?"

Lataste could not bring himself to look at the close-ups of Nadia's lifeless body, ravaged from the beating and bloated from the early stages of decomposition. When he did not answer, Vilar said:

"We are agreed, aren't we? That's her?"

"Yes . . . that's her," Lataste said in a whisper.

Daras slipped the pictures back into a file and ramped things up a notch.

"A routine question, but a crucial one: when did you last see her?"

"I don't remember exactly. Friday, maybe . . ."

He spoke in a distracted voice, his head bowed, his hands clasped between his thighs, as though thinking about something else, perhaps the repercussions of this whole business for him.

"What do you mean, 'maybe'?"

"What exactly was the nature of your relationship?" Vilar interrupted.

"I . . ."

"So when *did* you last see her?" Daras said. "I trust you realise how important it is that you answer truthfully."

"Were you having an affair? That might explain the tension between you and your wife."

Lataste looked from one to the other. He had begun to cower a little.

"Yes. We—"

"What do you mean when you say 'yes'?" Daras said.

"Yes, we were sleeping together," he said more loudly. "And we saw each other last Friday – I mean the Friday before last."

Vilar checked the calendar.

"That would have been the eighth. O.K., when and where?"

Lataste slumped back in his chair.

"We were together the whole day. I took her to Hossegor, I was supposed to be looking over a couple of houses we're selling there."

Daras came up behind him and hissed into his ear:

"And where were you on Monday, 11 June?"

He turned around and looked into her eyes. She jerked her chin, demanding an answer.

"Why the eleventh?"

"Answer the question."

"I was in the office, obviously."

"You didn't visit any houses that day?"

"Only in the city itself, you can check with my colleagues or with the clients I saw."

"Oh, we will check, Monsieur Lataste," Daras said. "Make no mistake."

"You're saying you're going to turn up at my office and question everyone about my schedule? Put calls in to my clients? That's going to start people talking. Basically you're going to destroy my reputation in a business that's completely dependent on trust."

"Yeah, because you're really trustworthy, aren't you?" Vilar said. "In our little meeting earlier today, you were – how shall I put it? – economical with the truth."

"My wife was there, I was hardly going to confess that I was having an affair with that girl."

"That girl, as you call her, how did you meet her?"

Daras had sat down behind her desk as she asked the question and now cupped her chin in her hands as she waited for an answer, obviously prepared for anything.

Lataste told the story in a monotone, betraying no emotion, and it was impossible to tell whether he felt nothing or whether he was struggling not to let it show. He and Nadia had met at the office one night. He was working late and they had slept together that same night. She had made all the running, and even now he wondered what it was about him that she had been attracted to, although at the time he had simply made the most of the opportunity and surrendered to a sort of feverish passion, watching himself live out the sort of sex scenes he thought only existed in movies.

The affair had gone on for about four months, made easier by Lataste's frequent trips in the region and the fact that they could use the properties he had to visit for his work: empty houses, quirky old cottages, luxury or dilapidated apartments, barely completed studios in buildings where labourers would sometimes be finishing work on the other side of the partition wall . . . It had been his idea, this sort of furtive, itinerant existence which he found exciting and which Nadia seemed to get a taste for, though it was hard for him to know what she really thought or felt, she could be secretive, sometimes mysterious, lost in her own thoughts, and there were days when she just let him drive her around and fuck her, as though she were not really there at all.

No, she had never asked for money – what a ridiculous idea. Although thinking about it, perhaps she had been expecting something else, she was never completely happy, but for the most part cheerful enough during their jaunts together.

"It turns out you didn't know her very well, then," Daras said.

Lataste stared at her, mulling over what he was about to say.

"I don't think I gave a shit about knowing her. For me it was almost a dream, meeting this young girl who put the moves on me and going . . . well, going around and screwing in all these different places, you can't imagine the freedom, the excitement . . . she was just a fuck buddy, really. That's all. If she had wanted to stop, I wouldn't have insisted on keeping it going. We didn't talk about our lives. I knew she had a thirteen-year-old son, she knew that I was married, and that's it."

"How did you feel when you heard she'd been murdered?"

Lataste shrugged slowly. He could not bring himself to look up at Daras and he stared down at the desk.

"I don't know. It felt weird. Like I was still in some sort of movie. Obviously I wasn't about to say anything in front of my wife. For me, it was like a break from the real world, something that happened once or twice a week, that's all. A sort of forbidden thrill."

"With death at the end, just like in the movies? Is that why you didn't get in touch with the police? Nadia's death was the inevitable fate of a misspent life, in some way? You must have known that we'd track you down, surely?"

Lataste bowed his head and sighed.

"Obviously, I was hoping you wouldn't."

Vilar tapped away at the keyboard for a few seconds, then, unexpectedly, all was silence. The printer suddenly clicked and whirred. It was Lataste who finally spoke.

"Can I ask you a question?"

"We're not bound to answer, but ask away," Vilar said.

"Why did you ask if she'd ever asked me for money?"

Vilar and Daras exchanged a look, found themselves in agreement.

"We have every reason to suspect that Nadia Fournier was working, at least some of the time, as a prostitute. When a girl like that hooks up with your type, she usually shakes him down one way or another."

"And what exactly is 'my type'?"

"Filthy rich and dumb enough to mistake your life for a fantasy. I thought you were an arrogant prick, but right now I think you're just a pathetic fucker."

"Well you're half right . . . I have been a bit of a fucker, and when my wife finds out about it I'll be royally screwed."

"Very good," Daras said. "Nice to see you haven't lost your sense of humour. You're resourceful. Here we are practically standing over the body of the woman you were fucking not two weeks ago, and you're making jokes.

"Maybe I'd make a good cop."

"For that you'd need to know which side you're on . . ." Vilar said.

He and Daras exchanged another look, and Vilar pushed the statement across the desk to Lataste. The man read through it and signed with a sigh.

"This statement will be on the case file," Daras said. "I hope you haven't forgotten anything, or kept anything from us. We'll call you in again if we need clarification. And obviously if we do call, you'd better make sure you come. Do I make myself clear?"

"Perfectly," Lataste said in a low voice. "Can I go now?"

The irony and superciliousness seemed to have drained from him. He trudged out slowly, closing the door softly behind him.

"So?" Daras said.

"So? We've found ourselves a true romantic, don't you think? Led around by his dick with his brain in his Y-fronts."

"Like most guys . . ."

Vilar smiled.

"Maybe . . . But he knows more than he's letting on, at least about how Nadia supplemented her income. I can't believe he didn't suspect."

"Agreed. We can keep up the pressure, but he doesn't look like the type to buckle easily. Just when you think he's about to spill his guts, he suddenly gets a grip. Funny guy."

The mobile in Daras' pocket rang. She took the call, heaved a sigh, and said she was on her way.

"I've got a meeting with Judge Dardenne in five minutes. I'd completely forgotten. It's about the two corpses we found two years ago, the couple we found bled dry in Montalivet a couple of months dead? Chaintrier has been working on the case. From the witness statements, we'd assumed it was a woman who cut their throats, turns out it was a transvestite, the husband's boyfriend! Sounds like it's turning into a bit of a farce – Dardenne and I always did have trouble taking the case seriously."

She went out, trailing a ribbon of citrus scent. Vilar slumped into his chair and sat motionless in the perfumed atmosphere, savouring the smell until the last fragrant molecules had dispersed. He thought again about Lataste, who had just had the shock of his life, a shock from which he might never recover because, at the end of the day, he was simply a middle-class pillock slumming it. An ignorant arsehole for whom ignorance was no longer bliss.

7

The two boys were forced to shake hands. They eyed each other suspiciously. Between clenched teeth, Nicolas muttered something by way of apology. His nose was still swollen, his cheek bruised, his hair had been cropped short to disguise the spot where Victor had ripped out a hank. They filed out into the hallway. Nicolas went first, and Victor stared at the muscular shoulders that moved as he swung his powerful arms. Outside, sitting in the shade, Nicolas' friends Lucas and Fabrice were waiting: the three boys hung around together, snickering and intimidating the younger kids or talking about pranks they had pulled or were about to pull. The two stooges got up as their leader swaggered out, and the three boys watched Victor head off towards the trees. He could feel their eyes burning into the back of his neck.

Once again the days began to pass in a muggy heat relieved only by the occasional thunderstorm, but by the following morning everything was parched again, tiny plumes of dirt rose from the footsteps of anyone walking along the garden paths, and football matches were enveloped in a grey dust cloud that looked as though it had been drummed up by stampeding herbivores pursued by predators on a sun-baked savannah.

Nothing changed. Victor was looked on with fear or respect, it all depended. Some younger kids came up, shook his hand and introduced themselves, waddling on their spindly legs but trying to swagger, like panicky wrestlers. One day the two brothers, the silent fraternal twins, asked permission to eat at the table where he had been sitting on his own. Without looking at each other, with synchronised movements, they sat down. Their names were Éric and Cédric, and, yes, they were twins. "But fraternal twins," Éric, the dark-haired one, insisted. "My mother always said that we were fraternal, that that's why we don't look like each other, and why we only look like our father."

"Where are they, your parents?"

The two boys looked at each other and buried their noses in their tomato salads. Victor was sorry he had asked.

"Papa is in Gradignan prison," Cédric said after a moment.

"Is he coming out soon?"

"He's only just gone inside," Cédric said. "And this is his second stretch, so . . ."

Victor did not dare ask about their mother. Here they were, too small for the chairs, there was no need to know the rest.

Nothing else happened. In the evening he liked to watch the night draw in over the grounds and to catch the stars as they appeared in the sky, surprise them at the very moment they began to shine or to flicker, like the one he had spotted just above the lime tree, not far from Venus. It was so delicate, its quavering light so easily masked by the thinnest veil of cloud, that he expected to see it suddenly gutter out in the terrifying darkness, snuffed out by the breeze, and no-one but he would notice. He wondered whether people reported the disappearance of stars the way they reported their discovery, whether you had to telephone the astronomers and announce your observation, or whether it was better to keep such an insignificant yet colossal death a secret.

He had been watching for a long time, waiting for it to appear, letting the star-spangled heavens wheel about him. The high clouds blowing in from the west meant that he could barely make out its quivering light. Just as he finally saw its tremulous glow, someone knocked at the door. Three faint knocks, followed by Cédric's plaintive "Open up!"

He was begging. The door shook with the weight of his body pressing against it, desperate to come in.

"What do you want?"

"It's the other boys. Let me in and I'll tell you."

"What boys?"

"Nicolas and his friends. They want to kill me."

Victor heard the little kid snuffling and pushing against the door with his whole body.

"Open up, they're coming for me."

"What about your brother?"

There was a silence. Victor heard the kid swallow painfully.

"I don't fucking know. I don't know where he is."

"Tell the social workers, I can't do anything."

"The social workers don't give a shit."

The kid let out a continuous wail, the lock juddering under his attempts to get in.

When Victor unlocked the door, the kid flinched and stood frozen in the middle of the hallway. Then he vanished, swallowed by a confusion of shadows that Victor did not understand.

"Shut your mouth, or I'll skin you alive."

Hands grabbed his shoulders and gripped his throat. He staggered back onto the bed, someone knelt on his chest, and he could no longer get air into his lungs. He wondered how long he could last without being able to breathe – or only barely. He focused on what was going on around him: he heard his door shut, saw Nicolas lean over him, whip out a flick knife, and press the blade to his throat. There were three of them. They were breathing shallowly, almost panting, like dogs. Soundlessly, wordlessly, the third boy rummaged through the wardrobe.

"Got it!"

Victor heard the boy pick up the urn and set it on the floor. He tried to move, but his body refused to respond. He thought he might suffocate beneath the weight of this thug. His eyes glazed over. He felt his strength ebb away, he no longer had the will to move or even to think. He thought about his mother, about what she must have felt and thought as she was dying. Had there been someone looming over her, was her killer's face the last thing she had ever seen? He decided to close his eyes, and when the weight was lifted from his chest and he could finally breathe he let out a groan, almost a sob, coughing, spluttering oblivious to the tip of the blade that was still pricking his neck.

He could see nothing, too busy gulping air, his eyes filled with tears. He felt them move, get up and sit down next to him, lift him up and stand him against the wall, twisting an arm behind his back. When he finally managed to open his eyes, he saw Nicolas taking out his cock, waving it around and sniggering.

"Next time I'll make you suck it, fuckface! This is what I use it for the rest of the time."

He started to piss into the urn.

"Jesus, you're really doing it? You're really doing it?" one of the boys said.

Victor howled and threw himself forward, only to be stopped dead by the blade of the knife, which left a nick just above his Adam's apple, the tip burying itself in his jaw, and at the same time he felt his arm being wrenched behind his back so hard he thought his shoulder might come out of its socket. He lashed out, kicking wildly two or three times and hitting empty air, impotently. Then panting with pain he slumped onto his side, his face pressed into the bedspread, moaning as he heard the sound of the piss as it hit the ashes, inundating the only thing he had left in the world, and then he wept, no longer aware of what was happening, not even reacting when someone kicked him in the ribs.

He did not hear them leave.

He went on sobbing as the silence returned, a hard, bitter lump of poison in his throat, the taste of it, like metal, in his mouth. He rolled heavily off the bed and lay, curled up, his face in his hands, lost in a fathomless abyss of grief.

And when he heard a commotion in the room, people asking what had happened, what they had done to him, when he felt someone gently take him by the shoulders and lay him down on the bed, mop his forehead with a damp cloth – *Victor, Victor, we're here, it's O.K.* – he let out a howl that made them recoil, a howl that sank its sharpened teeth into their privileged hearts, a howl that could have shaken the distant flickering star he had waited so long to see.

They got him to his feet and he stood, eyes closed, swaying like a punch-drunk boxer, then he passed out, dropping to the floor like a puppet with its strings cut, burning and feverish, and they could not support the dead weight of his body.

The following afternoon, while he was lying half asleep in his bed, Bernard came to tell him they had found him a foster family, good, kind people, they were used to looking after kids, they understood them. They lived near Pauillac, in the Médoc. The sea was close by. It would be nice.

The Médoc. All Victor knew about the area was sitting in traffic jams on Sunday night coming back from Montalivet or Soulac, his skin taut from the salt water, his shoulders scorched from the sun, looking forward to a shower, to a little coolness.

"Nicolas has gone. We couldn't allow him to stay here after what he did."

Victor silently vowed that he would find the boy and kill him. He had dreamed about it that night. A brutal dream from which he had woken with a start, afraid of himself. He watched the light shimmering in the cracks between the shutters. He could just make out the shifting leaves of the poplars. Everything outside seemed blinding.

"When?"

"Tomorrow. We'll take you there. Next week we'll go back to your house and get your things. The police have said we can."

"Tomorrow?"

His eyelids fluttered. He felt as though he had stepped off a cliff, the way Wile E. Coyote steps into mid-air but does not immediately fall.

He curled up again, turning his back on Bernard, waiting for him to leave, driven out by his silence. He thought about what Bernard had said, about this family who were going to take him in, these people he had never met and did not want to meet. These people who could change nothing, who would count for nothing. From now on, he knew, he was on his own, and the image that kept coming back to him was of a deserted world, peopled by whispering shadows that glided around him, whose words he could hardly ever make out in a fog of confused murmurings.

He waited for stillness to return, for the moment when the heat would gradually stifle all activity. He listened for the slightest sound, a creak of doors, laughter dying away. He heard snatches of conversation outside, a burst of music.

He picked up the urn, which no-one had dared touch, screwed the lid down tighter, and opened the bedroom door. He made sure the corridor was empty, listened again, then stepped outside.

He locked himself in a shower cubicle and immediately felt himself bathed in sweat, though it was no hotter there than anywhere else. He sat on the edge of the tub, tilted the urn and poured out some of the contents. The liquid ran almost clear, and he was glad that the ashes had sunk to the bottom. He poured away these dregs with the fastidiousness of a *sommelier* decanting a vintage wine. The acrid smell turned his stomach, and he nearly dropped the urn to bring his hands up to his mouth. He turned away, took a deep breath and swallowed hard. When there was nothing left, or almost nothing, he poured in some water and waited for a while for the ashes to settle again.

He was finding it hard to breathe, he gulped air with his mouth wide open, as if he had almost drowned. Keeping his lips pressed together, he began to pour again, but this time the stench had almost disappeared, and he could breathe more easily. He repeated the process three times, until he could no longer smell anything, and then slumped back against the cool, hard, tiled partition, whispering to the damp ashes as he clutched them tightly to him: *Don't worry, we're together, they can't hurt you, don't worry, we don't care about them.*

8

Somewhere in the apartment a mobile was ringing. Vilar wondered where the sound was coming from and quickly realised it was the pocket of his jacket, hanging in the hall where he had left it the night before. Given that it was Saturday and almost 9.00 a.m., he assumed that it was Morvan and felt that strange quaking in his heart he always felt whenever the retired *gendarme* called or he found an email from him on his computer.

A woman's voice. He did not know whether to be relieved or disappointed.

"Commandant Vilar?"

Vilar confirmed that it was he.

"Lieutenant Domergue, with the *police judiciaire* in Marseille. Sorry to call you on your mobile, but it was the only contact number I had. You requested information on Nadia Fournier and her parents, Souad and Michel Fournier? In relation to a homicide?"

"Yes, and—"

"I'll fax the paperwork through on Monday, but since it sounded urgent I took the liberty of calling."

The voice was gentle, a little indistinct, but there was something firm and resolute about the tone.

"Let me give you the bullet points: Nadia Fournier has a record here for prostitution and drugs offences. It started when she was sixteen. She had run away from home – it was almost a year before we tracked her down."

"She ran away?"

"Yes. Does that surprise you?"

"Do you know why she ran away?"

"Yes, I'll explain in a minute. She was found working for a pimp, a Tunisian, a violent little shit who kept his girls drugged up so they were easier to control. He's dead now . . . A bullet in the head, looks like he stepped on the toes of some Russian mobsters. Good riddance . . . Anyway, she was in a terrible state when we picked her up, but even then she was determined not to go home, which brings us to the reasons why she ran away in the first place, and I have to say the whole story's pretty vile."

Vilar sighed. Apparently the woman wanted to impress him with her diligence. He rummaged for paper and pen and sat in an armchair, scribbling notes. He stretched his bare feet into a patch of sunlight on the carpet.

"Her father, Michel Fournier, was a professor of maths at Aix University. And a serious alcoholic. It seems he took an unhealthy interest in his daughter's virginity. When he was pissed, he'd harass her and beat his wife, Souad, a primary school teacher in Marseille, her maiden name was Kaci. An all-round decent bloke. The upshot was that Souad committed suicide in '87. A year later Nadia took off. Left one hell for another."

"And no charges were ever brought against this guy Fournier?"

"Of course there were. From what I've read, he claimed that Nadia wasn't his daughter, that he'd brought her up, that's all. The case was dismissed shortly before the mother's suicide. Anyway Nadia retracted her statement, she was no longer a minor at the time, and then in 1990 she disappeared. So as you can guess, as far as we're concerned it's a cold case. Took me four days to dig this stuff up from under all the dust. But the fact that Fournier was a left-wing councillor and pretty well known – and that people still remember the case – made it not too hard to put together some bits and pieces."

"You know what happened to Fournier?"

"No. We've got nothing on him, so, well . . . You asked for

information, I've given you everything I've got. We're snowed under just now, so anything we can let slide, we do."

For a few minutes they bitched about the job, about how they were worked to the bone, then wished each other all the best and hung up. Vilar sat for a few moments, pen in hand, feeling the cool morning breeze from the window on the back of his neck, unable to think about anything.

He was postponing the moment when he would have to get up, get his things, get into the car and drive to Morvan's, convinced it would lead nowhere, that Morvan would show him photographs from C.D.s, magazines, internet sites, a catalogue of heinous acts in which the former *gendarme* thought he recognised Pablo. It had happened before: a year ago, he had shown Vilar a photograph released by Interpol of a young boy picked up by the police in Milan, an amnesiac, clearly a victim of abuse, who was all but mute but managed to stammer a few words in French, and it was true that Vilar had felt his heart stop when he saw the tanned face, the big dark eyes, the heavy lips half open in silent surprise. But he had quickly come back to earth when he summoned an image of Ana and realised this boy's face had looked nothing like hers. Pablo had always had his mother's eyes. This was why when he stared into Ana's eyes, he could still lose himself, despite the silence between them like a glass wall, despite the distance that separated them.

Vilar put the memory of last year out of his mind. He ran a hand over his face. In the back of his throat he felt a desperate urge to smoke. He closed his eyes and took deep breaths, shrugging off the torrent of unanswered questions. He leapt to his feet, his heart beginning to race: maybe this time Morvan really had a solid lead. He felt a familiar lump in his throat, and the three or four deep breaths he took were not enough to ease his grief, his pain.

"Pablo . . ."

He felt no calmer as he drove toward Morvan's place, but he was happy to be on the move, to be heading towards something he refused to think of as hope – he knew it was a counterfeit, like an artificial flower one feels the need to reach out and touch to dispel the illusion.

He drove, letting the mild morning breeze rush into the car, going over in his mind the various pieces of evidence he had about Nadia Fournier's death. He would pay another visit to Sandra de Melo, he decided, because she hadn't told him the truth, and because right now there was some guy roaming the streets of Bordeaux who might make her pay dearly for her tact.

He thought about calling Daras to let her know, but gave up on the idea because by now he was driving into Angoulême, and as he did so he felt himself entering the glass bubble into which he sometimes drifted, a place beyond ordinary space and time.

He found a parking space thirty metres from Morvan's house on a narrow street in the upper part of town. The sun beating down on the yellow stone facades dazzled him, making him squint, screwing up his face so much it hurt. He pressed the doorbell twice, impatient to be in the semi-darkness of the house, behind its closed shutters. He waited for a minute and rang again, assuming that Morvan was in the small back garden where he tended his rose bushes with painstaking care.

He listened but could not hear the slightest movement inside. He felt sweat trickling down his back, his forehead hurt from squinting into the sun. He glanced towards the street, stepping back to check the parked cars, and spotted the red Peugeot 306 the former *gendarme* had driven ever since Vilar first met him.

He did not bother to ring again, but pushed the door, which had not been properly closed and now swung open onto a dark hall, filled with the boxes of books and files that Morvan was forever promising he would sort out some day. Vilar closed the door behind him. As his eyes adjusted to the darkness of the house, still cool from the night, he walked down the hall towards the area Morvan had his office, in one corner of the living room.

He called out at the doorway, expecting no reply, and noticed that the lamp on the desk was on and the two large computers in sleep mode, displaying the same mountain scene. There was a faint smell of coffee. Vilar saw a red bowl and, next to it, a few crumbs of bread. The desk, which usually groaned under the weight of notebooks, maps, memo pads, diaries, pens and C.D. cases, was bare. All the tools of the former *gendarme*'s trade had vanished. It had been a thorough clean-up. Vilar was about to click the mouse to wake the computer, but his finger hovered over it. There might be fingerprints everywhere.

He moved through the house, flinging open doors. Not a trace of Morvan, nothing of the usual chaos, nothing that gave him the slightest clue as to what had become of him. Everything was filed away, with the obsessive neatness of an ex-soldier. The bed was immaculately made and the wardrobe, where everything was neatly piled and lined up as if for inspection, smelled of lavender. He had not really been expecting to find anything, but he would press on, in the teeth of the evidence, if it meant him getting even a few millimetres closer to Pablo.

Vilar was relieved not to have discovered Morvan's dead body and tried to feel hopeful that they might still find him alive, though every step he took in the empty house persuaded him otherwise. He had to believe the link was not yet broken, to maintain the dream that one day he might reach out his hand and clasp his son's. And perhaps also because he had more respect for the man than he realised. In the kitchen nothing was out of place. The half-full cafetière was cold, in the sink there was one plate and a glass. The bathroom smelled of lavender and soap. Two towels were spread out, dry and a little rough.

He went back and sat down at the computers, his head whirling with theories and questions. Morvan had spent a dozen years investigating paedophile networks and missing children, he had insisted that they meet in person, and Morvan was not the sort of man who insisted without reason, he was not impulsive, quite the contrary, he was quick to dash false hopes, quick to remember that he had to stick to the facts, follow the evidence, take no shortcuts . . .

Morvan was not here, and he had not nipped out to buy cigarettes – which he got by the carton for free from a friend who worked in Customs. Vilar could not imagine why this man might have disappeared, still less who might stand to gain, unless he really had found an important lead. Besides, no-one knew whether he worked alone or in a team, or whether he shared information with officers who were still on the force – something that would make his abduction, his death, pointless and deeply dangerous to anyone involved.

Unable to restrain himself, Vilar found a tissue and gently pressed ENTER on both keyboards. The hard drives whirred, and he heard the fans purring.

He felt his heart stop and lurch into his throat.

On an open document, written in huge letters, was the message:

I'VE GOT THE BOY
COME AND GET HIM!

He jumped to his feet, backed away from the desk, then turned to look at the screen, reading and rereading these two lines as though some encoded meaning might suddenly be revealed. He stood in the middle of the room, gasping for breath, his mouth open, whispering his son's name over and over: "Pablo", until his mouth was dry and he had to go to the kitchen and take a long drink from the tap. He had never felt so thirsty. He filled his mouth with water, spat it out, gulping more until he could not breathe.

When finally he stood up again, he felt faint and had to lean on the kitchen table.

"Pablo," he whispered again as he trudged back to the computers. He felt as though his son were the prisoner of this message and for an instant was gripped by the sort of fantasy that children have when they imagine actors trapped inside the TV and want to prise off the screen to let them out. He reached a hand towards the desk and exhaled violently, realising that he had been holding his breath for some time.

He explored the hard drives. Nothing. Everything had been erased, including the encrypted files Vilar knew about. He stared at the Welcome screen, at the flock of sheep on a mountain slope. He slumped back in the chair and closed his eyes. To get Morvan's passwords, someone had tortured him, forced him to talk. Vilar glanced around him, looking for some sign of a struggle, some clue as to what might have happened. No. That was stupid. There would be nothing, of course.

Someone had meticulously planned all this. Someone who was no doubt plotting his next move. Suddenly, it occurred to Vilar that the room might be bugged, that they might be watching him, and he peered into the shadowy corners of the room, studied everything on the desk looking for any sort of recording device, and once again felt like a fool and realised that this was an obvious mistake. He listened, watched, trying to detect the slightest movement in the air, searching for some trace of the man who had been here, who had probably sat in the chair where he was sitting, hoping that a whiff of cigarette smoke, a smell of aftershave or sweat, might cause whoever had abducted Morvan and his secrets to materialise.

For a long time he sat motionless, barely breathing, doing what he had been doing for almost five years: longing for some ghost to appear, believing that sometimes the air can still quiver with a long vanished presence. Nothing.

He went outside and phoned Daras. She only listened, did not ask for any details, simply said she would contact a *commissaire* she knew in Poitiers, who would send some people over, that they would some-how square things later. She made him promise to keep her posted, said, "Take care," and hung up.

An hour later a team turned up at the house, a young officer and two forensic officers from *l'Identité judiciaire* who wanted to know what they should be looking for.

Vilar explained everything: that the retired *gendarme* had dis-appeared some time between 9.00 a.m. and noon with all his research files, the evidence he had compiled over years, his work on Pablo's kid-napping; that they had agreed to meet this morning; that the hard drives had been wiped, including encrypted files; the message on the computer screen. The officer nodded, taking notes on a pad, asking no questions.

One of the forensics team was already pulling on his gloves, and the other was slipping on a pair of paper overboots.

"Can you tell me where exactly you've been in the apartment, what items you've touched?"

"The kitchen tap, I pressed the ENTER keys on both computers, but I used a Kleenex. I was careful not to contaminate the scene."

The technicians set to work, suggesting that the policemen might like to step into the garden for a while. Vilar picked up the tissue once more, so that he could raise the blinds and open the French door. The officer held out a packet of cigarettes.

"Sorry, I haven't introduced myself. Lieutenant Delvaille."

"Pierre Vilar."

The men shook hands, exchanged a brief smile, and smoked in silence in the muggy shade of a silk tree. Now and then, the scent of roses drifted on the still air.

"Where do you think Morvan is? He would surely have put up a fight? Was he a big guy?"

"A metre eighty-five at least, and about ninety kilos, I think. Yes, he would probably have put up a fight. But if he had, the house would be a bomb site. And there's something else: I can't see anyone dragging him unconscious into the street and stashing him in the boot of a car in broad daylight. None of it makes sense."

Delvaille nudged a twig with the toe of his shoe.

"How did you know him?"

"He was doing research into kidnapping and child trafficking. He was helping me to track down my son – he disappeared in 2000."

He managed to say this without becoming breathless. Realising he had used the past tense, he was about to correct himself, then stopped. The younger man said nothing. He was staring at a notebook in which he jotted down some things.

"I didn't realise," he said finally. "He . . . When was the last time you spoke to Morvan?"

"Yesterday. He called and said he had something to show me. Not a lead exactly, he said, but . . ."

Vilar tried to make sense of it. The erased hard drives, the missing C.D.s. All Morvan's databases were gone. It made no sense. Who could possibly have any use for such information? Suddenly he felt a wave of exhaustion, felt tension squeezing his skull.

They both started as the shutters suddenly flew open and one of the technicians appeared at the bedroom window.

"We've got something. Come and have a look."

Vilar walked ahead of Delvaille into the hall. The sun now streamed in through the open windows of the bedroom upstairs, spilling into the hall.

As he entered the room, Vilar saw one of the technicians bent over the unmade bed, on which he noticed a sunflower-patterned quilt and then a square of sky-blue sheet, while his colleague packed away the camera and rummaged through his case. Going closer, Vilar saw what the first technician was looking at: a bloodstain that extended from the edge of the bed right to the pillow, longer than it was wide, already clotted and brown, the outline almost crisp. There were other blotches spattered over the pale yellow surface, and on the top sheet.

"The mattress soaked up a lot of the blood," the technician said, lifting the sheet and pointing to an almost perfect copy of the same horror. "And look at this," he said, lifting a corner of the sheet. "It's like someone wiped a blade. See these lines? I'd say that someone was tortured here."

"That changes things," Delvaille said. "We're going to need backup."

"Now I'd be grateful if you could step away from the crime scene," the technician said, rummaging in his case.

The bedroom door closed behind him. Vilar's eyes took a moment to adjust to the crimson half-light. He leaned against the wall as Delvaille strode ahead, his mobile pressed to an ear. Vilar felt a suffocating nausea welling up in him, his head throbbed as though caught in a vice. He took a few blind steps, trailing his hand along the wall to guide himself, then a sudden spasm sent him running into the garden where he fell to his knees, though he retched up only bile. The noonday sun pinned him to the ground, he could feel the dense heat weighing on him, bathing him in sickly sweat. He lay for a moment on the scorched grass, trying to catch his breath and still the muffled pounding of the blood coursing through his body. He heard Delvaille ask if he was alright and he groaned that he was fine and struggled to his feet in spite of the dizziness. Delvaille was holding out a glass of water which Vilar gulped down, gagging and choking, and he managed to draw in enough air to bring himself round.

"Do you have any idea who might have done this?"

Vilar stared at the lieutenant for a moment without knowing whether he even wanted to answer. He could hear the two technicians in the bedroom above, pictured the patch of blood – so much blood – and felt a shiver run up his spine in spite of the heat which beat down on the little garden as though determined to scorch everything.

"What do you reckon?" Vilar said. "No, seriously, what do you reckon . . . ? D'you think I'd be standing here waiting for the cavalry if I had the slightest fucking clue which bastard tortured Morvan?"

"I'm just trying to understand," Delvaille said apologetically. "My colleagues will ask you some questions. You know the drill. A man disappears the day you're coming to visit him, and—"

"Yeah, I know the drill," Vilar cut him off. "I know it only too fucking well. I'm guessing Capitaine Daras explained the situation to your boss, right?"

"Maybe, but no-one told me. I got the call-out the same time as *l'Identité judiciaire*. All I was told was it was a missing persons case and here I am. And since I like to be thorough . . ."

He spoke softly, without hostility, with no arrogance. He seemed to Vilar to be a decent bloke.

"How about we go back inside?" Delvaille said. "We'll die of heatstroke out here."

He gestured for Vilar to go into the living room.

It was almost cool inside. The shade was soothing and, as one, both men took a deep breath.

"My son," Vilar said. "He . . ."

Delvaille was staring at him intently, as though he knew what Vilar was about to say.

In a low voice Vilar told him about Pablo's abduction, about the false hopes and the hopelessness, then he told him about meeting Morvan, told him he could only promise that he would never give up, that he had got results in three similar cases: one of the kids had been found alive in a brothel in Germany, and the other two had been found buried in the garden of a killer named Bernard Fédieu, who had thrown himself out of a window at the police headquarters in Rennes before it was possible to question him about the half-truths and contradictions in his confession to eight other murders.

"That's why I'm here," Vilar said. "I'm still clinging to a kind of hope. Though it's saner not to hope for much anymore."

He pulled up a chair. Delvaille, looking intently at the computer screens, hardly seemed to be breathing.

"But you manage to carry on working, you manage to care about all the shit we have to wade through?"

"I don't know if I really care anymore, it's more a kind of addiction. It's either this, or drink, or drugs. Or take up cycling – as long as you keep pedalling, you stay upright. In the past week we've had two big cases, and we're slogging our guts out. I've hardly got time to think, I've only been home to grab a bite. Drugs aren't the only thing that turn you into a zombie . . ."

Two cars pulled up outside, doors slammed, five, maybe six, Vilar was not sure, and Delvaille hurried to the front door. From the hall came the sound of heavy footsteps, muffled voices asking questions, and the young officer answering in a quiet voice. Vilar got to his feet with a sigh, realising that the nausea was gone, and turned towards the door as four men came in while the fifth headed straight for the bedroom, carrying a big black case, shouting to the forensics techs who told him that it was over there, they were almost done with the bedroom. A big man wearing a dark jacket and a fuchsia polo shirt came over and shook Vilar's hand, the expression on his face difficult to read.

"Capitaine Niaussat. Michel. Marianne Daras briefly filled me in. I have to warn you right now that she and I have agreed that, professionally speaking, you can have nothing to do with this case. So don't get in the way, please. For what it's worth, though, if I were in your shoes I'd be doing exactly what you've done."

"But you're not in my shoes."

Niaussat stiffened.

"Listen, I'm not trying to wind you up," Vilar said. "I don't care about your compassion, but I appreciate your support. You do your job, I'll do what I have to do. I won't get in the way. I've got more to gain than you in seeing Morvan found – alive and well preferably."

Niaussat nodded.

"Then we're clear. Can you tell me some more, so I know exactly what I'm dealing with? Because Daras was – how shall I put it? – pretty succinct."

They sat in the only two armchairs in the living room; Delvaille and the other officers had to fetch chairs from the kitchen. Over the next hour Vilar told them about his life since 20 March, 2000 at 11.30 a.m., when Pablo, who was almost ten years old, had disappeared on a street corner a hundred metres from his school gates. Never to return. He spoke in an almost placid voice as they stared at him, all knowing that this apparent gentleness simply masked the wound.

When he had given Niaussat all the information he had on Morvan's work, what he knew about his methods, his contacts and his habits, Vilar struggled to his feet and asked if he could go. Since none of them dared make him stay even a few minutes longer, he left quickly, as muted voices wished him a safe trip back to Bordeaux, before getting on with the investigation.

Delvaille walked out with him as far as his car and shook his hand, promising to keep him up to speed, regardless of whether or not his bosses said he could. Vilar smiled, patted him on the shoulder, then in spite of himself he studied the blazing street for some clue, something out of the ordinary, but as he sat in his sweltering car, breathing the muggy air, he felt as though any road he took now would run out to be a dead end.

9

The drive took a little less than an hour, and towards the end of the journey, after they had passed Saint-Laurent, there were vineyards as far as the eye could see, beautiful houses with turrets and slate roofs set in magnificent grounds, and the two adults – the director, who was driving, and Bernard – were marvelling at how close they were to the famous wineries advertised on the signs along the road. Victor, who had spent most of the trip dozing, turned around once to see a high-clearance tractor spraying copper sulphate, and the curious shape of the tractor surprised him at first, but then he remembered he had seen one before, though he could not remember where or when, and he stared at the machine, enveloped in a bluish haze, until it disappeared.

On the way into Pauillac they got lost, looked for the road to Saint-Estèphe, and ended up on the quays, driving along the swirling muddy estuary, past the forest of masts in the marina, until a woman gave them directions. Ten minutes later they pulled up outside one of the last houses in the village, after which the narrow road ran between the vineyards.

In spite of the heat that poured in as soon as the car doors were opened, Victor did not get out, leaving the two adults to go and ring at the blue front door. Almost immediately he saw a smiling woman with short brown hair, wearing floral-print leggings and a black T-shirt, bend down and give him a little wave through the car window. Bernard came back and gently told Victor he should come over and say hello, meet his new family, that he couldn't stay in the car all day.

The boy took a deep breath, got out, and walked towards the smiling woman who held out her hand.

"Hello, Victor. Welcome. My name is Nicole."

Victor looked at the woman, wondering how old she was. He felt an instinctive repulsion and was glad she had not kissed him. Obviously she was old, but he could not work out how old. Older than his mother, certainly. While she talked to the others, offering them a drink, Victor studied her plump features, her wide hips and her fat thighs in the floral-patterned leggings, the full breasts that heaved under her T-shirt.

"Aren't you thirsty in all this heat?" she said.

She invited Bernard and the director to come into the garden and briefly laid a hand on Victor's shoulder, urging him to come with them. She led them to a living room with drawn blinds where it was still relatively cool and told them to wait while she got some refreshments. When she asked what he wanted to drink, Victor mumbled inaudibly and had to repeat, "Some Coke", as he shook his T-shirt to dry the sweat from his back. Seeing him standing there, Bernard gestured to the spot next to him on the sofa, and Victor sat down and crossed his legs, fiddling with the laces of his trainers. The social worker asked if he was alright and he nodded, still staring at his shoes.

"It'll be fine," the director said.

Victor did not react. He felt as though he were being tossed on an ocean, floating on the surface, the way it might feel when a current pulls you out to sea or a whirlpool drags you under and you're shattered and don't know what to do, except wait out what little time is left and hope that something will float past for you to cling to. He remembered the last scene in the film "Moby Dick" – a teacher had shown it to them at school one day, and it had made him want to read the book – in which the hero is floating all alone at sea, clinging to the coffin of his friend.

Nicole came back with drinks, explaining that the kids were at the beach at Hourtin with her sister, that they were having a picnic there and would be home at about five o'clock.

"You'll have the whole day to yourself to get settled in," she told

Victor. "After that, we've got all the time in the world to get everyone introduced."

The boy raised his eyes to hers, then averted them straight away.

"How many foster children do you have here at the moment?" the director said.

"Just one, Julien, he's ten, and now Victor. And there's Marilou, our daughter, who's eleven."

She smiled to herself, looking down, the gentle look of a contented woman, then, seeing that everyone had drained their glasses, she jumped to her feet.

"Follow me, I'll show Victor his room."

She led them up a staircase that creaked as they went, and opened a blue door. Victor stood behind Bernard and the director, and they had to urge him to step into the vast attic room, furnished with a big bed, a desk on which stood a large red lamp, and a little shelf on the wall with two books whose titles he could not make out. The woman turned on the bedside lamp, which gave off such a soft, welcoming glow in the dark room with its closed shutters that the boy immediately wanted to be alone in what would at least be a safe, peaceful refuge.

"You'll be O.K. here," Bernard whispered.

Victor forced himself to smile. Obviously, it was better than the children's home, and obviously he had to live somewhere while he was waiting, though he did not know what it was he was waiting for, and suspected he might have to find it for himself.

Since he wanted to be alone, he mustered enough breath to ask the adults if he could go and get his things from the car and bring them up to his room, and they looked at each other in surprise and, smiling, gave their blessing. As he went downstairs he heard the director reassure Nicole that everything would be just fine, that there was no need to worry.

When he set down his two bags and his suitcase on the bedroom carpet, having refused to accept help, he shut the door and stood at the foot of the bed, breathless, letting the sweat drip from him, tiredness beating dully in his temples. He could smell clean sheets, old timber, and maybe damp. He listened carefully, but he could not make out the grown-ups' conversation downstairs. The shutters kept out the birds' distant muffled trilling and the luminous heat that pressed against the two diamond shapes cut out of the thick wood.

After a while he sat down on the bed, hands wedged under his thighs, looked around this peaceful room and nodded, perhaps in approval at the soothing half-light or perhaps at the vague notion that was gradually forming in his mind, less an idea than a foreboding that made his heart beat faster and brought a lump of bitter rage to his throat and made his eyes sting, a thought that he could not yet put into words, and one that he might never voice since he was beginning to think that words were futile, meaningless sounds whisked away by the wind like empty plastic bags to catch on fences and branches.

There was a knock at the door and he hurried to open it. It was Nicole, come to tell him that Bernard and the director were ready to go back to Bordeaux and wanted to say goodbye. He looked at her and realised she had a pretty smile that made those around her feel good, and made him feel handsome. The sort of smile a girl with a crush might give the boy she loved. He followed her downstairs and shook hands with the director, who said he was counting on Victor to build a new life for himself, a great future. Victor did not really understand what he meant by building a life, he often did not understand what the man was saying, with his flowery phrases and intellectual air. Then Bernard shook his hand and patted him on the arm, saying they were counting on him to be happy.

Victor did not go out to watch them leave, but stood for a long time listening to the car's engine as it faded into the distance, and when Nicole came back in, rubbing her hands, and asked if he would mind helping her tidy up the glasses and the bottles from the coffee table he carried everything into the kitchen, put the glasses in the sink and ran some cold water over his hands, drinking a mouthful from his cupped palm before splashing some on his face and neck.

Afterwards they had lunch, because it was already past noon, and then, having tidied away his things in his bedroom, he waited there in its tranquil shade. He did not know what he was waiting for, but he was no longer afraid. At some point he picked up the urn, held it close and pictured his mother's smile, her walk, the way she looked at him, the way she pulled her collar up when it was cold in winter, the smell of a tagine as she lifted the lid of the earthenware pot, eyes wide with hunger, then closing them to inhale the rich scent of the steaming broth.

He cried when he realised that all this was in the past. He cried that he did not have magical powers that could raise the dead or at least speak to them, so that he might be lulled again by her voice. He imagined finding a time machine in an old hangar and going back to that day, he would skip school, go home and force his mother to go out, even if she was furious with him, even if she was disappointed in him, at least she would not be there when the killer turned up. At least she would still be alive. Here. Her fingers running through his hair. My little boy. Manou.

He fell asleep. When the other children got back from the beach, Nicole came to wake him.

There was a girl and a boy. Marilou and Julien. Victor found it strange that they hugged him – they had probably been told to. The girl, who had wild black curly hair and big laughing eyes, put her hands on his shoulders and planted loud kisses on his cheeks, then sat on the sofa, holding a fizzy drink, and fluttered her long lashes at him. Victor felt obscurely flattered. Julien's glasses hit Victor on the forehead as he hugged him and he stepped back, embarrassed. Everything seemed to make the boy self-conscious. His eyes darted around, suspicious or fearful. Perhaps frightened of being scolded, or of some imminent danger.

Marilou told him about their day at the beach, the swimming, the helicopter that had whirred back and forth. About Julien digging a huge hole, burying himself in the sand and pretending to be dead. Marilou had found it creepy. She thought pretending to be dead was stupid.

Surreptitiously Nicole looked at Victor, who was still staring at the dark-haired girl.

The afternoon stretched on like this as he sat, his bare feet on the

tiled floor, in front of the television while the others went and shower-
ed to wash off the salt and the sand.

Then came dinner. Victor had to sit with these people, sit right next
to them, under their watchful eyes.

Victor felt as though he were at the bottom of a pit.

He was not hungry, and he felt again an acrid lump in his throat. He
weighed up these strangers one by one as they sat at the table, unable
to believe that they truly existed, that this meal – the five of them sitting around the big dining-room table with the windows wide open to
the night in the hope of a cool breeze – was not some sort of perform-
ance for his benefit, whose actors, completely engrossed in their roles,
intimidated him slightly. He longed to wake up from this nightmare in
which he felt himself shrinking, rooted to his chair, while the others
around the table seemed gigantic, distant, strange. He did not know
what he was supposed to do or say, he stared at his plate, eating slowly
so that no-one would offer him second helpings. He said, "Not too
much, thanks," when he was served, not daring to say that he could not
bring himself to eat anything, then he methodically chewed everything, making it easier to swallow.

Nicole had sat him next to Marilou, and he could feel her studying
him, observing the way he ate or maybe how he used his knife and
fork, anything that she could tell her friends the next day. He knew that
girls talked, teased each other, made up secrets about things they found
out, laughing and shrieking. Marilou constantly squirmed in her chair
as though incapable of sitting still, swinging her tanned legs, of which,
out of the corner of his eye, Victor could see only an area of thigh
between her shorts and the tablecloth. Victor had liked the way Marilou
smiled, the way she walked, twirling around the living room when they
got back from the beach, showing off her suntanned back, her stomach, her legs. But now as she sat next to him he suddenly found her too
quiet, too curious about his every gesture; he wanted her to go on talking in that soft, hoarse voice that made the boy want to clear his own
throat.

In fact no-one talked much over dinner, glued to the television that was broadcasting news from all over the world, images of famines, massacres and natural disasters which seamlessly segued into news reports about holidaymakers, of hoteliers and restaurant owners worried that their takings were down. But the babble of the television could not fill the long silences, interrupted only by the clink of cutlery and the smack of wet lips.

Then there was the man, silently bent over his plate, who sat up only to sip his wine or glance indifferently at the children. The conversations had already trailed off by the time he arrived.

This was Denis, Nicole's husband. He had got home just before seven, moody and exhausted, and had gone straight into the kitchen where he drank down two beers, standing in front of the open refrigerator, before coming into the sitting room to say hello, to shake the hand that Victor shyly proffered and ask how old he was.

"Thirteen."

"The awkward age. You'd better be careful. Otherwise . . ."

He had said this with a tired, forced smile, and Nicole had immediately said that of course he would be careful, that he was a responsible boy.

When Denis had turned his face towards him, slick with sweat, Victor had caught the sour smell of alcohol as if the man's sweat were made of the stuff, and he noticed a weary, doubtful gleam in his eyes, half hidden by his constant blinking. Victor had put it down to the fact that he was worn out after a day working on a building site near Bordeaux. During the afternoon Nicole had told him her husband was a builder, who had set up his own business three years ago, and he worked harder than the two labourers he employed because it was tough to make ends meet. It was not a job that Victor would have liked. Working under the heat of the sun or in the rain, as he often saw labourers do; they were badly paid too, his mother had told him, it was a shitty job.

Now everyone was watching a news report about the terrible fires in Portugal, huge flames leaping across roads, forcing the firefighters to flee while the locals complained about how their few belongings had been destroyed by the fire. Victor felt relieved that no-one was looking at him, and tried to make as little noise as possible with his cutlery so they might forget about him a while longer. Even Marilou seemed to have stopped studying him, and he could look up without risking meeting anyone's gaze.

Julien, sitting opposite Victor, was staring at the T.V. screen, his mouth hanging open, forgetting to chew, his almost translucent blue eyes wide behind his glasses.

"Julien!" Nicole said.

The boy flinched and swallowed noisily, then looked at Victor, who avoided his expressionless blue eyes. Julien was tall for his age and frighteningly thin. His bony arms moved with slow precision: he never let so much as a crumb fall from his fork and speared his food as though hunting animals on his plate. When not staring at the television, he managed methodically to wolf down a considerable amount of food. Nicole or Denis would ask whether he wanted more, and he never refused, always nodding, saying, "Thank you," in his shrill falsetto without looking at anyone.

Watching the boy furtively, Victor managed to distract himself from his own nervousness. Julien reminded him a little of the twins he had met in the children's home, and it comforted him somewhat to realise that there were children who seemed even more lost and unhappy than he was, whose misery was as evident in their faces and on their bodies as bruises or scars. He realised then that he was floating between two worlds, that he was just below the surface, yet close enough to it that he could see the light, while others were drowning and drifting into darkness and mud.

Marilou asked if she could be excused to watch the television in the living room until it was time to clear the table, and when she brushed against his back as she passed, Victor felt a cold shiver run up to his neck.

"You can go too, if you want," Nicole said to Victor. "You can go up to bed, if you're tired. It'll be time enough for us to talk tomorrow."

"Can I go outside? To the garden."

Denis assented by blowing cigarette smoke through his nose.

The moment he stepped onto the terrace, Victor felt as though he could breathe again; he sat on the steps that led down to the lawn, offering his face to the soft breeze that glided through the darkness, rustling the leaves of the trees. When he looked up, he was struck by the brightness of the sky in which he could even make out the gossamer shawl of the Milky Way. He picked out the three or four constellations he knew, then waited for a shooting star, as he used to do with his mother in their garden at home, on summer nights like this one, when the heat of the day forced them to stay up late into the night to gorge themselves on shade and cooler air. He waited several minutes, but nothing crossed the sky and he had the impression, as he sat here, that he could see the star-strewn heavens wheel around him with a crushing slowness until the tears misted his eyes, trickling down his cheeks and onto his neck, while the lump in his throat swelled again as though it would choke him.

He got to his feet, shaken with silent sobs, and walked onto the lawn so that he could surrender to them, wiping his eyes, his nose, his face with the hem of his T-shirt. He stood for a long while, his chest hiccupping in the silence, until he thought he could hear a sigh, the whisper of a breath, and when he turned he saw Marilou standing on the terrace, hands behind her back, trying to smile at him.

After that, she smiled at him constantly. Or at least that was how it seemed to Victor. Marilou's smile lingered for a long while, long after she had stopped smiling and moved on to something else. Like a cool balm on the skin, or the taste of a strong mint, her smile had a lasting effect. And it was something light and bright and utterly spontaneous, there was no hesitation, no guile. A sun appearing suddenly from behind a bank of clouds. It was probably the first scrap of happiness the boy had managed to claw back. It was unlike anything he had ever known. The simpering or the effrontery of the first girls he had had crushes on in primary and secondary school paled before this brilliance. He did not want to kiss or touch Marilou, it was nothing like that. He just wanted to take her in his arms and hold her, his face pressed into her black hair.

For the next few days he let himself be led around, listening as they showed him around the village and introduced him to their friends, telling him that they were the best friends in the whole world, you'll see, she's cool, he's really funny – Paola, Karine, Driss, Michael, and others whose names he instantly forgot – a whirl of children trapped there for the summer or waiting to go away on holiday, to get away from this godforsaken hole where they were already bored, cycling around on bikes and mopeds.

He thought they would get lost in this sea of vines whose carefully combed furrows he pedalled up, his legs stiff. He saw wine *châteaux*, spotted luxury cars he had only ever seen in photographs or on television. The rich drove past in solemn silence behind tinted windows or sped past in red or black sports cars. Marilou explained that vintage wines could fetch astronomical prices, and together they tried to work out how many bottles of Coke you could buy for the money and agreed that it was ridiculous, spending so much money on wine.

"Wine makes you drunk," Julien said. "It gets you plastered quickly. Papa used to fall over after three glasses."

The first morning when they stopped by the estuary, Victor did not recognise it as the Garonne. The river stretched away to the far bank in the distance, the water rushing, swirling past. Victor suspected that the roar he could hear was the ocean, but he was immediately drawn to the power of the river. It was the first time he had seen something so immense. It occurred to him that, at ebb tide, you could drift out to the sea. Go in search of this roaring, which must surely come from the rough waves and the wind.

Early in the morning they would head down to the beach. Nicole preferred to take them around 9.00 a.m., and Victor enjoyed walking in the still, cool shade of the pine trees, amidst the heady scent of resin with a sea breeze borne on the rising tide, that whispered in the high branches. Julien always walked more slowly, armed with a stick that he had picked up, poking through thickets for something interesting: a huge green lizard, an exoskeleton shed by a grasshopper, a coin. Nicole would call him back if he strayed too far. He would come right up to her then and take her hand and walk a few metres, head bowed, only to dash off again. Marilou hummed the songs she listened to on her MP3 player, and sometimes held out one of the earphones to Victor so he could share her enthusiasm.

He walked in front most of the time. He liked that there was nothing but the trees and brushwood and brambles with their ripening blackberries. Marilou told him that one day a roe deer had stopped on the path and stared at them before leaping into the undergrowth, and Victor hoped it would happen again, that he would be the first to see the animal so he might take a few steps closer, the better to see its big black eyes, its ears aquiver at any hint of danger.

One morning, seeing a woman in a blue summer dress coming towards them, Victor froze, and everything inside him stopped dead because the woman in the distance was his mother, carrying a red towel in one hand and a yellow bag in the other. He started to walk forward again, without saying a word to the others, suppressing the urge to run and at the same time unsure that his legs could hold him up. As he drew closer his mother's face became clearer, and in that moment he was convinced that she had come to get him, come back from some trip, from running away. He knew she had run away from home once when she was a girl; she had told him about it one night when she was sad and a little drunk, she talked about leaving home, about starting a new life somewhere else, and as she talked he had thought she was thinking of leaving without him, he had felt the blood drain from his body, and his head become so empty, so dead that his mother noticed and quickly hugged him and told him she would never leave, that he was her whole life. Ever since, he had been haunted by the fear that she might leave, might run away again from whatever was threatening to catch up with her, and so he was not upset to see her coming back now, having escaped the mortal dangers he had always sensed surrounded her. For a few seconds he felt a giddy, almost painful joy; all his sadness drained from him. Her death had been a dirty trick his mind had played on him, his mother was not dead, thirty seconds from now she would be hugging him.

He waved and smiled and he felt tears well up, because he had been scared that he would never see her again, because she was dead, because he had seen her body, had smelled the foul stench of death mingled with an impenetrable darkness.

The woman, who was astonishingly beautiful, stared as she passed the smiling boy, her face glazed over with surprise or amusement, and just as Victor stopped to watch her she gave him an icy, empty look that made him look away. He fell against the rough trunk of a pine tree, feeling the bark graze his palm, and a moment later Nicole was bent over him, cradling his head in the crook of her arm, asking him what was wrong, and Victor said, "Nothing, I don't know," as he watched this ghost disappear along the path.

"What is it?" Nicole said.

He shook his head and tears trickled down his cheeks. Nicole looked at him, nodding, perhaps she understood. She glanced back at the woman, and hugged the boy, who did not resist. "It's perfectly natural," she said quietly. Then she whispered something sweet which he did not quite hear, and he found the strength to get to his feet.

That was all. Nicole did not ask him anything more, and Victor never spoke of what he thought he had seen. But sometimes when she saw him stare at something or someone on the beach, shielding his eyes with his hand, staring over at the glistening strip at the water's edge, the luminous haze from which walkers sometimes appeared shimmering like will-o'-the-wisps, she would watch him, find some excuse to talk to him, trying to rouse him from his daydream, bring him back from this vision that held him spellbound.

Aside from this, every time he crossed the dunes, Victor always felt the same surge of joy, felt his chest swell with a kind of sob because the ocean as it lay upon the golden sands was so beautiful in the soft morning light, it was exactly how he had felt when he and his mother were out walking together and the elemental power of the landscape suddenly opened up before them. Everything was here, the insistent roar of the waves, the wide empty spaces glistening at low tide, the blue horizon where he could just make out the vast curve of the Earth. He would always stop for a moment to drink it in, while Marilou and Julien raced down the sandy hill to the beach, shrieking.

Several times he brought along his copy of *I Am Legend* and wandered through the uninhabited city with Robert Neville, frantically turning the pages when the vampires attacked. Sometimes, he thought he would have liked to be the lone survivor of an apocalypse, to be the absolute ruler of a dead world.

Lying on his front on the beach towel, in the drowsy shade afforded by his baseball cap, he worked out an elaborate scenario. He pictured himself wandering the streets of a Bordeaux full of stationary cars, their doors wide open, their occupants long gone or else lying rotting on the seats. He saw himself looting shops for food or anything else he wanted. He had trouble imagining the silence of a ravaged world. Would he be able to hear his own heartbeat? Would there still be birds singing and flitting from branch to branch? This was a question he returned to again and again. Of course there would be. He had seen it in the movie. They would land wherever they liked, having nothing to fear. They would peck at the open eyes of the dead. The world would revert to its wild state: animals would no longer be afraid of anything. He would have to arm himself, but that would be easy. He would find a house that was easy to defend. He would have to fight off starving dogs and even cats, since even the millions of corpses would not feed them for long. Maybe the wolves would come back, as in the olden days.

This terrifying solitude, of being hunted and living on borrowed time, seemed preferable to him to the shifting swampland in which, day after day, he felt himself sinking and where nothing he could do, no shouting, no waving, could bring him any help. He felt the urge to write. He even started one afternoon, in an exercise book, alone in his bedroom. He wrote *NOVEL* on the front cover and wrote a dozen pages without pausing, immersed in another world where he could forget himself.

Marilou knocked at his door one day when he had shut himself away, dozing in the half-light of his room and trying to finish reading *The Mysterious Island*.

"Come downstairs, Rebecca's here. You remember, my cousin, I told her about you. She wants to meet you."

By the time he opened the bedroom door she had gone, and he padded down the stairs, barefoot and still half asleep. There was not a sound in the house, apart from Nicole talking on the telephone. The girls had set up camp under the trees at the bottom of the garden, sitting on plastic chairs, near a table piled with blonde-haired dolls with pink and gold accessories. Rebecca looked at him with her big, black, needlessly made-up eyes. She looked like a woman. A woman who played with dolls. He couldn't tell. If Marilou had not told him Rebecca was at secondary school in Pauillac, Victor would have guessed that she was twenty. He wondered if she was beautiful or pretty. He did not have words to express what he was experiencing. By the time he reached them, Rebecca had lowered her eyes and was looking at a flaxen mane of doll's hair, spraying it with glitter.

Now he could see only her long, tanned legs, a little gold chain around one ankle, and her breasts beneath her sleeveless T-shirt, the curve of which he could see through the large armholes.

He immediately wanted to touch her. To kiss her. He had to restrain himself. He felt this desire stiffen between his legs. Never had he felt it so strongly. He found it disturbing and was scared she might notice, even through his baggy shorts.

When he reached them, Rebecca jumped up and hugged him, mumbling an apathetic "Hi". She proffered her round, firm face, on which he barely had time to plant a kiss. It felt like kissing a fist. He barely felt his lips brush her cheek. She sat down again and took a swig of Coke.

He sat a little way off in a hammock and watched her. Rebecca was dressing the doll in some sort of evening gown, biting her lower lip and frowning. Her hair fell over her face and she constantly had to push the heavy black locks behind her ear with a hand or a thumb, a gesture the boy decided he liked. Her fingers moved quickly, her rings shining. The plastic creature was soon dressed in its sequinned gown. Victor counted seven rings. He knew what his first present to her would be. She had crossed her legs and was nervously swinging her foot, a sandal decorated with coloured beads balanced precariously on the end of her toes. He did not dare look at her thighs, at the hem of the white cotton shorts that sometimes gaped over her brown skin.

"You want some more Coke?"

At first he did not realise she was talking to him. He emerged from a sort of daze to see that she was holding the bottle towards him.

"Here, I've hardly touched it, I wasn't really thirsty."

He got up, took the drink, mumbled his thanks. He took long gulps. The coldness and the sugar did him good. He stood there in front of the table. The girls paid no attention to him, bent over what they were doing, concentrating like couturiers. They did not talk to each other. They handled the tiny pieces of cloth with the deftness of skilled workers. It was like a job.

He sat down again, unsure what to do. Eventually, he stretched out in the hammock, turned towards the girls. He had tried to tear his eyes from Rebecca, to stop undressing her inch by inch, almost physically able to feel the touch of her skin beneath his fingertips. He decided to make her a character in his novel about the survivor. She would appear from nowhere on a motorway, dressed in rags, and throw herself under the wheels of his 4 × 4. Naturally he would swerve just in the nick of time, then comfort her. They would be alone in the world, amid the utter chaos. He liked this idea. Rebecca and him in the first days of the end of the world.

Marilou's voice pulled him from his daydream.

"Do you want to play with us? You can dress this one," she said with a big smile.

She waved a doll representing a man, or a boy, and Rebecca burst out laughing and hid her face in a tiny tulle dress which she balled up in her fist.

"That's Ken the gay boy," she said in a hoarse voice.

Victor shivered. He felt ill. He stood up, about to leave, and asked where Julien was.

"I wasn't talking about you," Rebecca said. "Shit, I was just joking. Wasn't I, Marilou?"

"Yeah, it's nothing," Marilou said, hunched over her mobile phone, tapping out an S.M.S.

"Who're you texting?"

"Paola. She's in Portugal at her nan's house."

"So are you happy here?" Rebecca asked Victor. "Denis and Nicole are so cool. I love them. Where did you live before?"

She didn't look at him, busy putting together some sort of pink camper van. Victor wondered whether there was any point in replying. He would have liked to see her eyes on him.

"I lived with my mother," he said eventually.

Bent over her task, the girl said nothing. She might not even have heard.

"She's dead," Victor whispered, feeling his lungs empty of every last atom of air, unsure whether he would ever be able to speak again.

"Oh yeah, that's right. Marilou told me."

She turned her eyes on him. Grey, or green, they captured all the light which stole between the leaves. She blinked twice, three times. She settled back in the deckchair and looked away.

Victor felt as though he were suspended in mid-air by a steel hook buried in his chest. The girls said something he could not make out, tapping away on their phones. He managed to get a little breath back, leaning on the table because his head was spinning.

"What about you?" he said.

Marilou put down her phone and looked at Rebecca.

"Yeah, I'm cool. Next year I'm going to study at La Maison rurale in Lesparre. To learn a shitty trade, so I can earn a shitty living. And so I can get out of here."

"Do you live with your parents?"

She shrugged and went back to listening to her voicemail. Marilou, her huge eyes wide, seemed to be trying to signal something to him.

He stared at the low neckline of Rebecca's T-shirt, at the curve of her breasts. He could not help himself. He was two metres from her, yet he thought he could feel the heat of her body, as if he was standing in front of a fire. She talked quickly, swallowing her words, her voice hoarse, and shrill. Her gestures were often brusque and her looks callous. She frightened him. She probably got into a lot of fights.

They did not say much more for a while. Then Rebecca got up suddenly, because she had to go, she said. She kissed Marilou goodbye and walked away without so much as a glance at Victor, and the boy did not know if he was disappointed or relieved to see her go.

10

As he pushed open the door to his building and stepped into the lobby, Vilar saw the letter poking out of the letterbox. It was a thin brown envelope with his name and address printed on it and no stamp. His heart skipped a beat, then he remembered that this was how the president of the housing association sometimes circulated the long-winded and detailed minutes he took at meetings with the building manager. He turned over the envelope, and noticed nothing out of the ordinary, except that the flap had been reinforced with Sellotape, so that it was impossible even to slip a finger inside to open it. Without knowing why, he sniffed the envelope but could smell nothing, then he started up the stairs, using his car key to open it.

Photographs. Six sheets. Three were contact sheets with twenty or so tiny images. The other three each contained two enlarged shots.

He stopped on the half-landing. Children. Innocuous images, portraits and happy snapshots, had been mixed with others. He held one up to the yellow ceiling light. He groaned, gritting his teeth, and slid the photos back into the envelope. He climbed the stairs to his apartment in a daze, plunged into the darkness, kicked the door closed behind him and stood in the hall without turning on the light, feeling the blood pounding in his veins, sending showers of sparks into his brain like struck flint. His arm was rigid, he could feel the envelope stuck to his sweaty fingers. The whole left side of his body felt paralysed, and he realised this was what a heart attack must feel like. It occurred to him that he might die right now, and discovered that, try as he might, he could not summon any memories of his life, not even an out-of-focus slide. The pictures he had glimpsed on the stairs made it impossible for any others to take shape.

Evil thwarting happiness.

The ringing telephone nearly made him lose his balance, and he had to support himself against the door frame before going into the living room to answer it.

"So? You see them?"

The man talked rapidly, roughly. The voice was hoarse, almost rasping.

"Who are you? What do you want?" Vilar bellowed, out of breath.

"Hey, hey, hey! Don't start kicking off, you're not down the station now, trying to intimidate some poor bastard. Shut your fat fucking mouth, or I'm hanging up, O.K.? Did you see them?"

"What is there to see?"

The voice let out a little high-pitched snigger that ended in a dry cough.

"Are you fucking dumb, or what?"

Vilar went over to the window, studying the street in the foolish hope of seeing the man he was speaking to. He took a deep breath and tried to control his voice.

"Kids. So what? I've seen thousands of pictures like this, these last few years, and that . . ."

Suddenly, he understood. He threw the photographs to the ground, clicked the switch of a lamp behind him and crouched down to examine them.

The voice of the man on the phone was mockingly sympathetic.

"Did you take a good look? You thought you'd never see him again, and here I am sending you a picture. What do you say?"

Vilar was trying to think what to say, how to deal with this, when his eyes fell on a photograph of a boy of about eight or nine, his face half hidden by a mask. Behind him stood a naked man, his thick hands on the boy's hips. Vilar could do nothing to stop the tears streaming down his cheeks. He set the telephone down on the floor and brought the photograph closer, peering at the small face, the tired, vacant eyes shining behind the mask. He saw the thin arms, the narrow chest on which the camera flash cast deep shadows, the jutting chin, his neck straining as he was raped.

He heard the stranger's voice reverberate in the earpiece and picked up the telephone once more.

"See what your friend the *gendarme* was jerking off to? I found loads of this stuff at his place, a whole sack full! This is what you went over to his place to look at, isn't it? But now you've got it, you don't know what to say, am I right? Never mind, I'll leave you to your happy reunion. Don't worry, I'll be in touch."

There was silence. Still Vilar sat on the carpet, clutching the hideous picture, not daring to look at the others, unable to take his eyes off the boy in whose face he thought he could see something of Pablo's when he was sad or sick; he thought back to the bad bout of flu Pablo had had when he was six, the chest infection that had sent his temperature soaring to 40°C while Victor and Ana sat up all night with ice packs by his bedside, terrified that he would have a convulsion, ready to dash to the hospital, dozing off whenever the fever allowed the boy to rest a little, only to jolt awake whenever they heard him whimper. By the following morning, Pablo's temperature had dropped almost two degrees, he woke up and beamed at them, dark circles around his bright eyes, which he quickly closed again, before sinking back to sleep.

Vilar lay on his back and wept, overwhelmed by visions of his tortured son, his mind teeming with every picture of an abused child he and Morvan had seen in the past few years, it seemed to him that Pablo was the victim in every one. At some point the tears and the sobs began to choke him and he coughed and had to sit up so that he could breathe, his chest crushed by a diffuse pain, a burning sensation that spread through his muscles and bones, an acid coursing through him threatening to dissolve him from the inside. He stood up, gasping, went back to the window and opened it. A cool breeze made the curtain behind him flutter. He stepped out onto the balcony and leaned on the railing, taking slow, deep breaths to calm his heart which was still pounding but could so easily stop, and once again he thought about the possibility that he might die right here, with no terror, no regrets about what he would be leaving behind, knowing that he had already lost everything that mattered, that his life was merely a limbo, an agonising twilight he could not escape either by plunging into darkness or returning to the light.

A car door slamming in the distance brought him back to his senses and once again he studied the street and the lines of parked cars, the curved windscreens gleaming under the lamp posts. He was convinced that the guy was out there, huddled in his car, spying on him, revelling in the grief he was causing, and Vilar weighed up his chances of catching him if he rushed outside right now, gun in hand, imagined bringing him back inside and making him talk. He thought about what he might do to him, about wounds he could inflict on this piece of garbage, he felt the sickness well up in him again, felt an icy shiver course through his whole body.

He went back inside and rolled down the blinds without really thinking, perhaps to avoid the eyes he could feel trained on him. Not daring to look at the images again, he put them back into the envelope and set it on the sideboard. He felt drained. He looked at his watch: almost 11.00 p.m. He turned on the C.D. player, intending to play whatever was in it, but the tray was empty and he did not feel up to choosing something. What could he listen to? Had music, especially when listened to on a machine, ever drowned out silence? He felt no desire to shut himself away in a bubble of sound and, not for the first time, he thought about explorers in novels trekking through the Arctic, who believed that by huddling over the flickering light of a fire, they could ward off the cold and the wolves.

He needed to hear a human voice. He would deal with the wolves later.

Pradeau answered on the second ring.

"Oh, Pierre. Hi."

He could hear music, a deep throbbing bassline. He could even hear Pradeau smile.

"What are you listening to?"

"Stuff you wouldn't like. Hip-hop."

"Do you like it?"

"I'm not really into rap. But I like this record. Kool Shen. Ex-member of Nique Ta Mère, every policeman's favourite group."

"You on your own?"

Vilar heard him light a cigarette.

"Depends on what you mean by on my own. Got a pack of fags, a bottle of Glenmorangie, a packet of crackers – I couldn't fucking face making something to eat. But, honestly, ossifer, I've hardly drunk a drop."

"You supply the company and I'll supply the food: pizza quattro stagioni, homemade liver pâté and a bottle of Graves to wash it down. But don't take too long, or I'll top myself."

"I love your sense of humour."

"It's not a joke."

Vilar heard Pradeau laugh nervously at the other end of the line.

"Have you got a choc ice in the freezer?"

"I do indeed."

"I'll be right over. We'll talk."

Vilar hung up. "Get a move on," he murmured. "It'll get cold." He sat for a long while, holding the telephone, then jumped up and turned on the lights, put Patti Smith's "Easter" into the C.D. player. He played "Because the Night" first, listening to her work her magic as he hummed along.

Pradeau showed up half an hour later with a carrier bag containing all the bits and pieces that helped him fill the lonely hours. He stood in the doorway for a long minute, his large frame silhouetted against the light, staring questioningly at Victor, then came over, patted him on the shoulder and asked what was up.

"Let's eat first," Vilar said. "Let's get a drink and I'll tell you all about it later."

They ate in the kitchen, sitting facing each other on rickety metal chairs at a bistro table, the rudimentary furniture he had kept when he and Ana separated, a throwback to the kitchenette in the studio flat they had rented for three years in Paris a lifetime ago. They talked in low voices, calmly, confidingly, about trivial and serious matters, and for two hours the silence was banished by the babble stirred up by cigarettes and alcohol.

At times the air of melancholy made them sigh, robbed them of speech as they dithered over what they were trying to express, scarcely knowing whether there was anything left to say.

At other times they laughed over some shared memory, some ludicrous case they'd had to deal with at work, those situations when people are no more than jesters in the tragedy of their lives, clowns watching their own downfall.

At about 2.00 a.m., Vilar stood up, rubbing his back, and suggested they move into the living room and have one for the road. Sucking his cheeks in, Pradeau announced that this was a fine idea, because they'd suffered enough for one day. He grabbed the back of his chair and shook it, laughing.

"The fucking chairs we force hairy thugs to sit on during questioning are sheer luxury compared to these death traps. So anyway, what was it you wanted to talk to me about?"

"Morvan has disappeared. Kidnapped, it looks like. And then this," Vilar said, cutting across Pradeau's questions and holding out the envelope. "The guy who shoved them through the letterbox called me two minutes after I got home. He couldn't have been far away. He had to be watching the building."

Pradeau studied the photographs, his face frozen, a waxen mask in the dim light. He breathed through his nose and, in spite of himself, Vilar could hear the revulsion in every breath. He jabbed a finger at one of the images.

Vilar was sat on the other side of the chest that served as a coffee table and did not move, just studied the frozen horror on his friend's face.

"You think this is Pablo?" Pradeau said.

Vilar grimaced.

"I hope not, but I think it might be."

"It's hard to say, you know . . . With the mask . . ."

"The guy took great pleasure in calling just after I got in. Gave me just enough time to look at them, then rang."

"He phoned you?" Pradeau's voice choked "He phoned you . . . !"

He shook his head, dumbfounded. This information seemed to shock him more than the vile picture he was looking at.

"Yes, he fucking phoned me, what's wrong with you?"

Pradeau suddenly seemed to regain his composure and took a slug of whisky.

"Nothing, it's just that this guy is . . . I mean, for fuck's sake, why take it this far? And look, some of the faces have been deliberately blurred. He's trying to confuse you."

He studied the photographs again as if he might discover some arcane secret.

"It's the guy who kidnapped Pablo," Vilar said. "I'm sure it is. Remember the message on Morvan's computer: 'I've got the boy'?"

"Give it up, Pierre. Guys like that don't do this kind of shit, you know that. But then what exactly does he have? Did he kidnap Morvan, is he holding him somewhere? What does all this mean? Besides, why the fuck would he turn up seven years later when the case is as good as dead and he's almost out of the woods? It's insane. You think maybe Morvan found a lead?"

Vilar shrugged.

"I'd be surprised. The one time he thought he'd got a lead somewhere down in Nice, he told me about it on the telephone, he didn't beat around the bush. You remember the case, four years ago? We found those twelve-year-old girls trafficked from Bulgaria. But if Morvan had any doubts about the photographs, or just wanted to tell me something, he'd get me to come over. And like I told you the other day, he sounded strange on the telephone. I had the impression he wasn't alone and he was trying to warn me."

"Trying to tell you not to come? But why? I mean he needed help. You think this other guy laid a trap for you? Does that make sense?"

Vilar stood up, walked as far as the rolled-down blinds, then turned.

"I don't know," he said, almost in a whisper. "All I know is that this guy knows what happened to my son and I'm going to find him and make him talk, even if I have to cut him into little pieces."

Pradeau looked up at him and Vilar held his gaze.

"I'll be there to hand you the knife," Pradeau said, breaking the silence. "In the meantime, we've got to tell Daras. We'll put a team on it. Don't you worry, we'll catch this fucker."

He poured them both another shot of whisky, lit a cigarette, coughed, took a swig for medicinal purposes. Vilar came over and sniffed the contents of his glass. He screwed up his face and set the glass down again.

"Shit, I'm dog-tired," he said. "I'm going to try and get some sleep."

He waved to the armchair where Pradeau was sitting.

"You can crash here, if you like. That way you don't have to drive back drunk."

Pradeau got up and stretched, yawning, then looked at Vilar with a sardonic smile.

"I don't think so. Me and Nathalie had separate bedrooms for two years. I'm not about to start again with you!"

They laughed. Their reeling shadows, drunker than they were, faced each other on the wall. Vilar walked Pradeau to the door.

"We'll start the hunt tomorrow," Pradeau said, turning on the landing. "We'll catch this guy and make him spill his guts."

They said goodnight and Vilar stood in the doorway listening to his friend lurch heavily down two flights of stairs, listened to the click of the electric front door, then closed his door and stepped back into the dim apartment made suddenly darker by the humming silence that throbbed in his ears.

11

He could stare for hours at the wardrobe where he had lodged the urn, the doors wide open, the red container sitting on its own shelf, him sitting on the bed, hands on his thighs, his eyes glimmering with the metallic reflections that glowed in the half-light of the room like the blood of some fantastical creature, focusing all the mental energy he could muster on this patch of crimson, trying to conjure the image of his mother so he could talk to her, beg her to come back right here, right now, Maman, because I need you, because through sheer force of will anything is possible and my will is boundless.

He waited for the ghost to materialise, to condense, a distillation of love and grief, to come and sit next to him, hug him to her chest, press her lips to his hair. Sometimes he could wait for hours in the heat of the afternoon, when everyone was taking a siesta and the house was so quiet it was possible to hear the shadows of memory sighing, but each time the unbearable anticipation eventually left him feeling shattered, and it seemed as if the air had been gradually sucked from the room, leaving him breathless, crushed by his own weight, crumpling in on himself, a burst balloon, an empty bag.

There was nothing he could do to quell the anticipation. It welled up in him at certain moments, when he was alone and at peace, when things seemed to him beautiful and harmonious. He did not believe in anything, neither in God nor in the soul, he knew the dead did not return because, for them, everything is over. But he was learning that memories of them could be insistent, because a bond still exists between the dead and those who live on, an echo, some lingering note like the vibrations of a bell which resonate long after the sound has faded, and he did not know whether he wanted it to go on or to stop, because he did not know whether it brought him pleasure or pain.

He ticked off the days on his calendar since it had happened. Forty-four. He tried to recall precisely what he had done on each day, then abandoned this impossible task, worried that the fragile archipelago of his memory seemed about to be washed away by a turbulent ocean.

All of a sudden he got to his feet so that the weight crushing his chest might fall to the floor. Barefoot, he took a few steps across the threadbare carpet, forcing himself to take deep breaths. A shiver ran down his spine, and he pulled on his T-shirt only to find he could not bear the feel of the warm fabric weighing on his shoulders. He went out onto the narrow landing and listened. He could hear faint music from Marilou's room. Rebecca was with her. Resisting the urge to go and listen outside her door, he knocked on Julien's instead, but there was no answer. He went downstairs into the kitchen and drank straight from the tap, and splashed water on his face and neck.

Outside, the light and heat were so dense that he stopped short in the doorway as though he had walked into something solid. He blinked, shielded his eyes with his hand and took a few steps, calling to Julien, who was probably working on one of the ridiculous projects that could keep him occupied for hours, alone, muttering mysterious curses.

He found Julien perched on some bricks near a shed in front of pile of wood, in the full glare of sunlight. He was wearing a football cap emblazoned with the logo of Olympique de Marseille, the team he claimed to support, though he could not explain why. "The others are idiots," he'd say, when anyone questioned him about it. One day he let slip that Marseille had been his father's favourite team, though he had been born in Roubaix.

"What you doing?" Victor said.

The boy put a finger to his lips and gestured to him to sit down.

"Look," he whispered.

He half opened the lid of a plastic box, pierced in several places. Seven or eight lizards were fighting viciously, sometimes drawing blood. He promptly closed the box again and set it on his knees, then jerked his chin towards another lizard that was poking its head between two logs.

"He's a big bastard."

Slowly, he picked up a piece of bamboo he had split so that it was forked. Victor stepped out of the way and held his breath as Julien gingerly moved the stick towards the animal with a stealth that reminded Victor of a predatory animal, capable of controlling its every movement, hovering for interminable seconds before the final attack. Sweat began to trickle down the boy's forehead, a droplet hung from the tip of his nose and Victor watched this scrawny athlete – eyes bulging, tongue poking between his lips – as he tensed his every muscle while insects crackled in the grass like thousands of tiny unseen flames baking the soil, in readiness for this primitive and preposterous hunt. The lizard looked up at this creature coming towards it and Victor thought he saw the animal's sides pulse faster and its translucent eyelids flicker as Julien froze, gripping the forked stick, and time stood still, or at least it seemed to Victor that for a moment the planet paused on its axis and that the sun plunged its white-hot blade into his back.

He barely saw the gesture – it made him start in surprise though he had been waiting for it for minutes. The lizard was struggling wildly, its head trapped between the bamboo pincers, and Julien carefully picked it up between thumb and forefinger to study it.

The animal opened its mouth, darting its tongue out, trying to identify the creature in front of it.

"D'you see that?" Julien said. "He wants to bite me. But it's not like the green lizards. I caught a green lizard once, but I had to cut its head off."

"How come?"

The boy did not take his eyes off the reptile.

"Because the little fucker wouldn't let go of my finger. So I went and got some secateurs and *snick*! It was five minutes before I could get it

143

off me. My finger was bleeding. They've got really sharp teeth. They kill snakes, you know."

"You ever caught any?"

"Any what?"

"Snakes."

Julien put the lizard into the plastic box. Then he mopped away the sweat from his face with his T-shirt.

"No, but I know where there are some. I saw some the other day. They're easy to catch. We can go there if you like. We'd have to take bikes, though."

Victor shuddered. Even the thought of snakes gave him gooseflesh.

"That would be good," he said, his mouth dry. "What will we do with them?"

The boy shrugged.

"I dunno. Kill them. Or put them in old Georges' house, stick them in his bed. Alive."

"Who's Georges?"

"He's Nicole's father. Marilou and Rebecca's grandfather. We're not supposed to go over there. We're not allowed. Apparently they fell out and now they can't stand the sight of each other."

"Why do you want to put them in his bed?"

"No reason. Just because he's a bastard, that's all."

Julien checked that the lid on the box of lizards was secure, then they both got up and stood in front of the woodpile without saying anything, looking thoughtful.

"What if they bite him? What if he dies? Imagine what would happen."

The kid pressed his ear to the box.

"Maybe. I can hear their hearts beating, it might make the plastic vibrate." He paused. "Nah – that son of a bitch would shit himself, but it's not like we have to. I was just thinking of something we could do with the snakes. It doesn't matter, we can worry about that later."

Repelled though he was by snakes, Victor could not help but imagine the viper biting the old man as he slipped his legs under the covers. He shuddered. He could almost feel the pain of the bite in his calf, the snake coiling around his ankle.

"You got a father?" Julien asked out of the blue.

The snakes disappeared. Something else bit him in the heart. He looked at the boy staring up at him, blinking against the sunlight, waiting for an answer.

"No idea. I never knew him."

Julien nodded.

"I've got one, but he's dead. Shot himself in the bathroom. I was the one who found the body. Shit, you should have seen it . . . I don't talk about it to anyone."

He screwed up his face, wrinkling his nose in an expression of disgust. He spat on the ground. Victor put a hand on his shoulder, felt the sharp bones beneath his fingers and realised how small and thin he was.

"Why are you telling me, then?"

"Cos I trust you. It's like you're like a brother. O.K., I haven't known you long and stuff, but, well . . . It's like you're protecting me".

Victor didn't know what to say, he groped for words and found none. In the end he aimed an affectionate punch at the kid's bony shoulder and smiled.

Julien announced that he was thirsty, and side by side they walked along the fence by the road back towards the house. Victor noticed a man in sunglasses watching them from a grey car, parked on the other side of the street. He recognised the man. He realised it was not over.

Seeing him pause, Julien turned to look in the same direction and asked who the man was.

"No-one," Victor said. "Some arsehole. Let's get inside quickly, it's too hot out here."

He laid his hand on the boy's shoulder again and steered him inside. He could feel the kid's hand clutching his T-shirt.

The girls were in the living room, slumped on the sofa, their feet up on the coffee table. The T.V. was blaring. Victor could see only shifting colours, bright flashes. Marilou called Julien over so that he could show her what he had caught and he went up and half opened the box. She shrieked in terror and delight.

Rebecca was playing with her mobile, texting. She turned to Victor, who was staring sightlessly at the deafening screen. Disdainfully she looked him up and down with a scornful pout, then turned back to the bluish glow of her phone. Victor did not understand – he guessed that her scorn was not directed at him, at least not entirely. The girl was weird, he thought, too grown-up already, though he did not quite know what that meant. He heaved a sigh then turned and went into the kitchen to get a drink. Standing in front of the open refrigerator, he swigged from the neck of the big bottle of ice-cold cola, almost choking. Then he stood in the middle of the room, inhaling deeply so he could catch his breath. When he came out of the kitchen he almost bumped into Nicole, who stopped him and ran her hand over his forehead.

"You're hot. Stay inside in the shade for a while. It's sweltering out there. Did you have something to drink?"

"Yeah. I'll be right back. I forgot something."

He ducked outside and walked cautiously behind the hedge, crouching needlessly, then rushed over to the car door and glared at the man, his elbow still propped out of the open window, smoking as he stared back at the boy.

"Hi, Victor. Remember me? Do you want to take a spin? I've got air conditioning. We need to talk."

Victor said nothing. The man tossed his cigarette. The smoke from the butt coiled and snaked along the tarmac.

"I don't want to force you, but . . ."

Victor bent, and grabbed a fistful of pebbles and, in a single movement that caught the man off guard, he hurled them at the car. Several of them hit the man full in the face, the others rattled against the bodywork and the glass. Victor wished that the windows had shattered, shards of glass ripping through the car, slashing the man.

The man's name was Éric; Victor had never known his surname. His mother had been scared of this man. Victor had seen him once, standing at the end of the hall, a tall, hulking shadow, with a square head and a thick neck. The guy had not even looked at Victor, but his mother had told him to go back to his room and stay there. She had snapped at him, something she rarely did, and Victor felt frightened and upset. The man had come round several times after that, and whenever Victor was there, his mother told him to play outside or to go to his room.

"I don't want you having anything to do with him. I don't want him to see you or speak to you. Just pretend he doesn't exist and everything will be fine. I'll explain when you're older. And you're not to mention him to anyone, do you understand? Not to anyone, because if you do then the whole world will come crashing down on both of us."

He knew only that he should hate this man. Hate him even more than he feared him.

More than once, he had heard raised voices from his mother's bedroom. One night, he had heard furniture being knocked over. Their heavy, muffled voices rumbled on late into the night, an ominous booming that made the walls shake. Victor had not slept a wink that night because he was frightened for her, even when their voices fell silent and Victor knew why they had and this terrified him even more than the blows and the insults he had imagined.

Éric drove off in a squeal of tyres and Victor bent double, gasping, acid churning in his stomach like dirty laundry in a washing machine. As he was spitting up bile and trying to catch his breath, he heard Nicole come up behind him and ask what had happened.

"What was that noise? That car? Who was that guy you were talking to just now? Do you know him?"

"No," he said. "Nothing. It's nothing. I didn't talk to him."

He was breathing hard, dripping with sweat. Through his tears he saw that the girls were watching from the doorway, shading their eyes. Nicole walked into the road and scanned the distant horizon from right to left, but could see nothing. She came back and asked Victor if he was alright, stroking him and wrapping her comforting arms around him. He roughly pulled away from her embrace, from her constant questions, and headed for his room. Julien was sitting on the bottom step of the stairs.

"I saw him," he said. "I've memorised the number plate, I'll write it down for you."

He slept deeply all afternoon, lying flat on his stomach. Marilou came to wake him, shaking his shoulder gently.

"Hey, you O.K.? You should come down and have something to eat."

He propped himself up on one elbow. The girl's big black eyes cast an invisible veil over him.

"Who was in that car?"

Victor sat up, his feet feeling for his espadrilles.

"You not going to tell me?"

He got to his feet. She stared up at him, waiting for his answer, then she stood up too, almost brushing against him.

"Is it a secret?" she whispered. "Seems like everyone's got secrets round here."

He laid a hand against her cheek. She took it in hers, kissed it gently then ran to the door in three elegant strides.

Before his sleep-befuddled brain could understand what had happened, she had vanished and he was left staring at an empty doorway.

They were all already sitting around the table when he came into the dining room. He said hello to Denis who, for once, responded intelligibly rather than with his usual mumble. Nicole asked again if he was alright and he nodded as he served himself some *salade niçoise* and tucked in straight away, his stomach growling and his head spinning with hunger. When he looked at Julien, the boy gave him a wink, then buried his nose in his plate and went back to eating in his curious fashion, at once awkward and brilliant, using the back of his fork and the tip of his knife. Victor wondered what he had done with the lizards. He thought again about the snakes, feeling the same shudder, thought how he wished that, instead of stones, he had thrown a fistful of vipers in the man's face.

After dinner, Nicole and Denis took him aside and asked if he knew the man in the car, and Victor insisted that he did not know him, had never seen him before, no need to worry. Denis said that was just the point, they were worried, they did not like seeing shady characters prowling around children like that. He told Victor to warn him next time he saw something strange, and said he had told Marilou and Julien the same thing.

Nicole, looking embarrassed, asked whether the man could be a friend of his mother's or something like that, and the boy bowed his head, hunched his thin shoulders and whispered, no, no, he couldn't be. He managed to look up, to look her in the eye without blinking for several seconds during which time he feared his tears would overflow and his heart would give out, unable to carry on. Standing next to him, Denis was leaning down as though to confide in him, breathing heavily through his nose, occasionally murmuring something in a voice that mingled worry with suppressed anger.

Nicole did not press the point. Denis went off with a sigh, to sit in front of the T.V., muttering vaguely about a gun and a bastard whose head he would blow off if ever he showed up round here again.

The following morning, no-one referred to it in front of Victor. They had breakfast in the shade of the terrace where something of the cool of the night still lingered. The sky was a harsh blue, criss-crossed by the chirp of swallows. Julien had brought out his box of lizards, and as he chewed on his bread, he lifted the lid from time to time to peer at the reptiles. When they left the table, Marilou asked Victor if he wanted to come to Rebecca's house to help them clean the windows.

"Why are you asking me?"

"Cos it'll be quicker with three of us. Besides, that way you'll see."

"See what?"

Marilou shrugged.

"Well?"

It was a low house on the outskirts of the village, almost invisible between the lush foliage of two big oaks. As they arrived, a cat darted off and crouched under a plastic garden table plonked in the middle of a yellowing lawn, watching them from a safe distance. They leaned their bicycles against the metal frame of a swing, faded by the sun and rusting in places, and walked towards the half-open front door from which Rebecca emerged, a cigarette in her hand, wearing a large T-shirt and cut-off jeans that came down to her knees. She did not seem surprised to see Victor and hugged him warmly. They followed her indoors.

"It's Marilou and Victor," she said as she went into the living room. "They've come to help me with the windows."

The room was in semi-darkness, the shutters barely open. Above the back of a brightly patterned sofa, Victor saw the top of a woman's head, her reddish-blonde hair piled up in a bun. She was staring at a widescreen T.V. on which sexy women were chattering beneath the blue Californian skies.

The smell of cigarette smoke was overpowering. Victor noticed that the windows were closed. The woman struggled to her feet. She was wearing red Bermuda shorts and an A.C. Milan shirt bearing the number "11" and the name "GILARDINO". She stubbed out her cigarette in an overflowing ashtray on the coffee table. The remains of breakfast were scattered about as were two empty beer bottles. She turned her lined and weary face towards them and looked at them with curiosity, or surprise. She looked a lot like Rebecca, Victor thought, and he did not like this image of her looking old and shrivelled. The woman shuffled over in her slippers to Marilou, put her arms around her and hugged her tight.

"Does your mother know you're here? What's got into her? Is she clearing out the house for a spring clean? Isn't she afraid you'll catch all our vices?"

She kissed the girl's face.

"It's so lovely to see you. One of these days, you'll be so tall I won't recognise you. And who's this boy?"

She stared at Victor, who murmured a greeting.

"That's Victor. He's been living with us for a fortnight."

The woman proffered a limp hand and Victor shook it, repeating his greeting.

"I'm Christine. You'll need to keep an eye on these two. Don't let them get up to any mischief, will you? And I don't want you taking advantage, being alone here with two girls."

She gave a wheezy laugh that degenerated into a bout of coughing.

Rebecca led Marilou and Victor down a narrow hallway, climbing over cardboard boxes stuffed with clothes and old rags, and invited them into her bedroom. Victor stopped in the doorway, but Rebecca waved him in.

"Come in, we won't bite! Is it what my mother said? If you listen to her . . . Anyway, by ten in the morning she's always drunk, spouting gibberish or running around all over the place."

Outside, a car honked its horn.

"There, that'll be Gaby, her best friend. They're off to the beach to show off their arses, and if they're really horny they'll end up in a club in Montalivet or Soulac getting shagged."

"Why do you always say stuff like that?" Marilou said. "I mean she's still your mother . . . You talk about her like she was just a piece of shit."

Victor looked at Rebecca; she had taken out a cigarette and lit it, her hand trembling. She was deathly pale, her eyes glistened with tears.

"Sometimes, I think I'd be better off not having a mother."

From outside came the sound of doors slamming and a car driving off.

Victor felt as though he could hardly breathe. He put it down to the cigarette smoke, but felt a bitter lump form in his throat.

"What about your father?" he managed to say.

He asked the question without knowing why. Maybe to stop Rebecca talking about her mother like that.

The two girls glanced at each other and in that look there was something invisible and indestructible, something so solid you could walk on it.

"Give it a rest," Marilou said.

Victor felt like running out of the room, like a character in a novel fleeing an accursed land, having come too close to uncovering its secret.

A little later, bored of the girls' chatter, he took his bike and rode north along the estuary towards the waiting ocean. He passed some jetties, some with boats moored, that jutted out into the muddy, swirling waters. At some point he stopped, clambered down the embankment, waded cautiously into the mud and stood listening to the faint sounds that the river made as it lapped at the bank, and a little further out he spotted a leaping salmon, enormous to his eyes. A blue and red plastic dinghy bobbed on the waves. Powerful and swift, the current glided towards the sea, and he realised that if he took a boat and allowed himself to drift, before long he would soon reach the mouth of the river, the furious backwash where it met the ocean. He would do it someday, he thought. He felt a longing, a call, that hovered in the air like a vast intake of breath.

12

They had coffee in Daras' office, making the most of a break between meetings, telephone calls, emergency callouts. They were settled in a corner where the *capitaine* had created a miniature living room with three armchairs and a rattan table that had been found in the street years before during a night-time stakeout. Daras spoke in a low voice, her chest thrust forward, arms folded in her lap. Vilar and Pradeau sat close to her, and together they looked like three conspirators, an impression reinforced by the intensity of their expressions.

"Whoever this guy is, he knows a lot about you. Pablo's abduction, your relationship with Morvan, your telephone number – despite the fact it's ex-directory – your address, and I don't know what else. He's mobile, he keeps tabs on you, leaves no fingerprints – at least as far as we know, the forensics lab in Poitiers haven't been in touch, but it looks like Morvan's house is clean."

"He might have a record, maybe that's why he's being careful," Pradeau said.

"Possible," Daras said. "We need a bit of luck: a print, a hair, anything. He must have spent hours at Morvan's place, there has to be some trace . . . I mean, he wasn't wearing latex gloves and a forensic suit, surely? Plus it's been sweltering recently, he must have been dripping sweat everywhere."

Vilar said nothing, content just to watch her long hands gesticulating to underscore a point, or pushing behind her ear an unruly lock of blonde hair that kept falling over her face. He had always loved these little gestures women made, these graceful details, the shimmering, pointillist beauty most women effortlessly exuded.

Pradeau lit a cigarette and got up to open the window. Immediately the morning heat spilled into the room.

"Who hates you enough to send you this sort of shit and then call you to gloat? It looks like this guy has some sort of plan, a strategy, don't you think?"

Vilar shrugged. "I don't even want to think about how many low-lifes there are out there who hate our guts. All the vicious fuckers we've banged up and who blame us and the judges for their ruined lives, their broken homes and God knows what else, I'm sure there's hundreds of them who would cheerfully skin us alive if they got the chance. We can't comb through every one of those we've ever pulled in or questioned in their homes. And how can we be sure it's not just some retard with a fixation for my ugly mug, like a limpet clinging to the nearest rock?"

He stopped and the other two burst out laughing, Daras shaking her head, muttering "Jesus, you're dumb!", and then they were serious once more, visibly racking their memories for some man – or woman – who might have cause to nurture such a deep-rooted hatred.

"And if he's so clued up," Vilar said, "we need to find out where he's getting his information."

"Or from whom," Pradeau said.

"Or from whom," Daras echoed.

She seemed to mull over the implications of this question, then said, "Thing is, it's not like an address or a telephone number is classified information. We give them out to people all the time, they pass them on, it's . . ."

Vilar waved to interrupt her.

"No, not to that kind of guy. He's got nothing to do with me, with us and the people we mix with, and he's certainly got nothing to do with the people I hang out with off duty – he can't have got my details from some chance meeting or conversation. As I said: this bloke has inside information. In other words, someone is informing him."

"In that case," Daras said, "draw up a list of all the people who might know your number and your address – although I think he probably just followed you – and you'll find the answer to your question. But you know better than most that nothing is watertight. And what do you mean by 'Someone is informing him'? Surely you don't think this is some sort of conspiracy? By who? For what?"

Vilar shrugged again. "To be the victim of a conspiracy, you have to hold a position of power, you have to have something to lose that the conspirators think is important: privileges, image, reputation, that sort of thing. What the fuck have I got to lose? No, I don't believe it's a con-spiracy, but . . . It's just . . . Jesus, here I go again, I sound like I'm paranoid."

"Stop it . . . You're overthinking this. No-one here is leaking informa-tion to that bastard. He overhead something, found out by word of mouth, maybe there was some sort of fuck-up, I don't know, but I do know it's not someone trying to hurt you. Because if that's what you think, it would mean the leak had to come from here, from the station – from a fellow officer if we're going to be specific. And that's something I cannot believe. Not with your history, which everyone knows, not with . . . not after everything you've gone through over the years. Who would . . . ?"

She had laid a hand on his arm, having spoken with that perfect blend of authority and gentleness that only she could use honestly, perhaps because it was something deeply rooted in her. Her lips were rarely graced with a smile, but her eyes could sparkle with wit, with joy or happiness. Vilar nodded and looked down at his shoes. It was not clear whether he was agreeing or merely masking his impatience, his anger.

"That's fine," he said at length. "Let's drop it. I . . . Well, what do I know."

"I'm not going to drop it. I'm going to go through all the cases you've worked on over the past ten years. We'll draw up a list of every-one you banged up, their sentences, what became of them. I'll put in a call to Toulouse for records of the two years you spent there. I think in a few days we'll have a clearer picture. I'm also going to ask the big chief if he can free up an officer to keep a watch on your apartment. We'll put a tap on your line and try to trace any calls."

Vilar nodded, in agreement or in gratitude, and got to his feet. Pradeau was already heading for the door when they heard Daras' voice.

"I had a call from the *procureur*. We need to make progress on the dead woman in Bacalan. It's been weeks and we've got nothing: no-one knows anything, no-one knew the woman . . . it's like she was invisible. And the kid, anyone know where he is? Wasn't he meant to be fostered?"

Vilar said he didn't know, but that he would see the boy again and try to get him to talk.

"I'll go over it all again. I'll interview the neighbour again, the woman who used to look after the boy sometimes. She wasn't exactly forthcoming last time, but she has to know something. I'll go see her now, in fact. And there's the woman she worked with, Sandra de Melo. I'm sure they told each other everything. I'll go and threaten to take them both in for questioning, see if that loosens their tongues."

Daras poured herself some more cold coffee. She could drink pints of coffee in a day, scalding hot or ice-cold.

"The girl worked as a prostitute. I can't believe she was a loner, that she didn't experience the pressure, the risks. There's something being covered up here. Something serious, something buried . . ."

Pradeau threw up his hands. "The formidable intuition of Capitaine Daras."

"You got a better suggestion?" Daras snapped. "Plus, I've got another hunch: I think there were two guys. I'm not sure why or how, but there are two of them. It's not easy to make an ex-policeman like Morvan disappear. Even if he was wounded, even if it was some hulking single-minded thug. I'm telling you, there's two of them. And I don't give a flying fuck what you think."

She smiled and Pradeau bowed his head slightly in surrender. She checked her watch, and got up to leave.

"Well, gentlemen," she said over her shoulder. "I have a meeting at the court, where I have to discuss some more of my intuitions with Judge Savy. She's a woman herself, she's more likely to understand."

Pradeau made no attempt at a comeback, and got up to follow her out. He waited in the hallway for Vilar.

"She really gets on my tits when she plays the great detective."

Vilar said nothing. He simply smiled and they walked together until Garcia called out to Pradeau, beckoning him into an office and immediately shutting the door behind them. Vilar was convinced Daras was right. Two guys.

Pulling out of the car park, he was almost surprised to find himself behind the wheel of his car. He had been acting on autopilot for several minutes and could not even remember the thoughts that had so engrossed him. The sunlight sparked a blinding migraine in his skull making him grope for a pair of shades so he could keep his eyes open without screaming in pain.

The rue Arago was deserted and the shutters on the houses were closed against the dense heat that slunk along the street and quivered on the pavements like a blinding jelly. Vilar rang the doorbell and pressed himself into the doorway, into the narrow sliver of shadow. A spy-hole clicked open and through it he saw a pair of glasses and the worried gleam of a blue eye. When he was asked what it was about, he held up his warrant card.

"Commandant Vilar. Madame Huvenne?

"Yes, of course," she said hurriedly and opened the door.

She was small and thin, with short grey hair, wearing a black blouse studded with little red flowers. She smiled pleasantly. Vilar tried to remember what Garcia, who had questioned her, had said about her age. Not far off eighty, most likely.

"Come in, it's too hot outside."

She led him down a dark hallway that was so cool he wondered whether the house was air-conditioned. Cool air wormed its way under his shirt and he felt a shiver run across his shoulders. Madame Huvenne ushered him into a kitchen that smelled of melon and mint. She pulled out a chair and gestured for him to sit at a large table covered with a wax tablecloth, sunflowers on a red background. There were some letters lying on it, open envelopes: some bills, a postcard.

"Would you like some lemonade? Or maybe a little aperitif?" the woman offered.

"Please, don't go to any trouble . . . whatever there is. A glass of water would be fine."

The old woman opened the fridge and took out a bottle of Muscat and a jug filled with an orange-coloured concoction. She took two glasses from the cupboard and came and sat opposite him. Her movements were swift and precise. Vilar had been expecting a lonely, sad old lady, still traumatised by the murder; instead, he found a sprightly, resourceful woman who even managed to keep the heatwave at bay.

"Help yourself. I make the lemonade myself. I add a few drops of grenadine for colour. Personally, I prefer it with a dash of Beaumes de Venise."

She poured a little wine, sniffed it, not taking her eyes off Vilar.

"One of your colleagues already questioned me," she said as he was about to speak.

"I know. I read his notes. You were close friends with Nadia Fournier and her boy. That's why I'm here to ask you a few more questions, in case there was anything you might not have remembered."

Madame Huvenne nodded. "I was fond of Nadia. She was a good girl. And I wasn't even there when . . . I was getting treatment for my legs. Maybe I could have . . . I don't know . . . Maybe it wouldn't have happened."

With the back of her hand, she wiped away a tear trickling down her cheek, turning the glass in the hollow of her hands, her head bowed. From somewhere in the house came the regular ticking of a clock. Otherwise all was silence. Vilar waited for her to speak, because he realised she needed to. Because this silence broken only by the swinging pendulum of the clock spoke of an aching solitude.

"I was really fond of her," she said quietly, turning her calm, clear eyes on the police officer. "She was like family. And Victor was like my grandson. My children don't live around here, I don't see them much anymore, nor my grandchildren. And since my husband's death . . . Yes, she was a good girl and I loved her, can you understand that?"

"Of course, but there are some things I don't understand quite so well. That is, who Nadia really was, how she and Victor managed to get by. That's why I wanted to come and see you here rather than bringing you down to the station."

"Bring me in?

She set down her glass. Vilar could hear the panic in her voice. No hostility, no suspicion.

"Oh, there's no need to worry. It's something we always do if we feel a witness hasn't told us the whole story. Normally they're released the same day."

She took a sip of wine, he sipped the cold, sugary lemonade that brought back childhood memories. Madame Huvenne looked him straight in the eyes, her hands flat on the table.

"What makes you think I didn't tell the other officer the whole story?"

"There's something strange about this case. Nothing quite fits. Nadia Fournier's life finally seemed to have calmed down after all the upheavals in her childhood." Madame Huvenne nodded, betraying no surprise, and Vilar was certain now that she knew more than she wanted to say. "Then suddenly she's butchered in her own bedroom. And there was nothing stolen – this wasn't a robbery that went wrong – there were no fingerprints, nothing. No D.N.A. we could use, she hadn't had sex with her killer. She was naked, her clothes neatly folded – indicating that she undressed voluntarily, without being forced. This tells us that she knew the man who killed her."

Madame Huvenne looked down and seemed to be studying the patterns on the tablecloth.

"Do you know how she made a living?" Vilar said.

"She cleaned offices and shops, at night. She worked for a company called S.A.N.I."

"Do you have any idea what she earned?"

"Not much, I'd guess. I never really asked her, but in that line of work, they treat their staff like dogs. Officious little bosses employing people cash-in-hand. Desperate women who have to take whatever they can get so they can feed their kids. Exploited, like serfs in the Middle Ages. Job insecurity, they call it nowadays. The only right they have is to remain silent. There's never any investigation into things like that. Think what Nadia and the other workers were earning, and then what their boss was pocketing. You should look into that, while you're at it."

"I already have. What she was earning at S.A.N.I. didn't even cover her rent, especially since she only worked part-time."

"What else could she do? That's shift work for you. They won't let you work more than twenty hours a week. She—"

"You talked to her about it? I thought you said you hadn't. Funny . . . I think the two of you talked about a lot of things. Or am I mistaken?"

Madame Huvenne stared at him, suddenly winded.

"Why don't you tell me how she managed to earn enough to live a decent life and afford to raise her son? I am sure you must have talked about that. It'll save everyone a lot of time and it might help us catch the man who did this. I imagine you want to see him arrested?"

He had raised his voice and spoke in a more staccato tone. He took a small notebook from his pocket and poured himself more lemonade: he wasn't thirsty, but it allowed him to maintain his status as a guest and subtly pressure the old woman without resorting to strong-arm tactics that might make her clam up. He deliberately set the jug down forcefully and saw her instinctively draw her head into her shoulders. He pulled his chair closer, the feet scraping across the tiles with a shriek that sounded menacing.

O.K., that should do it.

"I feel bad talking about her like this. It's like I'm betraying her. She trusted me. Sometimes she'd cry and more than once I had to put my arms around her, try to calm her down. You've no idea how terribly miserable she was, and how sweet."

"Tell me."

The woman took a breath, then shook her head with a sigh.

Vilar did not take his eyes off her; he leaned towards her. It was entirely possible she might take out a photograph of the girl with her arms around her killer. She knew so much about Nadia Fournier's life that she might well know the name of the man who had murdered her. Then he thought of Sandra de Melo, who had also been terrified of betraying Nadia. He jotted her name in a corner of the blank page in his notebook while Madame Huvenne drained her glass, sighed once more, and gently rubbed her hands, massaging the palm with her fingertips as though trying to crumple up a scrap of paper containing all her scruples and her qualms. It was not their affection and their friendship that made these women reluctant to talk. They were trying to protect Nadia.

"I don't know where to start," she said.

Vilar was about to suggest she told him how she and Nadia had met when the doorbell rang. The woman looked at him, alarmed. Then she got up, muttering to herself, wondering who it could possibly be. She stepped around the table, and as she passed him he caught the scent of her perfume, African violets, the smell stirred distant memories, of colours, the shade of a big tree in spring, but this hazy memory refused to crystallise.

From the hallway behind him, Vilar heard the lock click and the voice of a man apologising for disturbing her, explaining he was from the Electricité de France and had come to read the meter.

"I just had one of your lot here: are you coming every month, now?"

The man laughed, then his voice trailed off and he coughed.

"No, no. There was a problem with the readings. So we have to redo the whole street, see?"

When he saw Vilar, the man said hello, but the policeman did not respond, busy rereading the few notes he had made on his pad. At the back of the house, at the end of a long corridor, the old woman opened a cupboard door with a creak, explaining that she'd hardly used any electricity this last month. The meter reader cheerfully reassured her. There was a hoarseness to his voice, the chronic rasp of a smoker, perhaps. As they came past again, Vilar turned and looked at the meter reader, who looked away and did not say goodbye. He was tall, dark-haired, wearing a blue jacket with the E.D.F logo. He clutched a spiral-bound notebook to his chest, a bit like a schoolboy. Vilar found the fact he seemed to hide the notebook strange, but he did not know why, then decided he did not care: he wanted the man gone so that he and Madame Huvenne could pick up where they left off.

The front door closed again. He could still hear the man coughing outside.

"Dearie me, he had a terrible smell of smoke on him," the woman said, on as she came back into the kitchen. "Like he'd been sitting in his car chain-smoking for the past two hours."

Vilar leapt to his feet so abruptly that his chair toppled over. He jumped over it and raced down the hallway, banging into the wall. He flung open the front door and there, thirty metres away, saw the so-called meter reader climbing into a black Ford Mondeo that was certainly not an E.D.F vehicle. He dashed down the empty street, yelling as he raced after the car, which sped away, ignoring his order to stop. He reached around to the small of his back, instinctively groping for the gun he no longer carried, that he had not carried for years now despite the statutory obligation and the repeated reminders from his superiors.

He stopped as he saw the car turn into the rue Blanqui, feeling the pistol butt, his missing gun, like a physical absence in his hand. He retraced his steps, struggling to catch his breath, wiping the sweat from his face, reciting the number plate to himself. He realised he could remember nothing about the man's face: smooth, featureless, the eyes vacant, like the face in the nightmare that so often haunted his sleep.

Madame Huvenne was waiting on the doorstep. She looked up from under her spectacles as though to make sure he was unhurt, proposing she get him a glass of water, a chair, all the consolation she could offer.

"Dearie me," she said, holding out a bottle of mineral water. "Dearie, dearie me . . . All these strange, violent men . . ."

She kept nodding, her shoulders hunched, her movements slow, suddenly much older. Vilar gulped water straight from the bottle, feeling a burning thirst he thought he might never quench. He wiped his lips with the back of his hand, panting, his face flushed.

"Have you ever seen that man before?" he wheezed.

"Never, I swear to you."

The old woman's voice seemed about to crack.

"What is it? Please tell me, what's happening?"

"I don't know, but what I do know is that you're going to have to talk to me, madame. I've had enough of your little secrets. This whole case is starting to stink. You need to get it into your head that Nadia was murdered, do you hear me? She was beaten and strangled. Do you have any idea what that means? You call yourself a friend, but with your silence you're protecting the scum who did this."

"Of course, of course," the old woman said, brushing imaginary crumbs from the tablecloth.

She laid both hands on the table and sighed, then said something Vilar did not hear as he was fishing his phone from his pocket and stepping into the hall where he would not be overheard. He found himself standing in front of a door hidden behind a thick blue curtain, opened it and stepped through a sort of archway of wisteria which ran the length of the house. Bees buzzed around the flowers and, as he listened for Pradeau's greeting, he watched their tireless but comforting ballet.

He explained what had just happened, asked Pradeau to pull the records for the car. It had probably been stolen, but right now it was their only lead so they had to follow it. From Vilar's pauses, it was possible to intuit Pradeau's questions and surprise.

"Yeah, black Ford Mondeo. And put a rocket up the arse of the guys at Licensing to run a vehicle check, please. Yes. It was him. I'm pretty sure I recognised the voice. I don't know how. Maybe it was the hoarseness. The fucker's voice has been ringing in my ear since the other night. Yeah, I'm sure . . . I saw his face, but I'm not sure I'd be able to pick him out of a line-up. But what can you do? He knew I'd be there, I'm sure of it. He didn't turn up on the off chance. There's something very weird going on. This guy is able to follow me, to second-guess my every move. Now I'm wondering what the fuck he was doing here. And it's no coincidence: this means there's a link between Morvan's disappearance, the pictures I got the other night and the Nadia Fournier case, but I'm fucked if I know what it is. Yeah, obviously he's got it in for me, but what does he want? What's he after? Is he trying to get caught? He's taking a hell of a risk playing games like this. Correct, I'm heading home as soon as I finish up here."

He took a last look at the bees, thinking how nice it must be to sit in this garden of an evening, dismissed this ill-timed thought and walked back towards the kitchen. As he passed the living room, the unexpected sound of Madame Huvenne's voice made him jump.

"Why don't you come in here. We'll be more comfortable. You're quite right, I really should tell you everything I know."

The room was dark. He saw the glowing timer of a video recorder and could just make out the old woman sitting in a huge armchair that seemed about to swallow her whole. Here and there he saw the gleam of furniture. Picture frames traced dark rectangles on the walls.

He sat on a sofa diagonally facing the armchair.

"You can turn on the light, if you want to take notes."

He could barely see the woman in the big armchair and her voice seemed suddenly mysterious and anxious. It was no longer the clear, sprightly tone that had so surprised him when he first arrived. She sounded weaker now, breathless, she spoke more slowly, choosing her words carefully, it felt as though she were speaking from the dark shadows where all secrets lie.

He decided he preferred to listen in the dark, the better to hear every intonation, every quaver and every silence of the story she was about to tell, weaving a background murmur in which he might hear the whisper of truth.

This was how Pablo had liked him to tell stories, in a shadowy half-light where they could barely see each other. The sound of his son's breathing, its cadence shifting according to the perilous tales Vilar invented, filled the night with a fragile sweetness that would all of a sudden be overtaken by easeful sleep.

Vilar was not about to let himself be lulled. He settled back and listened to the weary voice speaking softly in the darkness.

Nadia had arrived in tears, one afternoon in January, clutching her jacket around her, her T-shirt torn, trembling with cold and fear. Éric had been around again, but this time he had brought a friend, apparently for a quick drink. Éric wants to marry Nadia. For months he's been pestering her about taking them abroad, her and Victor, taking them to Martinique where he's been offered a job running a hotel. It was some mad idea he'd got into his head. In fact, the guy's a loser, never has a penny to his name, he practically lives on the street. As for Martinique, well, Nicole never believed it, it was just another harebrained scheme – how could Éric manage a hotel when he could barely cope with the small change in his pocket? But Éric seemed to genuinely believe everything he told her, every future he promised her, always a different one; he used to say that he wanted to get away, to turn his life around. If she made fun of him, he would get angry and abusive, screaming that she'd die in the gutter and her son with her. Then he would get violent, he would smash things or beat her. As the old woman talked, Vilar pictured the scene. Anyway, the day I mentioned, he shows up with a friend and she serves them pastis, and they drink, but Nadia is keeping an eye on the other man, the one she's never seen before, a short dark-haired guy and there's something tired and sad about him, a bit like Droopy – you know, the dog in the cartoons – and at some point Éric asks Nadia if she's changed her mind about Martinique, so she plays dumb, she laughs, says it's too hot over there and what with all the pretty girls he would end up dumping her and her kid. Éric sighs, he's disappointed, as he is every time, and tells Nadia that if that's how it is, she has to make amends, and he nods to his friend, "Do what you like," he tells his friend, "And you, you little slut, you better play nice with him because otherwise I'm really going to get angry and you know what I'm like when I lose my rag." But Nadia refuses, she stares at Droopy and laughs and that's when it kicks off, the punching and the kicking, then they drag her into the bedroom and have their fun, they force her to do all kinds of filthy things and as they leave, Éric tells her he'll be back and that he won't be making the journey for nothing.

"No . . ." Madame Huvenne answers a question Vilar did not ask. "Nadia never told me why this Éric was such a danger to her. He had something on her, but she never said what it was. A hundred times I tried to get her to tell me; it was something she'd seen, something she knew, something she had no business knowing, but she never told me more than that. But yes, she was afraid. She said Éric was dangerous, said he was twisted, that he enjoyed hurting people. It wasn't her in particular, apparently that was the first time he'd got so angry, though thinking back he was obviously trying to pressure her. Most of the time it was just threats, they would argue at night in her bedroom after . . . well, you know, he was a regular, I suppose, so she put up with it. It was a habit . . . Once or twice she mentioned some people he knew, talked about how she felt caught in the crossfire . . . She was trying to keep a low profile, trying to make sure social services and Victor's school didn't notice anything. I think that's why he's such a good student, so gentle, almost too quiet, according to his teachers . . . I think that apart from . . . how can I put it? . . . aside from her *activities* – whoring, she used to call it, she wasn't proud, she said, but she wasn't ashamed because she'd sunk so low she had no shame left. That's exactly how she put it. Anyway, apart from that, I think she was mixed up in something that meant that in every other part of her life she had to be perfect, you know? And her son was just the same, he had to behave perfectly so he wouldn't be taken into care. They lived on a knife edge. Victor talked to me about it once. There was this boy in his class who lived with foster parents, he'd been taken away from his mother because she didn't look after him properly, he was always missing school and misbehaving, and Victor was completely terrified that he would be taken away, that he and his mother would be separated, the poor thing. And now . . ."

Madame Huvenne trailed off and in the silence that followed Vilar found his mind filled with the images conjured by her story. He could see the quiet, well-behaved boy heading to school with his bag on his back, the other children shoving and shouting. He could picture Nadia alone with her torturers, resisting them and then huddling up under the rain of blows, see her picking herself up after the rape, bruised and violated, her life once again shattered into quivering pieces, and running to find shelter here, in this very room. Vilar caught himself listening to the silence in the vague expectation that he might catch some ghostly echo of that day, the petrified young woman panting for breath, the words she had used to explain what had just happened to her.

Madame Huvenne shifted in her armchair and the creaking noise brought Vilar back to reality. He apologised, saying that he had been thinking.

"Do you think that Victor knows this guy Éric?"

"Of course. He would have been there in the evenings when the man sometimes came to the house. He would definitely have seen him. Though I do know Nadia did everything she could to make sure he didn't talk to the boy, she said Éric would taint him just by looking at him, that she didn't want her son having anything to do with that world. That's what she'd say. With those people, she said that too."

The woman sighed. She shifted her legs, rubbed her knee. Vilar asked again whether she remembered the other man's name, but she said no, she didn't think Nadia had mentioned it. Gingerly she got to her feet and massaged the small of her back. When Vilar stayed still, waiting for her to say or do something, she smiled.

"At my age, you've always got an ache or a pain somewhere. From spending too long on your feet, too long sitting down, lying in the wrong position . . . Your bones creak like a piece of old furniture . . . Never get old, that's my advice."

Vilar almost told her that this was his plan, that he had very nearly ended up remaining forever young. He thought about Pablo, about how time had passed for him, or rather how it had stopped. Then suddenly everything around him began to lose shape and form and he felt as though he were floating in a dark abyss, an astronaut cut loose from the cable tying him to his ship, doomed to drift forever, frozen instantly by the galactic void. He would have preferred not to think – not even to be capable of thought – because thinking about this was both necessary and impossible.

Shuffling, the old woman led him into the hallway, and once again he urged her to call at any moment if she thought of anything that she had forgotten to tell him. He shook her small bony hand and she took his and pressed it to her, and told him to keep his chin up because she feared he was hunting an evil man weighed down by terrible secrets.

The oppressive heat choked him the moment he stepped outside. He drove back to the docks with his windows rolled down, and in the fast-moving traffic, the air roaring into the car dried his sweat. Straight ahead, to the south, the opalescent sky was drained of colour, grey and dark, and Vilar hoped for a cloudburst, longed for a raging storm, that clamour of war erupting suddenly in a thunderous blast, in hail, rain and fire.

When he got back to the station, Daras told him they had tracked down the car he had called in about. It had been stolen two days before from a supermarket car park in Bègles. The driver had abandoned it on the street right in front of the skating rink opposite the police station, and walked off towards the cathedral while the duty officer watched, gobsmacked, blowing his whistle.

13

Every day Victor kept an eye on the road. He roamed the streets of the village on the lookout for the Peugeot belonging to Éric, since that was the name by which Victor knew him. He kept a knife with him, an Opinel folding pocket knife he had found in a drawer in the garage, honing and oiling the rusty blade until, though still a little tarnished, the grey steel gleamed. He was not sure whether he wanted the man to come back so he could plunge the knife into his throat or whether he dreaded the thought that he might reappear like some evil spirit. Victor thought he spotted him once in a supermarket car park, but the man disappeared behind a van and never re-emerged. He also thought they had passed the beat-up Peugeot driving along the narrow road to the beach, but once again a sharp bend made it impossible for him to confirm his suspicions.

He knew the man would be back. Because predators like that never let go. Never gave up. And every time he imagined this day of reckoning, he slipped his hand into his pocket and took hold of the knife, the blade safely folded into the handle.

At night, he would talk to his mother, leaving the wardrobe doors wide open so he could see the reddish gleam of the urn. He would whisper to her absentmindedly, then say nothing for a long time in case her answer, if it came, fell so softly that not a molecule of air would have quavered. He vowed to avenge her so that she could finally be at peace. He did not know where she was, but perhaps it was not so far away from where he was. "I know him, I've seen the guy who did it, he was here." He went on talking in a low voice, begging his mother to come back because he could not bear this emptiness he carried with him everywhere, the emptiness that had eaten away a part of him and threatened to suck him into the void. Then he would go to the window and listen to the night breeze playing in the trees, its quivering, tremulous voice like a weary sigh. Afterwards, he would manage to sleep, lying in the cool sheets, nestling into the pillow, suddenly so happy that it was almost as though his cheek was resting against someone's shoulder. He would smile in the darkness. And, though no-one could see it, as he slept, his face took on the relaxed expression of a small child, that happy smile they have when they know that everything is fine.

He would wake early but lie in his bed, watching the sun rise through the venetian blinds, and the long shadows of night disappear. He would hear Denis getting up and going to the bathroom, the rush of water or the rumble of pipes. Nicole was always up next. She would make breakfast and liked to sit for a while with Denis since it was the only time of day when they could talk in peace, untroubled by heat or exhaustion. They would smoke a cigarette in the cool air outside the French windows. Victor would hear them whispering, but he could never make out what they were saying. Sometimes they would laugh and try to smother their laughter so as not to wake the children. Victor loved this time of the day. Without knowing why, he was happy for them and he would find himself staring up at the ceiling, smiling at this little moment of happiness that made him jealous.

He would spend the rest of the day thinking about Rebecca. It was terrible and wonderful.

He lurked around her house, going back and forth on his bike, taking any opportunity to go into the village to fetch bread or take a letter to the postbox. He would stop on the corner of the two crooked houses and hang around waiting for her to appear at a window or in the garden, and when he saw her he felt his heart beat faster and something tightening in his chest, and even as he savoured these moments he also dreaded them. There was something about the girl that frightened him. He felt that at any moment she might turn against him and attack him. Perhaps he even hoped that she would.

One day he saw Rebecca's mother get out of a car, laughing loudly, stroke the head of the man behind the wheel and say goodbye. She went straight into the house, a red handbag slung over her shoulder, and slammed the door. The noise echoed along the empty street and Victor thought he saw the little house shake. A few minutes later Rebecca dashed out looking upset, slamming the door in turn. She cycled straight out into the road in front of a tractor whose driver yelled something at her.

She gripped the handlebars with one hand and, with the other, clutched a bunch of red flowers to her chest. She pedalled furiously, her hair streaming behind her like tattered black scarf. When she disappeared round a corner, Victor decided to follow her. There was more traffic on the little square she was now crossing. People stopped to gaze in shop windows. Three or four delivery vans were parking as cars came and went. She weaved between the pedestrians who crossed the road, barely slowing down. He gained on her and saw that the flowers were roses and dahlias. He occurred to him she might be visiting her grandmother, although he did not think it likely, and when he saw her take the narrow path that ran past the winery storehouses, he dismissed the idea. He let her pull ahead, now that she was riding between the vines. Sometimes all he could see was her dark, glossy mane flickering as she rode over the potholes.

And then she disappeared. He thought perhaps she had fallen off her bike, and pedalled frantically until he felt his legs burning with the strain, then, as he came up to a brick cottage, he turned and suddenly stopped. She was fifty metres ahead of him. She had set down her bike and was walking down the hill still clutching the flowers. Victor crouched and scuttled forward, stumbling over clods of dry earth that crumbled under his feet. He stayed close to vines in case he needed to duck and hide.

She was kneeling, her head bowed; he could see only the curve of her back, the purple sleeveless T-shirt clinging to her skin, her bare shoulders glistening with sweat, moving slightly as she reached for something in front of her. She looked as though she were gardening. He wanted to go over to her, but the thought that he would be entering unknown and forbidden territory held him back. He remembered the movies in which explorers ended up being tortured by some tribe whose secret they had profaned, and this unhappy mixture of curiosity and fear made him huddle deeper into the furrow. He pulled his bike after him between two rows of vines and camouflaged it as best he could, lying at the foot of a vine, its branches already drooping from the weight of the grapes.

Peering through the vines he saw Rebecca get to her feet. She rubbed her hands and stood motionless for a moment, then came back up the hill and picked up her bicycle. Victor sank down into the furrow as she walked past, leaning over her bicycle. He counted to a hundred then warily got to his feet and, bent double, walked back to the path. There was no-one. He listened but could hear only the drone of a faraway tractor and cars passing on the road. He walked over to the spot where Rebecca had been standing.

It was a carefully weeded patch of bare soil, a metre long and half a metre wide, forming a perfect rectangle. She had simply laid the bouquet of red dahlias and roses, their stems wrapped in damp kitchen paper.

He sucked in a lungful of air and wiped the sweat from his face. He stood in front of the little grave and the flowers that would soon wither, at once curious about what could be buried there – the body or the bones of a dog or a cat? – and surprised that Rebecca would have come to lay flowers on this pathetic tomb. He assumed she had been forbidden to bury the animal and had dug this hole in secret, deep in the vineyards where no-one was likely to see her.

He was happy he had discovered this secret, dismal as it was. It made him feel closer to her, so close he could look over her shoulder, see the things she saw, an intimacy they could only share when he plucked up courage to tell her that he had been spying on her. He knew something about her that no-one else did. Something they were the only two people in the world to know.

When he got back, Marilou was alone in the house, doing the dishes in the cool, bright kitchen. She was humming to herself and did not answer when he said hello. He offered to put the dishes away, but again she did not answer, pretending not to notice that he was standing next to the bowls and cutlery on the draining board.

"Well," she said. "I thought you were going to tidy things away?"

He opened a cupboard, put the bowls away one by one, taking care to line them up on the shelf. Marilou watched him, frowning.

He turned around and took a deep breath.

"What was Rebecca's dog's name?"

"What dog? Rebecca's never had a dog in her life. She hates dogs, she's scared of them."

He looked at the girl, gazing into the great dark eyes that stared back at him, trying to detect some lie, some hesitation.

"Why are you asking about a dog?"

He shrugged, turning away and putting the cutlery in a drawer.

"It's nothing," he said.

Marilou came up and touched his arm.

"What are you talking about? What dog?"

"It's fine, I told you – it's nothing. I don't know. It was just an idea."

"An idea, eh? You fancy her, that's what it is. And you're trying to find things out about her."

"No I'm not," he said in a whisper. "I'm not trying to find out anything. In fact, I couldn't care less."

She cupped his chin and turned his head towards her.

"Look at me: you can always tell these things by looking in someone's eyes."

She studied the boy's glistening eyes.

"You do fancy her. I knew it!"

She let out a shrill laugh.

"Stop it," Victor said. "Let me go."

He pushed her away and stumbled out of the room, dazed, ran into the garden and sat on the swing, which groaned under his weight. He could hear Julien in the garage, banging pieces of metal, hitting things with a hammer. He went to see what the kid was up to, standing in the doorway to watch. Tools were strewn all around, over the floor, over the workbench and every other surface large enough to hold a spanner or a screwdriver. He was beating at an old rusty, chrome-plated mudguard.

"What the hell are you doing?" Victor shouted over the racket.

Julien stopped hammering and shut one eye, checking the curve of the mudguard.

"Denis gave it to me. He said if I can get it working again, I can drive it."

Next to the boy lay the frame of an ancient orange moped with something that looked like half an engine attached. Wheel rims, tyres and inner tubes were leaning against a wall.

The boy stood up, hammer in hand, his vest smeared with oil, his grubby skin glistening with sweat.

"He said he'd help me, I've got everything I need, even new spark plugs. He'll give me a hand with the engine, because that's a ball-buster, apparently. What about you? What the hell are you doing?"

Victor screwed his face up and shrugged. "You thirsty?" he said. "You want me to get you a drink? Because there's no way Nicole's going to let you inside all covered in engine grease."

"Fuck, yeah, could you get me a Coke, I'm fucking dying here!"

Victor brought back two cans and they drank to the successful completion of the kid's mechanical jigsaw puzzle. Julien drained his can in one and let out a throaty, almost booming burp that astonished them both and then had them doubled up with laughter. When they calmed down, Julien announced he had to get back to work because he wanted to have the moped working by the weekend. Before he could start hammering at the buckled mudguard once again, Victor went over to him:

"How well do you know Rebecca?"

"I dunno, she's Marilou's cousin. Her father was Nicole's sister's husband."

"Where is he, her father?"

174

Julien shook his head. He sniffed and wiped his nose with the back of his hand, smearing grease on his face.

"No idea," he said feebly.

"He's banged up, isn't he?"

"Well, if you knew that already . . . Listen, Victor, I've got work to do."

"What's he inside for? Is he in for long?"

"I haven't a clue! Stop busting my balls! Go ask Nicole, she can tell you."

"Nicole won't tell me anything. On account of her sister."

"O.K. then, she won't tell you, and that's that."

The kid made the most of the silence and resumed his pounding, making a deafening racket. Victor grabbed the head of the hammer in mid-air and blocked the boy's arm.

"Did Rebecca ever have a dog?"

"Why you asking me?"

"Just answer me."

"She hates dogs. She thinks they stink."

"What about cats?"

The kid squirmed, trying to escape from Victor, who had begun to twist the arm.

"O.K., alright, she likes cats. She likes them. Can you let me go now?"

Victor found himself outside again, jolted back to earth, his head heavy with questions to which he had no answers. He pictured Rebecca in front of the grave and suddenly realised that he did not believe she was taking flowers to some dead dog. Nor could he believe it was a cat, a canary or a goldfish. He went and sat beneath the chestnut tree to think things over but all he could think about was that patch of bare earth and the bouquet of red flowers which were probably already withering in the sun. And he thought about what lay under the earth, about the hideous thing that it had become. He shuddered in horror, his mind teeming with gruesome images. He pictured dead children. Little children who might fit in such a grave.

He raised his head, desperate to look anywhere other than at his feet, where these grisly images swarmed, and, in the distance, he saw Marilou staring at him solemnly, brushing away the wisps of black hair the wind whipped around her face. He gave her a little wave, because he did not know how to behave, but she ignored him and turned away, head bowed, and slowly headed back into the house.

14

Vilar would sometimes wake in the middle of the night, convinced he had heard a car door slamming in the street. He would lie in the dark listening to the silence of the night, that white noise that conspires against sleep, then he would get up and go out to the balcony and stare at the line of parked cars, trying to pick out the shadow of the man spying on him, and in these moments he was so convinced that it had actually happened, or was about to happen, that sometimes he was sure he saw something move in one of the cars and he would stand, staring at the dark windscreen lit only by the glow of the streetlamps, his heart pounding, until he pictured himself, half dressed, on his balcony playing hide-and-seek with a string of parked cars. Then he would go back to bed, disappointed, humiliated, furious at himself, a lump at the back of his throat, weeping bitter tears.

This time he had leapt out of bed and waited for his heart to stop racing. The man in his nightmare had come back, rung his doorbell and run off again, and outside Vilar could hear a car starting and the shriek of tyres and in that moment, choking with horror, his arms still stiff from clutching Pablo's body to his chest, he did not know how to separate what was dream from what was real. For a moment he resisted the urge to look at the alarm clock because he knew dawn would be either too close or too far away, always discouraging, but when he saw that it was almost 5.00 a.m., he listened through the closed shutters to the chorus of blackbirds greeting the first rays of dawn, seemingly astonished by each new day.

He must have fallen asleep with his eyes open, because now light was pressing against the shutters, pushing at them with warm fingers. It was almost 7.00 a.m. Someone was knocking at the door, calling his name. He had dreamed that they were coming to arrest him, that there was no escape. Some confused story about the Gestapo screaming at him to open up. A story his father had told him.

The knock came again.

Laurent Pradeau seemed surprised to see him open the door. In the mornings he often had a stupefied look that made him seem surprised by everything. He must have something of the blackbird about him.

"They've found Morvan's body. We have to go. I'll make coffee, you get your shit together."

"What? Where?"

"He was found by a rambler in woods outside Poitiers yesterday afternoon. The body was lying beside a path. No attempt to hide it or anything."

Vilar shuddered. He watched Pradeau bustling in the kitchen, opening cupboards, rummaging around, not finding what he wanted. He tried to think, keeping his hands busy by making the coffee himself.

"Some lieutenant from Poitiers called the department. He couldn't get through on your mobile – why the fuck have you got it switched off all the time? Anyway, Daras told me to head down there with you to check it out. The autopsy is this afternoon."

"Do we know what state he was in?"

"I don't. But he was beaten and stabbed."

Vilar felt his throat tighten.

"No other details?"

"None, just that he was dumped at the side of a path in a wood. That's according to what's-his-name . . . Delvaille, I think his name is."

"Yes, Delvaille." Vilar pictured the calm face, the shy gaze of the young lieutenant.

The telephone rang. He glanced at Pradeau.

"That's probably Daras."

Vilar picked up and put the telephone on speaker. He recognised at once the voice that snarled from the receiver, as jolly as a friend who's just called to chat.

"Have you heard yet? Brave boy, that *gendarme* friend of yours. Hardly said a thing. Actually, he didn't know anything, so I probably shouldn't have got so angry."

"Why did you kill him? Did you enjoy it? Is that the only way you can get it up?"

"Here we go. From the off, the big talk. You really are a real fucking pig. You see, now I'm not sorry I bled him, the other little piglet. Shit, I actually feel pretty good about it. It's a bit like your son, I don't know what they're doing to him right now, but I hope you're thinking hard about it, that it fucks you in the arse like a red-hot poker!"

Vilar found enough breath, enough strength to speak.

"Don't you fucking talk about my son, you hear? I'll kill you, I swear I'll blow your fucking head off!"

His voice choked. He swallowed tears and snot, managed to gulp some air.

"Ooh, I'm so scared, I'm fucking pissing myself. You better aim carefully and shoot first, because I won't miss, you miserable fuck. Hey, if you like, I'll lend you my catapult since I've heard you're scared of actual shooters."

Pradeau was standing next to him, one hand on his shoulder, gripping through his T-shirt to hold him upright or to let him know he was not about to let go of his friend. Then he whispered in his free ear:

"I'll go downstairs and have a look around. I'll catch the fucker. He must have seen me arrive. He has to be nearby. Just keep him talking."

Vilar tried to signal to Pradeau that did not have the strength to go on talking to this guy, that it was pointless, but Pradeau lifted the flap of his jacket, tapped his gun with a wink, and headed out, closing the door soundlessly behind him.

"Hey! You still there? Listen, I gotta go. But don't worry, this isn't over. You're going to cry and shit blood. You're going to understand what it's all about."

The line went dead. Vilar tossed the phone onto the sofa and opened the shutters on the balcony to see if he could spot Pradeau, saw him standing in the middle of the road, waving his arms, stepping back onto the pavement to avoid a woman in a car.

"Come in, there's no point, he's hung up."

Pradeau looked up, then walked back towards the building, shaking his head. Gradually the street was coming to life: cars passed, the rumble of the city began. A cool breeze whipped along the front of the building, which was still in shade, and whirled around Vilar. He heard Pradeau coming back into the apartment, swearing and cursing this guy who kept getting away. He asked for coffee and a cigarette, carried the cafetière and two cups into the living room where Vilar stood, frozen, his mind empty, his head reeling, the ground beneath his feet a shifting quagmire.

*

Vilar could not suppress the shudder that ran down his spine when Lazzaro, the pathologist, showed them the body. Vilar hardly recognised Morvan's bruised face, his eyes were swollen shut from the beating. He found the pale, hairy, naked body almost embarrassing and it required a sheer effort of will to confront what was not yet real to him: the man lying dead on the slab was officer Louis-Marie Morvan, he had been beaten and stabbed in the stomach, a gash of about three centimetres was clearly visible just below the navel. The face was so bloated that Vilar, struggling to recognise the man he had known, did not even have the fleeting sensation, as he so often did, that the body might stir and come back to life.

Lazzaro detailed the bruises, the wounds and the contusions. The victim had probably been stabbed several hours before death, he estimated, and the knife wound had not been the cause of death. This was something he would need to confirm, but it seemed Morvan had been beaten while already in excruciating pain from the wound in his stomach. Given the circumstances, it might be described as torture. They were about to find out.

Watching the autopsy, Vilar stood closer than usual to the table, while Pradeau, pale and queasy, hung back, leaning against one of the sinks flanked by Lieutenant Delvaille, seconded from the local force in Poitiers so they could be kept in the loop: there had been two hours of outraged recriminations when it was discovered that Bordeaux were taking over the case, but then presumably there was some mention of Vilar and his connection with Morvan and maybe they suspected the case was a poisoned chalice anyway and everyone calmed down. The two investigations teams in Poitiers already had their hands full with a serial arsonist who had already killed four, plus a ring of drug dealers, so in the end they were happy to hand over this case.

Vilar did not tremble. His eyes were not misted with tears this time. He watched Lazzaro work with the meticulous attention of an eager student, leaning over when the pathologist pointed something out, nodding at the running commentary Lazzaro made so his assistant could take notes. Only his jaw muscles, quivering beneath his cheeks, betrayed his horror.

Vilar could not help but stare at the shattered eye socket, the bulging eyeball barely contained behind half-closed lids that revealed a dull yellowish membrane where once a human gaze had glittered. He contemplated the ruined face – multiple fractures to the facial bones, broken teeth, fracture to the right parietal bone exposing damage to the brain, dislocation of the jaw – and tried to recognise in the mutilated features, this rictus of utter agony, the peaceful, benign face of Morvan; and yet something prevented him from quite accepting that this mangled body was indeed his, the same one he had seen walk, move lithely, jump up and down if an idea came to him mid-conversation. As always, he found it difficult to accept that the person whose abdomen or whose skull was being cut open, rummaged through in the unbearable stench of viscera, was actually dead, was *the deceased*: was it really him, or was it someone else, someone anonymous, more or less abstract?

In its very horror, the probing, inquisitive attentiveness of the pathologist, this surgery not only dissected the corpse but made one forget this was a man at all: this body, whose most secret crannies were sounded and sliced by the scalpel, ceased to be a human being and became an anatomical inventory. A harrowing litany of death. Vilar did not believe in an afterlife, nor in any supernatural being, but it seemed to him that the dead man was no longer here, that he had departed his sundered body even as his dying agony was being described with horrifyingly clinical coldness.

Eventually, the pathologist stopped. He lifted his visor, pulled off his mask and wiped his forehead with his sleeve. His hair was white and cropped short. A short salt-and-pepper beard covered his cheeks. Vilar could not put an age to him. Sixty, perhaps.

"He was beaten, slashed. You can see the wounds here, probably made with a razor or a Stanley knife. I was told he was kidnapped ten days ago? It's reasonable to assume he was tortured every day and that he died from the beatings, having been weakened by the deep stab wound to his stomach. I'm astonished that he survived as long as he did – seven, possibly eight days . . . He has been dead for seventy-two hours at least. I'll know more tomorrow. I'll be able to give you the details when we've run some more tests."

He seemed to be talking to himself, staring down at the face of what had once been the Maréchal des Logis Morvan, then he shrugged, checked the time on the clock hanging above the row of sinks. He began removing his gloves.

"Did you know him well?"

"Yes," Vilar said. "For a couple of years now we'd been working on an investigation together. We met up regularly."

"Ah, yes . . . I heard something about that. Your son, wasn't it?"

The pathologist looked Vilar in the eye, unblinking. Vilar reeled a little from the shock. He was not used to people talking about Pablo so bluntly.

"He suffered a great deal, you know," Lazzaro said.

Vilar shuddered and stared at the pathologist, puzzled.

"No, no. Him . . ." Lazzaro said, jerking his chin towards Morvan lying on the slab. "You know, I find this very upsetting."

Pulling off their scrubs and tossing them in a bin, they followed

Lazzaro out of the morgue, and Vilar was surprised by the heat and the noise: from everywhere came laughter, snatches of conversation, the creaking of doors, and, curiously, he began to shiver as sweat once again began to trickle down his back. The pathologist led them to a coffee machine and offered them espressos, which he paid for, after a fashion, using copper tokens which the machine initially accepted as ten centime pieces.

"Not to be repeated," he said, smiling. "You're now guilty of receiving stolen goods."

The officers smiled too, noses in their plastic coffee cups. Lazzaro fumbled in the pocket of his white coat and took out a pack of cigarettes which he offered around.

"It's my round. Cigarettes kill the stench. These I acquired honestly in Spain. Cancer is cheaper on the other side of the border."

"Sounds tempting," Pradeau said, taking his pick.

Vilar accepted one in turn. Only Delvaille, tipping back his empty cup in search of sugar, declined. They savoured the cigarettes in silence, staring out through the picture window at the trees in the grounds. After a moment, Lazzaro announced he had work to do and would not be seeing them out. He briskly took his leave, shaking their hands without meeting their eyes, distant now, remote.

As soon as they got outside again, Delvaille ran to a small mound and doubled over, retching. Some distance away, in the shade of a chestnut tree, Vilar and Pradeau waited, dripping with sweat, their breathing laboured in the sweltering air. None of them dared to speak of this malaise, this fever that would unexpectedly come over them, causing stabbing pains all through their bodies and pounding in their heads like a migraine.

When he rejoined them, the young lieutenant was deathly pale, but he managed to smile as he apologised.

"It's my third corpse, but every time it's the fucking same. I'll never get used to it."

"I hope not," Vilar said. "It's not something you should get used to."

In the car park they went their separate ways, undertaking to keep each other up to speed. Vilar thanked Delvaille for having got in touch and asked him when he was planning to request a transfer to Bordeaux. The young lieutenant mumbled something about his wife, a teacher, his two daughters and having a house where everyone seemed happy.

"Forget I mentioned it," Vilar said as a tremor of grief ran through him. "Make the most of what you've got."

Watching him walk away in the blinding sunshine, he envied this young man whose slight frame seemed almost to melt in the harsh light.

*

They had been driving for a while in silence.

Vilar could not get Morvan's last days out of his mind, imagining the torture, the terror and the abject despair of knowing death was inevitable while that psychopath prowled around him with his knife, thinking of new ways to inflict pain without killing him, keeping him on the brink, on that threshold where the heart still beats, where speech is still possible, the limbo that torturers the world over know how to prolong, pulling their punches, deferring their pleasure the better to enjoy it later, often with the collaboration of doctors, dishonourable rather than deranged, who live to a ripe old age and die peacefully in their beds surrounded by their families.

Vilar allowed himself to be overwhelmed by questions flooding his mind. Was the man they were looking for a skilled torturer? If so, at what "school" had he learned his trade? Or had the need to persuade Morvan to talk been so urgent that he had used any means at his disposal? What could Morvan possibly have known that might pose such a threat?

After a moment, he slumped back in the seat and, somewhat dazed by the blast of warm air from the rolled-down window, he stared out through the windscreen at the ribbon of tarmac flashing past at 150 k.p.h., registering small changes in the landscape as they approached Bordeaux.

Pradeau dropped him outside his building, though not before trying to insist they stop off to eat at a trendy restaurant and then go hang out in some fashionable Cuban bar to check out the girls practising their salsa.

"Just to cheer us up, after all that," he said. "Come on, it'll take our minds off all that shit . . . Make a bit of a change to see living people who are a bit brainless because they think they're happy, instead of dead people who've suffered."

Vilar almost accepted so as not to disappoint his friend or leave him to drink on his own, but he thought about the noise, the crowds, the heat and realised what he really wanted was the opposite; his head was heavy, fatigue spread through his body like a scalding liquid. He wished Pradeau good luck in not going to bed alone and said goodbye, then closed the car door and almost ran to his building.

The silence in his apartment surprised him. He stood for a moment in the doorway of the living room, dark because the blinds were drawn; he liked this neat, tidy room which contained no ornament, no superfluous object. He had settled on this spartan existence when he moved after his separation from Ana. Nothing hung on the walls, nothing sat on the few pieces of furniture. A magazine, maybe, or a newspaper left on a chair. Two racks of C.D.s next to the mini hi-fi system. The room that served as his office was exactly the opposite. There teeming confusion reigned, a private chaos in which he liked to lose himself at times.

He sighed, slipped off his jacket and hung it on the coat stand. He went into the kitchen, took a bottle of orange juice from the fridge and drank half of it, feeling a slight twinge from the cold on a sensitive tooth. His head was throbbing by now with a full-blown migraine.

He was thinking about nothing. In fact he could not manage to think about anything, his mind refused to function, filled as it was with the vision of Morvan's gaping corpse, the putrid stench of viscera still lodged in the back of his throat.

He took a cold shower, closing his eyes and leaning against the shower wall trying to control his rasping breath. He scrubbed himself with a mint-scented soap, dried himself quickly and almost immediately felt the weight of the heat in the apartment settle on his shoulders. He swallowed a pill and drank long gulps of water directly from the tap. He pulled on a pair of shorts, decided against a T-shirt, splashed his face again with cold water. Pain throbbed in his temples and he went back into the living room to get a breath of air. He turned on the stereo as he passed and put on a C.D. Slumped on the sofa he listened as the energy of blues rock filled the room, the guitar tearing at the walls, sinking its steel claws into the carpet.

He stayed like that, half dozing, his mind blank, finally emptied of the nightmarish visions that recently had a tendency to find a home there, playing their grisly slide show. He was barely aware of this stillness, through which floated images of American highways, of horizons ringed by steep bluffs, of seedy roadhouses with an old pick-up truck parked out front and a pretty, sad girl behind the till. Every note of the music triggered some new image and he drifted into sleep as though slouched in a cinema seat.

Perhaps it was the silence that roused him from his doze. Or the rivulets of sweat tickling his skin. It was pitch black outside and he could not tell what time it was. Through the half-open window he heard the soft murmur of his neighbourhood, the distant bustle of the city. He remained absolutely still, listening to this background noise like a man in a submarine might listen intently to the sonar so he can pinpoint the enemy.

15

Alone, he went back to the grave. He ducked and weaved through the vineyards, making sure he was not seen. At first he circled the path of bare earth without coming close, glancing about him as though the vines or the copses of trees here and there might shed some light on this mystery. Once, he was even tempted to dig, as he bent down and touched the soil, laying a bunch of wild flowers he had collected along the way. He scratched at the earth with his fingernails, then straightened up again, overcome with terror, because he knew it was not an animal buried there. It was a child. He was convinced of it. Probably a child Rebecca's mother had had in secret; hardly surprising given the number of men she'd spread her legs for. Stillborn maybe, or worse, a screaming baby suffocated by its mother and dumped into this hole. And Rebecca would come to visit this little creature who had barely lived, who may not even have had time to open his eyes. Her little bastard brother.

The rest of the day he hung around Marilou, unable to pluck up the courage to talk to her. She pretended not to notice his little game, or perhaps she was truly oblivious: she scarcely looked at him, besides she was busy making jam with Nicole. He lurked around on his own since Julien hardly set foot outside the garage these days, though his restoration job on the moped was making very little headway as he bounded like a dwarf on springs among the confusion of engine parts, one minute excited, the next discouraged.

That evening, Victor went up to Marilou, who was lying in the hammock playing on her mobile phone.

"I know about Rebecca."

The girl sat up quickly and turned towards him, her legs dangling over the mesh of rope. She stared at him, trying to work out how to react.

"You know about what?"

"About her little brother."

"Her little brother?"

Marilou was rigid, leaning her weight on her arms, her eyes wide.

Victor knew he had hit a nerve. She sat on the end of the hammock, clutching the ropes, her feet on the ground. Suddenly she looked as though she were carved of wood or stone.

"Can you just stop it about Rebecca? Leave her in peace."

"Her little brother is buried at the other end of the vineyards, where the grove of trees is," he said. "I saw the grave."

"What grave? Where?"

"You know what I'm talking about. You've known all along. There's flowers on it and everything, just like in a cemetery."

"I don't know anything about it, I don't even know where you mean."

"I'll show you."

Marilou got to her feet and glanced back at the house.

"Is it far?"

When they got to the grave, breathless and soaked in sweat after cycling in silence without stopping through the oppressive heat of the evening, Marilou took Victor's hand, squeezed it hard and moved so close to him that he could hear her breathing and feel her warm breath on his shoulder.

"We shouldn't go too close."

"Why not? Are you scared?"

She did not answer, but pressed herself against him.

"What does Rebecca do when she comes here?"

"I only saw her once. She knelt down and put down some flowers and then she just stayed there."

"You think she's praying?"

They were whispering now. A sudden breeze from the estuary almost drowned out their voices.

"I don't know any prayers – if I did I'd say one," Marilou said softly.

"To pray there has to be a god, and you don't believe in God. You'd just be talking to yourself. Actually that's what people who pray are doing, because God is just bullshit."

"No, but I could talk to him, to the little boy there. Tell the poor thing we're thinking about him. Sometimes they like it when you say things to them."

"He probably wouldn't even understand what you said, I mean he died when he was only a baby, he wouldn't have been able to talk or anything."

They stood there, pressed against each other, while the wind carrying its acrid smell of mud swirled around them like a spirit. They said nothing for a moment, because they could find no words, then Marilou started to sob. When Victor asked her why she was crying, she said she was thinking about Rebecca and the baby and she cried harder, letting go of his arm and turning away, her shoulders now shaking with sobs. The boy was silent for a minute, then he said that maybe they should head back now, because Nicole would wonder where they'd been and ask awkward questions.

When they got back to their bikes, Marilou put a hand on Victor's arm.

"I have to tell you something."

She sniffled again, wiped her eyes with the hem of her T-shirt. Victor tried to meet her gaze, but she stared back at the place from which they'd come.

"The dead boy . . . he's not Rebecca's brother."

Victor felt something stab him in the back, leaving him unable to breathe.

"It's her son. She had him when she was thirteen."

Victor shook his head. He grabbed his bike by the handlebars then let it fall back onto the grass. The bicycle bell rang faintly and he stared at the little chrome casing, unable to move.

"It was her father, he . . . Ever since she was little he did things to her, you know what I mean . . . Her mother went to the police and now he's in prison. But Rebecca told me that Grandpa Georges used to try and touch her up whenever she went to his house, so now she doesn't go anymore, but she never told anyone about it. She says she wants to kill him herself. Anyway, he's just old paedo, everyone knows that. Apparently he got in trouble when he was younger and his wife even left him because of it."

Victor managed to find a gulp of air and could speak again.

"How d'you know all this?"

"Rebecca told me. She tells me everything. We tell each other secrets, even really private things."

"But she didn't tell you about the grave?"

Marilou finally looked at him, her eyes still glittering with tears.

"No. She told me she got an abortion . . . you know what that is? She had it in Lesparre from some woman."

Victor nodded. His mother had explained it to him once.

"She didn't come to school much that year, her mother didn't want her going, said she was too ashamed. She never really cared about school anyway . . . Even in primary, she used to wind up the teachers and fight with everyone. Then, the year she got pregnant, well, that's when they came and arrested Christophe, her father."

Without thinking about it, they had sat down side by side on a bank of dry grass, and Victor was almost shocked to find himself sitting there, dazed, with a buzzing in his head that made it impossible for him to hear Marilou's soft, droning voice. They had begun to whisper again as though the wind might carry their secret all over the village, but now they said nothing, hunched over, suddenly years older.

When finally they got to their feet and picked up their bikes, Marilou grabbed Victor roughly by the neck of his polo shirt.

"If Rebecca finds out I told you, she'll kill me, O.K.? And I'll tell her you showed me the grave and she'll split your skull. She can be really cruel, you know . . ."

190

"What do you take me for? You don't talk about stuff like this, you just don't."

"All the same, I'm glad *we* talked about it. This way, there's two of us."

Nicole was grappling with a supplier on the telephone and Denis was not home yet, so they did not have to find an excuse for being late. Marilou went to set the table and Victor ran into Julien on the patio.

"Where were you? Fuck's sake, been looking for you all over the place."

"We went for a ride, we felt like cycling."

The boy laughed and gave him a wink.

"Yeah, yeah, I believe you. Just the two of you, was it?"

"Don't say anything, will you?" Victor whispered.

"No sweat! I'll even lend you my moped. I'll have it working soon."

*

Victor had trouble finding sleep, so overwhelmed was he by the confusion of sinister and violent thoughts and images. As dawn began to break, he felt that the sadness that had haunted him for weeks was now giving way to something that welded his jaws shut and made his heart pound so hard he could feel it in the pit of his stomach. It seemed to him that such evil could not go unpunished; he did not know how, did not know whether he would be capable, but he knew he could no longer make do with being sad.

It was while talking about old Georges with Julien that the two of them decided to catch vipers. There was a tumbledown house to the north, on the road that ran along the estuary. There were thousands of them there, Julien assured him. They spent the whole morning plotting, settling all the details of their expedition. The kid prepared by practising the intense concentration of great hunters, or of warriors in a movie before a decisive battle. He wielded his forked bamboo stick, tested the bottom of an old canvas bag he had found in a cupboard in the garage. Victor surprised him, off on his own, learning to control his breathing, swelling and emptying his bony ribcage.

The smaller boy forced his way through the brambles in rubber boots so big his skinny legs disappeared into what looked like the mouths of subterranean monsters, then he stopped and balanced on the crumbled foundations of the ramshackle house, only one wall of which was still standing among the broken beams; he bent down, hands on his knees, forked stick tucked under one arm, to peer into the dark corners, stir up a mound of gravel with his stick, looking for any vipers nesting there. Victor stood a few metres away, legs slightly apart, clutching a piece of wood, vigilant, ready to repel anything that might appear, telling Julien to be careful, feeling a cold shudder run down his back in spite of the fire falling from the incandescent sky.

Suddenly, Julien started and seemed to plunge into the rubble. He poked about for several seconds that to Victor seemed interminable. All that was visible of him now was the curve of his back, the vertebrae poking through the faded T-shirt that had probably once been red.

"Got one! Quick, gimme the bag!"

Victor crept closer and saw the snake writhing between the supple tines of the forked bamboo. About fifty centimetres long, it was coiling and uncoiling itself furiously around the stick that held it captive. It had been trapped a few centimetres below the triangular head it was struggling to lift, its mouth wide, its tongue flickering in short, quick darts. Victor bent lower and saw the vertical pupils, like those of a cat, but lifeless, cold, and he felt an urge to trample the terror this lethal gaze inspired in him. It was the first time he had seen a snake up close without being protected by a wall of glass and his whole body quivered with an almost painful tremor and he thought that this might well be the feeling caused by the poison from the bite as it circulated through a living creature before it died. He felt sweat pour from him, saturating his T-shirt, trickling down his temples. He sucked as much air as he could into his lungs, grabbed the snake just behind the head and held it at arm's length, studying it. The long, tepid body coiled about his wrist, embracing it with a sort of gentleness that made him whimper with disgust. He tightened his hand around the neck of the beast and felt beneath his fingers the firm muscles harden and move beneath the rough skin.

Julien stared at him open-mouthed. He looked terrified.

"Careful! Don't let it go! Jesus Christ, you're mad, you are."

His voice was choked, he seemed lost, swaying in his huge rubber boots, still balanced on the rubble.

"Open the bag," Victor said in a low voice. "Move it!"

The kid did as he was told, pulled apart the edges of the jute sack, which as soon as Victor had dropped the viper into the bottom he quickly tied again with string.

They walked away from the ruins and sat on the parched grass. Julien set the bag down in front of him and stared at it as he took off his boots and wiggled his toes, red from the friction and the heat. Inside the bag, the serpent was still moving a little.

"One should be enough," he said, wiping sweat from his damp ankles. "Why did you do that?"

Victor did not reply. He all but turned his back and looked through the trees and the swirling, foaming waters of the river. His legs were trembling and he pressed his knees together to control the shock wave that fear still sent shuddering through him.

"Me, I never touch 'em, I kill 'em. I only touch them when they're dead," Julien said. "One'll be enough, won't it?"

He slipped his bare feet into an oversize pair of trainers, then jumped to his feet. The thick soles, doubtless designed to break world records or make one believe this was possible, made his spindly legs look like two matchsticks planted in pieces of chewing gum. He walked back to his bike, picked up his bag.

"We should go there, while the bastard's not in."

Once on his feet, Victor found that his legs supported him without weakening. He grabbed the sack containing the snake and hung it from the handlebars. Then they headed off, riding breathless along the road towards Artigues where the old man lived.

They leaned their bicycles against an E.D.F. substation next to a vineyard and wiped their sweaty faces on their T-shirts. They gulped warm lemonade from the flasks they had brought, finding it delicious, then decided to keep some for later because the sun was beating down, and a heat haze drifted above the rows of vines heavy with grapes which were already ripening here and there.

From where they were, all they could see of old Georges' house was the rooftop rising above the shrubs and trees of his garden. They had encountered the old man on his moped, a rifle slung over his shoulder, a juddering trailer hitched to the back. He was heading towards the estuary wearing a faded cotton sunhat. He often went down there to hunt river rats off the fishermen's wharf with his .22, then feed them to his dogs. They walked along the narrow deserted road, its tarmac melting in pools that Julien carefully avoided because he was afraid of getting stuck.

"What if it suddenly went hard? I mean you never know. You could be stuck there with a car heading straight for you."

"Then you get out of your shoes, dumb-ass," Victor said.

The kid slowed his pace, glanced over at Victor, pulling a face beneath the huge peak of his baseball cap, then bowed his head, staring at his shoes, perhaps, or at the road.

"Yeah, but then you'd be in your bare fuckin' feet on the hot tarmac. Think about it, you'd end up with blisters on your soles! Fifth-degree burns!"

Victor put a hand on the kid's shoulder to shut him up. They were no more than thirty metres from the house now. Here and there pyracanthas spilled out through gaps in the broken railings and this botanic barbed wire represented a barrier more impenetrable than a wire fence – even an electrified one. As they stepped towards it, a blackbird flew out of the tangle of thorns with a raucous cry, making them both jump. They stopped in front of the gate, a crude metal frame, set with bars, some of which were warped as though someone – or some animal – had tried to escape without bothering to jump the gate. A few smudges of black paint were still visible on the rusted ironwork.

They never heard the dogs approach. From Victor's scream it sounded as though one of the beasts had its jaws around his throat, and Julien started violently and found himself sitting on the road. A pair of Rottweilers had leapt at the railings, pushing their jaws between the bars. The two boys had felt warm breath and wet drool on their faces. They had seen the fangs up close, seen the jaws snap right under their noses. The gate shook from the dogs' assault.

"Fucking dogs!" Julien screamed.

Victor watched the dogs leap and howl, their dead eyes rolling back in their heads. He had brought his hand to his heart to calm the terror in his chest, the hammering fit to break his ribs; he tried to catch a little breath, just enough to give him the strength to get away from here.

"C'mon, let's get out of here!" he managed to say. Julien had moved closer to the railings and Victor tried to drag the kid away.

"Hey, don't panic. I know this kind of dog. Papa used to have one. They're fine with me most times."

"Well, this isn't most times, Jesus, you can see for yourself they're fucking savage! They'll eat us alive! Now, come on!"

Victor screamed when he saw Julien place his hand flat against the gate. Rearing up on his hind leg the larger dog, the male, was taller than Julien; it sniffed loudly at the little fingers, forcing its snout between the bars. The other dog, a bitch, stood back, barking frantically, teeth bared, muscles trembling, moving beneath her sleek coat like fists. The kid whispered gently to the dog, calling him "Pépère", his nose only inches from the gaping maw.

"Let's get out of here," Victor said again. "Shit, that thing'll rip your face off!"

But the dog had stopped growling. It was now licking at Julien, whose hand was stroking its head, scratching between its ears, disappearing into its huge mouth. With his other hand, Julien lifted the latch on the gate and pushed gently.

"Come on," he said without looking around. "It's all cool. Follow me."

They walked across an area of gravel that crunched under their feet. Tufts of grass had tried to force their way between the pebbles, but the drought – or a dose of weedkiller – had completely shrivelled them. The bitch lumbered over to a sort of tumbledown lean-to, moving slowly at first as though exhausted; she thrust her snout into a bowl and lapped greedily, then trotted back, describing a semicircle, her nose pressed to the ground, her eyes fixed on Victor. The boy froze, arms pressed against his body so as not to agitate the animal as it growled and sniffed, first at his ankles, then at the bag.

"She can smell the snake," Victor said.

Julien turned, one skinny arm wrapped around the neck of the other dog as it strained to lick his face.

"Don't worry about her. She's scared. Don't say anything, just ignore her."

He whistled. The bitch looked up at him and yapped, jumping up and raising a small cloud of dust.

"Fucking hell, how d'you do it?" Victor said. "Are you using some kind of magic words or what? It's like they know you."

The kid nodded proudly then launched into a little routine to demonstrate his control over the dogs. The male followed him meekly, walking to heel, but the bitch simply ran in circles around them giving little barks, sniffing at Victor, stretching her neck towards him, eyes fixed on his.

Julien walked around to the back of the house. They passed two cars so patched and mended with salvaged parts it was impossible to determine their original colour. They were old large Peugeots with rusting chrome bumpers and windows grimed with dust. Victor glanced inside the first wreck and, where the back seat had once been, he noticed a filthy pile of empty cans and bottles, dirty rags and plastic containers on top of which lay a chainsaw. He looked away because the mess disgusted him and, though he did not understand why, it frightened him a little. He decided not to look inside the other wreck, vaguely thinking that he might just as easily have seen a nest of rats or maggots devouring a corpse. His mind filled with grisly images, he hurried to catch up with Julien, who was already rounding the corner of the house, bouncing along like a puppet on his spindly legs and his huge trainers, followed by the huge dog.

Behind the house – the one part of the grounds where a little order seemed to reign – a well-tended vegetable garden, protected from the dogs by posts and wire fencing, ran along the right-hand wall to the

196

end of the lot with rows of tomato plants, lettuces and other vegetables that Victor did not recognise. The rest of the garden was an overgrown area of grass overlooked by three peach trees laden with fruit, and a cherry tree. Beyond the back fence, stretching away interminably, were the vineyards, their dark green leaves shimmering in the sun. Victor wanted to steal some peaches, but Julien was already inside the house and holding the door open for him.

They stepped into a narrow hall, the dark blue wallpaper was patterned with big pink flowers and the damp had left brownish stains and streaks that ran down from the ceiling. The place smelled of mould, stale tobacco and perhaps urine. A khaki oilskin coat hung from a lopsided coat stand, and a pair of rubber boots crusted with dried mud stood on the floor. Julien, who had been peering into each room in turn, now pushed the door opposite, drawing his head back at the terrible screech of hinges as it swung open to reveal a dark corridor at the far end of which was a glass-panelled door leading into a room bathed in sunlight.

"Down there, that's the kitchen," Julien said in a whisper. "That's his bedroom, it's got his bed in it."

"What about that one?" Victor pointed to the door on their left. The kid opened it.

"The living room? Let's take a look."

The room was dark, Victor fumbled for the light switch and found it under a painting depicting a hunting dog with a pheasant in its mouth. Three of the five bulbs flickered on in a fitting shaped like a cartwheel. The room smelled of wood and dust. The board cracked under their feet as they walked slowly across the creaky floor, gazing around them with the astonished air of explorers in a pharaoh's tomb at the furniture covered in curios and framed photographs, the geometric orange and black wallpaper hung with gilt-framed paintings bought from supermarkets and furniture shops. They were rural landscapes, meadows ringed by tall trees in which cattle grazed, country scenes from a far-off time: cows down by the river, a couple of shepherds with their sheep.

Victor studied the paintings in this pitiful gallery. He did not know what to think of them, but the luxuriant vegetation reminded him of scenes he had seen in cartoons, only uglier. They exuded a curious sadness he found somehow fascinating. Eventually his contemplation was disturbed when he felt the snake jerk inside the bag and he continued quickly on his way.

Everything was grey with dust. He blew on the table raising a cloud that prickled his throat. With a fingertip, he traced the word FUCKER on a dark wood tray whose varnish made the word shimmer.

Julien wandered over to a bell jar enclosing a figurine of a flamenco dancer playing castanets. A souvenir of Toledo. Next to it, in a large frame, a bride and groom smiled out of a photograph. Julien studied it in the light from the chandelier and laughed.

"That's him there with his slut of a wife."

Victor came over. He looked at the photograph, then threw the frame against the wall where it shattered in a crash of breaking glass.

"What d'you do that for?"

Victor turned away without answering. He stood in front of a sideboard on which stood a stopped carriage clock garlanded with tarnished gilt. Around it was a crowd, a sort of tribe, peering out of photographs in black-and-white or in washed-out colours, most of them in dusty frames. He could see mouse droppings on the frayed doilies.

"It's disgusting," he said, and, with the back of his hand, swept the whole mess onto the floor in a deafening crash.

Julien shouted something at him, alarmed, but Victor did not hear because of the racket made by the carriage clock as it shattered on the floor. Cogs and springs bounced and rolled. A clear, shrill note pierced the sudden silence as the two boys hesitated.

"You're mad!" Julien whispered, "What the fuck did you do?"

Victor walked over to an armchair, unzipped his pants and started pissing on it. He shook himself off then spat on the back of the chair.

"You do it too," he said. "Shame I don't need to take a shit."

Julien went over to the window and pissed on the curtains.

"Fuck, this is so cool!" he said.

Victor was already opening the door of the sideboard and peering in at the crockery. Bone-china plates, soup tureens and sauce boats, serving dishes decorated with floral patterns: a whole dinner service, probably given to the couple as a wedding present. He rummaged about brutally.

"Shit, that's enough," Julien said. "He'll come back."

Victor shrugged and kicked the sideboard closed.

"Stop it!"

He waved the sack he had been carrying all this time.

"Where should we put it?" Julien said, his eyes wide.

Victor opened the kitchen door. The smell of rancid oil mingled with the stench of piss made his stomach heave. He knocked over two bottles next to the fridge and the sudden crash made his heart skip a beat. Boxes and crates covered the work surfaces and were piled up on top of the cupboards. The gas cooker was covered with a brown film and there were brown spatters on the hood. In the sink, plates and cutlery were soaking in murky greasy water. Everything was caked in grime. The floor was stained with a slick film that sometimes squeaked underfoot: probably a mixture of oil and dirt.

"Jesus, this place is scuzzy," Julien said. "Can you imagine what it was like for Rebecca?"

Pinned to the wall were yellowed press clippings, one of which was a large photograph of a bunch of grape pickers, wooden baskets strapped to their backs, posing in front of horse-drawn carts piled high with fruit. Victor read that a warm welcome had greeted the owner, an important, indeed a legendary figure in the Médoc, who had come to implore the pickers to take great care with the precious harvest which would once again be transformed, through the magic of winemaking, into an illustrious vintage that would be served at the most prestigious tables the world over. The boy peered at the image and saw, amid the fly specks, men with moustaches and women in scarves doing their best to smile while, in the middle of the crowd, a man in a large hat and polished boots posed with one hand on his hip and the other holding a pipe to his lips. The boy was surprised to discover the man's name was double-barrelled and clearly aristocratic, then remembered that the French Revolution, for all its good intentions, had not managed to chop off all their heads.

"Over here," Julien said from behind him.

He had just opened a drawer in the table. Cutlery, a napkin in a napkin ring. The oilcloth was worn here and there where the old man rested his elbows.

"This is where he sits when he's eating, look," said Victor. "Well tonight when he goes to get his fork the viper will bite his hand. And apparently when you're bitten on the hand the poison goes straight to your heart."

He opened the drawer wider and started untying the string around the bag.

"What if someone finds out it was us?" Julien said.

Victor stopped what he was doing and looked at the kid, trying to think of an answer.

"It was the snake. They'll find him, see he's been bitten by a snake and that's that. The bastard could have been bitten out in the garden, couldn't he? Besides, the snake will slither away, no-one's ever going to find it."

The kid looked at him, chewing his nails.

"But what if someone saw us?"

"Fuck's sake, shut it! This was your idea, so stop whining! We'll tell them the whole story about Rebecca and that'll be that. Justice is done. Anyway, at school they told us that if you're a minor you get like half the sentence. What have we got to lose? Nothing."

Julien was still staring into the drawer. "Shit, we should have caught two. With one, we can't be sure he'll croak."

"We haven't got time now. He'll be back soon. Come on, let's do it. Shut the drawer as soon as the snake's in there."

He shook the bag and they immediately heard the viper wriggling among the knives and forks as Julien slammed the drawer shut.

They stood for a moment by the table, staring at their trap. Victor put a hand on Julien's shoulder and the kid nodded imperceptibly, struggling with some private conflict or perhaps nodding at his own determination.

They were still standing transfixed by the drawer when the dogs began to bark. The boys heard them run to the railings, heard the iron gate clang, shaken by the strangled rage of barks and cries. Victor went to look out of the window but could see nothing but the thorny hedge hiding the road and the bounding dogs.

"That's probably him now," Julien said. "They heard him coming."

Without consulting each other both boys dashed through the dining room, tripping over the jumble of objects strewn over the floor. The carriage clock went flying under the sideboard in a last jangling crash as they rushed out into the warm air just as both dogs gave a howl of pain and began to whimper pitifully. Victor saw the dogs coming towards them, tottering clumsily as though drunk, shaking their big heads. The bitch slumped down in the shade of a tree, rubbing her eyes and her snout with her paws while the male, a little further off, rolled in the dry grass and moaned.

"It's not him," Julien said.

Victor turned away from the dogs and saw the man, the one called Éric, closing the gate behind him, leaving his grey car parked by the side of the road. He was tucking a canister into his pocket. Tear gas. Julien ran over to the dogs, grabbing them by the scruff of the neck, shaking them and shouting "Attack!", but the animals lay there sneezing, panting and choking as they whimpered.

The man took out a knife, a flick knife, released the catch and the blade snapped into view.

"Careful with them dogs of yours or I'll gut them, you little wanker," he said to Julien. "Now take your bike and get the fuck out of here, and keep your mouth shut unless you want me to come around and torch your place."

"Who is it?" Julien said. "Is it the guy from the other day?"

He came over to Victor. The man stopped about ten metres away from them, half sitting on the bonnet of one of the Peugeots.

"Fuck off, and don't say anything," Victor said. "This is none of your business. If you say anything I'll kill you, I swear, I'll fucking do it. You got that?"

Julien picked up his backpack and walked quickly towards the gate, head sunk into his shoulders, trembling on his scrawny legs. He had to walk past the cars to get out and tried to give the man a wide berth, but not wide enough because the guy had only to reach out to give him a slap across the face that sent him staggering back two paces.

"Don't fucking threaten me again, you little son of a bitch, you got that? Now go home and fuck your mother before I do it for you!"

The kid ran, pressing a hand to his cheek. He turned briefly to Victor, eyes wide with fear, blood dripping from his face and staining his T-shirt.

The man did not take his eyes off Victor. He did not move, did not blink. He waited, arms wide, the palms of his huge hands turned towards him, until Julien was out of sight. He kept his thumb pressed against the handle of the flick knife. They heard the gate close, the soles of the kid's trainers slapping along the road. The dogs lay slumped on the grass, their sides quivering in the heat.

The man lit a cigarette. He exhaled a cloud of smoke and jerked his chin at Victor.

"So what you gonna do now? Throw stones at me? Gonna call the dogs? Not so tough now, are you? You're just like your mother. Soon as I showed her who was boss, she caved. Nothing but shit on my shoes. That's whores for you. They open their mouths and spread their legs and they don't even know why. Am I right?"

He closed the flick knife and slipped it back into the pocket of his trousers. He ran a tentative hand over his close-cropped hair, glanced up at the white sky, blinked and pulled a face. He stepped towards Victor, skirted around him without making eye contact and leaned against one of the window shutters in the shade. Victor had to turn to look at him.

"What did the pair of you come here for? To steal stuff? Who lives in this shithole anyway?"

Victor shrugged. He thought about the viper now probably coiled up around the old man's napkin, or wriggling about looking for a way out. Then he calculated his chances of escape, of retrieving his bike or running through the vineyards, making it as far as a storehouse or a winery. No chance. He was sorry he had left his knife in his bag rather that slipping it into the pocket of his shorts. He would have started a fight with this guy, stuck the knife into his throat or slashed his face. He pictured the scene and a shiver ran up his arm and down his back.

Éric opened the door and gestured for him to come over.

"Get inside. Don't make me come over there."

Slowly, Victor walked towards him and stepped into the filthy hall. The man came in behind and quietly closed the door. Victor could hear him behind him, breathing. He bowed his head. Waited for the blow.

"Jesus fuck, I don't believe it," the man said.

He opened the door to the dining room and stopped dead when he saw everything smashed on the floor. He turned back to the boy. His piercing blue eyes shone in the darkness. He made a sort of grimace. Perhaps this was how he smiled.

"Been behaving like a little chav, have we? You mother would be disappointed. Did you think about that?"

"So what? You're not my papa, what the fuck's it got to do with you?"

Victor said this in a breathless rush without a second's thought. Instantly, he dreaded how the man might react.

The man did not move. He grimaced again.

"How would you know, you little bastard? How would you know who your papa is, with all the guys who fucked your mama over the years? D'you ever think about that? You see, that's the thing with a whore's kids, they never know who they are. You're old enough to think about it now, aren't you, now you're all alone in the world. Maybe I should give you a hug, my son."

He gave a soundless laugh. He spoke quietly, almost gently, but every word hit Victor like a kick in the stomach. The boy thought of a knife being twisted in a wound. He knew for a fact that this man had killed his mother and had enjoyed it. He knew for a fact that he would kill this man. Or this, at least, was what he vowed as the man looked to see how much pain he had inflicted with his words, and this is what gave him the strength to stand there, to stare him down.

"So what did you kids come here for? There's nothing worth nicking here."

Éric stood in the middle of the kitchen glancing around suspiciously, looking for some clue that might betray the boy's intentions. Then he grabbed Victor by the neck of his T-shirt and pulled him towards him.

"What's the matter, you little queer? Got nothing to say?"

Victor lashed out, jabbing an elbow into his belly, probably surprising him more than it actually hurt. The man pushed him against the table, slammed his head down between a dirty bowl and a hunk of stale bread. Victor let out a high-pitched scream and started sobbing, his jaws clenched tight, his face lined with pain and rage. The man almost lay on top of him, pressing his lips against Victor's ear, still forcing the boy's head down on the filthy tablecloth.

"Readies, is it? The old bastard stashes his cash here and you little shits came here to rip him off? Where is it, then, where's the money?"

"No, no," Victor gasped, "it's not money."

Outside the dogs began to whine, the gate squealed and there was the sound of a car rolling across the gravel, its engine turned off, probably being pushed by the old man. Victor tensed, he felt sweat stream down his back as though someone had poured a bottle of water between his shoulder blades. Éric stood up and pressed an ear to the door leading in to the hall. He took out his knife, placed his thumb on the catch and waited.

The dogs fell silent. There was a sound of metal, the noise of things being moved around in the shed. The man was grumbling, muttering to himself, or maybe talking to the dogs. The front door was opened slowly, then the old man seemed to stand for a moment on the threshold as though listening for something suspicious. Éric was breathing through his mouth, his lips formed an O, his eyes stared at Victor without seeing him, or tried to drill through doors and walls so he could know exactly what the old man was doing as he wandered into this house that had suddenly become a trap, sensing the danger and muttering to himself to allay his fears. The living-room door opened and there was total silence as the old man surveyed the wreckage, paralysed with shock or choking with rage while Éric, knife in hand, looking less vicious now, less arrogant, stared at the door behind which the old man still stood, reeling from the shock. He kept giving Victor quick sidelong glances and the boy realised he no longer knew what to do and thought perhaps he might make the most of the anxious hesitation he could see in Éric's eyes to try and make his escape. He was trying to summon strength to his trembling legs when suddenly he felt a draught on his face as the living-room door was wrenched open and the old man bounded into the kitchen with a furious roar, waving his rifle, firing wildly at Éric and missing, cocking the rifle again, cursing and swearing as his target rushed at him, one hand grabbing the barrel to deflect it or yank it from him, while with the other he slashed the old man's face and throat with the flick knife.

Victor had backed away against the fridge and if he could he would have slipped between it and the wall because by now the old man was covered in blood and bellowing, still clinging to his rifle, occasionally finding enough breath to swear at his assailant. Another shot rang out and hit the tiled floor a metre from where Victor was crouched. The bullet must have ricocheted because one of the windows exploded with a crash that made him cower in panic. It was then that he realised that the door was still open and he turned, preparing to make a run for it, and when he saw the two men rear up, both clutching the rifle, and whirl around the room like two drunken dancers, he dodged past the table, shuddering as his hand grazed the drawer in which the snake was lurking, then ran and ran, knocking into furniture, bumping into doorframes, slipping on the filthy linoleum in the hall before finding a foothold on the gravel outside while the howling dogs dashed through the door he left wide open.

Back on the road, looking around for his bicycle, he realised he was deaf. He stood stock-still but could hear nothing but a dizzying buzz underscored by the frantic pounding in his veins. He shook his head, stuck his fingers in his deafened ears, but it made no difference. This scared him a little and he turned back towards the house, expecting that at any moment it would explode or go up in flames, then spotted the E.D.F. substation, ran over to it and got on his bike. The breeze on his face brought him round and he concentrated on the effort he had to make to pedal, he felt sweat stream down him, felt sensation return to his body, something more than the trembling and the cold that had gripped him in the kitchen where the two men were fighting. Gradually his eardrums also recovered and the muffled buzzing was replaced by a permanent whistling which seemed to come from the depths of his brain. As he passed the water tower, he saw the village at the bottom of the hill and this reassured him as, almost happily, he allowed the bike to freewheel down.

When he got back, Nicole, just back from doing the weekly shopping in Pauillac, asked him to help unload the car. She did not notice anything was wrong, and he could breathe easy again. He felt as though he had been reborn, as though everything around him was returning to its proper size and place, to a stillness that did him good. He carried the drums of mineral water and the heaviest bags, and was careful to bolt the doors behind him. When he had finished, Nicole slipped an arm around his neck and hugged him to her chest, kissed the back of his damp neck. He let himself be hugged, smelling the perfume that seemed to come from her breasts and he thought about Rebecca and his groin ached with a terrible desire for her.

Feeling suddenly exhausted, he wandered aimlessly into the living room, where the television was chatting to itself, and as he passed the sofa he saw, leaning against the high back among the cushions, the small, skinny figure of a sleeping Julien, his mouth hanging open, his face slick, his hair plastered to his forehead with sweat. He wanted to wake him, to make sure he had said nothing about what had happened at old Georges' place and his heart beat faster at the thought that by now the old man was probably dead, slaughtered by Éric. In the end he gave up, not knowing what to do; Rebecca would be happy when she found out that piece of scum was dead. Reassured by that thought, he went upstairs leaving the scrawny kid sleeping.

In his room, he quickly fell asleep in the darkness that was almost cool.

He was woken with a start by raised voices which had merged with a sad dream in which his mother did not recognise him. He wiped away the tears from his nightmare, touching only his dry cheeks, then went to the door to listen.

Denis was there, Victor could hear him talking loudly, probably into the phone. Nicole was also saying something unintelligible. Victor held his breath for what seemed like forever when he heard that old Georges' had gone up in flames, that it had been almost completely razed by the time the fire brigade arrived. Slowly, he went down the stairs and immediately he saw Julien, still on the sofa, staring at him wild-eyed, a panicked look on his face.

16

He and Pradeau had decided to go and forget their troubles "somewhere pumping with sound and fury" and they found such a place; from the moment they stepped inside they had been bludgeoned by the deafening howl of feral rock music and overwhelmed by the oppressive heat and the swirl of smoke.

Right now, Pradeau was talking to him, but he could not make out what he was saying, catching only a word or a syllable here and there and attempting to string them into something that made sense, but more often than not the crushing wall of sound which kept them pressed against the bar almost as effectively as the people crowded around them reduced all human language to gibberish, so Vilar simply nodded and smiled, or adopted a serious look, trying to coordinate himself with the alternately satisfied, excited or distraught expressions flickering across the face hovering above a pint of Guinness less than fifty centimetres away. From time to time an arm would be thrust between them only to immediately withdraw clutching the handle of a tankard, and they would have to step back or duck their heads to make way for the countless beers of varying hues being swilled by the gallon all round. The place was pounding to a fusion of rock and heavy metal with shrieking guitars and a thumping bass that hit you in the solar plexus like a dozen Lilliputian boxers let loose among the clientele. Vilar thought he recognised a Gary Moore song he used to listen to long ago, the high-pitched harmonies sounding horrible at this volume.

Vilar blinked, trying to keep his eyes open in the thick, acrid pall of smoke that clung to his sweaty face and even seemed to compact the glare of the spots into tangible slabs of light through which hazy shadows moved. From the moment they arrived, his mouth had been filled with a coppery taste which he did his best to wash away with long swigs of beer, only to immediately light another cigarette since there was nothing else to do, because he had long since lost any desire to do anything at all tonight.

Pradeau began by talking about his ex-wife, how he still did not understand why she had left, yet still he felt vaguely guilty – miserable, wretched – and Vilar could hear the mournful intonations in his voice as it grew hoarse from drinking, smoking and having to shout in order to be heard. Then he talked about his sick mother, whose memory was completely gone, his distraught father trying to take care of her, stooped, shrunken in his grief, constantly by her side, a shadow of the shadow she had become. He looked up and Vilar saw the heartbroken look of a little boy, then he smiled bravely as he lit his umpteenth cigarette. He and his brother sometimes met up at their parents' house, but found they had nothing to say to each other.

Once or twice he had talked bitterly and regretfully about the brother with whom he had cut all ties.

Pradeau trailed off and sipped his beer. He shook his head.

"He'd be better off dead."

"It can't be that bad, can it? He's your brother . . ."

"Oh, not really . . . If only you knew. A toast," he said raising his tankard, "to traitorous brothers and true friends!"

They clinked glasses, forcing themselves to smile, but their pinched faces, their eyes red from the smoke, suggested only weary melancholy.

When the music stopped, suddenly, brutally, Vilar felt relieved, as though some guy who had been sitting on his chest for the past hour had finally got up. Even Pradeau was quiet, his momentum lost, plunging his nose into his beer. It seemed that the sea of faces was thinning out, bodies straightened up and remnants of the crowd stood, revelling in this precious moment. At the far end of the room, he saw a group of musicians setting up on a small stage. There were five of them: guitar, bass, lead singer with bodhrán, violin and drums, flanked by an impressive battery of speakers from which one could but fear the worst. Vilar emptied his glass, felt a cool breeze on his face: someone had opened the door onto the street. It was at that moment he realised he was drunk, because the cool air rekindled the embers smouldering inside his head. Then someone tapped his hand and he looked at his fist curled around the handle of the tankard and up into the eyes of the waitress who wanted to take the glass; she smiled at him and asked if he wanted another. He nodded and, leaning towards her, felt a smile stretch his face, which probably looked like a crumpled sheet of paper suddenly smoothed out to reveal a message you did not want to read a moment earlier, because this girl was beautiful, luminous in this murky light, in this fetid atmosphere, singular amid this sweaty crowd. He was surprised not to have noticed her earlier, probably because since he had come into the bar, he had moved in a bubble, the sort of diving suit or survival suit into which he often withdrew to try to keep on breathing.

It was precisely the sort of beauty that, once seen, makes every other human presence disappear. Some guy ordered something and Vilar felt a fleeting pang of hatred for this intruder, hated the way she leaned forward, almost touching the man, so that she could hear what he was saying as though oblivious to the fact the music had stopped and it was possible now to be heard without having to scream. The girl shared some joke with the stranger and they both burst out laughing, then she went back to the beer pump. She must have felt Vilar's eyes on her shoulders, bare in her sleeveless black T-shirt, because she turned and shouted, "Be right with you!", shaking her dark hair. She had a slim figure and to Vilar it seemed that behind the bar strewn with barrels, the boxes and the crates, she moved with the grace and suppleness of a dancer.

"Camille," Pradeau suddenly whispered into his ear.

He looked at him for a moment, puzzled.

"Her name's Camille. And her boyfriend's the guitarist."

Vilar shrugged. The girl came back to them, wiping her forehead with the back of her hand. She addressed him, asking what they wanted in a hoarse, cracked tone that made him think of scratches made by a cat.

"Same again," he said, nodding at the glasses.

He racked his brain for something halfway intelligent to say to her, but all he could find in his addled brain were tedious platitudes. She turned away and walked off. Pradeau too stared after those shoulders, that back, that waist.

"Just looking at her I feel better," he said with a sigh.

Victor was about to say he felt the same thing when a guitar chord exploded from an amplifier. Both men simultaneously shrugged and smiled. The drummer started warming up.

"Let's finish this one and get out of here," Pradeau shouted. "Too bad about the beautiful Camille, I'm sure she'll survive without us. It feels like he's drumming right into my brain."

The waitress came back with their beers and set them down. Vilar quickly whipped out a twenty-euro note but she was already at the far end of the bar. As the band started playing, Vilar felt the phone in his pocket vibrate. He put a finger in one ear, yelled into the mouthpiece for the caller to speak up, shook his head. Pradeau realised something was happening and leaned forward, staring at him worriedly.

He did not understand the first words, but he recognised the voice as that of Daras.

"Sandra de Melo, in Pessac."

"What do you mean, Sandra de Melo? What about her?"

Even as he asked the question, he knew the answer. The connection was bad, Daras spoke haltingly as though she were walking briskly.

"A massacre. Some kid had his throat cut. The neighbours called the police . . . Around 9.00 p.m."

Vilar felt his heart stop. He sucked in a lungful of air.

"What do you mean, massacre? Who?"

"Shift your arse. We'll meet up there. I'll call the *procureur*."

"I'll be right there," he yelled twice, so loudly that people turned and looked at him in astonishment. He caught the stricken gaze of the waitress, whose beauty now seemed like a lantern disappearing into the darkness. He swallowed a long draught of beer, not taking his eyes off her until, with Pradeau stumbling after him, he elbowed his way through the crowd, this bunch of morons, determined to smash the face of the first person to hassle him. As soon as they were outside, he tried to run, but his stomach lurched, he felt completely breathless, panting as he told Pradeau what little he had learned and why they had to hurry.

They walked in silence back to the car, Pradeau's, which was parked by the gardens outside the town hall. Both stopped and leaned on the bonnet to catch their breath, shaking themselves in an attempt to shed their inebriation, coughing up the cigarettes they had chain-smoked, sweating in the summer night filled with the bustle of pedestrians making the most of the illusory cool of evening, whereas to them the warm air felt muggy, heavy and squalid, and waiting at the end of their journey was another corpse. More blood.

It was Vilar who drove, since he felt a little less drunk than Pradeau, and he barrelled down the empty city boulevards and through the deserted suburban streets, windows rolled down, running every red light with every ounce of concentration he had left. Both men sat rigid in their seats, eyes wide and staring, neither of them spoke. It was difficult to tell whether they were drunk or aggressive, since the alcohol set their expressions in a scowl and exhaustion made them blink more even than did the hot air reeking of tar and motor oil that whipped at their faces.

They were stopped a hundred metres from the tower block by three officers in riot gear who had set up a roadblock with their van and glanced up from time to time at the windows, most of which were lit up. A little further on, there was a patrol car parked beneath the trees with four men in plain clothes armed with tear gas.

"O.K., go ahead," the officer said, after checking Pradeau's warrant card. "That your own car? Well watch out, we had beer cans lobbed at us earlier tonight."

Vilar drove on and parked behind a fire brigade ambulance. There were police everywhere, he could see about thirty posted around the tower block, patrolling the green areas or climbing back into their patrol cars and driving off slowly.

As he got out of the car, Vilar heard yelling, a commotion that echoed harshly off the buildings. At the far end of this stretch of road that ran alongside the building a group of about fifteen figures was being kept at a respectful distance by uniformed security guards. Daras' voice from behind made him start. She was accompanied by Annelise Leroux, the deputy *procureur*, who watched dazed as the two officers approached.

"Sorry . . . I'll never quite get used to this."

Daras was watching the small groups of busybodies chatting at the foot of the building.

"I see the French underclasses have crawled out of their holes . . . Nice around here, isn't it?" she said with a sweeping gesture of her hand. "And then we wonder why they kick off . . . I had to talk down the C.R.S. captain from mounting a baton charge. Fancied kettling some chavs . . . I mean, Jesus, twenty cretins screaming 'police scum' and throwing empty coke cans. If they'd had gone in, we'd have cars burning and truncheons flailing all over the crime scene by now. What a tosser! He brought the C.R.S. to 'secure the scene' as they say. O.K., come on, we need to get a move on. There's someone waiting for us. *Madame procureur*, I'll call you tomorrow morning, O.K.?"

The young woman nodded, tight-lipped, and took her leave without a word.

"Poor girl's got a weak stomach. But I've got a lot of time for her, she's straight up," Daras said as she watched the deputy *procureur* walk back to her car. "Shall we go take a look? *L'Identité judiciaire* got here about five minutes ago."

She walked towards the entrance of the tower block being guarded by two officers.

"So what's the deal?" Vilar said.

"Some kid from the estate. Sofiane Khalef. Stab wound to the throat. I called you in when I realised it happened in the block your witness lives in."

"And where's she?"

Vilar climbed the four steps leading to the lobby.

"No-one knows," Daras said as she stepped over the threshold.

"Before we set off, I asked for an officer to be sent around to her apartment, but the place was empty. The door wasn't locked."

The police in the lobby were doing very little, as were the various witnesses, who seemed to be setting up some sort of shrine. As they turned to look at him, Vilar felt the hostility they reserved for all intruders.

A body lay beneath a blanket at the foot of the stairs, a pool of blood spreading next to the head. There were also long blood spatters on the wall above the body. Vilar lifted the blanket and shuddered: it was one of the three little thugs who had tried to wind him up the day he came to interview Sandra de Melo.

"Was he with his mates?"

"What mates?" Daras said, astonished. "You know this kid?"

"They were hanging around the first time I came here. They did their best to piss me off. Might be worth checking if these brave gentlemen were present when it happened and took off after the kid got shanked to avoid any grief."

Daras jotted this in her notebook.

"We haven't got the manpower. Door-to-door will have to wait for tomorrow, but I'll put a call in to Ferrand anyway . . ."

Vilar did not let her finish. He stepped around the body and took the stairs three at a time until, reaching the first landing, he felt sweat course down his back, his legs buckle and his head spin. He tried to catch his breath, grabbed the banister and hauled himself to his feet, panting, then spat bile onto the ground and carried on up.

When he got to Sandra de Melo's door on the third floor, he hesitated for a moment, listening to the sounds coming from the neighbouring apartments, then stepped inside.

He flicked the light switch with a fingernail and peered about the hallway. The kitchen was directly opposite him, then the living room and two bedrooms. He took the kitchen first, it was spotless, glowing in the warm light of the red and yellow lampshade, everything meticulously tidy. Nothing was left within reach of little José, nothing with which he could hurt himself or someone else. Then, under the table, between the metal chair legs, he saw the clown. Seen upside down, the painted smile on the little cloth head looked like a rictus.

"Toto the clown."

He ran into the kid's room. It was not the usual jumble of toys, stuffed animals and Action Men. Here too, nothing that could be swallowed or thrown had been left within reach. Vilar thought about Pablo's den, the almost primeval cave teeming with bug-eyed creatures and stuffed animals over whom he ruled as the gaudy, plastic lord of the jungle. Here, everything was spartan; in one corner sat a large, bored teddy bear, with a stuffed snake wound around it. Vilar sighed, attempting to concentrate, because the urge to lie down anywhere and fall asleep all but cut the legs from under him.

As he expected, the bed was unmade. One of the dresser drawers was open, someone had hurriedly taken some clothes. Sandra de Melo had run away. She had made the decision in a matter of minutes. She had forgotten the clown, and the boy, half asleep, had not noticed. When he woke up later, or tomorrow morning, little José would throw a tantrum and perhaps the only way of calming him would be to sneak back to collect the toy. Someone would have to wait here to see if she came back for it.

The woman had to have been pretty scared to forget this particular object, the rag doll her son kissed instead of her. This extension he had dreamed up, this image of her in which she wanted to believe. A grotesque effigy. Whoever had thrown Sandra into a panic had had his way barred by the little thug hanging out in the lobby – this time without his friends – and had despatched that little problem without a qualm: a single stab wound to the throat. But what about the screams? What about the tenants hanging out of their windows, or the ones out making the most of the cool evening? It was hardly discreet.

He had killed Nadia, he had come here – for what? To kill Sandra too? To intimidate her? To keep her quiet, obviously.

Vilar went into Sandra's room. White walls bare but for a large framed photograph of a street in the Alfama district in Lisbon. On a dresser like the one in the kid's room there were two photographs: Sandra sitting on the beach, holding José's hand, José holding Toto the clown by its floppy arm. The kid stares into the lens, though clearly unaware of it. He is listing, as though weighed down by the doll. It looks as though were his mother to let go he would drop like a stone without using his hands to break his fall.

Vilar leaned down to get a better look at this elusive stare. The other photograph showed Sandra arm in arm with another woman, someone perhaps a little older who looked a lot like her. Two pretty brunettes. Her sister. The picture had been taken on the streets of some nearby seaside resort. Soulac, Lacanau. Behind, beside and all around them were people in beachwear. Stands selling rubber rings, beach balls, sunhats, beach towels. The colours garish. The sky an unreal blue. Vilar took the photograph out of the frame and turned it over: PAOLA AND SANDRA, LACANAU, AUGUST 2005. FOR MY LITTLE SISTER.

He opened a drawer, lifted up the pile of T-shirts and blouses, but found nothing underneath; he opened the second drawer, full of underwear, which he rummaged through gently with his fingertips.

"What the hell are you doing?"

Daras was standing in the doorway of the room; reflected in the picture frame he could also see the ashen face of Pradeau.

He extracted his fingers from the lace and pushed back the drawer.

"She's at her sister's place. We have to find her. The guy who killed Nadia came here tonight. He's the one who killed the kid downstairs."

Daras walked over to him. Pradeau leaned against the doorframe slowly massaging his temples.

"And you were expecting to find him among her bras and knickers?" she said mockingly. "We're good now? You got a good sniff? You're sobering up?"

He ignored the sarcasm and stared down at the lingerie.

"She left in a serious hurry. She even forgot to take her autistic son's clown. I don't know what happened, whether she actually saw the guy, whether she pushed him or what . . . But we need to get her sister's address and get round there fast . . ."

"We'll talk about it downstairs. We've got three witnesses who say they saw something."

216

Daras turned to Pradeau.

"Laurent, you deal with this place, see if you can turn up anything that could help us track her down. Addresses, telephone numbers, whatever. We'll go down and talk to the witnesses, you never know."

The witnesses, who had been left standing in front of the letter-boxes, had mostly heard noises. They thought it was a fight or some kids making a ruckus; it happened a lot. They had looked out of the window but had seen nothing.

All three were men, one of whom had visibly had an alcoholic Friday night bender, explaining that his wife was already in bed asleep because of the pills she took for her panic attacks. He probably drank every other day of the week, mornings too. It was impossible to guess his age, his drunken face was slick with sweat, his puffy red eyes glistened with tears, but he tried to shrug it all off with a sad smile, hunched over his cigarette, tottering on his feet. From time to time as he talked his horrified eyes flicked towards the corpse on the far side of the lobby, where the forensic boys from *l'Identité judiciaire* were now at work.

Another witness, tall and broad-shouldered with close-cropped hair, biceps bulging under a black sleeveless T-shirt, seemed pleased to be helping the police with their inquiries. He spoke in an affected, ponderous tone, clearly attempting to lend gravitas to his words, but came off sounding like a character from a badly written T.V. show. Vilar and Daras quickly sent him packing and when he gravely asked whether he should remain available for further questioning, Vilar patted him on the shoulder and thanked him for the valuable assistance he had given in tracking down a dangerous criminal. They would not hesitate to call on him if necessary. The man announced that he was merely doing his duty as an upstanding citizen and that if everyone did likewise, everything would be fine, then headed for the lifts, which had just been made operational again.

"I saw something," the last witness said. He took a step towards Vilar and said his name was Éric Gauthier and that he lived on the fifth floor. "I saw a guy doing a runner. I told the other officer earlier. He went that way."

He pointed towards the end of the street and the whole town beyond.

"Did you see what he looked like?"

"Dark hair, not very tall. He was wearing a denim jacket."

"His hair was long or short?"

"Short."

"Did you get a look at his face?"

"It was dark, all I could tell was he was young. I mean he wasn't *young* young. Thirty, thirty-five maybe."

"No car?"

"Like I said, he left here on foot. After that, I didn't see. Was he the killer?"

Vilar's mobile made a sound like a foghorn. It was Pradeau. He turned away from his witness and took a few steps.

"We've got about a dozen addresses where she might have gone."

"Do what you need to do, sort it with Daras. We have to get there before he does. I'm sure he's looking for her right now. He might even have been in the apartment, I mean she didn't close the door when she left, remember? He might have the same addresses we've got."

"Fucking hell," Pradeau said, and rang off.

Vilar went back to the witness, who had not moved and was waiting for him, smoking a cigarette. The smell of the smoke made him feel sick, and he felt his stomach heave slowly into his throat.

"What were you doing at the window?"

"Nothing. Just looking out. Getting some fresh air."

"Did you know Sandra de Melo?"

"What did you say the name was?"

"Sandra de Melo. She lives on the third floor."

"Neighbours, well, you know . . . I've not been living here long. What's she look like? I must have run into her in the lift."

"Short, brown hair, with a little boy."

"Oh right, yeah, I know her. Really sweet, the kid. José I think his name is. Really polite, always smiling, he says hello to everyone."

Vilar tried to conceal his surprise: the kid was not the sort to say hello to anyone, but this man, Éric Gauthier, clearly knew José by name. He was about to question him a little further about this when he heard shouts outside, the sound of people running, charging into the lobby. As the harried officers tried to restrain her, a woman rushed over to the body and howled, then fell on her knees, pulled off her hijab and used it to gently wipe the face of the dead boy. She lay down next to him, stroking him and covering him in kisses, letting out a long wail broken by sobs. Two young girls tried to lift her up, but she clung to the shoulders of her son. Her lamentations mingled Arabic and French and the girls seemed at a loss as to which language to speak in to make her see sense.

"Don't touch me! Let me go!"

A man appeared, struggling with the security guards who tried to hold him back. Daras stepped forward and told them to let him through, then took him gently by the arm. He stood, frozen, before the body of his son, now covered by that of his wife who went on wailing while the two sisters hugged each other and sobbed. The forensics team responsible for collecting samples had retreated into a corner, gloved hands limply by their sides, petrified, as though shocked that anyone might grieve for a corpse. Vilar stepped forward to where Daras was standing next to the father and laid a hand on her shoulder.

"Come on. Leave them."

"This is a complete cock-up. Let's get out of here, there's nothing useful we can do now. I'll tell them to move the body."

The lobby was now full of police and bystanders, all united in a solemn silence broken only by sobs and the whispered voices of the daughters begging their mother to get up.

Vilar turned as he felt someone touch his shoulder and was rewarded with a cloud of alcoholic breath from the first poor bastard he had interviewed. Nose to nose with this angular, unshaven face weathered by drink and tired of living.

"What is it? What do you want?"

The man's lips quivered, his wild eyes rolled, still glistening with tears.

"That guy. The one you were talking to a minute ago."

Pradeau appeared on the stairs and stood, staring at the scene of mourning. He was very pale. He shot Vilar a weary smile.

"Yes, what about him?"

"He's never lived here. I've never seen him before. I heard what he said to you, but he doesn't live up on the fifth or down in the cellar. I don't know him and I know everyone around here, me and the wife have been living here nearly thirty years."

Vilar looked around half-heartedly to see whether the man was still among the small group of people bustling around the door.

"Did you see where he went?"

"Outside. About three minutes ago. That's why I came to say something. I think it was him . . ."

Vilar laid a hand on the man's shoulder. He tried to smile at him to express his gratitude.

"Thank you . . . Thank you."

Pradeau came over.

"Look after this gentleman. We'll need to take a statement. The guy talked to me, pretended to be a witness, he's outside there somewhere on the estate . . ."

"What? What are you talking about?"

"The guy who did it, for fuck's sake. The guy who cut the kid's throat, the guy who's after Sandra de Melo. He was right here not five minutes ago, he wormed his way into the group of witnesses, he's still toying with us, the bastard."

Vilar was already heading for the door. A uniformed officer asked if he needed a hand, but he did not reply.

"Where the fuck is he going?" he heard Pradeau calling after him.

Outside, there was no-one. All the night owls were inside, gathered around the body of a boy with his throat cut. Vilar could not see any of the riot police who had been milling around when he and Pradeau arrived. He turned right and quickly crossed the road, running past the cars parked along the tree-lined central reservation. Acacias. He shivered at a gust of warm air. Through the foliage, Vilar could see the tower block opposite, the few windows still lit up at this hour of the night. Snatches of music, of muffled bass reached him. He came to a crossroads: directly ahead on the right were tower blocks like the one he had just passed. To the left, a few shops grouped around a car park with about twenty cars.

Turning his head, Vilar saw a figure standing on the pavement, diagonally opposite, watching him perhaps. Suddenly he felt out of breath. He could not make out the face, but he was convinced he recognised the false witness. And when he saw him take off, running around the building, he ran out into the road without knowing whether his body could hold out more than five metres. As he crossed the road, a car sped past behind him, but he barely heard it. He slowed to a walk in order to ease the pounding of his heart and the terrible racket in his brain, the blurry mélange of alcohol and fatigue. He struggled to try and hear anything beyond the buzzing that engulfed him, and after a moment found himself in a sort of park planted with groves of trees whose dark shapes he could barely make out in the gloom. A few street lights were still working, but the faint bluish glow served only to stir the shadows that gathered around him, urged on by the wind that whirled around the tower blocks.

He stopped, hearing a slight rustle to his right. He peered into the darkness, saw the page of a newspaper slithering past a bench like one of those languid predators you see grazing the seabed in search of sustenance. He realised that he was standing at the foot of a pylon strung with a mesh of wires that reminded him of the complex rigging of a pirate ship in a movie. Again, he peered, tried to make something out in the darkness; he saw a roundabout, a see-saw, wooden horses set on huge springs. He listened for sounds above the cacophony of his exhausted body and found it ridiculous to find himself here, standing by a playground in the dark, searching for a suspect who had drawn him here precisely in order to toy with him, a suspect he would not find tonight. He decided to turn back, to go back to the others, he no longer felt the need to lie down, to rest his weary head on something soft and let sleep come.

The blow to the back of his neck sent him reeling and he crumpled to his knees, then down onto all fours, trying to work out what was happening. There was no pain. He felt as though he were floating, dazzled, deaf; he could no longer feel the heft of his body and for a moment he thought his head had been severed and in sheer terror threw himself to the ground, lying on his belly. Scarcely conscious, convinced that he was dying, he felt a knee against his back and someone slammed his head into the ground. Stones and gravel embedded themselves in his forehead and pain now awakened all his senses and brought him jolting back to a reality flooded with panic. He opened his mouth to scream, and felt a ball of paper being forced into his mouth; the smell of ink and the feel of the paper against his palate made his stomach turn. He felt bile rise in this throat. For several seconds he struggled and groaned, unable to breathe, his face ripped and torn by gravel.

"You looking for me? Calm down, you dumb shit, breathe through your nose! I don't want you dying on me just yet. Besides, we ain't got time because your buddies will be here soon."

The man whispered the words into his ear. Vilar could feel his warmth, could almost feel the damp of his breath. Something sharp jabbed him between the shoulder blades, then sank a few millimetres into his flesh. Blood ran down his spine into the hollow of his back. He moaned, trying hard to swallow.

"I'm glad I caught you. You see, I know everything about you . . . I've been following you, I come and go at your place and make myself right at home, sometimes I'll be standing there right next to you and you don't even know it. When they said I'd get a taste for it, I didn't believe them, but they were right. I'm like your shadow, but a shadow capable of getting there before you because I can anticipate what you're going to do. Now isn't that amazing?"

The knife twisted in the wound. Vilar felt blood run into his shirt. He realised he was trembling.

"Nothing to say? Not as cocky as when you're down the station with your buddies, are you? Doesn't matter . . . See, I decided to make you suffer, we've got a score to settle, you and me, and you're going to pay dear. Providence – divine providence – put you in my path, and that's too bad for you. Hey, you listening to me? Now . . . I don't want to kill you. That's not my style. So listen carefully: right here under my knife is your backbone. And I suspect that one sharp jab between the vertebrae and I'll hit your spinal cord, and you know what happens then, don't you? Given the blade's position, you'd be happy just to be able to breathe by yourself. But I guess you'd probably be able to work the buttons on an electric wheelchair. Nothing to say? Cat got your tongue? Ah, I get it, you don't find me funny? If you like I'll come and push your little mobility vehicle and call you a cunt. You'll have your whole life to wonder every morning whether you've got the courage to live or whether you should top yourself. That's a pretty serious question, isn't it? I had a lot of time to think about it when I was banged up."

The blade stopped twisting. The man shifted his position, now he was sitting astride Vilar, who was just about managing to breathe in spite of the paper choking him.

"Don't move! Drop the knife and put your hands in the air!"

Pradeau's voice, close by.

"Like I give a fuck, I'm going to end this bastard."

The pressure on the blade increased. Vilar groaned. The pain spread through his thorax. This psychopath was going to cut him in two. Was actually going to sever one part of his body from the other. Was going to half kill him precisely so that he would be alive to witness the state he was in, to endure this amputation of self, the living corpse he would become. Suddenly, he was dazzled by the beam of a torch. He heaved his hips, trying to unseat the guy straddling him, and just then he heard the gunshot, felt a fearful judder as the bullet entered the man's body even as he pressed himself against the ground, almost ready to dig himself to safety with his nails, his teeth. Deafened, dazed, unable to move, he heard nothing else. That was when he knew he was truly sinking, a scream and his last breath stuck in his throat.

17

Victor gripped Julien's throat, his fingers locked either side of the boy's larynx, aware of the hard, dry feel of his scrawny neck, this living bundle of bones and tendons that quivered every time the kid tried to swallow. The boy's eyes rolled wildly, pleadingly, and his head, nodding frantically to let Victor know he agreed with every word, banged against the side of the bath into which the two of them had fallen after they grabbed each other around the neck and started tussling.

"You just keep your trap shut, you little shit. This is nobody's business but mine, so you don't say anything, you don't know anything, otherwise I'll drill a hole in your head, you got that, dickface? Did you hear what that guy said? He said he'd torch this place if we talked. D'you see what he did to the old man's place? So you know he's perfectly capable of doing it. And besides you were there with me so you're an accomplice. I'm not going to take the heat for this alone."

Julien blinked. He face was flushed red, he seemed unable to move.

Victor loosened his grip around the boy's throat and helped him to his feet. Julien sat motionless on the side of the bath, his head down. He was gasping, his mouth wide, his chest heaving violently.

"Oh, come on, you're O.K. Fuck's sake, I hardly touched you."

The kid shook his head as though he did not quite agree. Gradually his breathing subsided. Tears began to trickle down his cheeks, then a huge sob shook his body and he let out a high-pitched wail, almost a shriek, his mouth stretched into a horrible rictus.

"You hurt? I didn't ..."

Julien got to his feet and took a step towards the door.

"Shit. What's the matter with you?"

In two minutes, Nicole would come up to see what they were up to. "Don't cry, O.K.? Let's go outside."

Julien nodded and they crept soundlessly out of the bathroom, Victor putting a hand on the boy's shoulder to reassure him or to prevent another crying jag.

Once outside, they went and sat on the bench under the oak tree. Fretfully they watched a hornet circling above their heads in the leaves, then seeing it fly off, both boys heaved a sigh of relief.

Julien was still sobbing and sniffling. He stared straight ahead of him, his eyes vacant.

Victor asked him what he was blubbering about and the kid looked up at him with sad eyes.

"You do understand what I was trying to tell you?" Victor said. "We have to keep the secret, otherwise we're screwed. We'll be hauled up in front of the judge again and everyone will be pissed off. They'll send us off to another foster family and we'll be in the shit."

Julien said nothing, staring into space. The hornet was back, buzzing loudly, and Victor could not take his eyes off the insect's fat yellow body.

"You scared me," Julien said, "I thought . . ."

The hornet disappeared into the foliage.

"You thought what? You thought I was going to strangle you, is that it?"

He shook his head. He wiped away another tear and sighed heavily.

"Maman used to do that. Sometimes she'd get really mad with me and she'd squeeze my throat like you were doing. Then after she'd hug me and she'd be crying. But, really, she wanted to kill me. That's why I was taken into care."

Julien picked up a stone and threw it at a plastic chair which gave a hollow rattle as the pebble rolled around and then came to a halt. The boy stared at the chair, clearing his throat. Victor laid a hand on his bony shoulder. He struggled for something to say, but it was difficult because he was suddenly convinced that his mother was listening to them and he did not want to disappoint her.

"I was lucky," he said.

Julien leaned back against the bench. He sniffled, wiped his mouth and his nose on the sleeve of his T-shirt.

"When Maman was sad, she used to hug me and tell me she loved me. She said it was our secret."

Julien looked up at him, his eyes still glistening.

"You've got a lot of secrets, you."

"No, not really. Now you know them all."

"Just me?"

"Yeah. Just you. That's why . . ."

"I'd never give away a secret."

"I hope not."

The muffled roar of the vacuum cleaner broke the silence between them.

"When are they burying him, the old man?"

"Dunno. Tomorrow, maybe. They had to do an autopsy on him."

Julien pulled a face.

"You mean like in films when they cut dead bodies open? That happened to Papa. But the old guy died in the fire, didn't he?"

"He might have been dead before."

"On account of the snake?"

"Of course not. Because of the other guy, I told you already how they were fighting and everything."

"Jeez, this is serious."

"Yeah, it's serious. That's why we can't say anything. We're witnesses, you get it? We saw the guy. But being a witness just gets you in more shit. They'd ask us what the fuck we were doing up there."

The kid hunched his shoulders.

"Do you think it got burned up, the snake?"

Victor shrugged. "Yeah, sure, along with everything else."

"But Denis and Nicole said there was still furniture and stuff up there. The police go through everything in cases like this. With tweezers."

Victor looked at him. The boy was biting his nails and looking around with wide, astonished eyes and it was obvious he was lost in his own unfathomable thoughts. They sat in silence for a long moment amid the hum of insects bustling in the summer morning and the wind moving through the dense foliage. The sun was high already, it must have been about 10.00 a.m., and the light was searing, the warm breeze blew on them now and then tracing a line of sweat down their necks.

"We'll go up and see tonight," Victor said, "when it's not so hot."

Julien nodded gravely, pursing his lips, then slowly got to his feet.

"I need to pump up my bike tyres," he said decisively.

Victor looked up towards the leaves of the oak where the hornet had reappeared. It seemed even bigger now and its abdomen looked like a blister filled with venom. The boy fought the shudder running down his back and decided to stay where he was, under the circling poisonous insect, to master his fear as he had with the snakes, because his mother would have been proud of his bravery.

They grew bored and they lingered in the shade, seeking shelter from the scorching heat beneath trees or in the house, which was only slightly cooler. Then Julien suggested that they go down to the estuary because he had spotted the burrow of a river rat you could see only if you stood out on a pontoon. They got their bicycles and arched their backs against the sweltering sun.

After half an hour's ride they dismounted and scrabbled up a grassy bank from which, between the trees, they could see the still expanse of thick, muddy water flowing out to sea. It was low tide. The mud stank, and they walked carefully between the reeds on the hard crust of mud that dried in the heat of the day between tides. They easily got through the makeshift gate – a metal frame with a wooden door painted khaki – which Berlan, who owned the fisherman's hut, had installed to prevent people wandering onto the pontoon. They sat down and caught their breath for a moment in the shade of a tree that grew out over the water from the bank.

Julien showed Victor the burrow and whispered that they had to wait, to be patient, because the river rats did not come out much during the day.

"But they've got babies," he said. "The mother takes them out swimming with them on her back while they feed."

"They swim on their backs?"

"No . . . She carries them on her back. The females have their teats on their back, so they can feed their babies while they swim."

"Are you kidding? Teats on their backs? Where do you come up with this shit?"

"Denis told me. And anyway, I read about it in a book. River rats are also called muskrats. They come from America."

Victor nodded. Not taking his eyes off the burrow. He did not believe this story about them having teats on their back, but he did not want to argue with the kid. Julien took a catapult out of his backpack.

"Here."

Victor looked at the forked stick with the ribbon of thick black rubber but did not touch it.

"What about you? Have you not got one?"

"This is for you. I've got another one for me. I found this yesterday when I was rummaging around."

Victor grabbed the catapult and tried it out several times, drawing back the rubber as far as he could, then letting go. The wood was still rough and uneven, it had not been dirtied or worn smooth by any hand. It was brand new. The kid who had made it for him now watched him toy with the catapult, swinging his legs in the empty space below the jetty.

"Where's yours?" Victor said.

Julien rummaged in his bag and took out a second slingshot that was almost identical.

"I know how to make them. A friend taught me. You know Felanzino?"

Victor pulled a face.

"Ferreira. Marina's brother. He's the one who gave me the elastic. And he gave me ball bearings too, look."

He opened his hand and the steel balls glittered and clacked sharply as he rolled them around his palm.

"You can use these to hunt," he said. "You can kill animals. Even people."

Victor took a ball bearing. It was heavy and warm. He rolled it between his fingers, brought it up to his face to study it more closely.

"You ever tried?" he said.

"Yeah. With cats. But I don't kill them, it just hurts them. Jesus, you should hear them squeal, the little bastards!"

The kid was squirming, excited at recounting his heroic deeds, and the jetty rocked a little, shaking under his bony arse. Victor did not try to persuade him to stop shooting at cats. He did not want the kid's high rasping voice drilling into his ears. Julien must have realised this because he said no more and turned back to the burrow, catapult ready for action, a steel ball bearing in the pocket of the elastic.

They sat there in silence, but for the faint rustling of the tree above their heads, and from beneath, the sound of the river heading for the sea, lapping at the bank. Victor gazed at the dark, pungent silt encircling them and he felt he could almost taste mud at the back of his throat; he spat twice and coughed vainly, trying to get rid of the taste. He remembered his adventures on the Garonne near his house, and the vast Cité Lumineuse building he had watched being demolished as a child. He and a gang of other boys used to wander among the reeds below the embankment and every now and then rats would scuttle out of nowhere, their shrill squeaks terrifying the children who would try to hit them with sticks, or goad a dog into giving chase, and sometimes the rats would fight back, rearing up on their hind paws, baring their teeth and uttering piercing shrieks. The smell of silt was the same, that sickly stink of shit carried on the water, rising from the wastes of fetid mud that sucked at their shoes and threatened to trap and swallow up anyone who ventured into the sludge, before drying in the heat to a brownish-grey dust like the skin of a dead animal.

The river rats appeared after half an hour, first the one Julien called the mother, who sniffed the air, sat up on her hind paws, scraped her big yellow teeth with her claws and then trotted along the dry riverbank with two little black rats dashing after her and disappearing into her fur. The ball bearings disappeared into the mud, raising clouds of dust. Julien cursed his slingshot every time he missed, then the animals themselves when they disappeared back into their burrow and refused to come out again. The boys waited around for another half-hour, slingshot elastic taut, then, without exchanging a word, they got to their feet simultaneously. The tide was rising and the estuary seemed to swell with a low murmur of wind and a rush of water as though the ocean's dull roar reached even here.

"Let's go, yeah?" Victor said.

The kid nodded without looking at him, already terrified at the idea of going back to the house where the old man had died. They passed through the fisherman's gate and walked back between the reeds across the crusted rivulets of sun-baked mud.

"What about the police?" Julien said anxiously as he picked up his bike.

Victor shrugged and stood up on the pedals as he set off. They rode quietly through air so still, so warm, that their sweat did not dry. They got off their bicycles just before the last turn and cut around the back on a dirt track between the vines so as not to be seen.

Just about all that was left old Georges' house was a scorched wall, its empty windows gaping like huge eyes ringed by streaks of soot that looked like lashes. A police car was parked in the drive and the two boys, crouching on the far side of the road, saw a man wearing white overalls sifting through the rubble. They set off again, skirting around the vineyards to get to the other side of the house, where they might get a better view. They ran, bending low beneath two rows of vines already heavy with green grapes. Here, the wall had partly collapsed and the shed where the old man had stored his equipment was nothing but a black and tangled mass in the midst of which stood a bicycle frame. Nothing in the house had been spared and the two policemen nosing about inside had to stoop to duck under the charred, collapsed beams of the roof.

"That snake's gone for good," Victor said. "Look, there's no table there anymore."

Julien heaved a sigh.

"They said the old guy was completely black and shrivelled up," he said, "so a snake . . ."

"I told you we were never in any trouble."

"What are they looking for? Money?"

"I don't know. Fingerprints, maybe."

Julien almost cried out in fright. Victor reassured the kid, telling him he was only joking, that everything had been burnt to a crisp, that the police always did this, he had seen it on T.V.

They watched in silence as the forensics officers bustled about, raking through the blackened rubble, sometimes showing each other charred artefacts that the boys tried in vain to identify. Then Victor signalled it was time to leave, giving Julien a little tap on the back of the head to shake him – nose pressed to the chicken wire, crouching behind a mimosa – from his rapt contemplation of the painstaking comings and goings of the two men in white amid this expanse of blackness. Calmly they walked back to their bicycles, pausing here and there to pilfer a few warm, pink grapes that were already sweet. The sun had dropped and already a little shadow began to pool at their feet and in the deep furrows, but the heat was still sweltering, and they could feel the sunlight coming over the leaves of the vines and hitting their faces. They shivered as a cool breeze blowing in from the estuary caught their bare legs. On the road down to the village, they let out whoops of joy, letting go of their handlebars, sometimes freewheeling, sometimes pedalling like demons. As they approached the house they slowed down, let their breathing settle to normal. Denis was sitting on the kitchen step smoking a cigarette, still covered in plaster dust, his hair almost grey. He hardly acknowledged their greeting.

"We've been waiting for you so we can eat," he said as they passed. "What the fuck were you up to? Where have you been at this hour?"

"We were watching river rats," Victor said. "We didn't notice the time. Sorry . . ."

"Well, don't do it again. Round here we eat on time, understood? Just look at yourselves, you're filthy."

The man blew a long stream of smoke in the direction in which he was idly staring. They went into the silent house. The T.V. was turned off. Nicole was in the kitchen making a large pizza, and as they went to get a drink from the fridge, she asked them where they'd been. They told her about the river rats. Nicole said how much she loathed the little beasts.

"Honestly, have you nothing better to do with your time? Those filthy things are full of diseases. And look at you, you're all red and sweaty. Go on, go wash your hands at least. Have you seen the time? I was wondering what you were up to."

"Where's Marilou?"

"She's with Rebecca. Out the back. Go and tell them dinner's ready."

Victor felt his skin tingle. He went out onto the back terrace and saw her, sitting on a bench, her black hair hastily pinned up into a bun. Marilou was lying in the hammock chatting to her, but she trailed off when she saw Victor arrive. He said hello and took one of the white plastic chairs, his damp skin immediately sticking to it. The girls did not reply and they sat for a moment like this, not saying anything, Marilou almost dozing, her tanned legs crossed, Rebecca sitting cross-legged on the bench playing with her mobile, her back straight, almost stiff, her shorts hitched up over her thighs. A gust of wind darted between the branches above them and Victor hoped it meant there would be a storm tonight. He longed for a downpour, for thunder, for something violent that would shake everything from the torpor in which it was mired, a torpor into which he could feel himself sinking. Here, gazing at Rebecca's mute, headstrong beauty, he longed for a cataclysm that would sweep everything away, leaving behind it only desolation and sobbing and the despair of the survivors. He looked up at the drab sky, greyish-green perhaps, but leaden in the west as though something were brewing over the ocean.

Nicole called for them to come and eat and they got up without a word. Victor could feel Rebecca walking behind him, her breath almost ruffling his hair, so close that he had to resist the temptation to turn around suddenly so she would bump into him, and he let his hand dangle next to his thigh in the hope that she might brush against it.

They ate out on the terrace, talking quietly and laughing from time to time at the stupid things Julien came out with as he squirmed in his chair, blathering away, talking so fast that Victor worried he might betray them, and so gave him the blackest look he could muster.

It was cooler now, and from time to time the wind whipped up and they could sometimes smell salt or pine resin and sometimes the particular smell of damp pine needles, and Denis thought it was probably raining along the coast and that would put an end to the heatwave. Then Victor watched out for distant streaks of lightning or the rumble of thunder but nothing came and after a while his disappointment hardened into the familiar lump in his chest that had tormented him over the past three months. He caught Marilou's worried glances, she could always tell when he was sad, and now she turned her dark gentle eyes on him and he responded with a blink, because between them there was the unspoken bond that he had noticed the first time they met.

When dinner was over and Julien had taken his turn at clearing the table, they stayed out in the garden watching the last flashes of sun that managed to steal between two grey banks of cloud as night drew in. Rebecca was lying on the bench, knees raised, arms folded over her stomach. She was staring at the sky, a look of disgust on her face.

Victor and Marilou talked about storms. They hoped there would be a violent storm tonight.

"You coming?" Rebecca said suddenly to Victor.

She was already on her feet, hands on her hips, almost impatient.

As soon as they set off, she took and squeezed his hand, her fingers interlaced with his, and pressed it against her leg. They walked in silence away from the village, which disappeared as they rounded a corner. Victor found it difficult to breathe, feeling her warm skin against the back of his hand, his mouth was dry and tiny shivers ran through him like insects driven mad by the cool gusts of an evening breeze.

"He's dead, that old sack of shit," Rebecca said. "Can you believe it?"

Victor nodded. He wanted to tell her everything. "So now you've had your revenge," he said.

She turned towards him with a start. "Why do you say that?"

"No reason . . . just from the way you talk about him, I always thought you hated him . . ."

"I fucking despise him . . . And that's putting it mildly. I would have slit his throat myself if I could have."

She set off walking again, taking long strides. Victor could hear the soft swish of skin rubbing together with every step she took.

As soon as they came to a path between the vines, she pulled him in and started walking quickly, almost dragging him behind her. To the west, a dark purple mantle stretched across the sky. Victor glanced behind him.

When they reached the middle of the carefully tended field, its monotony broken only by branches coiling up in search of something to cling to, Rebecca flopped down onto a grassy bank and told Victor to sit too. He sat next to her, panting, his face red, feeling slightly feverish. She slid closer until their hips were touching and he felt her weight as she leaned towards him, instinctively hunching his shoulders when she put her arm around his back and pulled him towards her, letting her head fall against his neck, her lips seeking out his salty skin.

He had only to turn towards her. He closed his eyes and aimlessly thrust out one arm to encircle her waist, something he had seen in films. He felt her tongue flick between his lips and he did the same, something he had done before with girlfriends at school, though he knew this was something new, especially when she took his hand and slid it under her T-shirt and his palm found the curve of her breast.

She lay back and pulled him against her. He dared to slip his hand between her thighs and his throat tightened as his fingers fleetingly brushed the cleft mound through the sheer fabric. Rebecca squeezed her thighs shut, trapping the boy's fingers and moaned softly, then said, "No," her mouth pulling away from his.

Night had fallen without them noticing. They lay side by side beneath the now dark sky in the midst of which a storm rolled and thundered, shooting pale sheets of lightning over the river. Rebecca got to her feet, saying it was going to rain. Above him, in the vanishing light, Victor could make out her long legs and felt the urge to press his mouth where they met to taste what he had felt. She turned away and walked off without a word and he bounded after, afraid of losing her in the darkness.

They walked in single file across the uneven ground, twisting their ankles on dry clods of earth. Rebecca touched his hand, nothing more, as she turned to make for her home, and Victor stood, watching her disappear, head bowed, beneath the grubby light of the streetlamps. He set off again, his head still reeling. As he walked, he sniffed his fingers and brought them to his mouth.

In the two days that followed, he felt a little stunned, as though he were recovering from a fever. Sometimes he would see Marilou staring at him quizzically. She obviously suspected something. Sometimes he wondered if it had really happened and wanted to know whether it would happen again, whether it was possible for such pleasure, perhaps even happiness, to last forever.

That first night, he did not dare touch the urn or talk to his mother. The following day, in the dark, allowing the cool air filtering through the venetian blinds to lap over him, he wept. He begged forgiveness from this life that pushed him so hard, distanced him, attracted and compelled him. He felt so miserable that he could see no choice but to go away, become feral so he would no longer know anything, no longer say anything and subsist like an animal on instinct and silence. Far from everything.

Old Georges was buried two days later. Rebecca called around to the house while Mass was still being said for the filthy old pervert (as Denis called him at dinner one evening), but she gave Victor only the same distant look she had always had for him and barely spoke to him, just wandered down the garden, chatting and laughing with Marilou and humming silly songs.

18

As he came to, he realised scissors were cutting away the back of his shirt and was aware of the silent agitation that reigned around him. He was lying on his stomach and when he tried lift his head to see what was happening, a woman's voice told him not to move.

"How are you feeling? My name is Doctor Ferrière, I'm a paramedic."

He tried to answer, spat out soil and gravel. He felt a damp patch between his legs, at the top of his thighs. It was not blood.

"I think I'm O.K.," he managed to say. "I just want to go home. What did he do to me? Oh fuck, I've pissed myself."

He moved his legs, tried to lean up on his elbows.

"Please, don't try to move."

He was vaguely conscious of comings and goings in the convulsive light of the torches and the blue strobing from the police cars. A cacophony of voices, shouts and arguments was suddenly superimposed over the doctor's voice. He felt fingers pressing on his back around the wound the man had made. People were talking over his head and he could not understand what they were saying.

"It's superficial," the woman said. "It's nothing more than a scratch."

"Pierre? You O.K.? Jesus, you gave us a scare. Are you taking him to hospital?"

Daras was crouching next to him. She took his hand and was forcing herself to smile.

"Where's the guy?" he asked. "Did you get him?"

"He took off. We're looking for him everywhere, but I'm not exactly hopeful. Pradeau managed only to wound him."

She stood up quickly and Vilar felt himself being lifted and put on a stretcher.

He said that he could walk, thank you, but one of the men carrying the stretcher advised him not to move until they got him into the ambulance. Daras mumbled something into her police radio, an order maybe, Vilar could not make it out. He felt as if he were floating in a soporific haze.

"This guy . . ." he managed to say. "He can't have slipped through our fingers just like that. You said he took a bullet?"

"Yeah. But Pradeau was only shooting to wound, and the guy managed to run off. We were this fucking close to catching him."

The paramedic was blonde and rather young. She sat next to him and looked at him with a gentleness that softened the curt tone of her deep voice.

He realised he was trembling. He tried to take a deep, calm breath, to focus entirely on that breath. He could still feel the tip of the knife in his back.

"He tried to hit the spinal cord."

"Don't worry, he didn't get that far. He slashed you a little, the wound is about two, maximum three centimetres, nothing serious."

She was smiling. She seemed competent. She explained that she was going to give him an injection to calm him. He did not bother to answer, simply closed his eyes. He let her do her job, he felt the injection, felt himself being swabbed with a cold liquid, felt the sutures pinch his skin. He felt alert to the slightest sensation in his body and was surprised to discover he felt no pain.

The doctor asked him again if he was determined to go home and had him sign some sort of discharge form, apologising that this was something she was obliged to do.

He found himself in the back seat of his own car without knowing how he got there, looking out at his fellow officers talking on the pavement while the security guards climbed back into their vans and their patrol vehicles. He felt sleepy, stupefied, and remembered that the blonde woman from the S.A.M.U. had given him a sedative injection to stop his tremors. The alcohol he had drunk earlier was turning off his brain, like the lights in a village hall after a party, when eventually all that is visible is the glow of the green exit signs.

He woke up the next morning in his own bed with no idea who had put him there or how. As he rolled over, he barely felt a twinge from the wound. Sitting on the edge of the bed, he waited for the first shooting pains signalling a migraine, but nothing came, so he stood up and found himself steady on his feet with a craving for coffee and buttered baguette that made his mouth water. He felt none of the panic he had experienced the night before. He felt a trilling of residual adrenalin, nothing more.

He was tucking into bread and jam, waiting for the coffee to brew, when the doorbell rang. He started, the hand clutching a spoon froze in mid-air. From outside he heard Pradeau call out. When Vilar opened the door, Pradeau waved a bag of croissants under his nose.

"Jesus, you're looking good. Did that blonde from the S.A.M.U. stay behind and administer intensive care, or what?"

He flopped down in a chair and demanded coffee.

"You on the other hand don't look so hot," Vilar said. "You're the one in need of critical attention."

"Too much booze, too many fags, too much brooding. I didn't nod off until gone seven this morning. Still, plenty of time to sleep when I'm dead."

He sipped his coffee, lit up a cigarette. Vilar took one from his pack and went to open a window. They smoked in silence. Pradeau stared out of the window, lost in thought.

"We didn't even find the fucking bullet. I hit him in the neck, I'm pretty sure, but it was only a flesh wound. It can't have been a through-and-through or he'd be dead. Now I've got to fill out some fucking report explaining the incident. I'm going to have Internal Affairs crawling up my arse."

"There's a guy dead, isn't there?" Vilar said. "The only one taking any serious risks was me. They're not going to hassle us over this, are they? You get to save a colleague's life, the guy gets to do a runner, everyone's happy, no?"

Pradeau said nothing, staring at the ashtray into which he was stubbing out his cigarette. He stifled a yawn and poured himself more coffee.

"What is it?" Vilar said, "You really don't look good."

Pradeau sighed and gave him a beaten, helpless look.

"My father called at about five this morning, completely hysterical. I'd only just nodded off and the phone scared the shit out of me. My mother collapsed in the toilet and he couldn't manage to get her up. Wanted me to come around. Shit. I told him to call a neighbour and he started sobbing down the line that it was too early to go waking people . . . Can you believe it? It's not O.K. to wake the people next door, but it's fine for me to drive a hundred kilometres on fuck-all sleep just to help my mother stand up? Fuck's sake, what am I supposed to do? He refuses to put her in a nursing home, he doesn't want to be separated from her, but there are days when he wishes she would just die quickly so he could have a bit of peace because he can't take it anymore. And if that wasn't bad enough, these last six months she doesn't know him from Adam. The other day when she saw him in the kitchen she was terrified he was a burglar. She recognises his voice sometimes, so when he talks to her she calms down. It's like she's just found something familiar she thought she'd lost forever. I tell you, it fucking does my head in, all this shit."

In the silence that followed, a bird trilled, a fire engine siren honked in the distance.

"Why don't you take a week off, go sort things out with your father?"

Pradeau shrugged and shook his head. He smiled sadly.

"You've no idea what you're talking about. Just leave it."

Vilar stood up. There was nothing he could do for Pradeau. He wanted him to leave. There was nothing anyone could do for anyone. "I don't know what to say."

"Then please, don't say anything. Each to his own. You've got your shit, I've got mine, that doesn't make it *our* shit. I never know what to say to you either."

Vilar was desperate to find some way out of this blind alley they were in.

"Last night, the guy . . . did you see him? What did he look like?"

At first Pradeau stared at him dumbfounded, as though he didn't understand what he was saying. Then he nodded slowly.

"Tall, light brown hair, bright eyes, a prominent chin. I got a good look, I talked to him while he was crouching over you with the knife."

Nothing like the guy he had seen at Madame Huvenne's place, nothing like the witness he spoken to in the lobby of the tower block. A shudder ran down Vilar's spine. He felt as though the wound had suddenly developed a nasty itch.

"The guy I saw before had dark hair. There are two of them, I'm sure of it. Two at Morvan's place to make him disappear without a trace. There's the one I had on the line who talked to me about Pablo, and the one who killed Nadia. I don't know how, but they found each other and they're in this together."

"That just brings us back to Marianne's woolly theories. I don't buy it. There's one guy, he's clever, but he'll end up getting himself caught. End of story. At Morvan's house we found fibres, two hairs, nothing concrete. You and Marianne, you're too determined to make this two people. And if there were two of them, then why would they put themselves to so much trouble? Take so many risks? I think you're both kidding yourselves. It's all bullshit."

"Call it bullshit if you will, but it's unlikely that the same guy would be going around abducting a kid and terrorising whores."

"Unless he's a pimp . . . Someone trafficking women and kids. What do we know?"

Vilar leaned back against the sink and nodded.

"Obviously, we don't know anything. I personally don't think it holds up, but it's not so far-fetched. If you're right, though, I'll kill the guy myself when we track him down. I don't give a shit about anything else. I want to see him grovelling at my feet, I want to look him in the eye while he lies there bleeding. Shit, how could you have missed him? You were what? Three, four metres away?"

"I was trying to wound him. We need him alive. And anyway, it all happened so fast, you know what it's like . . . I saw him sticking a knife in your back and I did the best I could. I hit his shoulder, or maybe his neck, like I said. The bullet must just have grazed him."

Pradeau fell silent and looked thoughtful. Between his fingers, he held an unlit cigarette.

"You O.K.?" Vilar said. "You want to talk about something else?"

Pradeau shuddered, as though someone had jabbed him.

"And what exactly do you . . . No, it's fine. Carry on," he said wearily.

Vilar decided to ignore Pradeau's apathy.

"So who is this guy?"

"Which one?" Pradeau said, smiling crookedly.

"I don't know. The man from last night. Or the one I saw at the old biddy's place in Bacalan. Maybe they're the same guy."

"That's something we won't know till we've got him in front of us and we can beat seven bells out of him – and no bullets, because that won't answer any of your questions."

"Last night I screwed up," Vilar said, who seemed to be thinking aloud, staring vaguely at the impressionist landscape on the calendar hanging on the wall. "I should have twigged, when he said that the kid used to say hi to everyone in the building . . . He gave himself away, and I missed it. Instead of ducking the question, he raised the stakes. He's not afraid of anything. And what with everyone blubbing and screeching behind me and the kid bleeding out on the floor, I lost control. Shit, he was right there in front of me, I could smell the cigarette smoke on him. What is he looking for, the bastard?"

Pradeau's face contorted.

"Intense emotions. Maybe he wants to feel alive. Maybe it's a game to him?"

"If it is, it's Russian roulette, with all the chambers loaded."

"Could be there's something in that," Pradeau said, getting to his feet.

He pocketed the cigarettes and his lighter.

"I have to go. We have to question the dead kid's friends – what was his name again? Ah, yes, Sofiane – they're probably the same two little thugs you saw him with in the lobby that time. The neighbours gave us their names and addresses. You never know, maybe these two clowns were there when it happened and ran back home to Maman without saying a word. They act like big men when they're in a group, but when they're on their own or they're faced with a really vicious fucker, they shit themselves. We'll shake them up a bit, the cowards, teach them a bit of respect. At least we won't have made the trip for nothing."

He said goodbye, promising to call later, and left, closing the door quietly behind him.

It was almost 10.00 a.m. Vilar drank some more lukewarm coffee, cursed the fact he had no cigarettes. Then he turned on the T.V. and watched an American thriller on a cable channel, "The Deep End", the story of woman who kills the man who has been abusing her son and then goes after everyone else involved. The movie was set beside a lake in a majestic, tranquil landscape, lovingly filmed in luminous, saturated colours. Vilar pictured himself in that house. He wondered if he would have the courage to do what the mother in the film did. Of course, he thought. As he did every time the question was asked, every time it occurred to him when he woke from a nightmare or from a deep depression. He would kill anyone and everyone who . . . He had no words to finish the sentence forming in his mind. Impossible to imagine doing anything else. Impossible to imagine himself resisting the urge to destroy that sort of predator. And yet he understood the law, and he agreed with it. Self-defence . . . he abhorred all those brainless vigilantes – in films and in real life – including the ones he himself had banged up. He had always despised what they had become, a ragbag of savage, snivelling impulses motivated only by grief or hatred, inadvertent psychopaths who were almost happy to have found, in stalking a killer, their *raison d'être*.

And suddenly, as always, reason, or perhaps some mad hope, came and placed a hesitant finger between the bullet and the firing pin. What if he ended up killing the one man who knew where Pablo was now?

242

His very last hope? He had spent whole nights wrestling with this question, feverish with exhaustion, nerves wound like barbed wire around his body.

He turned off the T.V., irritated by the very things that had drawn him to the film. The plot seemed hackneyed now, the scenery grandiose. He got up and stood for a few moments in the middle of the room, arms hanging by his sides, unsure, his mind a blank. He ran a finger over the picture frame from which Pablo smiled out, his head resting on Ana's shoulder.

"I'm here, I'm right here with you."

Early in the afternoon, he managed to speak to Daras, who informed him that Sandra de Melo was nowhere to be found. Her sister had indeed spoken to her on the telephone the night before, but she noticed nothing out of the ordinary. The boy had not turned up at school.

"She can't have disappeared into thin air, not with a kid," Daras said. "She has to resurface."

Resurface. Archimedes' principle as life force.

"Obviously. Though that would require the people who are hiding her to let us know. If they're as scared as she is, they won't say a word. We've seen it before. They'll think they can protect her better than we can."

"Well, we haven't done such a great job up until now. We just have to hope this guy isn't planning to destroy everything in his wake. You saw what he did to the Sofiane kid last night. And still we've got nothing on him. We've been chasing a shadow for the past two months."

"And the shadow is chasing me. But I'd like to see exactly whose shadow it is."

"The two-man theory?"

"Laurent doesn't go for it."

Daras sighed.

"Laurent doesn't go for much these days. Things are bad with him just now."

"I think his mother's on the way out."

"Yeah. He mentioned something about it once," Daras said. "He doesn't confide in me. I'm just some stupid bloody woman."

They said nothing for a few seconds.

"So what are you up to?" Daras said eventually. "You getting some rest?"

Vilar hesitated.

"I'm staying put. Though I feel fine. I'll be in tomorrow. I'll call you later."

They hung up at the same time. Sandra would turn up, sure. Vilar thought about the little clown. She would not be able to stop herself. It was almost 4.00 p.m. He went into the kitchen to drink what was left of the coffee. The sky was leaden – he had not noticed while he was in the living room, where the shutters were closed, but now through the kitchen window he could see the wind whipping at the trees.

He pulled on a jacket with lots of pockets, slipping a blister pack of tablets into one of them in case the pain came back. He was about to leave when he took out his mobile and called Ana. His heart pounded a little as he listened to it ring. The click made him start.

He could leave a message after the beep.

Vilar reminded himself that it was August. Holidays. Other climes. She had said something about Tuscany.

Traffic was light on the boulevard and he could easily keep an eye on what was going on behind. Several times he changed his speed to see whether anyone was tailing him, but there was nothing. He parked fifty metres from the block where Sandra de Melo lived and walked, taking a roundabout route. He rang the bell for the caretaker, flashed his warrant card and demanded that he hand over the keys. Dressed in shorts and vest with a pair of canvas slippers on his feet, the man said nothing, did not even respond to Vilar's greeting, simply gave him a suspicious, hostile look. As he went back into his apartment to collect the keys, a wolfhound – or maybe it was a Malinois – came and sat in the doorway, ears pricked, nose to the ground, staring up at Vilar with eyes that burned in the half-light with an unsettling golden glow. He could hear a T.V. somewhere. An American crime drama. The sirens of a police car.

"He's not generally dangerous," the caretaker said without much conviction, nudging the dog with his foot. "Depends on the person."

He held the keys out to Victor who thanked him and turned on his heel. He had already gone down a couple of steps when he heard the caretaker's voice:

"You planning to be long?"

He turned. The man had spoken through the half-closed door.

"I don't know. Why? Do you really need to know?"

Vilar went back up to the landing. He thought he saw the caretaker ease the door close. The dog poked its nose between its master's legs.

"I thought you didn't want to talk to me," Vilar said. "Or that you didn't like the look of me – you didn't even fucking say hello . . . And me, I don't like to impose."

"It's not that," the caretaker said. "It's just, you get so you don't trust anyone. And it was weird, that kid getting himself killed. I chucked them out of here, you know, him and his mates, twenty times I threw them out, the little wankers. Sometimes they'd get wound up, call me a dickhead, threaten to cut my wife's throat, or my mother's, threaten to fuck them, it depended . . . That sort of drivel. Twelve years I've lived here. I watched them grow up, every one of them. They don't scare me, they're not so tough, but when they're together they think they're big men, I don't know, they get arrogant, try to start laying down the law and I'll tell you there's been times when I wished I could get a shotgun and sort them out."

"That bad? Did they threaten people?"

"Not really . . . But they were always hanging around, smoking weed and making smart remarks, and over time people feel intimidated, they're afraid to walk past, and the more people are scared of them the more they think they're gangsters. That's what they used to say, the little bastards: 'We be gangstas' . . ."

The man paused, because this long speech had left him breathless.

"Obviously I feel sorry for him, and for his parents – they're good people, they worked hard for their kids. The sisters are both at college. One of them is going to be a nurse. The kid didn't deserve what happened to him. A good kick up the arse, yeah, a clip round the ear, but not that . . ."

"And not someone coming after him with a shotgun like you were suggesting."

"No, of course not. That was just the anger talking . . . Sometimes you just have to grin and bear it."

The man had opened the door a little wider. The dog had disappeared.

"In any case, he didn't die because he was hanging around doing fuck all," Vilar said. "He was just in the wrong place at the wrong time. He ran into a man we were already looking for . . . I don't suppose you saw anything unusual? I realise you've been asked that already, but you never know, if something came back to you . . ."

The man shook his head.

"No, nothing. But don't think I spend all day hanging out on the stairs watching people come and go. I'm responsible for taking out the bins, doing minor repairs, looking after the grounds. It's a full-time job! But the little woman on the third floor, the one with the handicapped son, I knew her. She was really sweet, very shy, and she was a pretty little thing too."

He glanced furtively behind him as though some jealous shrew might suddenly appear and claw his eyes out.

"You don't know if she had any visitors, people who came to see her?"

"As I said, I've got too much work to be meddling in the tenants' private lives. Unless I'm asked or unless someone complains, I keep my nose out, I say good morning, I say goodnight and that's all. I know what goes on in my world, I've got a keen eye, but I'm not the type to go playing detective . . . I mean . . . sorry . . ."

"That's O.K., we wouldn't expect you to. I'm going to take a look round her flat. Don't worry if I'm a while. I'll bring the keys back to you."

He walked up the stairs, watched by the caretaker, who could not seem to bring himself to close the door. Once in her apartment, he headed straight for the kitchen: as he expected, the clown was no longer lying under the table between the legs of the chairs. He went into the boy's room but could see nothing different there. A quick tour of the other rooms gave him no more information: Sandra had been inconspicuous, stealthy in invading her own privacy. She had to be nearby. Probably upstairs with a neighbour. He felt like calling for backup, instigating another door-to-door, finding her so he could talk to her, so he could get her to talk, get her to tell him whatever it was the other guy had been trying to find out so as to be one step ahead of him; but the thought of his colleagues showing up, all that manpower combing every floor, sparking panic across the whole estate, was not bearable. He would have to play things out alone this time. No-one knew he was here apart from the caretaker who, from what Vilar could tell, was not involved. Which probably meant that for the first time in this investigation he was acting without the killer's knowledge.

He flicked off the light and sat in an armchair in the living room. Here, in spite of the loud pulsing of his heart and crackle of the nervous electricity he could feel coursing through his limbs, alternately searing and freezing, he was overcome by a torpor that kept him floating on the surface of sleep, in the shallows where dreams come skimming and where, of course, Pablo appeared and spoke to him. Pablo's voice was clear and bright, and when Vilar found the words to answer him, his own voice was tremulous with sobs.

He was ripped from this desolate happiness by the soft creak of a door being opened above or below him, and he held his breath for a long moment in the half-light, not knowing the time, refusing to check his watch, then he drifted off again, vainly trying to reconstruct the heart-rending illusion of the dream.

He was woken with a start by something moving. At first he thought he was at home in his bedroom, but he quickly came to himself. He did not know how long he had slept. It looked dark outside: no light filtered through the shutters. He could not possibly have slept for five hours. The darkness was such that he could not read his watch.

He had heard nothing, yet he was convinced there was someone in the apartment, perhaps even in the room. He sat, motionless, breathing through his mouth.

Behind him. Sitting in this armchair, there was nothing he could do.

When the light was flicked on it felt as though he had been electrocuted: his heart stopped, his brain was little more than a feverish pulp. Sandra de Melo screamed, her finger still on the light switch. She was deathly pale and stared at him terrified and gasping for breath.

He stood up, tried to calm his nerves, fumbled for words. Here he was standing before the woman he had come to find and yet, dazed with sleep, he did not know what to do.

She took a step towards him.

"What the hell are you doing in my flat? I thought you were him!"

Her shrill, hoarse voice cracked. Her tousled hair framed a face that looked drawn, the eyes ringed with dark circles.

"Jesus!" he said. "Don't scream at me like that. I've been looking for you, and looking for him. Where did you get to? What's with your little game of hide-and-seek?"

"Oh? You think I'm the one playing hide-and-seek? So what are you playing at? I'm betting you have no right to be here."

"Calm down . . ."

"I will not calm down! That guy the other night, he was coming here to kill me, wasn't he? He slit that boy's throat just like that, just because the kid got in his way! Bloody hell, that's a good enough reason not to sleep soundly in your bed, don't you think? And what about my son? Did you even stop to think about him?"

He let her finish. He felt the knife wound throbbing in his back. He could hear the two of them breathing, hear as they struggled to swallow. Sandra sighed.

"I came to pick up some things for José. Is that O.K.? They're in his room."

She did not give him time to answer. She walked down the corridor and he followed her. She rummaged through a wardrobe, took out some T-shirts and some underwear, which she stuffed into a plastic bag.

"What do you want to know?"

"Where have you been hiding?"

She closed the wardrobe door.

"I'm thirsty. There's cold water in the fridge. You want some?"

She took out two cans of sparkling water and offered one to Vilar.

They opened them without a word and drank in long gulps. Sandra sat down, wedged between the table and the wall behind her, and Vilar lowered his stiff body into a chair.

"Now that's what I call thirsty," Sandra said, "but to answer your earlier questions, I've been staying upstairs with a neighbour, Madame Fadlaoui. José's asleep right now. He knows her, he's calm when he's around her."

"And he has his clown . . ."

"You thought about that? You noticed I forgot it when I left?"

"Who is this guy you're so terrified of?"

"His name's Éric. He's the one who killed Nadia."

"How do you know that? What's his surname, this Éric? Do you know where we can find him? You were happy to feed me Thierry Lataste's name without worrying whether that might make him a suspect. Were you trying to confuse me? Why should I believe you now?"

"Because I'm telling the truth. And I didn't lie to you about Thierry. I just told you about him, and left you to make up the rest. I didn't tell you about Éric because I was scared of him, that's all."

"Éric what? Is that even his name?"

"Yes. At least I think so . . . Just Éric. Nadia used to talk about him and that's what she called him and it never occurred to me to ask her his surname or his address. He's not exactly the kind of guy you would want to drop in on. But he killed Nadia, I know that much. I've no proof, but I know it's true. He's sick in the head. A vicious thug who can't control himself. She was terrified of him. He wouldn't let her go. Told her he was in love with her. He wanted them to go off and live in the Antilles together . . . I don't know, he was planning to open a restaurant, or manage one, or something – I don't remember. It was some idea he had. But Nadia, she wouldn't even talk about it. And then recently, he got it into his head that the kid was his."

"What are you saying? Had they known each other a long time?"

"Since '93. When he got out of prison."

Vilar did the calculations. It could tally. And now he knew the guy had a record – the fact that he had been banged up meant he was no longer merely a shadowy presence. They almost had him.

"Which prison?"

Sandra de Melo sighed, pulled a face. "Oh, for God's sake, how would I know? I don't even remember whether Nadia told me! Besides, when it comes to ex-cons – especially that one – the less I see of them the better . . ."

"Why, do you know a lot of ex-cons?"

"I don't have to answer that, do I?"

"We'll see. But think hard, because if we know which prison he did time in, then we can find out who he is."

She drank some water, and crushed the empty can.

"No, I don't know. I'm sorry . . ."

"How did you meet him, this Éric?"

Something moved above them. A chair being dragged across the floor. Sandra sat up, rigid, staring at the ceiling, then relaxed and leaned back again, one elbow on the table.

"It's nothing. It's just I'm always scared that . . . What were you saying?"

"I was asking you how you met Éric."

"Through Nadia. They already knew each other and Nadia had told me what she was doing to earn a little cash. So one day when I was finding things tough – I didn't have a penny to my name, my son was having fits every day and down at the centre they didn't know how to deal with him, they'd started talking about putting him into a psychiatric unit to try and control the fits . . . Anyway, Nadia mentioned some party where they needed some girls who were not too ugly and not too shy, told me it was well paid, about a thousand euros, all that money just for allowing yourself to be touched up by a few big shots, I mean customers, politicians, that kind of thing, and she said if I wanted I could come along . . . I started screaming at her, saying what did she take me for, I wasn't some whore, and she didn't push it, in fact she apologised and explained that as far as she was concerned it wasn't a big deal."

"What wasn't a big deal?"

As she'd been talking, Sandra had folded her arms across her chest and was now hugging her sides. Vilar thought she was trembling.

"I don't know how to explain. But suddenly I felt bad about what I'd said. Because whores are just people . . . We talked about it a lot. As far as she was concerned her body didn't matter. She told me she was paralysed from the waist down . . . That's how she put it. She couldn't feel a thing. Like it was no longer a part of her. And she hated men. She said having some guy put his hands on her made her feel dirty, so you can imagine how she felt about sleeping with them. She said she'd kill one of them someday, bleed him like a stuck pig. I could never have imagined such hatred. She told me that ever since her father . . . When she talked like that, it was like I didn't know her at all."

"In that case, how could she stomach the visits from . . . from Éric? And her fling with Thierry Lataste?"

"I don't know . . . Habit . . . Or money, maybe."

"How did it work? I mean, she didn't do it at her place, with her son in the next room, surely?"

Sandra looked away.

"I don't know. We never talked about that."

Vilar sprang to his feet, making the woman flinch in fear and surprise. He paced the room, trying to think of some way he could get her to talk.

"Look, do me a favour and stop fucking me about, alright? 'I don't know', 'I can't remember . . .' It's one step forward and two steps back. I'm not here for the good of my health, you got that? A guy you know comes around here one night planning to kill you, but you, you don't know what it's about, you play the innocent . . . I don't mind you taking me for a fool, I mean in my job I get it all the time, but just know that right now you're guilty of perverting the course of justice, you're protecting a criminal on the run, and that's more than enough for me to make your life very difficult."

Sandra tried to say something. She stood up. He waved for her to sit down.

"Let me finish. I reckon you know a lot more than you're saying, about Nadia, about her activities, and I think you probably did what she did sometimes, when you needed cash, and you often need cash, don't you? It's as you said, whores are just people. So now you're going to tell me everything, very calmly, because if you don't I'm going to arrest you and have your son taken into care by social services. Think about that. It's another thing you have in common with Nadia, trying to protect your sons from the shit you've had to deal with, am I right?"

"I see, so that's your attitude?"

"Maybe. But let's talk about yours, because I'm losing time and patience."

She got up quickly and stalked across the room. As she passed him, Vilar could smell her perfume, though he did not recognise the dominant fragrance. Nor did he react to her swearing at him behind his back.

Then she went back and curled up in the chair again, her eyes fixed on the tray on which the glasses stood.

"We hit it off the first time we met at S.A.N.I., we worked in the same team that first month, we joined at about the same time. There was this foreman, Castets, who was desperate to fuck us, so we stuck together. He'd do his round every night in a company van and he'd ask us out for a drink, or for something to eat at Les Capucins, as if we really wanted to party at eleven or twelve o'clock at night when we had kids at home. Every night, the same thing. We'd say no, he never pushed it and he never held it against us, never tried to blackmail us, nothing. It was weird . . . Let's just say it was friendly persuasion, or maybe that dickhead was waiting until one us felt desperate enough to fuck him, I don't know. And then he stopped. So anyway, Nadia and I, we'd laugh about it, and she'd say that we could make serious money out of a nerd like that, then she started talking about what she did so she could make ends meet, so she could save up to buy her apartment. One day, she told me she'd found a little studio flat on the cours Balguerie – it's number 145, if you want to check – and she'd go there once or twice a week with clients who contacted her on a mobile phone she kept only for that. It was cheaper than the hotels on the bypass where she used to go. Sometimes, she'd stay overnight, especially Saturdays, and she was making good money. She also had a network of guys who'd call her up if they needed to close a deal with some foreign client. She'd pretend to be a secretary at some meeting, or over dinner and she'd be all over these guys, spend a couple of nights with them while they were here and mostly it worked out pretty well . . .''

"Did that happen a lot?"

"Three or four times a year . . . maybe more, I don't know. It was well paid."

"Why did she go work at S.A.N.I.?"

"To have a payslip, so as not to attract attention at school, with the civil service. She did it for her kid . . . She wanted him to have a normal life – a normal mother, as she put it. She didn't want a social worker coming around poking her nose in."

"What about Éric? Was he collecting the takings?"

Sandra smiled bitterly and shrugged.

"No. Nadia worked alone. She wasn't some whore walking the streets, competing with girls from Africa and Romania with some bastard of a pimp running the show. Besides, Éric never gave her any grief about what she did, he told her he loved her, that he'd never hurt her or her kid. Let's just say that from time to time he borrowed money that he never paid back."

"Did she ask for it back?"

"He's not the kind of guy you ask for anything. But she must have done, once or twice, and from what she told me that's when things got ugly. He'd get angry, they'd fight."

"Where? At her place? At her studio flat?"

"It depended. Wherever. Every time it happened she'd try to get him to forgive her. Or he'd bring round a few of his mates to punish her, if you know what I mean."

Vilar knew. He tried to see where all this was leading. He would have to go and talk to the boy, Victor, who might know something about this man who thought he was his father. He took two large swigs of water to wash the bitter taste from his mouth. He desperately wanted a cigarette, and vaguely hoped that maybe the young woman might take out a pack so he could ask for one. He glanced towards the closed shutters, wishing he could look out at the scenery rather than at these blank boards: a lit window in the tower block opposite, the halo of light that hovered above the city at night. Suddenly he felt boxed in. Trapped in a blind alley. Only Sandra de Melo's gentle face, the shimmer of her dark eyes, stopped him from getting to his feet and leaving right now. It had been a long time since he had taken such pleasure in looking at a woman's face.

At the same time, he wondered how she could have sold her body to these men, allowed them to touch her, penetrate her, pollute her. In spite of everything he had seen in his years with the police, he still found it difficult to imagine the terrible plight that could lead people to debase themselves like that. At what point does a person think that there is no other solution than this self-abnegation, this leap into the void, this poison that seeps into you, that you try to wash away, to mask with perfume, this self-loathing that kills more swiftly than any illness since with each new humiliation something in the body, something in the soul dies? Nadia was already dead long before she was murdered. Her body no longer mattered to her. All she could do was try to keep a small part of herself, that part of her mind that included her love for her son, her last vestige of dignity, safe from this mental necrosis. As someone might clutch their most precious belongings to them as they are swept away by a landslide.

He wanted to go on talking to her, if only for the simple pleasure it afforded him, and the curious sensation of helplessness he felt when she looked at him.

He came up with one more question, a pointless one in all probability. One way or another he would track down this Éric, it was only a matter of days, he had only to find the man's police record.

"These special . . . parties, what was Éric's role?"

"He was the one who told Nadia about them, he always drove her there. From what she said, he checked out the place where it was being held. Apparently there was some cop who helped him out."

"A cop? What do you mean, a cop?"

"What do you want me to say? Some officer he knew. Maybe they were friends. I mean sometimes criminals get to know policemen, don't they?"

"Did you ever see this officer?"

She shrugged and gave him a mocking smile.

"It bugs you, doesn't it, the idea that there's some colleague mixed up in this shit?"

He thought back to his conversations with Daras and Pradeau. The possibility of a leak.

"What kind of places were these parties held? Did she tell you?"

"A couple of times it was a villa in Cap-Ferrat, or one down near Pyla, there were politicians there and people off the television. The sort of arseholes who get their pictures in the paper when they spend their holidays or the weekends in the area. Famous people, she said, but she never mentioned any names. A lot of guys off the T.V. are happy to pay for a hooker for the night, as long as she doesn't look like a hooker . . . The sort of girls who play walk-on parts and are happy to get fucked for a thousand euros, or two thousand, in the hope that one of these bastards might call and ask her to work on his fucking show. I tell you, there's no shortage of slappers who dream of being on T.V. Nadia used to try and persuade me to come, telling me I'd see loads of famous people, that it was totally safe. About how there was lots of champagne and coke set out in little bowls. Not that she ever touched the stuff, but she saw those bastards doing coke. And she told me . . ."

A telephone rang, the ringtone made a mooing sound like a cow and Sandra jumped to her feet and took a small black mobile from her pocket. She was pale now, her hands fumbled to open it and her fingers hesitated over the keys. She looked at bluish glow of the screen. Vilar stood up, and they stood staring at each other, the mobile and the ridiculous mooing sound between them. On the screen he saw a picture of little José.

"Who is it?" Sandra said to Vilar.

"Answer it and you'll find out. Doesn't it tell you on the screen?"

"No. This is my new phone. I haven't had time to set it up properly."

She tried to bring herself to answer.

"What if it's him?"

She stared at Vilar, wild-eyed, leaning towards him. He tried to think of something to say.

"If it's him, give me the phone. Keep calm."

She answered the call and gave a little cry of surprise.

"Paola? What's happening?"

Paola. Sandra's sister. From where he stood, Vilar could hear her voice crackle through the receiver. She was talking quickly and loudly.

"So what was he like, this guy? Yeah, I know him, kind of. Say again? Yeah, obviously."

"Let me speak to her."

Vilar introduced himself, explained why he was there with Sandra. The woman told him that a guy had turned up asking for Sandra at about six o'clock, saying he was a friend of hers, and was worried because she wasn't at home. Charming, polite, with a big bandage on his neck. Since Paola could not tell him anything, he did not press the point and left, wishing her a pleasant evening. Too polite to be genuine. "I can spot that kind of bullshit artist from fifty metres," Paola said, "I watched him leave, he got into a big car, a metallic grey estate. I stood behind the curtain and watched him drive slowly past the block. Given that Sandra had phoned me this morning and told me a bit about what had happened – she's a magnet for this sort of trouble, I don't know how she does it – anyway, I thought I should call to warn her. So who is this guy?"

"You said he had a bandage on his neck?"

"Yeah, a big thing like surgical collar. So who is he?"

"Someone we've been looking for. He's got a grudge against your sister, but we're protecting her. Did you call the local police? And what about the car, did you see what make it was?"

"No. I don't know anything about cars. It was an estate, really big, too . . . Pretty new, I guess, because it was gleaming. But no, I didn't call the police. In our family, we sort out our own problems, we don't get the police involved. When it comes to Sandra, I'm kind of used to situations like this." She hesitated. "I'm all alone here with the kids. My husband's a truck driver, he's not here at the moment. Do you think we're in any danger from that guy?"

"No, I don't think you're in any danger. He's just trying to track down your sister, but we'll be waiting for him if he shows up. But give the local force a call, they'll keep an eye on things. Meanwhile, if you see him hanging around again, give me a call, maybe we can collar him."

He heard the woman sigh, clearly relieved. She trotted out a few hollow platitudes about the world we live in, then asked if she could have another word with Sandra. Vilar handed the phone back and left the two sisters to say their goodbyes. Eventually Sandra rang off and set the mobile gently on the table in front of her, still open, as though her life depended on the next call, or the next, or the next.

"How did he know my sister's address? He didn't even know she existed!"

"You're sure you never mentioned her?"

"Of course I'm sure. I would never get her mixed up in my shit. She did more than enough for me when I was young, when I moved out of my parents" place and all she got for it was grief. And it's not like Éric could have looked her up on the internet, her last name is Ménenteau, not de Melo.'

Vilar looked at his watch. I was 8.50 p.m.

"He's coming here," he said.

"Who?"

"What do you mean, who? Éric whatever-the-fuck-his-name-is. Who did you think I meant? We have to get out of here. Let's go up to your neighbour's place. You get the kid ready, and I'll get another officer to take you somewhere. We'll put you in a safe house."

The neighbour, Madame Fadlaoui, opened as soon as they knocked, looked at them wide-eyed and ushered them inside quickly, glancing anxiously along the walkway before she closed the door. She was a tall woman with a face like a knife, an aquiline nose. In the immaculately polished living room decorated with brass plates, intricate lamps, leather cushions and sofas, she invited them to sit down and offered them something to drink. In a corner of the room, a little girl was staring goggle-eyed at a flat-screen T.V. and jiggling the buttons on a games controller. Little characters were running and jumping and shooting at each other.

"You're the police officer, is that right?" Madame Fadlaoui said. "My name is Sihem. And this is Amel."

The little girl barely tore her eyes from the game to greet them with an extravagant flick of her eyelashes.

"What's going on?" Sihem Fadlaoui said.

"We need to leave," Sandra said. "I'll explain everything later."

The woman looked at Vilar questioningly. He turned away and keyed a number into his phone.

"Marianne? Something's come up . . . No, nothing, I don't have time to go into it right now. I need you to put out an alert for a man named Éric, surname unknown, released from prison in '93, probably from the Gironde area . . . No, that's all I've got. We're not talking some minor offence here, it had to be something major. Yeah, that kind of thing . . . Anyway, Sandra de Melo. I found her, she's here with me. We need to get her into a safe house, I'll sort that. O.K.? I'll call Laurent. I don't want news of this getting all around the station. This guy knows too much, he's got someone on the force feeding him information, I have confirmation of it . . . I'll tell you later, I've no time now. You have any idea where Laurent is at the moment? O.K., well that's not too far. He should get her quickly. I think our guy might come back. We need bodies here. I'll hang around to wait for reinforcements. Yeah, that's good."

He hung up and keyed another number.

"Laurent?"

He gave a detailed account of the situation, told him that they had identified the suspect, Éric, and had officers looking for him. Pradeau seemed overwhelmed by so much information, his uneasiness was palpable. Vilar felt as if he were dealing with a swimmer, overcome by exhaustion, plunging into the murmuring depths of the ocean. He told Pradeau to get a grip, said he needed him. Pradeau quickly composed himself and promised to get there within half an hour, and he kept his word.

By the time Pradeau rang the doorbell, José was half asleep, slumped against his mother, the clown in his arms. As a precaution, it was Vilar who opened the door. They said goodbye to Sihem Fadlaoui, thanked her for her help and warned her to lock the door and not to open it to anyone, and to call the police if she saw anything suspicious. The building would be under surveillance in case Éric came back. The woman turned the almost gentle steel of her grey face on the policemen and gave them a sceptical smile.

"My husband and my son will be home soon; that way I'll feel safer," she said.

Sandra stepped out into the walkway behind Pradeau who was already on his way down the stairs, waving for the woman to follow him. Vilar brought up the rear. Little José was clinging to his mother's neck, his chin on her shoulder, staring behind her, looking up only when they passed a ceiling light. When Vilar appeared in his field of vision, the child raised his head, his mouth half open in surprise, then reverted to his previous position. Sandra de Melo was panting, José was a heavy child and she frequently had to hitch him up, having trouble finding a comfortable way to hold him.

It was now almost 11.00, nothing was stirring in the building. The buzz of television sets, the sound of muffled voices, music and laughter followed them to the ground floor, but they encountered no-one. Sandra and her son got into the back of Pradeau's car; he was to drive them to the police station until someone could find them a place for the night. As Vilar was heading back upstairs to hide out in Sandra's apartment, Pradeau insisted he take his weapon and pressed the pistol into his hands.

"You never know . . . this guy sounds like he's completely out of control."

He did not give Vilar time to answer, quickly putting the car into gear and driving off. Vilar stared at the gun, watched the street light cast copper reflections on the steel, then he tucked it into his belt.

He was hardly back inside Sandra de Melo's apartment when his mobile rang.

"I see you're visiting that Portuguese slut . . . Did she give you a decent blow job? You do know that's her speciality?"

Vilar ran to the windows, cursing at the fact the shutters were closed. The guy was downstairs. How was it possible?

"How do you know that?"

"That she sucks cock? Guess! I've even got it on video. Just like I've got one of your son."

Vilar almost ripped the handle off the door as he flung it open. He dashed along the walkway, took the stairs three at a time, slamming into the wall, because the mobile pressed to his ear threw him off balance.

"Doing a little jogging? You think you can catch me, dickhead? What, you think I'm going to be waiting outside the door? You dumb fucks didn't even set a trap – or 'stake the place out', as you'd say. Jesus, even I feel embarrassed for you."

Vilar arrived outside and looked around, started back towards his car, trying to catch his breath. He could hear the guy laughing on the other end of the line and he tried to think of something to say to needle him, to get to him somehow.

"She talk to you, did she?" the voice growled. "Tell you who I was? That little whore knows nothing. I suppose she told you my name's Éric? Well, good luck hunting. Makes no odds . . . I'm about to kill her anyway. I've got your mate's car about fifty metres ahead of me. Just wait till you see the expression on her face when I'm done. Maybe later I'll show you some more stuff about your son. Have to keep my priorities straight, can't do everything at once. You got to understand, I'm taking a risk here with a guy like you. Then again, I get off on it, so I can't really complain. O.K., shitface, see you round."

Vilar ran the last few metres and jumped behind the wheel. He called Pradeau, but the call went straight to voicemail. He left a brief message, knowing it was pointless: hide, make a run for it, do whatever you have to because this psychopath is right behind you and more than capable of creating a bloodbath. Then he called the station to tell them an officer was in danger and to ask that patrol cars be despatched to secure the likely route. The duty officer promised to do the necessary. Pradeau had probably taken the most direct route to the police station. At this hour of the night, it should take him about fifteen minutes. Vilar floored the accelerator as hard as he dared, one hand pressing the mobile to his ear, trying again to get through to Pradeau, the other hand gripping the steering wheel. He negotiated every red light at speed and quickly found himself at the intersection of the boulevard Georges V and the rue de Pessac, where heavy traffic forced him to slow to a crawl. Cars honked their horns angrily at the way he was driving. All he needed now was for the local traffic police to arrest him or give chase, try to breathalyse him. He called the station again, narrowly missing a moped that shot out of a side street, and waited to hear if Pradeau had got back safely.

"He's not here," the officer on the phone said. "He took the woman directly to a safe house."

By now, Vilar could see the police station up ahead, rising up in the darkness, immense, white as an iceberg. He parked on the kerb, jerking the handbrake.

"What? What safe house?"

"Ah, that I don't know. No-one's told me."

"Where the fuck is he? I called not five minutes ago to say there's an armed and very dangerous bastard on his tail, and what the fuck have you done about it? Would it really be so hard to get off your arse and do something to stop him being killed?"

The guy mumbled, called someone over. There seemed to be a commotion. As though an alarm had finally gone off, Vilar thought.

"Commandant Castel," a voice said suddenly. "The officer has just been located. Place Jacques-Dormoy. We've got two units on their way to the scene. Bystanders thought it was a fight between a couple of drunks and called the police."

"What happened?"

"We don't know yet. We've paged Capitaine Daras."

It took him less than ten minutes to get to the place Jacques-Dormoy, weaving through narrow, potholed streets lined with parked cars where he several times had to swerve to avoid hitting vehicles parked haphazardly on the pavement.

There were police everywhere. A dozen patrol cars. Every squad out tonight had clearly shown up the moment they heard that one of their own was in trouble. The metallic chatter of the radios mingled with that of the officers, while around the little square people peered out of their windows or gathered in groups along the pavements, waiting in this muted cacophony for some dramatic or tragic announcement. As he got out of his car, Vilar spotted a dog handler wearing blue fatigues getting his Alsatian to piss against a tree. Surveying the scene, illuminated by the convulsive blue flashes of the squad cars, Vilar felt his blood run cold because he knew all too well what was at the centre of this chaos of flickering lights: a place where nothing moved, where the noise and the voices suddenly fade, as though muffled by a wall of glass.

He flashed his warrant card to silence a driver yelling at him to move his vehicle. From behind, he immediately recognised Pradeau's car which had piled into a black Mercedes, hitting the driver's door and smashing the window. The doors on the other side were open onto the road and as he drew closer, he saw someone in a white coat leaning into the back seat and, just then, he heard the scream, a long wail broken by groans and splutters coming from inside the car. He walked more quickly, dodging between the cars, weaving between the officers standing talking, breaking though the semi-circle surrounding the screaming child and the five or six men working the scene. One of them, a lieutenant called Gallin working with Mégrier's team, a stocky blond man as short as he was fat, was just about to push Vilar aside when he recognised him.

"Where's Pradeau? Is he O.K.?"

"We don't know. There's only the kid. Your partner's not here."

"What do you mean there's only the kid? Where did he go?"

"We have a witness who says he saw two men fighting and that they then got into the other guy's car."

"They just got in? Pradeau wasn't injured? Where is he, this witness? And what about the woman?"

"She left with them. The witness didn't see much. He heard the car slam into the Mercedes, and he heard the screams, but when things got ugly he legged it."

Vilar felt his mouth go dry.

"Are we looking for them?"

"No," a voice behind him said. "Why on earth would we be doing that?"

It was Mégrier. He was snapping shut a mobile.

"I mean, obviously we just came out to get a bit of air, go for a spin. We'll give the kid a little injection so he keeps his trap shut and then we'll all go home to bed. I mean, you hardly expect us to disturb the whole town at this time of night, do you? We were just waiting for you to tell us what to do. We knew you'd be worried."

The officers giggled silently at their commander's comeback.

"Do you take us for complete idiots or what? And where's the beautiful Marianne Daras? Doing the horizontal mambo? I'm sure she'll get here the moment she gets her knickers back on."

Vilar could think of nothing to say; he shook his head. He walked around Mégrier and stepped closer to the Peugeot where José was still wailing. Officers were taking fingerprints and collecting evidence around the vehicle and inside the car itself. A S.A.M.U. paramedic kneeling on the back seat climbed out shaking his head, he sighed, ignoring Vilar's questioning look, then moved aside to let him pass. Now Vilar could see the boy, huddled on the back seat of the car, clinging to an unbuckled seatbelt that was bizarrely wound around him, thrashing about like a terrified animal whenever anyone tried to come near or speak to him. Vilar leaned one knee on the back seat, slowly reached out his hand and called the boy by name. He looked around for Toto the clown, saw it on the passenger seat, picked it up and handed it to the little boy who hugged and kissed the doll, no longer wailing. Vilar watched as the boy looked up at him with big eyes, looked right through this stranger leaning over him, staring into the distance at some place no-one else could reach. He curled up again and began to howl sadly, banging the clown against his forehead. Vilar withdrew his hand and got out of the car. He was shivering, in spite of his sweat-soaked shirt, in the sweltering heat of the night.

"I don't think there's anything else we can do," the doctor said. "I'll have to give him a shot. He'll end up hurting himself. Do you know the kid?"

"His mother is a witness in a case I've been working on. The boy's autistic, as far as I know. He looks like he's in shock. He must have been terrified . . ."

"We'll have to take him to a psych unit. The children's hospital won't take him."

"A psych unit?"

"You got a better solution?" The man's tone was curt, impatient. José was wailing now and sobbing.

"No, I've no solution."

He looked back at the boy, his eyes were wide with fear, crouching in the back seat of the car.

Pablo. Different shadows, a different fear. Vilar felt himself choking, everything around him was suddenly floating. He leaned on the bonnet of the car and shook his head.

"You O.K.?" the doctor said.

"Yeah, yeah . . . Just look after him. Don't leave him crying in the dark like that. Give him something so he can sleep, so he can get some rest."

He felt sweat trickle down his back. His eyes were blurred from the dizziness – from the tears – and he stood for a moment, head bowed, hands resting on the warm bonnet. All he could hear now was the boy's wail, shrill, deafening, right beside him in the darkness. A woman in a white coat came over and set a first-aid kit on the roof of the car. Slowly, she opened the door against which José was leaning and began whispering to him gently. The doctor Vilar had spoken to was also leaning into the car and they discussed what to do while the boy whimpered softly.

Vilar walked away, watching as one by one the officers left the scene. An ambulance moved slowly off. Mégrier was giving orders to his men, juggling two mobiles simultaneously. In his pocket, Vilar's own mobile rang. It was Daras.

"Mégrier told me about Laurent. Shit. What the fuck did you do?"

"We were trying to get Sandra de Melo somewhere safe. The guy must have followed her. He called me. He was tailing Pradeau's car, threatening all sorts. What would you have done?"

He heard Daras sigh.

"How do you expect us to find them in the middle of the night when we've got nothing to go on?" she said. "We could put an officer on every street corner but we'd just be pissing in the wind. Besides, by now they'll be long gone."

"So what are you planning to do?"

"Nothing. I don't know. We can't do more than Mégrier. He's already got bodies on the ground. He has promised to call me the minute he hears anything. He's been in touch with the big shots, the *commissaires* and the directors and they've told him to do his best, to get out all the officers he can. Jesus wept! I think I'm just going to take a pill and get some sleep so I can start again early tomorrow. Not that there's anything we can do. We're already trying to track down details for this Éric guy, we can't do any more. With a bit of luck, we'll have some information tomorrow."

"Tomorrow, yeah." Vilar echoed her words mechanically, incapable of forming a coherent thought.

"What about you?"

"I'll hang around for a bit. Tire myself out, because the way things are I won't get a wink of sleep, and that wouldn't help."

He broke off as he saw the frail form of the boy being lifted gently out of the car like some sacred effigy. Surrounded by doctors and police officers, his body seemed as though it might disappear. A huge fire-fighter was cradling him in his arms. To such a giant he barely weighed anything, he barely existed. Vilar wondered whether this boy would ever truly be aware of his own existence.

"If you'd seen the kid screaming in the back of the car . . . The guys from the S.A.M.U. are just taking him away, sedated like an elephant. They didn't know what else to do. There was nothing left of him but this howl. He saw everything, his mother was taken away from him, while he was there, bawling in the dark. You remember, I told you about him? And the girl, his mother, she's a decent person."

They both hung up. Vilar turned away from the line of police officers and headed back to his car. He drove towards the train station, his mind blank, unable to think, then he went along the cours de la Marne, found a place to park in a narrow street next to the Marché des Capucins. All the windows in the alley were dark, the heat was stifling. From the vast mouldering dumpsters by the market came a stench of rotten meat and fish that made his stomach heave. He walked back towards the cours de la Marne, where the greasy smell wafting from a steakhouse forced him to double up between two cars, but he could only manage to vomit up a little bile. He headed towards the place de la Victoire, his eyes blurred with tears, an acrid taste in his mouth, weaving between the crowd that was gathered around the stalls offering various kinds of food. The place smelled of fried onions, pizza, grilled meat and hot fat, and as he walked he caught snatches of conversation – this seemed to be a nocturnal race of people who communicated only in monosyllables and in the rumblings of their bellies. Their faces were dazed, tanned or flushed with sickly colour by the garish neon lights. He stepped aside for five guys who came swaggering along, taking up the whole pavement, wearing baseball caps or bandanas in a pathetic attempt to look like American "gangstas". He passed an African woman dressed in a red and gold *bubu*, pushing a buggy with a baby who stared out, wide-eyed at the garish lights and the milling crowds. Two little girls, their hair braided in cornrows, walked alongside, sometimes pressing themselves against her hips.

Through the square, which was marked out like a landing strip with recessed lights, weaved a host of shadows, chattering into mobile telephones, publicly declaiming their most private thoughts, some with the faint blue glow of a Bluetooth headset winking at their ears, others with their heads down, listening to music on their phones. From here and there came cries or laughter in this darkness spangled with lights and teeming with sleepwalkers. Vilar stopped in the middle of the square, its cobblestones transmitted all the heat of the day to the legs of the passers-by and, for a brief second, he had the precise impression of being surrounded by the dead. By a crowd of people who did not realise they had died. Oblivious and sombre, quickly swallowed by the darkness and dispersed into the void. He allowed himself to sink into this vertiginous feeling, his breath coming in gasps, an urge to cry caught in the back of his throat.

Then a boy walked past. Ten years old, maybe, pushing a bicycle that was too big for him.

Pablo. Vilar shuddered at the idea that his son could be right here, alone in the darkness, drifting in limbo, unable to see or hear him, while Vilar could do nothing to bring him back to the light. He felt himself choking, wanted to cry out. He spun around, shook his head in an attempt to ward off this nightmare.

He headed for the bars with their dazzling terraces, not daring to look around him, crossed the street, weaving between the cars, and walked into the first bar he came to which was huge, heaving, deafeningly loud. He tugged the sleeve of a barman who initially tried to extricate himself, arrogant and aggressive, but seeing the man half slumped over the bar, he served Vilar the beer he had ordered. Vilar had to force himself to breathe, otherwise all his internal workings would have stopped dead. In that moment it seemed to him that to stay alive he had to make a conscious effort to breathe, to constantly check his heart was still beating, just as someone in the hold of a sinking ship – he had seen this in films – has to keep working the hand pump that both drains the breath from him even as it prevents him from suffocating.

Breathless, Vilar gulped half of his beer so quickly he had a coughing fit that had him doubled over. When he finally managed to catch
his breath, the thick wall of cotton that had been smothering him had
melted away. Pradeau's pistol, tucked into his belt, was digging into his
back. He thought about the evening, about Sandra de Melo somewhere
out there in the darkness at the mercy of that psychopath, separated
from her son; about the little boy separated from himself, torn away,
torn apart, a boy who right now was bludgeoned by sedatives, thrashing in terrifying sleep. He wondered how Éric – since this seemed to be
his name – would manage to cope with two hostages, one of them a
police officer who would grab the first opportunity to take him down.

He thought again about Pablo, about limbo, about the nightmare
vision that had overwhelmed him in the square, and he knew that if
one day he began to believe in these images, began to talk to them, a
conversation with shadows, he would go mad.

He looked around, because there was nothing else for him to do.

Apart from a couple of old lags sucking in their stomachs to hide
beer bellies while they chatted up drunk students, he had to be the old-
est person in this milling crowd. He listened, but heard only a general
hubbub in which he could not make out a single word, and once again
he had the insistent sensation of being in a foreign country with an
unfamiliar language, a feeling that faded as he gradually came back to
the surface of things, of himself. He could now make out isolated
words, voices, the throaty, sensual laugh of a girl standing behind him.

All this was life. And nothing else. It was this or nothing, perhaps.
These loud, pretentious young people crowded in here to exorcise a
working day, a week of grovelling, self-denial, resentment and humiliation; to forget everything they have been forced to meekly accept; to
drown the insidious sorrows that govern their lives. Young people who
are already resigned, already wrinkled beneath their smooth, glossy
skin, their limber backs already bowed. Reduced to silence, or to the
scarcely articulate gabbling of drunken crowds. Vilar looked at the
laughing faces, the shocks of hair, the bodies of the girls naked under
bodysuits; curvaceous breasts and muscular abs visible through

cropped T-shirts. He saw three or four faces of extraordinary beauty; suddenly he desperately needed a woman, right now; he felt his cock harden in a way it had not done in a long time and he thought about how he would like to grab one of them, fuck her roughly, right here, pounding into her, howling more with rage than with pleasure.

He drained his glass, dropped a five-euro note on the bar and walked away. As he made his way to the door, he brushed against one of these beautiful girls, felt the curves of her body, the heft of her breasts pressed against him. He gently pushed her away, wrestling with the urge to shove his hand between her legs and drag her away with him.

He wandered around for a while, shocked by the violence of his feelings, of his desires, he drifted towards the dark corners of the square past lurking groups of thugs, walked a little way along the cours Pasteur then turned back and walked back down the cours de la Marne oblivious to everyone, paying little attention to the fight that broke out on the opposite pavement, only dimly aware of shouts, jerking movements, a body collapsing into the road. He needed to get back to his car, suddenly overwhelmed by the feeling of being clumsy, drunk, pathetic, his stomach lurching queasily. He slipped behind the steering wheel with a groan of exhaustion and relief and drove off, all the windows rolled up, happy in this silence, this solitude. He crossed the city in his air-conditioned bubble, the radio playing a Mozart concerto he happened upon while flicking through the stations. He allowed himself to be filled with the grace of this music. By the sudden joy that formed like the cool condensation on a glass when you are thirsty.

As he got home and was fumbling in his pockets for his keys, the telephone in his apartment rang. He slammed open the door, crashing through the dark flat, winded and wheezing.

He recognised the voice. He listened.

"It will be all over soon," the man said, "You'll see."

"What do you mean, 'over'?"

"For everyone. You, me. The time we've spent together. This is the moment when everything comes together."

"What about Sandra? What about my partner?"

"It will be over for them too. Don't worry, I'm taking care of it right now. You tried to fuck me over, but you're not in control of anything, you shower of shits. I've been in control, ever since the beginning. Oh, and I've got some stuff about your son. You'll like that."

Vilar had to sit down. He slumped into an armchair, feeling suddenly dizzy. The darkness whirled around him.

"Hey, you listening to me?"

Vilar sought some reserve of air within himself.

"Yeah, I'm listening. One of these days, I'm going to kill you."

"Whatever. But maybe you should wait till you find out about your son, because if I'm dead, you'll never know."

Vilar closed his eyes. The man had stopped speaking. There was nothing now but the hum of electrical static, a meaningless buzzing.

Then, without another word, the call was cut off.

Vilar threw his head back. Tears trickled into his throat.

Late that night, the telephone rang again and immediately a dream came to him in which Ana was saying that they would be home soon and telling him she was about to pass the phone to Pablo, and Vilar, half asleep, leaning over the nightstand, receiver pressed to his ear, smiling at the thought of hearing his son's high-pitched voice, could not understand why Daras was talking to him in a muffled, distant, barely audible voice as though she were calling from the bottom of an abyss; he had to ask her to repeat what she had said.

"They've found Sandra de Melo at the Cité du Grand-Parc. It's not pretty. You have to get here."

19

Victor was sitting in the sweeping shadows cast by the mulberry tree and the oaks at the bottom of the garden where, at this time of the evening, it was so dark that it seemed it was from here that night welled up and spread irresistibly across the face of the earth. He abandoned himself to the muddled thoughts and chaotic images which seemed to sum up his situation. Once again he felt as though he were trapped in a deep hole, with no means of escape. At times the hole seemed to be filling with water, or to be flanked by steep powdery sides where his hands could find no purchase to climb out.

Then he thought about Rebecca, about her hands on him, about what she had allowed him to do, what he had glimpsed. He ran a finger over his lips trying to recapture some trace of the pleasure he had experienced. But he felt nothing, alone and stupid in the silence that had suddenly swelled around him; there was not a breath of air and he looked up at branches of the trees which seemed impossibly still, tried to listen for the sound of the television in the house but heard nothing, not even the noise of the plates clattering in the sink.

When finally he did hear something, it was too late. A hand was clamped over his mouth, a blade pricked at his throat. He recognised the voice whispering in his ear. He smelled the boozy breath that reminded him of the stink of cheap plonk that often hung around the wineries.

"Keep your trap shut. You're coming with me. You know who I am?"

Victor nodded.

"No . . . you don't know. But I know. I'm sure now. I'm your father, you got that? I'm the one who had you with that whore and now you're coming with me."

Victor felt his head being pulled back, the man's hand was still clamped to his mouth so the boy decided not to resist and allowed himself to be dragged backwards, toppling the deckchair where he had been sitting, knocking over a plastic chair. The man was behind him, panting suddenly out of exhaustion or fear, following Victor's footsteps, walking so close behind him that he stumbled and trod on his heels. They moved towards the house, passing the shed where Julien had finally got the engine of his moped working, and Victor remembered the kid's whoops of joy that almost drowned out the backfire from the engine as he sprang from his den, stripped to the waist, slick with oil and sweat, coughing and spluttering from a cloud of exhaust fumes that looked as though they were coming from a big diesel truck rather than a moped. He recalled these whoops of joy perfectly now, the reek of engine oil, he could see Marilou hugging the kid, kissing and congratulating him like a little brother.

Victor felt nothing. Neither fear nor anger. He tried to understand what was happening, but things were moving too quickly. All he knew was that he was drifting away. Everything suddenly seemed distant, remote. He was sorry it was dark because he would have liked to see the world flash past.

As they passed the terrace and the golden glow that streamed from the open French window, Victor heard the familiar sounds of evening, Denis' voice, loud and clear, saying to everyone "Hey, come look at what this guy's doing on the telly," and Victor was not sure whether he wanted someone to suddenly burst through the door and save him, chase this evil bastard out of his life or whether he wanted them to stay inside, safe and happy in this beautiful summer evening. The familiar sounds died away and Victor quickly found himself out on the road in the gathering dusk, faintly lit by a distant streetlamp. The man pushed him towards a large estate car whose make Victor did not recognise, but he thought it might be the car he had thrown stones at the other day. The man stopped when he clicked open the vast boot filled with boxes, bags and tins, he hesitated and Victor felt the grip on his mouth and his throat ease a little, but he did nothing that might anger the man or arouse his suspicion, he forced himself to remain completely still. He was terrified that someone might come out into the garden – probably Denis, who was always worrying where the kids were at night – might call him, come out to the gate and see what was going on, might see this guy trying to bundle a boy into his car, rush over and get into a fight or – worse – the guy might turn round at the last minute and stick the knife into Denis' chest, so Victor let himself be manhandled, he tried to imagine Marilou and Julien sitting wide-eyed in front of the television with Nicole and Denis commenting on what was happening because someone on television was clearly doing something extraordinary, almost beyond belief, and he knew that this peaceful world was over now, that one way or another, he would be done for.

"You scream or make any sudden move and I'll cut your throat," the voice behind him said. "I don't give a fuck."

The man took his hand from Victor's mouth, reached into the boot to get a roll of duct tape, which meant he had to let go of the boy, keeping him pressed against the bumper only by the weight of his body, struggling to locate the end of the tape.

Victor did not know what the man had done with the knife, but he knew he needed to use both hands to unroll the tape so he drove his elbow back hard and the man staggered back in surprise, allowing Victor to run out onto the road away from the village. As he turned away, he could clearly see the house he was leaving behind and he thought about the people inside, happy that he was able to keep them out of this. He heard the man curse and run after him, then dash back to his car. As he heard the engine start up, Victor came to the little path he and Rebecca had taken a few nights earlier, he plunged down the embankment as the utter darkness closed its huge jaws around him. He made no attempt to get his bearings, he simply ran across the soil rutted by tractor tyres and when he felt the ground rise again he stopped to catch his breath and listen, but he could hear nothing save the silence of the night pierced by stars with a pink moon rising over the estuary. He realised he could make out the shadowy mass of the vines and the dark track of the path running gently uphill from here. Feeling thirsty, he picked a heavy bunch of grapes, feeling each one with his fingers and eating only those that were soft and ripe. He loved the taste of the sweet juice filling his mouth and he walked on more slowly now, almost calm, hearing nothing but the night wind whispering in the vines.

He carried on walking with no concept of time, skirting around the vast fields of the vineyards, along paths that criss-crossed one another; the moon, rising behind him, cast the faintest shadows that alerted him to any obstacles he had to negotiate, the furrows or the hillocks where he might trip and fall on all fours, pricking his hands on the brambles or thistles. His feet were bare, he had been wearing only a pair of old espadrilles that Nicole insisted they use when coming and going between the garden and the house, but the canvas had ripped while he was running so that they barely stayed on his feet, and more than once he had to hop around in the dark looking for the one that had come off.

His only thought was to move forward. The darkness made him invisible and this entirely suited his desire to vanish, to cease to exist, to be able to watch unseen, as the dead do, perhaps, to eavesdrop on what others say about you, to know their secrets, to be close to them without their knowledge. He plunged into the balmy darkness and felt weightless.

Then he stopped. He thought about his mother, he had left her behind, and his heart beat wildly as he pictured the urn in his wardrobe. "Manou," he said aloud, "Manou, I'm not leaving you, I'll come back to get you. You saw the guy. I had to run, I had to." Once again he waited several seconds for her answer, but there was nothing but the wind tickling his neck.

After a while, his legs began to tremble each time he needed them to jump a ditch or a stream, and he wondered where he was going to sleep. He scrambled up another bank and found himself on a narrow tarmac road, which he thought he recognised from having cycled this way once or twice – to the right, it led down to the estuary. He was afraid of that expanse of water gliding in the dark, afraid that it would swallow him up or carry him away, so he turned left and walked uphill for about a hundred metres, then cut back into the vines. He was hurrying now and turned his ankle in a rut, breathless and aching and suddenly so exhausted that he wanted to lie down and try to sleep, but when he felt the rough, dry grass prick his hands and his knees, felt the soil radiate the accumulated heat of the day against his skin, he gave a disappointed groan and limped on.

Further on, just as the moon disappeared behind a wisp of fog, he almost ran straight into a trailer lying in the field; the boy hoisted himself into the back and lay down on the rough bare boards. He peeled off his shirt, rolled it into a pillow and the moment he lay down on his stomach and pressed his cheek to it, he was asleep.

20

If Sandra de Melo was not dead, it was only because an old woman out walking her dog at about 1.00 a.m. had started screaming when she saw the guy kicking and punching something she dimly recognised as a human being, Only as she drew closer did she realise it was a woman. The yapping dog had dragged its arthritic mistress towards the hulking figure who was raining blows on the broken body that jerked and twitched but made no sound. The man had made his escape in a large estate car of unknown make, possibly grey – the old lady had very bad eyesight, and had been unable to make out anything at all of the number plate.

When the ambulance arrived, Sandra was lying curled up in a gutter, her head in a pool of blood. The paramedics quickly noticed a deep wound to the occipital bone and several fractures to the face – the nose, the jaw, the supraorbital arch – and diagnosed an intracranial haemorrhage. Her heart stopped beating but was restarted with a defibrillator. Vilar, who arrived just as she was being lifted into the ambulance, did not recognise the misshapen face with the bruised and swollen eyes, the split lip. He felt as though he were seeing Nadia as she had been on the day her body was found. Once more, the two women seemed determined to merge into one, but when he commented about this to Daras she shrugged and turned angrily away.

"I don't give a damn about your disturbing insights, Pierre. I want this bastard stopped right now, do you understand? He kills, he murders victims, he kidnaps one of ours, shit, this guy didn't get to be who he is in the space of a month. He has form, he's got a record and I'm guessing not just for assault. Jesus Christ, I want a name at the very least, and before tomorrow night."

She was trembling. For all the horrendous crime scenes the two of them had witnessed together, Vilar had never seen her so distraught. Without waiting for a response, she walked over to where Mégrier and his men were cordoning off the area and, since there was a whole team working the scene, Vilar decided to go home.

He had driven, oblivious to the chaotic tangle of cars around him, with the sensation of slowly emerging from the weight of this muggy night, as though stepping through a curtain of cobwebs which were impossible to brush away, that dusty glue that sticks to the hair, clings to the eyelids, the filthy hands, the futile gestures. He had slept for two or three hours with no dreams, no nightmares: perhaps, realising that he was exhausted, his little ghost had decided to leave him in peace for once. He had taken a barely lukewarm shower, drunk half a cafetière of coffee and polished off a packet of sponge fingers and felt almost fine by the time he went down to the garage to find himself in his car, out on the street, back in this city where he could no longer bring himself to look at anything. He needed a cigarette, and indeed would have liked another coffee and something to eat to go with it, he desperately wished he were anywhere but here, behind this steering wheel, and he tried not to think about the place he would like to be, because it was too far away and there was no way back.

He called the hospital. Sandra was still in a coma. The charge nurse in the intensive care unit, who spoke in a gentle, slightly weary voice, told him not to give up hope, that sometimes they saw catastrophic situations improve in a matter of hours. For the moment, the patient was stable. It was a promising sign that her condition had not deteriorated. They would have to wait. When she did not say anything else, Vilar suggested a time frame, though he knew it was pointless.

"Forty-eight hours?"

"Yes, that's about right. Let's say forty-eight hours. Well, if you'll excuse me, someone's calling on the other line."

She had already hung up by the time he could say thank you. From what little he could guess of the extent of Sandra's injuries, Vilar started weighing up her chances of surviving, and the long-term consequences if she did manage to pull through. He set the mobile down on the passenger seat and weaved between a parked bus and a truck that sat on the edge of a vast building site that had transformed this part of the ring road into a disaster area. He turned onto the cours de Médoc, slowing to a crawl in the early rush hour traffic. He called the station and discovered that Pradeau was still missing. They were moving heaven and earth to find him. "But given what he did to the girl, who knows what that fucker has done to Laurent. Everyone's really worried," Ledru said, a young lieutenant whom Vilar liked – somewhat nervous, but always reliable. "Otherwise, there are three of us combing through prison records for a con named Éric released between '92 and '94."

"And?"

"So far, we've got seventy-six. We're cross-referencing against the crimes they were banged up for."

Vilar got him to promise he would call the minute they found something.

"Daras was looking for you five minutes ago," Ledru said.

"I'm on the cours Balguerie. I'll be there as soon as I can be. Tell her. She'll know what I mean."

The studio flat Nadia had used could not have been more than twenty square metres. Vilar sat in a corner watching the forensics team from l'Identité judiciaire taking prints and bagging evidence. At present, all he could hear was their surprise at the lack of any useable prints.

"Someone's scrubbed this place spotless," Lopez said after about five minutes, holding up a fingerprint brush. "We'll see what we can get, but it doesn't look promising. It's like being in a sterile laboratory."

The interviews with the neighbours had produced nothing: no-one had seen or heard anything. No particular comings and goings. The studio was on the first floor, making it easy to enter or leave without anyone else noticing. The police had found two champagne bottles in the fridge, a few snacks in the cupboards, two glass champagne flutes and some plastic tumblers and plates. In the bathroom, there were some clean towels. A tube of toothpaste but no toothbrush, some cotton buds and a dried-out bar of soap.

Vilar tried to get in touch with the owner of the building, and only reached his secretary. She tried to contact her boss on his mobile, Vilar could hear her talking on the other line, but could not understand what she was saying, perhaps because she had put her hand over the receiver or stood up to use her mobile. When she came back on the line, she told him that he could dial the number she was about to give him and Monsieur Vacher would answer straight away. Vilar rang off without saying goodbye and dialled the number.

He could hear machinery, men's voices, banging, a plank falling, an engine starting up. A voice yelled down the line asking who was calling. When Vilar introduced himself, the man told him he was looking for a quieter place to talk because just now he was on a building site. And suddenly the racket faded and he stopped shouting.

Vilar explained to him that a studio flat in his building on the cours Balguerie had been rented by a woman engaged in prostitution, and that he needed more information because there was no record among Nadia Fournier's papers of any rent having been paid.

"That's probably because I never received any rent for that studio, monsieur."

"May I ask why?"

"Because it hasn't been rented for the past seven or eight months. I've been planning to do some work on it – the place is old-fashioned and doesn't meet the typical standard of luxury in the area. So, to be honest, I'm wondering what you're talking about."

There was no trace of irritation in Monsieur Vacher's tone. He sounded polite and surprised, and Vilar decided to be tactful because he sensed something was about to open up beneath his feet. Perhaps, as he expected, some kind of pit with an unpalatable truth at the bottom.

"I am in your studio right now, Monsieur Vacher, with two forensics officers, because the person who was living here was murdered two months ago. Which is another reason I find this story of a phantom tenant a little hard to credit."

"She was murdered in the flat?" Vacher shrieked.

"No. But she was present in the flat on various occasions, as I said earlier."

"This is dreadful. The poor girl . . . But she hadn't been squatting, there was no forced entry? Nothing damaged?"

"The place is immaculate. There's not so much as a fingerprint."

"But I don't get it. A.C.I. didn't get in touch with me, something they usually do if they've rented out one of my properties. Honestly, I don't . . ."

"A.C.I.? And who are they?"

"Aquitaine Conseil Immobilier. They're reliable people, they manage all my properties. You have to understand, when you're a property owner . . ."

"Thierry Lataste runs the company, doesn't he?"

"Yes, he's the managing director. Do you know him?"

"A little."

Vilar cut short the conversation so he could calmly think things through. Before hanging up, Vacher expressed the hope that all this was not going to cause him any problems. Vilar reassured him, slipped the mobile back into his pocket and stared, without really seeing, at the two technicians packing away their equipment.

"We haven't got much," Lopez said. "Couple of hairs, half a thumb-print . . . We ran the forensics vacuum to pick up any trace evidence, but I tell you, I'd like the telephone number of their cleaning woman, I'd give her a couple of hours' work around my house. Even cleaned the U-bend, if you can believe that."

When they were gone, Vilar sat on the edge of the bed and looked around him at the banal décor: the wall at the head of the bed plastered with a huge poster of mountains, the thin, rough, royal blue carpet, the two armchairs upholstered in bottle-green velvet.

He stood up and covered the bed that his colleagues had unmade in order to run the vacuum cleaner. A telephone rang and rang somewhere in the building, but no-one answered. Outside the window he saw a small courtyard with a climbing rose. Virginia creeper covered one wall. Somewhere a pigeon was cooing. Vilar looked up at the misty sky where the sun was already beginning to swelter. The room was pervaded by a vague smell of dust, dirty laundry and other things he did not recognise. He tried to imagine how things would play out with Lataste, struggled to find the words that would shut him up, preferably in front of witnesses so he would be forced to back down. He called directory enquiries for the number of A.C.I. and dialled it to make sure that Lataste was there.

He was working in his glass-walled office which looked out onto five or six cubicles, divided with partitions, within which people were busy making money for the business. He recognised Vilar immediately, blushed and leapt to his feet to come and meet him, hand outstretched, a cardboard smile pasted on his face. The policeman was about to take out his I.D. when Lataste moved to stop him, assuring him that he recognised him, that there was no need, glancing around him, but Vilar ignored the gesture and flashed his warrant card. "Commandant Vilar, police," he said, and felt a wave ripple around the office and in each cubicle voices dropped to a whisper or fell silent, the click of fingers on computer keyboards slowed.

Lataste led him into his office and closed the door. He offered Vilar a seat, sat down himself and the smile vanished from his face like a mask that had suddenly crumbled to dust.

"What's going on?" he said.

He seemed genuinely worried. He was better at feigning panic than nonchalance and Vilar felt like wiping the stage make-up from his face.

"Did I hear you right?" he said. "You're asking me what's going on?"

"Of course! You show up here unannounced, let everyone know you're with the police, trying to embarrass me a little more, so I think I've got the right to know why, don't you?"

Vilar stared at him hard, at once puzzled and astonished. He did not know whether this guy had the nerve of a true gangster or whether he was completely reckless and stupid.

"Are you familiar with a studio apartment at 145 cours Balguerie belonging to Monsieur Jean-Philippe Vacher? I'm guessing you remember Nadia Fournier, with whom you had a relationship for several months and who was murdered early in June? Well, this is what's going on: we've just discovered that Nadia was using that studio flat to meet clients, because as I'm sure you're aware she frequently worked as a prostitute. And we discovered that she paid no rent for that studio flat because, apparently, it was provided to her by Aquitaine Conseil Immobilier. And since I suppose you are the only person at A.C.I. who knew her, I have inferred, somewhat simplistically I'll grant you, that you may have, let's say, committed a breach of normal practice in your profession and loaned this studio, located in a building managed by you, to Nadia, so that you could meet her there and so that she could more easily carry on her professional activities. Do you have any comment you would like to make? Have I made any mistakes, left anything out?"

He reeled off this long speech without pause, knowing that in doing so he was suffocating Lataste. The man had slumped back in his seat, arms clamped to the armrests, and was staring at the calendar hanging on the wall behind Vilar.

"Monsieur Lataste?"

"No, no mistake. It's all true."

He took a paperclip from the desk which he began bending and twisting.

"So what's the problem?" he asked after a few seconds.

Vilar shivered. An ominous shudder ran down his back and through his limbs. He wanted to step around the desk and slap this son of a bitch. Or maybe smash his face. Violently. Leave him bruised and battered on the floor, blood streaming from his mouth, his nose broken. He took a deep breath then got to his feet and opened the door.

"The problem," Vilar said in a loud, clear voice, "is that in the eyes of the law you are a pimp. To be more precise, you are the pimp of a murdered woman and that makes you an obvious suspect. And there's more: I believe you lied to me during our first interview to conceal the fact you were implicated in this murder. That's the problem. So now, you're going to get up and come with me to the police station where I plan to detain you for questioning. Now, Monsieur Lataste, I'd be grateful if you could come with me without offering any resistance."

Vilar took out his handcuffs and showed them to the man who got to his feet, deathly pale, his face glistening.

"Couldn't you spare me that?" he whispered.

Vilar gestured for him to put his hands behind his back.

"I could, but I don't want to. I don't trust you an inch and the only respect I owe you is that set down by law for the treatment of suspects."

The man turned around and proffered his wrists. Vilar snapped the handcuffs shut.

When they got to the station, Vilar led Lataste to his office, empty at this hour, and handcuffed him to the wall, then went to ask where he might find Daras. He was told that she had rushed off to the quai de la Souys because the headless body of a woman had been discovered on the riverbank. Vilar remembered the body that had been found by a rambler by the river behind a shopping centre in Bègles. The woman, who was very young, had been decapitated, almost certainly with an axe given the deep impact wounds on her shoulders and upper back. They had still not managed to identify her. Daras had come to the conclusion that she was probably a prostitute from Eastern Europe, but their investigations among the pimps and the working girls in Bordeaux had led to nothing more than a handful of undocumented immigrants being deported, something even the requirements of an ongoing police inquiry had been unable to prevent.

Vilar found Lataste leaning against the wall next to the metal ring to which he was handcuffed, massaging his wrist with a grimace of pain.

"O.K.," Vilar said. "Let's get this over with quickly because I think you've wasted enough of my time already. Question one: why did you lie to me the last time we spoke?"

"Because I was scared."

"Scared?"

"Yes, scared. Do you never get scared?"

"No. Never. Now answer my question: why did you lie?"

"When I found out Nadia was dead, I knew my whole life could come crashing down. My wife, my kids . . . I knew I'd ruined everything and I was terrified of losing it all . . . I don't know . . . I was trying to put on a brave face, slip through the net maybe."

"How old are you?"

"Thirty-six."

"At thirty-six, you're still behaving like a kid who thinks that if he covers his eyes no-one can see him, is that it?"

Lataste looked down. He was still rubbing his wrists. Vilar got to his feet, removed the cuffs and offered him some water. He went to fill two cups from the water cooler humming in a corner of his office. Lataste drained his cup in one. He took two or three deep breaths, then tears began to roll down his cheeks. Vilar also drank, his throat felt dry and sandy, and he went back to the dispenser. Proffering another cup, he asked Lataste what was the matter.

"Nothing," he said with some effort, swallowing hard. "Just that cold water. It's so simple, so good."

Vilar observed him and had the distinct impression he was witnessing a man in free fall. He had seen men fall before, but never from such a height. A slow-motion plunge that he could not bring himself to think of as tragic. He let Lataste finish the cup of water and decided not to wait until this guy collapsed in on himself like those fierce galaxies that become black holes.

"Right now, you will certainly be charged with procuring, passively at least, since in the eyes of the law you were providing accommodation to someone working as a prostitute. Secondly, I think I can say officially you are a suspect in the murder of your lover Nadia Fournier. I have to agree with your observation that your life is completely fucked. Aggravated murder can get you fifteen years because, as it turns out, being her pimp is an aggravating factor in the crime. Do you understand?"

Lataste nodded.

"I know who killed Nadia," he said so quietly, so quickly that Vilar, sitting up in his chair, had to ask him to repeat himself.

"His name is Éric Sanz. He's married. His wife's name is Céline, he has a daughter called Manon."

Vilar picked up the phone and called Ledru.

"O.K., I think we've got him. Éric Sanz. S-A-N-Z, yes. Can you check that immediately? And put out a call for a Céline Sanz."

He hung up. Lataste was now staring at him, his eyes still red.

"Do tell me about it," Vilar said, "and be very careful what you say."

He did not know how to breathe to remove the weight pressing on his chest. His heart was pounding so hard that he could feel it in his spine.

"He's this guy, he kind of stalked her. She'd slept with him once but when she told him it was over, he wasn't having it. First thing I thought was that he was the one who had killed her. That's why I was scared."

"He knew you? He was aware of your existence?"

"In theory, no. Nadia said she had never mentioned me to him. But with a guy like that you never know. He could have decided – I don't know – to cover his tracks, to get rid of anyone who could identify him, that kind of thing happens."

"How did she come to mention him to you? I thought she had her life pretty neatly compartmentalised?"

"It's complicated . . . I . . . She knew his ex-wife, Éric had nothing to do with her anymore, and she and the kid were having a rough time of it. Nadia asked me if I could find the wife somewhere to stay because they were living in a trailer in Mérignac. She had a job – I think she worked as a cleaner at the airport. Since I've got a mate who works at Habitat Girondin, I gave him a call and he managed to sort something. His company had just evicted a family with two years' rent arrears in Mérignac, so as long as she was prepared to take the apartment as is, with no work done on it, he was prepared to let her have it straight away. And—"

"This mate's name?"

"Why do you want to know? You're not going to hassle him, are you?"

"Like I said, we cross-check everything. Mate's name?"

"Jérôme Fontan."

Vilar wrote down the name on a piece of paper already criss-crossed with notes.

"What did Nadia tell you about this guy Sanz?"

"She said he was really violent, that he'd beaten her in the past . . . That he'd been banged up for it . . . For that kind of thing, I mean. She said he was a bit sadistic in his tastes. He liked to humiliate people, and when that wasn't enough, when he got pissed off about something, he'd lash out. And he'd got the idea into his head that he was going to take her away somewhere, some island, and run a bar or a restaurant, I don't remember. Some friend of his had money invested over there – Martinique, I think it was. He used to hassle her about that. She was completely petrified of him, she thought about leaving the area to get away from him, but it was difficult, what with her son. She managed to postpone this whole Martinique thing by saying she had to put her son first, and that seemed to work, Sanz didn't push it, but she knew it wouldn't last, that he'd always find some new way to try to persuade her. One day, he even told her that the kid was his son. It was another idea he got into his head. Apparently he wouldn't stop talking about the kid."

Vilar tried to remember the face of the boy, Victor. He remembered the frail body lying in a hospital bed, the trembling figure standing next to the coffin as it rolled towards the crematorium furnace in the whirring silence. But no face appeared on the moving screen of memory.

"What did Nadia think about that? Did she think it was possible?"

"She never said anything to me. All I know is she got scared, she thought he was losing it, he was completely obsessed. I told Nadia I'd help her, told her I knew people all over the place and I could find her a place to live, even a job, in Brittany or Normandy for example, I've got a couple of friends in senior positions who would have been able to pull some strings. But she wasn't sure. She was waiting until she'd saved enough money to leave and start over. Nadia liked to dream, she was always coming up with these hare-brained ideas. She thought it was possible to start your life over, to begin again from scratch. That's what she wanted for the kid . . ."

He trailed off, shook his head angrily, staring into space. He spoke of Nadia warmly, almost tenderly.

"How did you feel when you heard that she'd been killed?"

Lataste did not answer immediately. He snorted and shrugged.

"I was afraid, I think. Not so much for me, I mean, not for my own safety, but for the life I'd built with Mireille, my daughters . . . I knew it was the beginning of the end . . . That one way or another this whole affair would catch up with me."

"So why make things worse by withholding evidence?"

"I don't know. I panicked. I was trying to plug the holes on a sinking ship."

Vilar looked at the man slumped in the chair, hands folded in his lap, and remembered the arrogant executive who had welcomed him in his hallway that first time, who had tried to send him packing him like some vacuum cleaner salesman. He remembered the body in the morgue, and the man's impassiveness even in the face of the cold rage and the contempt of his wife and he felt an urge to grab him by the scruff of the neck and slam him against the wall just as he had that day in order to take him down a peg or two. He forced himself to take a deep breath, to stare at a poster on the wall in which an emerald river snaked through thick jungle, and he told himself that one day he would canoe through that lush vegetation. So he stifled the rage welling inside him and found the strength to say in a flat voice:

"If you'd said something sooner, a woman wouldn't be in a coma in intensive care right now, an officer with the *police judiciaire* would not have been abducted; instead, we know that Éric Sanz abducted them. And I can tell you right now, that if anything fatal happens to either of them, you'll pay for it, and you'd better hope you don't run into me in a corridor, or even in jail, because I'll smash your fucking face. Do you understand? Doesn't matter that I'm police, doesn't matter about the law, I'll make you pay for your lies and your silence and I'll do everything in my power to have you formally charged with procuring, for obstruction of justice and for sheltering a criminal, since by your silence, as you yourself just admitted, you protected him. And if either of the people I've just mentioned dies, we can add manslaughter. You were scared you might fuck up your life? Congratulations, job done."

"Why are you talking to me like that? What did I ever do to you?"

"To me? Nothing. I don't give a fuck. No-one can hurt me anymore. As for the rest, I just told you."

Vilar stared at Lataste who was staring at nothing, his eyes fixed on the clutter of notices pinned to the wall. He was slumped in the chair, his shoulders drooping, his suit suddenly seemed too big for him.

He glanced at his watch.

"I'd like to call home. I know I don't have the right, but . . ."

Vilar pushed the telephone across the desk, and Lataste dialled a number.

"Clem? It's Papa. How's my big girl? What did you have for dinner? Was it nice? And how was school today?"

He stared out of the window as he listened to his daughter's answers, a smile on his face, with the slightly inane expression of a zealot talking to God. He asked his daughter how her little sister was, said sweet, silly things and all Vilar could hear was the catch in his voice, something his daughter clearly heard too because at one point Lataste had to reassure her that he was fine, that everything was fine, then had to admit that Maman would explain everything. "Can you put Maman on the phone for me? Yes, darling. Big kiss . . . Yes, I promise."

He wiped his eyes with the back of his hand and shifted the receiver to his other ear. There was a tightness in his voice now that choked the air out of the end of his sentences, the words faded and he had to clear his throat and start over.

"Was it Caroline who called you? Yes . . . since eleven o'clock. Here at the police station, you know, opposite the skating rink. Yes, that's right. His name is Commandant Vilar. Yes . . . Call Sylvain, see if he knows any criminal lawyers, because he works mostly in corporate and company law . . . I don't know. No . . . It's not good . . . I've got myself involved in a nasty business with that girl who was . . ."

He fell silent. Listened to what his wife was saying. He closed his eyes, nodding his head regularly every time another blow hit home.

Vilar remembered the small, hard inscrutable face of Lataste's wife, the strained jaw muscles.

"Slag me off if it makes you feel better, what do you want me to say? But there's something else . . . apparently, because I didn't tell the c—" He hesitated, then went on, ". . . didn't tell the police everything, a whole bunch of other shit happened. It's a complete clusterfuck . . . Yeah, all because I didn't say anything . . . Of course I've told them everything now. There's nothing I can say to defend myself, Mireille . . . When will I get out? When do you think I'll get out?"

He was breathing hard through his nose, his eyes filled with tears.

"Listen to me, Mireille, listen to me . . . You hate me, you despise me, fine, I can understand that, but don't tell the girls I'm a bastard, they're only little, let them keep their father more or less intact, I might be a swine, but I'm not a complete bastard. Please don't tell them that . . ."

He listened to her answer. His eyes and his nose were streaming, he did nothing to dry his face so that he looked like a small child so distraught it becomes little more than a paroxysm of tears and snot. "I . . . I love you . . . I love you all," he stammered and slowly hung up, his hand still resting on the receiver, whimpering. Vilar told him to calm down, then called an officer to take him to the cells because he had seen enough, had enough of listening to this guy whine about himself, about his fucked-up life, his ruined career, what his kids would think of him, and because Vilar knew that people often feel self-pity because they are afraid to die or because they are forced to live, and we see ourselves weeping and sometimes it appeals to us, this tragic stature we think we attain in such situations, as though finally we have found our place in the endless, shifting vortex of the tribulations of this world.

When Lataste had finally left, and the office was silent once more, Vilar tried to call Daras but was told that she was on her way back to the station having stopped off at the court. As soon as he hung up, the telephone rang. It was Ledru.

"We've tracked down the wife. Well, when I say wife . . . They're not married. Her name is Céline Bosc, she lives in Mérignac, at Résidence Paul-Éluard, Apartment 28, Block D."

Vilar had the man's name, an address, almost a whole family. He could see a figure begin to form around the mocking voice that had been hounding him; soon he knew he would put a face to the voice. He felt the man was close, almost within his grasp. It was a feeling he had had once before, in Paris while tailing a suspect in the *métro*, a serial rapist: Vilar was standing right behind him, less than two metres away, inhaling the clouds of cheap aftershave the suspect had a habit of wearing.

He reread the note he had jotted on the piece of paper: "I'm coming, you little shit, I'm coming."

21

The sky widened as it paled, and racing towards the daylight from the west a vast flock of clouds came galloping, their flanks first bronze, then pink, then blood red, fleeing some terrible massacre that had just occurred. From where he was lying, on his back, his head against his rolled-up shirt, Victor could see nothing of the world but this massive heavenly exodus. As he sat up, there suddenly appeared the quivering outline of a small thicket of trees in which he could hear birds bickering. He sat on the rough boards of the trailer and, feeling cold, slipped on his shirt and hugged himself as he watched the daylight bleach away the last blue wisps of night. The silence was broken by cries and birdsong, Victor could hear the occasional car passing on the invisible road at the foot of the hill, the gusts of cool air sweeping in from the estuary without disturbing the neat rows of vines in between the trellises.

He heaved a loud sigh. He felt at home here, beneath the sky now wreathed with light, completely alone, and far away. He would have liked to stay right here, completely still, and wait for the heat to pour down on him and wash away the early morning chill that clung to him. He noticed that since he had woken, he had not thought about anything, that no memories had come to him, as though his mind had been wiped clean under the star-strewn blanket of darkness which had kept him warm, and whose powdery glow had startled him when he woke in the night, disoriented, bathed in sweat. Knowing only who he was. This was something he had never felt before, this sensation of time suspended, a pure instant in a world that might easily have stopped turning.

He lay down again, arms behind his head. His chest heaved with two or three sobs that caught in his throat and which he managed to dispel by breathing deeply though his mouth to catch his breath.

A laugh rang out in the distance, clear. A pretty, girlish laugh. And shouting.

Rebecca. Marilou. It all came back to him. It was not over.

He jumped down from the trailer, his feet raising a little puff of dust as he hit the ground and immediately he felt the heavy heat, slick on his neck. He turned away from the village and ran towards the other side of the hill, heading north. He arrived at a small tarmac road that ran down to the estuary and he set off that way, panting for breath, his stomach rumbling, with a craving for hot chocolate or cereal that made him slow his pace as he passed an isolated house and imagined the people inside sitting around the breakfast table. As he ran along a fence, a dog suddenly hurled itself against the chicken wire with a shrill bark that made him jump. He kicked out at the wire, hitting the dog on the snout, sending it bounding away shaking its head.

He walked on, and felt in his legs the heat already radiating from the tarred road. The air was still and the sky had the glossy whiteness of metal. Before he saw it, he could smell the estuary, the stench of mud that forever hung over it. Then, behind a curtain of trees, he glimpsed the glassy, murky water and raced to get into the shade. When he arrived at the water's edge, he sat at the bottom of the bank so he could not be seen from the road and he watched as, with not a ripple or an eddy, the vast coffee-coloured torrent ran sluggishly to spill into the sea.

He tried to get his bearings. The nuclear power plant was just to his right, shimmering white in the sun. There were a few fishermen's shacks like the one where he and Julien had fired pebbles at the river rats, but he remembered that they had cycled a long way that day. He knew the village was south of here, to his right. He enjoyed orientation, liked always knowing where the cardinal points were. It was something his mother had taught him. All the time she would ask him: "Which direction is Marseille, where I'm from? What about Paris? So if we go there some day, you'll know which direction it is." And he would answer without hesitation, proud and happy to know his place in the world. More often than not, not far from her.

Cars passed from time to time on the narrow road that ran behind him and he wondered if the police were looking for him and whether they might search along the riverbanks, so he climbed down the bank to the water's edge and watched the lapping of the water between the withered reeds and rubbish covered over with a crust of dried mud. He sat on a tree trunk that had been washed up at high tide and contemplated the indomitable force of the river which seemed capable of carrying off all the soil with it, washing everything away to leave nothing but sharp, jagged rocks. Before long, sleep overcame him and he dozed off, his head resting on his knees.

He was woken by the banging of a gate and lurched unsteadily to his feet, then threw himself on the ground next to the tree stump, amid the tall, prickly grass. From here he could see the top of the bank and the strip of sky beyond and, framed against the light, he saw the figure of a man who stood, staring down at the river's edge, glancing to left and right. He moved his hands from his hips to his flies and began to piss, sighing with relief. Victor shrank back, afraid the stream would reach him, disgusted at the sight and at the splashing sound it made as it hit the ground, of the repulsive, ridiculous lump of flesh the man was now shaking with a sort of groan.

The car drove off and the boy looked around him at the debris washed up on the shore by the river. Dead trees, branches, twigs, reeds, hunks of plastic, shoes; he realised he was reduced to hiding out in this rubbish tip after the magical night that, despite his fear, he had spent in the open, in that crystalline solitude. He spun around several times and knew that everything here was dead, and indeed would soon be buried beneath the patient shroud of water gorged with mud. He thought about the dead dog he had found one day with Julien and Marilou, a gaping carcass crawling with vermin that had made them start back in horror, then creep forward in spite of the smell, hands clamped over their mouths, so they could see the devastation washed up by the high tide. Suddenly he was afraid to stay where he was. From time to time a sickly stench caught in his throat and filled his mouth with a taste of putrefaction he could not spit out. He climbed a little way back up the bank and listened to the murmur of the water. A mute, relentless keening, almost a shriek. Here and there were large eddies. The tide was rising; this was the ocean's unceasing effort to plug this current of shit, to prevent itself being polluted. Victor pictured a convoluted struggle between two mythological giants of the sort he had been told were merely hidden forces constantly at work in the world.

He came back to the road, but he did not know what to do. He felt as though he had escaped the insidious threat of putrefaction, but here, in the dazzling sunshine, he was at the mercy of those who were looking for him. He dashed across the road, jumped the ditch and plunged into a dense thicket of acacia trees and brambles. He could just make out an overgrown path which he followed, gingerly at first for fear of snakes, then running hard to escape their fangs. He came to a dirt track that ran along a vineyard and he stepped with relief between two rows of vines from which he once more picked a handful of grapes that were nearly black, and whose sweet juice hit the spot. He rubbed them on his shirt to remove the sulphate and examined the firm, glistening berries before biting into them.

He could hear the whirr of tractors, the sound of voices shouting or calling. He dodged between the vines, ran past the storehouses, inhaling the pungent smell of wine, then found himself at the foot of the water tower that dominated the village and the estuary. He tried to pinpoint the house, wondering what Marilou and Julien would be doing now and whether Rebecca had eaten lunch alone again with her mother sprawled on the sofa in front of the television.

A cold hand gripped his heart, alternately shaking it and stopping it from beating. He thought about her, alone in the wardrobe. The secret glow of the urn that such a long time spent in darkness might have extinguished forever.

He blindly ran down the hill, his eyes filled with tears. Before he came to the road, he turned left and ran on, hidden by the vines. There was a high-clearance tractor up ahead. He could just make out the driver, stripped to the waist and wearing a red cap, amid the blue clouds of sulphate. As he approached the village, he could already hear a dog barking. He hunkered down in a ditch and waited until there were no cars, then dashed across and ran to the nearest house. He leaned against the back of a truck, catching his breath.

Just as he stepped onto the pavement, he saw four police vans drive past followed by a covered lorry. He knew what was happening. He had seen searches for missing children on the news. The officers would move forward in a line through fields and woodland with dogs on leashes. He knew that within half an hour he would not be able to move without being recognised. Rebecca's house was nearby, so he ran there, rushed inside and stood, pressed against the front door trying to think.

Suddenly he saw her at the far end of the hall, a cigarette dangling from her fingers. She was wearing shorts and a sleeveless T-shirt, her hair had fallen over her face. She brushed it away.

"Shit, I was wondering who it was. What the fuck are you doing? Everyone's looking for you. Come on!"

She dragged him into her bedroom. From the sofa, her mother called to ask who was at the door.

"No-one. Go back to sleep."

She locked the bedroom door behind her, sat on a garden chair piled high with cushions, jerked her chin towards the bed and Victor sat down.

"What happened? Marilou told me some guy came and kidnapped you, everyone thinks you're with some paedo or something. Can you believe it? She saw the car drive off and she was crying when she called to tell me about it."

Victor shuddered.

"You got anything to eat?"

"Don't move."

She came back three minutes later carrying a tray with a bottle of milk and a packet of biscuits. Victor painfully swallowed the saliva flooding his mouth. Rebecca took a biscuit and handed him the packet.

He wolfed them down two at a time and washed them down with long gulps of milk.

"I've got to go back and get my mother's urn. I can't leave her like that."

"The feds will be looking for you everywhere, you'll be lucky to go to the bog without them finding you. You have to go back and explain everything – don't you realise Nicole and Denis think you're dead, or that some fucking pervert is molesting you, Jesus, you can't let them go on worrying."

Rebecca picked up her phone.

"I'll call them and they'll come get you, O.K.? That way you don't have to go back and be all ashamed."

"I'm out of here." He got up and stepped towards the door, but Rebecca grabbed his arm and he liked the feel of her hand around his wrist. She was standing next to him.

"I just need to go back and get her," he said in a whisper. "Don't tell on me, Rebecca, please."

She snapped her phone shut and looked at him seriously. He sat down again, brushing away a tear with the back of his hand, drank a little more milk. It left him with a white moustache and Rebecca came over and ran a fingertip along his upper lip, then she leaned down and kissed him tenderly.

"You're so sweet, and you're really handsome."

Then she took his head between her hands and forced her tongue between his lips. She pushed him back and lay on top of him, gripping him with her thighs, moving on top of him so that he did not know what to do with his hands, suffocating under the weight of her body rocking slowly above him and then she wriggled, rolled off him onto her back and guided his fingers into her shorts and said, "Just there."

Victor immediately felt the warm, welcoming dampness, his fingers slipping in and out of the folds of flesh he could only dimly imagine but whose secrets he already seemed to know, because Rebecca was now moaning softly, eyes closed, biting her lower lip. He wanted her to touch him too, even though he felt sure that he would not be able to withstand even the slightest touch and he shivered when he felt her put her hand on his crotch and massage it gently. He almost said "no", but he could not summon the breath; he did not know whether he wanted her to carry on or give up, to finish or to stop.

He was moving inside a bubble, no longer knowing if anything existed in the world other than the body pressed against his. He could feel her kisses on his face, his neck, could feel each of her fingers as they fondled his penis through his shorts, could hear her breathing, the little cries that lodged in her throat like a nest of baby birds; felt these intense, prickling sensations coursing through him, these pinheads, these grains of sand that tingled all over his body.

Then Rebecca suddenly sat up, got to her feet almost brusquely and Victor studied her face, glistening with sweat and streaked with wisps of hair, waiting for her to say something rude; instead, she unbuttoned her shorts and in a flash she was naked, then, making the most of the boy's shock, she unfastened the belt of his shorts and he lifted himself up and, motionless, almost comatose, allowed her to undress him. The little room was bright. Everything was yellow. Rebecca's face was expressionless now, her eyes half closed and the boy did not know whether she was concentrating or whether she was thinking about something else. She straddled him and slipped him inside her, her face and her mane of hair like night suddenly falling around his neck as she told him not to move.

When it was over they lay, their skin fused together by sweat, still, silent, their wet, parted lips pressed against each other's necks. Then slowly, Rebecca sat up on the edge of the bed, her head down, her back curved, her hair falling over her face. When she stood up silently to get dressed and Victor saw her again after what they had just done, her whole body, her legs, her arse, the soft curve of her breasts, he felt something surge through him, a pleasurable electricity that swelled his chest with a huge sigh.

He felt light-headed and he swayed a little when he stood up. She turned away from him, rummaging in one of the dresser drawers so he quickly pulled on his clothes, ashamed now to let her see his thin, puny body, his penis which seemed now a hindrance, heavy, useless and out of proportion. As soon as he was dressed, she turned to him and gave him an almost astonished expression and smiled and he realised this was the first time he had seen her smile.

"I'm going to take a shower. If you want, you can go after. My mother is probably asleep, so you don't have to worry. She'll likely be there until noon, as usual."

He sat on the rumpled bed, ran his hand over the sheet to feel the warm imprint of their bodies. He felt dazed, as though he were a different person. This had not happened to him. Not to him, maybe to someone else, to his double. A fantastical creature that came and interposed itself between him and happiness. And yet he could feel it drying, tugging slightly at his skin as it did so. He was about to slip his fingers down to check when the door was flung open.

"Who the fuck are you? Where's Rebecca? What the hell are you doing here?"

For two or three seconds he could do nothing, say nothing. The woman stood stiffly in the doorway wearing a pair of white, low-slung trousers and a sort of short red jacket so that her belly was bare all the way down to her pubes. She seemed to be looking for something in the room, glancing around, observing every detail.

"Oh, I know you, don't I?" she said, wagging her finger at him.

Victor threw himself at her, his hands on her shoulders pushing her back. She hit the wall with a loud cry and her head struck the wall with a dull thud. She stood there, rubbing the back of her head, dazed, an expression of fear or pain creeping over her face slowly as though the shock had delayed her reflexes. The boy ran out, then came back into the bedroom and looked around for Rebecca's mobile. He spotted it on the dresser, just as the woman began to swear and scream for help. Victor dashed out into the hallway, tripping over cardboard boxes and then suddenly found himself outside in a glare of sunlight that forced him to look down and squint as he walked as far as the garden gate. He could hear the woman shrieking behind him, but as soon as he reached the streets, the screams stopped and he walked quickly, keeping to the strip of shade next to the houses, not daring to look around. While he was still in the village, he resisted the urge to run so as not to attract attention and he soon noticed that the people he passed barely seemed to see him. Once he was past the last of the houses, he jumped the ditch and plunged between the rows of vines. He wondered what time it might be, looked up at the sun and decided it had to be close to noon, then it occurred to him to check Rebecca's phone. It was barely 10.30. Time had slowed to a crawl. He kept moving away from the road, from the village, crept past a group of labourers bent over the vine stocks, noses buried in the dense foliage, talking loudly and laughing. He went into a small coppice and sat at the foot of a tree. He found Marilou's number in the list of contacts in the phone.

She answered straight away and stifled a cry when she recognised his voice.

"I thought it was Rebecca. Are you with her?"

"No. I've got her phone is all."

"Have you seen her?"

"What the fuck do you care?"

"When are you coming back?"

"I'm not coming back. It's over."

"What do you mean, over? They're looking for you everywhere, the police, everyone. They think you were abducted by a paedophile and that you ran away. I saw this car driving off, I thought the guy had kidnapped you. Julien said it's the same guy who came here before. They've been questioning Julien and me all morning. Where are you?"

"I can't tell you. But I need you to help me."

"Why don't you just come home. Everyone's been worried sick. Especially me."

Victor listened to the long drawn-out breath with which Marilou said this. She sighed.

"Where are you going to go?"

"No idea."

"So who was that guy last night?"

"Some guy my mother knew. Some psycho."

"Is he the guy whose car you threw stones at?"

"Yes, that's him."

"So what does the bastard want with you?"

"I don't know. Look, you have to do me a favour. Where are you now?"

"In my bedroom. I'm tidying up. Maman threw a fit and now Julien and me aren't allowed out . . . He's playing on his Xbox."

He pictured life carrying on, quiet, sheltered, and he smiled in spite of himself.

"What did they say to you?"

"Who?"

"Your parents."

"Nothing. They're in a complete state. Maman's been crying."

"You have to meet me."

"I can't, I told you. And anyway, what for? You're the one who left, you can come back if you want to see me."

"I need the urn with my mother in it. I want to have her with me. Can you bring it to me? In a bag. And something to eat."

There was a silence. In the distance he heard Nicole's voice asking Marilou what she was doing. "Nothing," Marilou said. "Making my bed."

She came back to him. "O.K. Where?"

"At the grave. And don't say anything to Julien."

"Right, but I'm not touching that urn, it's too weird, and anyway, Julien won't say anything."

"Tonight?"

"O.K., but I don't know what time."

"I'll wait. Remember to bring me some water."

She hung up. He bowed his head and leaned back against the tree. A helicopter buzzed overhead. He saw it pass slowly, just above the treetops, and dip lower as it flew over the vineyards. He shivered in spite of the heat gusting through the leaves, he arched his back and stared for a long time at the helicopter tracing circles high in the sky, or hedgehopping over the vineyards. Just as it dwindled to a black speck disappearing into the west, Victor heard a dog barking and a man shouting orders.

22

No-one answered Vilar's pounding – he had to knock, since the door-bell was obviously not working. He pressed his ear to the door to see if he could hear anything, but, as far as it was possible to tell above the hubbub of the building, the apartment was silent. The door to the stairway opened and a moment later a woman emerged, panting, a large blue grocery bag in each hand, followed by two young children. Vilar waited until she had reached the landing and set down her burden in order to look for her keys in her handbag, before showing her his I.D., rattling off his name and rank.

"I'm looking for Céline Bosc."

The woman barely looked at the warrant card and nodded, catching her breath. She was young, her curves squeezed into tight jeans, her large breasts bouncing beneath a low cut sleeveless T-shirt. The children, a very blond boy and girl of about the same age, were hungry, thirsty and hot. They were clamouring for something to drink; their mother told them to calm down, wait a minute, but they insisted in their shrill voices and started searching through the grocery bags for fruit juice. The woman decided to take care of them before answering Vilar's questions and the policeman nodded, took one of the heavy bags for her and set it down inside the apartment. He waited at the door while the woman got her children something to drink. She spoke to them in a loud voice, probably to drown out their incessant chatter. Shouting at them to pipe down and watch television, she came back to Vilar, planting herself in the doorway.

"I'm sorry, but the kids are always on at me for something. So, anyway, Céline doesn't live here anymore. Left about two months ago."

"Do you know where I might find her?"

The woman cocked her ear to hear what the children were up to.

"The thing is, I don't think she really wants to be found . . ."

"Why not? Did she leave without paying the rent?"

"Right, let's say that . . . Listen, I have to get back to the children, so if you don't have any other questions . . ."

She was about to close the door, but Vilar blocked it with his foot. On the doorbell he read the name Rayet.

"What is your first name, Madame Rayet?"

The woman looked surprised and let go of the door.

"What is it you wanted?"

"I want you to stop playing me for a fool and answer my questions. I am working on a criminal investigation and, if we are going to make this official, I should warn you that obstructing the police is a crime. There are other ways I could show you how serious this is, but I wouldn't want to upset your children. It can't be easy, being a single mother with two kids, so I don't want to make things any harder. Besides, I'm in a hurry. So, your first name?"

The woman sighed and leaned against the frame of the door, her arms folded.

"Caroline."

"Married?"

She gave a lopsided smile.

"I wish. No, I'm raising the twins by myself. What with Céline being on her own and having to fend for herself, we hit it off, if that's what you want to know."

"What I need to know is where she is now. You told me she didn't want to be found. What did you mean by that?"

"It's because of him. That bastard."

"Which bastard?"

"Éric, her ex, he's the father of her little girl."

302

Vilar felt a burning sensation in the back of his neck that coursed through his nerve endings.

"Did you meet him? Did he come round often?"

"No, but the couple of times he did come were more than enough. The last time, he nearly killed her. In fact I called the police – well, I mean . . ."

"Did they show up? Did she press charges?"

"Sure, they came, but they got here too late as always . . . The ambulance took her to Casualty, she had a broken arm and two cracked ribs."

"When was this?"

"Beginning of March."

One of the children called out, whining that Mélissa had stolen his biscuit. There was shouting and the sound of banging on the walls. The woman turned away, craning her neck towards the far end of the apartment. She yelled at the children to settle down.

She sighed, shaking her head.

"Do you want to come in? That way I can keep an eye on them."

Vilar closed the door behind him and followed her down the hallway to the kitchen, where the two children were drinking fizzy drinks and staring in open-mouthed stupefaction at a small T.V. Caroline Rayet turned back towards him.

"What is he like, physically?" Vilar said.

"Tall, dark hair, big hands . . . He has green eyes. He would have been pretty hot if it weren't for . . ." She paused. "He'd come around sometimes and stay the night, but if he'd been drinking, or if he was on something, he'd get nasty. He still wanted to sleep with her, but she didn't want him touching her. She used to say he was sick in the head. And it would always end in a fight. But Céline's not like me, she's short and skinny, so you can imagine . . ."

"Did he come back, after that time you called the police?"

"No. Wouldn't have mattered if he had because she was so terrified that by two weeks later, she was gone. And anyway, she couldn't afford the rent here anymore. She found a caravan for rent out in the sticks, in Beutre, on the rue de la Princesse – you couldn't make it up! You can imagine what a dump the place was, especially with Alexia, but at least it wasn't too cold that winter . . . I went to visit them once, and I tell you it depressed the hell out of me."

"How old is the daughter?"

"Seven. She's a lovely little girl. If it weren't for her, I don't know how Céline would cope."

Vilar nodded. It was a story he had heard before. Nadia and Sandra and now Céline, all of these women could only survive because they had children with bright futures ahead of them, something they tried hard to believe in since, at thirty, they felt their own futures were nothing but a dark sink. Vilar desperately needed to get away from this misery memoir, and tried to think of some way to take his leave of this woman who would have happily poured out her whole life story now that someone was finally prepared to listen to what she had to say, even if it was only some detective who seemed panicked, his face pale and slick with sweat.

"I have to go," he said almost curtly, as she launched into telling him about how tough life was, how it was no picnic.

She trailed off in mid-sentence and looked at him in surprise, then nodded her head.

"I'm sorry," he said. "I really need to find Céline. You understand . . ."

He felt as though he were fleeing. He felt as though these days he did only two things: hunt and flee, in his role as a staunch guardian of the laws of the jungle.

*

Twice before he had been to this part of Mérignac, away from the main road and the motorway. He needed a map to find the rue de la Princesse, which looked more like a country lane and ran through a no man's land of woodland, fields overgrown with brambles and illicit rubbish dumps. There were a few houses, most guarded by fierce dogs, surrounded by ramshackle wooden outbuildings.

The caravan park was at the end of a tarmac drive lined with acacias. Under the trees, it was possible to imagine in the soft afternoon sunlight that this was a holiday camp. Vilar parked his car at the gate and walked in. Lined up along a central path were some fifteen caravans of various sizes and degrees of disrepair, ranging from large mobile homes to rusty tin cans. At the far end of the site was a brick building, which probably housed the showers and laundry facilities from which two women were exiting, carrying baskets piled high with washing. When they saw Vilar approaching, they stopped. He asked where he could find Céline Bosc and the younger woman, tall and slim with an angular face, wanted to know who was asking. Vilar flashed his warrant card.

"The blue and green striped awning over there," she said pointing towards a long caravan whose roof was green with moss and lichen.

He walked away, feeling the worried glances of the two women boring into his neck. A little further on, three kids were laughing and swinging on a purple and pink porch. The children's laughter sounded strange in the oppressive silence that reigned beneath the thick foliage of the oak trees.

Coming to the awning, Vilar wiped his feet on the tatty doormat that read HOME, SWEET HOME, then stepped onto linoleum with a pattern mimicking a wooden floor. Under the awning was a makeshift living room. A brown plush sofa stood next to the caravan underneath an open window, next to it was a camping table and three chairs. In one corner, a wicker chair with a couple of cushions sat facing a switched-off television. On the other side, a plywood dresser sat on a wooden pallet. He did not need to knock, because the door opened suddenly, and a woman appeared in a fog of cigarette smoke. She was wearing a navy blue Girondins de Bordeaux football shirt and a pair of cut-off jeans. Her dishevelled hair was dark with streaks of red, her puffy features made it look as though she had been drinking, or had just woken up. Or both.

"Céline Bosc."

"Yes, that me. And who are you?"

Vilar introduced himself. No sooner had he mentioned Éric Sanz than Céline Bosc peered nervously out through the transparent plastic sides of the awning.

"Come in," she said quickly. "We'll be more comfortable inside, and anyway, it's not so hot in there."

Inside, he felt the floor tremble and perhaps bow slightly under his weight. The woman gestured to a bench draped with a dark red slipcover.

"Would you like something to drink? Beer? Mineral water?"

Vilar felt his mouth water. He accepted a beer. At the other end of the caravan, the banquettes had been pushed together to make a bed, covered by a duvet decorated with cartoon characters. On the shelf above were a dozen children's books next to a pile of neatly folded clothes. A single glass and a plate sat on the draining board of the tiny stainless steel sink.

The woman sat down opposite him and with quick, precise movements opened two bottles. She handed Vilar a beer and took a long gulp of her mineral water. Then she lit a cigarette and offered one to the policeman, who declined.

"I'm looking for Éric Sanz, your ex. We need to—"

"How did you find me? Was it Caroline?"

"Yes. But don't blame her, I leaned on her pretty hard."

"Yeah, I bet . . ."

She smiled scornfully, pretending to study her bottle of water

"So what's the dumb fuck done now?"

"He's suspected of murder."

With a sigh, she exhaled a cloud of smoke, stared out of the window and shook her head.

"It was waiting to happen. That's what he was banged up for, or pretty close."

"For grievous bodily harm."

"Yeah, you could call it that. The girl he beat up is in a wheelchair now. Paralysed. I'd rather be dead, wouldn't you?"

Vilar said nothing. He was studying Céline Bosc. She flicked the ash from her cigarette with such force it was as if she wanted to flick out the tobacco too, she rolled her shoulders like a boxer warming up. The exhaustion in her face was so striking that at first you did not notice

306

her large grey eyes, her delicate features made sharper by an aquiline nose.

"That son of a bitch," she said at last.

"Tell me about him. Tell me where we can find him so we can put an end to this."

"Why? Are you going to shoot him? Because I'm telling you, that's the only fucking way. Rid the world of that bastard. But no . . . You slap the handcuffs on him and he'll be remanded until the trial and he'll get, what? fifteen years max, right? And seven or eight years from now he'll be out terrorising women and pimping whores to make money. You can take it from me, that's what'll happen."

"Was he different when you met him?"

"He used to be the gentlest, most handsome man in the world. He was working as a barman in a club, where me and a gang of girls used to go for a laugh, for a break. We were twenty-five back then, working on the checkouts at Carrefour, so to let off steam – to forget the crappy job, the bosses, the long shifts – we would go down this club on a Saturday night and we weren't scared of anything, maybe because we already knew we'd never get far in life. I don't know . . . Anyway, he was working behind the bar and he had this amazing smile and we got talking. And that was that. For two years, he was fantastic. I knew he'd been inside, he insisted on telling me, wanted things to be clear. Some nights he didn't come home and I suspected he was still in the life, but I ignored it because otherwise I was happy."

The ghost of a smile flitted over her face and then her features hardened again.

"Alexia was born, and that's when he changed. He never took to her. Once, when he was really pissed off, he told me she wasn't his. But anyway . . ."

She fell silent, leaned back in the seat, her eyes down. From outside came the sound of children playing.

"She's not here, your daughter?"

"I put her in the outdoor day-care centre. It's not good for a kid, being shut up in a caravan. Just look around – I do my best to keep the place clean, but it's like living in a shoebox. At least at the centre they look after her, she can have fun. When you've got a social worker, it's pretty much free. And it saves on food. And it means when I'm at work I know where she is. One of my neighbours picks her up and looks after her till I get back."

She stood up suddenly, grabbed her cigarettes and lit one.

"There is one place you might find Éric. At his foster parents' place in Saint-Martin-du-Puy, over in Entre-deux-Mers. An aunt of mine lives nearby, she's from Sauveterre, that's how I remember. He put them through hell when he was a kid, but every time he goes home they take him in with open arms. The father worked in the post office, and she looks after kids placed with her by social services. That's how they ended up looking after Éric until he was eighteen.

"What are their names?"

"He must have told me, but I can't remember . . . Pralon? Something like that . . . Oh, I've got it: Pradeau. He even mentioned the mother's name was Irène."

A painful shudder ran through Vilar's body.

"Has Éric got a brother?"

"Yes, but they fell out. Pradeau's son, his biological son. I don't remember his first name. Éric never talked about him. It was like he was ashamed. Like he was hiding something. And no-one was ever allowed to bring up the subject. It was taboo."

Vilar stood up and immediately felt so faint he had to lean against a cupboard to stop himself from falling. The woman noticed his malaise, the hand bringing a cigarette to her lips froze in mid-air, but she said nothing. Vilar mumbled something like an apology or a farewell and rushed outside. He stared up at the leaves of the towering oak trees, peaceful, dappled, rustling gently, and headed back to his car, his mind blank, the heat clinging to his shoulders like an attacker weighing in him trying to wear him down.

He drove to Langon at an almost steady 150 k.p.h., sirens blaring. He had the front windows open and the noise left him dazed. He did not even try to think about Laurent Pradeau's betrayal. He knew only that he had been betrayed, and that that was reason enough to floor the accelerator, drive to some tiny village of whose existence he had only just learned, turn up on the doorstep of these people and see what happened, improvise. He felt as though he were driving through a tunnel. Not a dark tunnel, one that was dazzling, blinding. A light had been turned on in his darkness and he could not bear it; nor could he work out anything other than that this journey was necessary.

He bought a local map at a petrol station and pored over it, smoking a cigarette from a pack he found in the glove compartment. With some difficulty he found the village, circled it in pen and set off again through this peaceful, verdant countryside with the almost childlike feeling – a mixture of excitement and anxiety – that he was advancing into enemy territory. He took two wrong turnings and had to negotiate paths that led into deep woodland. He drew up outside the little village, at the junction of two narrow roads, turning the car so it was facing back the way he had come. He continued on foot and spotted an old woman in a large straw hat sitting in a garden chair in the shade of a catalpa tree.

She started at the sound of his voice, roused from her doze, she narrowed her eyes and glared at him, her mouth a black hole of astonishment. He repeated his question; she appeared to give it some thought then raised her arms and hesitantly pointed to the right.

"Down that way, the last house, the one with the blue shutters and the car outside."

He wished he could calm the confused hammering in his chest. He wished he did not feel so out of breath, wished that the heat would let up. He wondered whether he might not collapse, right here in the middle of the village street. He walked around the car, an old Renault estate whose right-hand doors were dented. The inside of the car was a jumble of boxes, empty water bottles and plastic bags. A duvet was spread across the huge boot. Someone had slept in this car. Éric Sanz had slept here. He lived in this car, forever moving about, travelling alone, impossible to pin down, the more so since his brother the policeman was keeping him up to speed about their investigations. And now he was in his parents' house. Vilar kept walking, past the house and towards the fields and the vineyards which stretched as far as the line of tall, dark trees. As he walked he tried to decide on a plan of action, given that he was alone and unarmed. He thought about phoning Daras, imagined the melee, dozens of uniformed officers, Sanz being led away in handcuffs to the waiting police van, taking any information he had about Pablo to his cell. He saw himself standing in the confusion of a major police operation, watching the man being led away without a word – because guys like Éric, the ones who talk tough, who like to spew threats and insults, rapidly become silent as a tombstone as soon as they're caught, somehow let fall scraps of information, just enough false leads to keep the investigating magistrate happy without ever giving up the truth. At any moment now, he might pile into his car and drive off and Vilar had no way of stopping him.

He turned back up the lane. He knocked on the door.

The man who opened looked at him wild-eyed, his jaw dropped, his chin quivered – it was so obvious he knew exactly who was standing on his doorstep that Vilar did not feel the need to flash his warrant card.

"My son has just left," the man stammered.

He was tall and thin. His long neck was nothing more than a bundle of tendons in the midst of which his Adam's apple bobbed like a ball in a fountain. His eyes, set into his tanned face, trapped in a web of wrinkles, were bright and piercing.

"Let me in," Vilar said. "Reinforcements will be getting here any moment now."

Pradeau senior let his arms fall to his sides and led him down a long corridor adorned with small picture frames, but Vilar did not so much as glance at them. They went into the living room where a television was blaring.

Vilar saw the elderly woman sitting in an armchair, her head propped up on a large cushion as her husband moved over to take the remote control and turn down the sound. She gave a bad-tempered scowl and then stared blackly at the policeman.

"May I present Irène, my wife. She's been ill for five years. She's always complaining she can't hear the television, so she steals the remote and turns up the sound. She can't manage to wash herself any more, but she can still steal the remote . . . The doctors are mystified. This gentleman wants to speak to Éric!"

He shouted and Vilar realised the message was intended not only for the old woman. He listened carefully. The rest of the house was silent.

"Give him the bread money," the old woman said, "I put it on the shelf in the kitchen. I thought the loaf he brought on Tuesday was overbaked. The boys don't like it like that, I don't know how many times I've told him."

She nodded and turned back to the television, picked up the remote control and turned the sound up again, but even so Vilar heard a faint creak outside the living room. He dashed out of the room, but did not even have time to turn before he felt a tremendous blow, someone slamming him against a chest of drawers. He felt himself being lifted up and thrown to the ground. His head banged against the skirting board, pain shot through his body and his stomach heaved as someone kicked him.

"What on earth is going on?" the old woman screeched.

Vilar vomited up a little bile, forcing himself to breathe because he could feel himself slipping into a bleary darkness. He inhaled almost with a roar, felt a hand grab his throat and heard a shriek echo through the house, dimly aware that the shrill, cracked voice was screaming: "Help, son! Help!"

Then a face pressed itself against his and he saw the green eyes staring into his, the hesitation in the stare, the uncertainty that flickered across the face each time the scream started up again. And the mixture of hatred and moronic brainlessness. His breath smelled of menthol. The guy was chewing gum. Vilar focused on this because he could focus on nothing else.

"So you managed to track me down . . . a nice piece of police work. I heard you were good, but even so, I have to fucking hand it to you.

I'm not going to kill you. Not here. Not in front of them. You already scared my mother and I should rip you apart just for that, you fucker. Not here, but soon, I'll tell you where to meet me and then we'll see. And anyway, you're not done yet. What's his name again? Oh, yeah, Pablo! Think about him. I'll be in touch soon."

Sanz slammed Vilar's head against the floor and Vilar saw him clamber over him, but did not hear the door bang or the car drive off. He lay there, barely conscious until the old man pressed some ice against his forehead. When he came round, he had no idea how long he had been unconscious. He struggled to sit up, leaning back against the wall and pressed the bag of ice to his head. The old man said nothing. He came and went between the hall and the living room, fussing anxiously around Vilar, shuffling about in his slippered feet. He brought a glass of water which Vilar drained. The old woman sat in her armchair moaning over and over, "Oh God, oh God."

Vilar slowly tried to get to his feet and was surprised to see blood on the tiles. He wondered where he was bleeding from, his fingers felt a wetness at the back of his head and another wound above his cheekbone, blood trickled from his chin down his shirt and onto the floor.

"I'm getting blood everywhere," he said to the man who reappeared with a sponge, and knelt down to clean him up.

The man got to his feet again and disappeared into the kitchen. Vilar followed him, in spite of his headache and the dizziness that almost did for him again. He tore off a sheet of kitchen roll and pressed it to his cheek, then dropped the bag of ice into the sink.

"Monsieur Pradeau, I need to call Laurent."

Pradeau looked at Vilar sadly.

"What difference will it make? Just look at this mess . . . this catastrophe. My sons."

"I knew nothing about it. Laurent told me that his mother was ill, he told me sometimes he couldn't bring himself to come and see you."

"I know. He doesn't visit much anymore. It hardly matters, she hasn't recognised him for the past couple of years . . . And, well, he and I have never known how to communicate . . . It's been a month since

I've seen him. No news. Not even a phone call. I called his mobile the other day, but there was no answer. I don't know. But Éric, he visits all the time. He's the only person she still recognises. It's very strange. She didn't give birth to him, he didn't come to us until he was four, but every time he comes, she gets out of her chair and takes a few steps so she can hug him. And every time he leaves, she cries. Five minutes later she's forgotten he was here, but every time it breaks her heart to see him go."

He pulled out a chair from the kitchen table and sat down heavily. His pale eyes bored into Vilar as he asked why he had come.

"I came to arrest your son Éric."

"What did he do?"

The old man clung to the table with both hands, leaning forward waiting for Vilar's answer.

"We believe he killed a woman."

Pradeau closed his eyes. His knuckles were white from gripping the sides of the table so hard. "It's not true," he murmured. He shook his head slowly then opened his eyes again and looked at Vilar through tears that welled in his eyes but did not flow.

"I'm listening," he said in a whisper.

"It took us three months to trace it to him, to here. I also came because I wanted to find out why Laurent lied to me for so long, and why he disappeared a week ago. There are other things I'd like to know too, but there's no guarantee I ever will."

Vilar sat down because the room was spinning.

The old man took a pack of tissues from his pocket, wiped his eyes and sniffled. He was struggling to breathe. His voice quavered a little.

"They really were brothers, you know. They really loved each other. Laurent used to protect Éric, he stood up for him at school when the other kids bullied him, and Éric would barely talk. Years it went on, until he was in the *sixième* he hardly said a word, the only person he'd talk to was his big brother . . . He was very affectionate with us, he'd come and snuggle up to us on the sofa. He was like that for a long time. And then when he started getting into trouble in his teens,

313

Laurent covered for him, as they say ... He lied for him. I'm sure he was even in on some of his brother's pranks. But there was nothing anyone could do. Not us, and not Laurent. It was as if there was something broken inside him before he ever came to us. As soon as he turned eighteen he moved out, we weren't able to stop him. He promised he'd come and visit ... It was three years before we had any news from him ... Laurent was studying for his law degree at the time. He'd already decided he wanted to join the police, it was all he ever talked about."

"And did they see each other? I mean other than here?"

"I think so. It's something I only realised a few weeks ago. Laurent knew about one of his mother's funny turns, even though I'd never mentioned it to him. But Éric was here the day it happened. That's how I knew that there was something – that they were in touch with each other. When Éric was sent to prison, Laurent said he never wanted to hear his name again. All the time he was inside, he would tell us to shut up if we so much as referred to his brother, and it broke my wife's heart. Éric being in prison and our sons not speaking to each other ..."

"Did you know that Éric had a daughter, that he had lived with a woman for two years?"

"Yes ... He mentioned it. But he said it was his life and none of our business. So we had no choice but to accept it."

Pradeau got up and went and looked in the living room.

"How is she? All this has shaken her up."

The man shrugged and sat down again.

"She's asleep. I gave her a tablet. One of the advantages of the disease is that you tend to forget your troubles. I doubt she'll remember anything about what happened. Or maybe she'll have a nightmare or an anxiety attack, but she gets those all the time over such trivial things, or sometimes when she realises that she's slipping away ... I don't know how it's possible, those moments of lucidity. Sometimes, she'll look at me, she'll take my hand and squeeze it hard enough to break a bone and she'll say 'What's wrong with me? What's happening to me?' And it's like seeing her sink into quicksand. I don't know how to explain it. She's so far away and at the same time she's so close. She's alive and she's already dead . . . She's still here and yet all I have of the real her are memories."

He trailed off, out of breath.

"They all leave and there's nothing I can do to keep them here. Even her . . . It's like when you catch someone's hand as they're falling and you feel it slipping and there's nothing you can do, you know?"

"But you can still touch her, still talk to her . . ."

The old man shook his head angrily.

"You can't possibly understand. She's not the woman she used to be, she doesn't even remember who she used to be. I don't know how to explain . . . You don't touch someone, don't kiss someone just for your own pleasure . . . It doesn't work like that. And she doesn't react, doesn't react at all. Sometimes she gets frightened when I get too close to her and she screams. And sometimes I'll hold her in my arms like a big doll. There are times I'd rather be alone than have to live with someone who exists only because she has still has "vital signs", as the doctor puts it. Sometimes, when I have to change her or wash her, I get these terrible thoughts. I shouldn't really tell you that, you being police and all. I've never even told my son. He pretends he doesn't understand. That way he doesn't have to deal with it."

Vilar tried to summon an image of Laurent Pradeau from the description his father gave. He found it difficult to reconcile it with the man he thought he knew. He gulped air like an exhausted swimmer forcing himself to stay on the surface.

"What's going to happen now?" the old man said.

"We'll put your house under surveillance, put a tap on your phone in case Éric gets in touch. That's all. One way or the other he'll be arrested. He's been playing a game and he's bound to lose in the end. I'll need a photograph of him, the most recent one you have. We've probably got a mugshot, but you know what they're like, your own children wouldn't recognise you in one."

Vilar made no mention of Laurent because he did not know what would happen, and he did not want to overwhelm the old man slumped in the chair. He got to his feet and realised he no longer felt dizzy and his legs seemed able to support his weight.

"Will everything be alright?" Pradeau said.

Vilar nodded.

"Could I have the photo please?"

He heard the man open a drawer in the dining room and rummage around. Finally he came back and handed Vilar a photograph.

"That one was taken three years ago."

"It'll be fine."

Vilar walked to the front door. As he passed the living room, he glanced in at the old woman sleeping, her head resting against the back of the chair, her mouth open. He turned to the old man.

"Don't worry. Well, what I mean is . . . Just take good care of her, Monsieur Pradeau."

He went back to Bordeaux the way he had come, dazed by the speed, the noise and a headache. Driving through the city centre, he found it difficult to convince himself these places were familiar, that he had spent years patrolling these streets. He felt almost as if he were a stranger, a traveller who had returned after a long voyage. Out of sheer reflex, he saluted the security guard as he turned into the police station car park and, when he got out of the car, he was startled by the sound of voices, car doors slamming, tyres squealing as a squad responded to a call.

People stared at his bloodstained shirt, his swollen face. He smiled at them to throw them off the scent, told them it was nothing. He asked after Daras and was told that she had been looking for him.

She was in her office.

"Close the door," she said as soon as he appeared.

He sat facing her and she stared at him, pretending not to notice the gashes and the lumps on his face that had now turned black or blue.

"I'm not going to ask you what happened," she said. "I'd rather believe you walked into a door, because you've been pretty distracted recently. So much so that I've got someone in the cells, a certain Thierry Lataste, without mentioning any names, and I have no idea what he's

316

doing there – is he under arrest? Is he being deported? Or is he just here to see how comfortable our cells are? And where are the notes of the interview? You go to this guy's office, you arrest him, you drag him here single-handed, you interrogate him, you toss him in a cell, you request an arrest warrant for someone named Éric Sanz, all this without consulting with anyone? Who do you think you are? Dirty Harry? What sort of shit is this? I've got the *juge d'instruction* screaming down the phone at me because some lawyer is accusing us of arbitrary arrest and detention, I've got Garnaud busting my balls wanting to know where my officers are, one of whom disappeared a week ago and the other isn't answering his phone . . . I mean, fucking hell! Right now, you're going to go home and wait there until we've dealt with you. That's all. You get out of here, get yourself stitched up and you don't go around playing cops and robbers until I say you can, got it?"

Vilar stared at her. His cheeks were flushed with anger and it gave him a healthy glow. "You want me out of here right now, or do you want to know what happened? Might help you do your job."

"Go on, then, spill . . . Jesus, you haven't got a fag, have you?"

He found a crumpled pack in his pocket and tossed them onto the desk.

"You're lucky I didn't bleed all over them."

"Yeah, yeah, you'll have me in tears in a minute . . . Right, so what have you got to tell me?"

She smoked with obvious relish, inhaling deeply and blowing clouds of smoke above her head. Perhaps she was also trying to calm herself.

Breathlessly, he told her about what had happened and what he had found out. Daras, not knowing where to stub out her cigarette, ground it under her shoe so as not to interrupt Vilar as he talked on and on, eyes fixed on her though probably without seeing her; she did not want to break the fragile silence that swooped down on every sentence as though to pin it to the ground, to stop it having its effect or even being heard. When he had finished, she said nothing, she did not move, she stared at the map of the city on the wall as though searching through that maze for some way out. After a moment, she sat back in her chair and spoke quietly.

"What I don't understand, what I can't even imagine, is where Laurent is now and what the fuck he's up to. I just hope . . ."

"I've thought about that too. But if he has, we'll never find the body. It would be just like him to disappear without a trace, to piss everybody off even when he's dead."

"Jesus, for months he's been keeping his brother up to date about our every move, all that so you couldn't arrest him? There we were wondering how his aim was so bad that night he shot at the guy who attacked you in the playground. He didn't even manage to put him out of action, remember? We were thinking of clubbing together to send him on a training course. We didn't realise that actually, his aim had to be perfect to graze him in precisely the right place so you could testify that he'd been hit."

"To say nothing of making Morvan disappear. You always knew it must have taken two men to do it, and the crime scene, not a hair, not a fibre – same thing in Nadia's studio."

Daras got up and leaned on the desk next to Vilar.

"How could he? Morvan was tortured. I just can't imagine Laurent doing something like that, it's out of the question. And all those calls winding you up about Pablo? Shit, you guys were friends, Laurent knew the kid."

"I know. Maybe things got out of control."

"But why, for fuck's sake? Why take all these risks, why attack you, his friend, and why bring your son into it? How can someone change so much, so quickly? There's something between those two bastards that goes way beyond the fact they're brothers. There's something else. We'll have to go through everything. Go back over their lives, now we know there's a connection. There's a skeleton buried somewhere."

"There was some officer who used hang around the high-class orgies organised by those big shots – Sandra de Melo mentioned it. I'm not sure exactly what his role in the whole thing was, it was Sanz who did the pimping. But I'm sure the officer was Pradeau."

"What the hell would he be doing there? Looking out for his little brother? Stopping him doing something stupid?"

"I could imagine a little erotic game going wrong, things getting a little extreme, a girl dying."

"It's pointless to speculate, that won't get us anywhere. There's always rumours and people shit-stirring. Besides, when did they take place, these orgies? We'd have to go back over the files of every missing girl, every unsolved murder . . . It would be a nightmare. And besides, there are plenty of other psychos out there – right now, we've got a guy running loose in the city murdering girls. He's decapitated two, and there's a third case we can probably pin on him . . . Are you really suggesting – with no proof, trusting to a hunch – that we start reopening cold cases and combing through missing persons files going back years? Besides, like I said, I can't imagine Laurent as some psycho."

Vilar said nothing. He was trying to take in was she had just said, trying to gauge the scale of the investigation it would represent. He knew the past was never dead. That it dies only with memory.

"Yes, I can see him being involved. Now I can."

He tried to sit up in his chair, but felt a terrible shooting pain in his side. He pulled a face, struggled to catch his breath.

"Don't you think you should get yourself looked at?" she said, concerned. "Do you want me to take you to Casualty? That bastard's broken at least one of your ribs."

Vilar waved away the offer and got to his feet. His whole body ached and he stood motionless for a moment, waiting for the pain to subside. Daras rummaged in a desk drawer and took out a blister pack of tablets. She went to fetch a glass of water.

"Here, take two of them. That way you'll be able to stand up."

He swallowed the pills and drank some more water. He felt as though he could drink litres of the stuff.

"Go home, get some rest, sleep if you can, I'll call you as soon as I've got anything. You're no good to anyone in that condition. You've done enough for today, don't you think? For three months we've been floundering and now we know the guy's name, we know his haunts . . . that's not bad, is it? I'm going to go organise surveillance units to keep an eye on the parents' place and the caravan, even though I don't think either will do any good. If he takes his brother's advice, he's not going to fall into that sort of trap. But it may be our only hope.'

Vilar went home, took a shower, cautiously soaping his aching body. The pills Daras had given him made it possible for him to move, to breathe without too much difficulty, but his skin burned beneath his fingers, like a touchscreen, sensitive to the slightest movement. He tried to remember where Sanz had hit him, wondering how he could have landed so many blows in such a short space of time. Or had he gone on beating him after he passed out?

He examined the wound on his head: a two-centimetre gash which did not look particularly deep, and a large swelling. He dabbed it with Betadine, found some antiseptic powder in the bathroom cupboard and shook some over the inflamed area. Then he rubbed his bruises with an ointment that smelled of mint and camphor and remembered that Pablo, when he had to have ointment applied, loved to bring the tube to his nose, close his eyes and smell it.

He had just managed to dress himself when the telephone rang. Of course, his heart stopped and for a moment it seemed as though it might not start up again. Of course, he made for the telephone as though nothing else existed, as though he were walking through pitch darkness along a girder suspended high in the sky.

It was Daras.

"The hospital just called. Sandra de Melo died an hour ago."

The girder swayed on its cable. Vilar had to dig deep into his chest to find the breath he lacked.

"And the kid?"

His voice was hoarse. He cleared his throat.

"What?"

"Her son, José. The little autistic boy. He was admitted to a psychiatric unit the night it happened and now . . . Well, it's no place for a kid."

He hung up without another word. He took the photograph of Éric

Sanz from his pocket and studied it, hoping for some magic revelation, some vision of the man at the wheel of a car and of where he might be right now, but all he saw was the thin face, the grey eyes smiling into the lens, looking gentle and shy, standing in front of Arcachon Bay at low tide, and here and there on the sand, glistening in the sunshine, boats large and small lying on their sides.

23

The barking had stopped and this only worried him more, because the dog might appear at any moment, jump at him, tug at his shirt, knock him to the ground and keep him pinned there until the police arrived. He ran straight ahead, dazzled by the sun, his weary legs straining at every little hill, his ankles twisting on the rough terrain. He stopped so he could get his bearings and work out the way to the grave. He got his breath back. He could hear nothing now, not even the roar of the tractors, or the cars passing on the road, and for a second he imagined the whole village had downed tools in order to look for him. He found the silence ominous and set off again towards the meeting point, hoping Marilou would not keep him waiting long.

He hid in a copse of trees from which he would be able to see her arrive. Sitting on the ground, his knees drawn up to his chin, arms clasping his legs, he realised his body was beginning to give off a smell of sweat, of muck. In two or three days, he thought, he would stink, like a tramp he and his mother had passed one night outside the sports stadium; he remembered that the stench – like ripe cheese and stagnant water – had stayed with him for days. He remembered the dark figure lying motionless, remembered turning away, terrified and disgusted while his mother tried to tug him away. When he had said something to her about how the man smelled, she did not look at her son, she simply said: "That's the smell of someone who doesn't know if he's dead or alive."

Now Victor knew what death smelled like. It smelled like his mother's mangled body.

He closed his eyes and began to count in his head, setting targets such that if Marilou arrived before he reached them it was a good sign, and if she arrived later it was a bad omen. He whiled away the time, frequently having to start over because Marilou had still not turned up and he could not quite bring himself to believe that such a childish ruse could influence fate.

In the meantime, he cleaned the black crud of dust and dirt that had collected between his toes, then he wandered away from his observation post and began to collect twigs which he made into a neat pile. He cleared the whole area of brushwood and marked it out with stones he found in a hole from which an acacia tree grew. As he busied himself, he began to daydream about strange adventures. He imagined becoming a living legend, the wild boy of the forest, the boy no-one had ever found, and he thought perhaps he should head north towards the Médoc to lose himself in the forests and the swampland where no-one would ever see him again.

He was sitting in the middle of his makeshift campsite when, through the leaves, he saw Marilou's red dress appear at the top of the hill. She stopped, picked a few grapes and set her backpack down in front of her. She shielded her eyes with her hand so that she could scan the area around the grave and as soon as she spotted Victor, she ran to him and hugged him then, taking the boy's face in her hands, breathlessly she kissed his forehead, his cheeks, his mouth. Surprised at first, he let her, not knowing what to do with his hands, not daring to touch her, then he put his arms around her and they stood for a moment, huddled together without saying a word next to the patch of ground where Rebecca's secret was buried.

They went into the copse. Marilou opened the backpack and stepped away in fright as the crimson urn cast an eerie, gentle glow in the shadows where they stood, something they took to be a miracle. Then Victor crouched down, took the urn out of the bag and examined it before setting it on the ground and stroking the curved sides. A few feet away, the girl watched in frozen silence. Victor rummaged in the bag and took out two tins of pâté and some sliced bread and two big bottles of water. He opened one, clicked his tongue and took a long swig.

At the bottom of the bag he found his knife and two packets of paper napkins. He thanked Marilou for the knife which he opened up, holding the glinting blade close to his eyes.

"Thanks for that too," he said gesturing to the urn.

"I didn't touch it. It was Julien. I couldn't do it, it's too weird."

"What's he been up to, Julien?"

"He's repainting his moped. He said he'll show it to you when you come back."

Victor smiled. His face took on a wistful expression. Marilou came towards him, bent down and laid a hand on his arm.

"Where did you sleep?"

"Over there, in the vineyards, in an old trailer."

"Weren't you scared?"

"No. Scared of what?"

"I dunno. It's scary in the dark. There's animals and things . . . Why don't you come back? Come back with me, it'll be fine."

Victor hunched his shoulders.

"No."

He stared at his feet, toying with a piece of wood. The dense foliage of the trees was no longer able to bear the weight, the sweltering heat suddenly descended on them.

"Why not?"

"I don't know. I can't stay. I'm better off out here."

"What happens when it rains? And when it gets cold in winter? You can't just become a tramp. You have to stay with us and go to school. And anyway, my parents are really fond of you, I can tell. Papa doesn't say anything, but I know he really likes you."

Victor struggled to his feet and put the urn back in the bag. Then he packed the food and slipped the knife into his pocket. He could feel her tapping on his leg.

"Hey, isn't that him?"

A man was walking down the hill, following a vine row, heading

324

straight for them. He was wearing a white T-shirt and a jacket with a lot of pockets. He was walking rapidly.

Victor carefully closed the backpack and hefted it onto his shoulder. Marilou looked at him questioningly, waiting for him to make a decision.

"This way."

They took the only path not choked with brambles and emerged between two rows of vines and ran west. Victor took the girl's hand as she bounded along the hillocks in her leather sandals.

"Where we going?" she said.

Victor did not answer. He ran straight ahead, bent double, then turned onto another path that ran between two vines, dragging Marilou who gave a grunt of pain or surprise, but she said nothing, did not protest. They arrived, breathless and exhausted, at a small stone hut with a pointed slate roof and a hole in the wall like an arrow slit. On the other side gaped another opening with no door. The ground was covered in plastic sacks that had once contained sulphate and over time not only the ground but the walls had taken on a bluish tinge. From here they could see nothing save the straight rows of vines, nor could they hear anything.

Leaning in one corner was a dented old iron hoe, eaten away by rust. Victor picked up the handle, the wood was shiny and hard, and he decided to keep it. They sat by the wall and drank some water in silence, panting hard. Their feet and their ankles were grey with dust and Marilou thought they looked like socks or leggings. She licked a finger and traced dark lines on her tanned skin. Then, since neither of them had said anything, meditating on the silence, Victor said, "He'll never find us. He's too dumb."

"Yeah, but he must have followed me to get to the grave, and he knew you were living at our house. How do you think he worked that out? He can't be as dumb as all that."

"You scared?"

Marilou shook her head.

"We'll be fine. It's two against one."

Victor stood up.

"Let's go. You have to get home."

They set off along a path rutted with tyre tracks from the tractors. They made a long detour before turning back towards the village. They passed a bottling plant and heard the hum of machinery and the clink of bottles brought from the storehouse. They saw a forklift truck working in the yard and crouched down for fear of being spotted, small amid the dark green leaves of the vines. They crossed two roads without knowing where they led. Victor kept his bearings relative to the estuary on their right, meaning they were heading towards the village.

"Maybe we'll meet a policeman," Marilou said.

Victor shrugged. He walked a little faster, brandishing the shaft of the hoe like a rifle.

In the distance they could see a crossroads. A police car was parked on the verge, all the doors open in the blazing sunshine.

"Come on," Marilou said. "We're safe now."

"No, you go. I have to leave. I can't stay here."

She walked towards the road, jumped the bank and turned back.

Victor had crept back into the furrow and was lying on his belly between the vines. He could see her looking for him, standing in her red dress on the boiling tarmac. She pushed a wisp of hair behind her ear, looked at the ground as though trying to decide what to do, then shrugged and walked down the middle of the road towards the village. Victor stood up again and watched her over the tops of the vines as she grew smaller before she vanished among the houses.

He felt as though he would never see her again and he stood for a long time staring at the point where he had lost sight of her, down in front of a house with a blue shutter. He would have liked to tell her how empty he felt, right in the pit of his stomach, and how he was a prisoner of that emptiness which followed him wherever he went, keeping him in a bubble that he could neither puncture nor burst. But she could not know, still less understand. She could not see the shadow that he sometimes saw at night in the darkness of his room. Could not hear that voice. And yet, a little earlier, when he had held her in his arms, he had felt her thin, hard, gentle body imprint itself, interlocking precisely with that void, nestling in the cleft of that emptiness, but it had lasted only for a moment and then she had become a nuisance and he had wanted to push her away but could not bring himself to, because he loved the feel of her hair against his neck.

He followed the line of the estuary, taking narrow paths that led through the reeds or across the fields of hard mud, dry and cracked from the heat. He recognised this place from the afternoon he spent here with Julien, watching the river rats and the fish leaping sluggishly in the water. He trudged for more than an hour along crude paths that skirted the vines, their leaves blue with sulphate, or disappeared into fallow fields, barren and baked by the sun. Sometimes he caught a glimpse of the estuary on his right between the trees, and he thought that he could walk as far as the sea and wake up tomorrow morning on a sand dune watching night sink below the horizon.

He passed a group of three caravans clustered beneath a thicket of trees, they were so dirty and mud-spattered that at first he thought they were abandoned until he heard a squalling baby and a dog barking, a huge brute probably, and – fearful – he took a detour. With the rusty old hoe he could defend himself, he thought, but this place was so desolate, so empty that he felt a faint uneasiness pushing him onward without his knowing what he was doing or where he would stop.

He passed the village, saw the church spire in the distance, and drifted closer to the estuary before suddenly spotting a blue fisherman's cabin, the glare of a corrugated iron roof in the sun. He moved closer. The boat was still there, tied up, resting on the mud. A path, or rather a wheel track in the dirt, stopped some fifty metres from a flat area of ground where the fishermen probably turned their cars. An old banger sat rusting, propped up on breeze blocks, surrounded by rusting steel rods and even older tyres. He walked along this path to see whether it might not lead to the back of a house or a storehouse and saw that it came out onto a wider dirt track, the one they had taken when they cycled here. The tracks here seemed to be older, since many were over-grown with grass.

No-one would come here. He felt as though he had come to the end of the world. He wondered what time it was and turned on Rebecca's phone which told him it was just after four. There was a long time still before it would be dark. Suddenly he felt exhausted and walked to the shade of some trees growing near the fisherman's jetty. There, he sat down, opened the backpack and drank a little water, careful to leave some for later. He was sitting facing the muddy water, he heard it lapping against the shore and leaned against the trunk, legs stretched out. He closed his eyes, slowed his breathing and listened to the murmuring all around him.

He felt as though he might fall asleep here, so he got up again and walked to the fisherman's hut. The door was nothing more than a salvaged piece of board, the varnish worn away, fastened by a bolt and two padlocks. The board did not reach the top beam; he pushed the point of his hoe under it and using it as a lever, he managed without much effort to ease it off its hinges. Then he had only to push and the door fell onto the floor of the shed, overturning a camping table and two folding chairs. He opened the shutters on either side of a huge cogwheel – used for reeling in the nets – turned by a handle which operated a windlass to which was attached a steel cable. He liked the breeze on his face, and the fact that from here he could see the whole breadth of the estuary.

The water shimmered yellow in the sun and the blue of the sky was reflected as grey shards that shifted on the waves. A fish leapt above the water not far from him and the boy stood watching, hoping he might see another. The far shore was nothing but a dark line, above which rose an expanse of sky more vast than anything he had ever seen. Even the towers of the nuclear plant seemed insignificant, like pebbles placed along the shore. He quivered to feel so alone, faced with the expanse of the horizon, proud to be standing staring at it even as he was crushed beneath the vastness and the weight which he could feel bearing down on him. He turned around, picked up the chairs and the camping table, then opened the doors of an old formica cabinet: he found crockery, some knives and forks, a bottle of pastis, four or five glasses stacked on top of each other, salt, pepper, a bottle of olive oil and two tins of sardines. In the drawers, there was a ball of string, a pair of rusty scissors and a jumble of nails, screws and wire. In the bottom cupboards he found nothing interesting other than a hacksaw.

He stood in the middle of the hut, turning slowly around, wondering whether it would be possible to survive here, especially in winter. He had no clear answer to this question. He set the chairs facing each other and sat down on one, putting his feet up on the other, grabbed his backpack, rested it on his legs and began to rummage through it. First he took out the urn, laid it on his belly, placed one hand on it. He closed his eyes. It was warm. He took one of the tissues Marilou had brought and wiped the urn clean of fingerprints, then, wetting the tissue with spit, polished the red surface until it shone. "There you go, Manou," he whispered.

They sat for a long time, lost in a daydream, a rush of chaotic images mingling old memories of Marilou, Rebecca and Julien, but also memories of Nicole and Denis, and he could no longer distinguish his previous life from this one. He had gone on living without quite knowing how. But there was still this pain, this tightness in his heart, this insurmountable void. This desert heat followed him like a shadow.

He was struggling to breathe, so he looked out at the river again, the powerful waves and eddies of the water, and took a deep breath, shaking his head with a groan. Suddenly he felt unbearably hot. He ran out of the hut and the air outside felt cooler as it whispered in the leaves. He went down to the boat and saw that it was chained to one of the piles supporting the jetty. He sat in it, his feet resting on a hillock of ropes. He looked around for the oars, went back to the hut in case he had missed them, then decided it was probably normal for the fishermen to take them home so no-one would steal the boat, as he had been planning to do. He wondered what he could use to steer to boat. The estuary was murmuring now with a thousand jets of spray as the waters swelled, the waves breaking in a spume of muddy water that glittered in the sun. The rising tide pushed against the river, the powerful current rippling the water.

Victor went back up onto the bank to explore around the old abandoned car. It was a veritable rubbish dump: old tyres, scrap iron, gravel and a few long planks that he dragged back to his den. There, he set to work on them with the broken hoe and the hacksaw. He had no skill and not much strength. Before long he was sweating profusely, perspiration burned his eyes and left his lips tasting of salt. He stopped from time to time to drink some water, finishing off the first bottle. He watched the rising tide, observed the inexorable patience as it encroached on the dry ground.

Eventually he fashioned a piece of wood that would serve, flattened at one end. He threw it into the boat and began slowly cutting through the first link of the chain, the steel ring shifting under the hacksaw which was reluctant to bite into the metal; the boy grunted and groaned as the boat rocked under his movements.

When he checked the time again on Rebecca's phone, it was almost 7.30. He decided to eat in the boat which he had now reattached to the jetty with the length of rope. From the hut, he got an old blanket that smelled of paraffin and threw it onto the seat. He opened a tin of sardines which he ate using the tip of his knife, then sopped up all the juice with some of his bread. He did not eat all the pâté, nibbled a few of the crackers. Finally, in small sips, he drank half the second bottle of water.

He felt happy and tired. He lay down in the bottom of the boat and looked up at the leaves of the trees above him. There were noises from the bank, a crackling in the dry reeds, river rats probably. He heard the fish leaping in the water, carried in on the high tide, which was calmer now the ocean had the upper hand.

Then he heard the shout. It was Julien. And another voice, muffled. A car door closing. Victor dashed to the hut to get his bag. He had trouble fitting the urn back into it, got tangled with his shoelaces, grabbed the hoe.

As he stepped out the door he saw the man running towards him, and behind him Julien scurrying down the bank shouting something he could not make out. The man was no longer paying any attention to Julien, who raced to the water's edge. Victor took his knife from his pocket and leaned his weight against the boat towards the current, forgetting that it was still tied to the jetty and had to fumble to loosen the knots he had tied himself. He was still pushing the boat, his feet already in the water, when the man grabbed him by the hair, jerked him backwards and clamped a hand over his mouth in case anyone might hear a scream in this godforsaken spot, then he put an arm around his throat. The boy felt his face flush and gulped as much air as he could. He still had his knife, but did not know where or how to strike and he knew the man could easily disarm him, so he lashed out, stabbing behind him at random, feeling the blade hit something hard; he pulled it out and stabbed again. He felt a warm wetness on the fist gripping the handle that made him feel nauseous. The hand over his mouth disappeared and he heard the man stumble back and fall. Victor turned and saw him get to his feet and walk towards him, his trousers stained with blood. The pale, slick face betrayed no emotion. He looked like a robotic creature, executing a mission it had been programmed to perform. Watching him lumber forward, head down, dragging his injured leg, it fleetingly occurred to Victor that the man might be immortal, eternally destroyed only to be reborn. At that moment Julien leapt at the man, only to receive a punch in the face that sent him reeling; he fell onto his back, motionless, as though dead. Victor let out a cry. He called out then turned and jumped towards the boat which was drifting into the current. He fell into the water, trying to grab the length of rope, his hands sank into the mud and were cut on something sharp and jagged that made him think of bones. When finally he managed to grab the rope, he pulled the boat towards him, moving deeper into the water as he did so, then clambered over the side and fell onto his stomach.

The man was behind him, clinging to the back of the boat, the water up to his waist, trying to climb aboard. Victor got up on all fours, grabbed the hoe and lashed out with all his strength but he only struck the man's shoulder with the handle, the rusted metal barely grazing his shoulder blade. The man arched his back, leaned his weight on his hands, but he seemed unable to hoist himself, sinking back into the mud. The boy stood up, unbalanced by the man rocking the boat, he took the hoe in both hands. This time he was careful to keep his eyes open, but as he struck out he stumbled and had to steady himself against the side of the boat and the blow caught the side of the man's head and he saw the metal scrape across the scalp, seeming to rip his ear off, Victor could see nothing in the gush of blood. Screaming, the man clamped his hand over the wound, staggering in the water, clumsy and heavy, his whole upper body now spattered with blood, bogged down in the mud, the water lapping around him.

Victor paddled as best he could with his makeshift oar, and the boat moved away from the stupefied man who shook his head and slowly turned back towards the bank. The boat slipped into the current and was carried, askew, far from the bank, so Victor stopped paddling, his arms stiff, his back aching. He could still see the fisherman's hut, but the man had vanished. He wondered whether Julien had come round, picturing again that brutal punch that would have stunned a rabid dog. He felt like a coward, running away like this, but did not know what else he could have done. He knew he had to disappear. And here, in the middle of the estuary, being carried upstream on the tide towards Saint-Estèphe and Bordeaux, he was going back in time, going back to the place he had left and as he lay exhausted in his little boat there was nothing he could do about it – he could not fight the power of the tides which, tomorrow, might drag him back and fling him into the roaring ocean.

24

The telephone. Vilar did not dare to move, as though the device were capable of detecting his presence and would stop ringing if it thought he was not there. He dearly hoped this was just another dream. Go back to sleep. Everything will be fine. This is what he and Ana used to say to Pablo. Pablo was often scared during the night. Perhaps scared of the night itself.

His mobile. Slowly he emerged from the delirium of sleep. It was almost 2.00. He found the telephone. The call was coming from a landline.

"Were you asleep?"

Vilar had not turned on a light and yet around him the darkness began to pale to the point that the room seemed to have been sprayed with phosphorous. He blinked and now the shadows were lit by spots before his eyes that darted in time to the pulsing in his veins.

"What do you want?" Vilar asked.

"To get this over with. I don't want to play anymore."

"So this was a game?"

"Sometimes, yeah. I think it was the same for you. At least it keeps your mind busy, all your police bullshit, the corpses, the investigations, all that shit. That's what gets you up in the morning, dickhead. If it weren't for that, you'd have put a bullet in your head long ago, am I right?"

Sanz was interrupted by a hiccup. Vilar could hear his breathing.

"Where are you calling from? Have you gone into business as a shrink?"

"I'm in the Médoc, if you can believe that. I came to get my son, but the little bastard doesn't want anything to do with me."

"Your son?"

"That's right, my son, Victor – ring any bells? I'm sure you know, they placed him here with a foster family . . . Just like his father before him. We've got a lot in common. But this is the second time he's got away from me, so fuck it, he can drop dead just like his whore of a mother . . ." He paused, took a breath. "Anyway, we're coming to the end of the road."

Vilar tried to think, but his mind was blank. All his concentration was focused on this voice in which he thought he could finally hear a crack, a supressed quavering.

"Where's the kid? Is he with you?"

Sanz sighed.

"I . . . Are you fucking dense or what? I just told you, he got away. I don't know where he is, and I don't give a shit, you got me?"

"Where are you right now?"

"I'll tell you. Come and get me . . ."

Vilar wondered if this was a request or an order. The voice had trailed off towards the end. There was none of the manic triumph, the overweening arrogance with which Sanz usually imbued every word.

"You want me to come get you? Don't you have a car?"

Sanz sighed again and mumbled vaguely.

"No petrol. And I'm not heading out in the middle of the night, the place is crawling with cops."

"Cops? Looking for you?"

"No. You're the only one looking for me. No, they're looking for the kids. Probably think I raped them or killed them, fuck knows. Get me out of here. You have a warrant card, you can get through the cordons."

"You said kids. What kids? Victor? Who else?"

"It's no big deal, I'll explain later . . . Come get me and I'll take you where you want to go."

Vilar felt an excruciating current course through his body. The bruises from the previous day's altercation ached as though Sanz were beating him again.

"And where is it you think I want to go?"

"You know perfectly well. You've known for the past five years."

"I'm tired. Why should I go anywhere with you? What do you know about what I want? I should rip you apart for what you've said about my son, what you've done. I . . ."

Suddenly he had no more breath, his chest felt as though he were suffocating.

"It's not like I'm not tired too. Chill out. You're not going to rip anyone apart because you're not like me, you don't have that rottenness in your brain."

Vilar tried to marshal his thoughts. It was like trying to catch and hug the driving rain. *He's trying to suck up to me. All psychopaths do it. But I've got him. He's got me.*

"Tell me where you are. If I can't find you, I'll get directions from a local officer."

He turned on the light, reached for a piece of paper and a pen. Out of the shadows the lamp conjured a familiar reality and he feared his nightmare might fade away. Vertheuil. A remote house with a blue door on the road to Cissac. A white Golf parked out front. Some sort of pine in the garden. Vilar may have stumbled across the names of such villages on the labels of wine bottles. In the chaos on his desk, he dug out a sufficiently detailed map and went down to the car.

He did not know what he planned to do when he found him. He did not know what his promise was worth. The urge he had had to shoot him in the stomach and watch him die slowly was gone now: perhaps because something in Sanz was exhausted. The way you might say a seam of coal is exhausted. Vilar was about to come face to face with this man he had dreamed of slaughtering for months, and it was this man he was now allowing to guide him. He felt like a blind man in the darkness led by a mad dog. Perhaps he would get to watch Sanz die without having to touch him, watching this blaze that had consumed everything gutter out of its own accord. And it would happen in the darkest hour, there where the earth petered away, where the Médoc narrows to a jagged point and buries itself in the ocean.

He took the pistol Pradeau had given him before he disappeared. He checked the ammunition. Fifteen cartridges. He put the gun on the passenger seat and, as he drove along the dark, straight road, passing the occasional speeding car, his fingers caressed the placid, warm steel.

A little way past Pauillac, he came to a police roadblock. He slipped the gun into the pocket of his jacket and submitted to the questioning without mentioning he was one of them. The *gendarmes* were wearing bulletproof vests and some of them, who remained in the background, were hefting rifles, butts tucked into their armpits, fingers on trigger guards. He allowed them to open the boot and shine their torches inside. The number plate of Sanz's Renault estate had obviously been circulated that afternoon so they were probably on the lookout for the car, and for the missing boys, but it was unlikely that Sanz's mugshot had been sent to every patrol unit.

Afterwards he strayed onto narrower roads, driving through pitch darkness interrupted only by the street lights of deserted villages, stopping three times to consult his map. When he got to Vertheuil, he made a tour of the village to get his bearings, passing the house where Sanz was waiting for him. He parked some fifty metres away and, engine and headlights off, found himself in shadows as thick and murky as oblivion. He suddenly felt a weight on his chest, and he had to inhale deeply two or three times to catch his breath. Through the rolled down windows, he could hear crickets. The night was warm, without a breath of wind. Nothing moved, nothing seemed to exist anymore. Vilar realised he could not even see his hands and was struck by the idea that his body too had ceased to exist, dissolving into the blinding void that surrounded him, that he was dead and had only just noticed.

He opened the car door, leapt out and stood, gasping and feeling foolish as the light inside the car automatically came on, casting a dim glow on the grassy verge. He worried that Sanz was watching for him, perhaps could see him standing here, so he closed the door soundlessly and walked towards the house. The starry vault above his head cast no light.

336

The gate opened without squeaking. The windows were dark, the shutters open. Vilar wondered if Sanz could see him. He also wondered where the people who lived in the house were now. He curled his hand around the pistol and circled the house, keeping his distance, trying to make something out through these windows that seemed to be staring at him like vacant eyes. From time to time, he saw the green or red L.E.D. of some device set on standby. Gradually, he became convinced that he was not circling a sleeping house, but a dead one.

He found himself back at the front door and decided to open it. It swung noiselessly open and he waited for two or three seconds. He could hear nothing in the silence but the muffled ticking of a clock. He stepped inside, pointing the gun this way and that as though it might cast some light on things. He felt ridiculous gesticulating in the dark like this. He found a switch and the light immediately alleviated the pressure in his chest and he could breathe normally once more. He moved towards a door behind which he could glimpse the hulking form of a sofa and cautiously stepped into the room. He smelled stale cigarette smoke. He felt certain that Sanz had laid a trap for him and would jump out at any minute. He slid his feet across the floor, skirted around the sofa and, just as he reached the fireplace, a lumbering movement and a creak of wood made him start and turn towards the sofa.

"Shit, you're here . . ."

Vilar fumbled for a light, switched on a lamp.

Sanz sat up blinking. On his right temple was a huge gauze bandage soaked in Betadine, held in place by a piece of tape that ran across his forehead such that one eye was almost closed. The top of his T-shirt was brown with dried blood and the right leg of his trousers was also stained above the knee. Next to him was a hunting rifle and a cartridge pouch. He looked at Vilar, nodding, a twisted smile on his face.

"What the fuck are you doing in the dark with that gun? You come to arrest me?"

His voice was slurred. He blinked constantly in the dim light.

"Where are they?"

"Who?"

"The people who live here. What did you do to them?"

"I scared them. One look at me and they were shitting themselves. So I nicked their rifle before I passed out completely and I made sure they wouldn't piss me off anymore."

"Where are they?"

Sanz brought a hand to his thigh and gritted his teeth. Then he slumped back against the sofa.

"I buried them in the garden."

A forced, guttural laugh wracked his throat.

"I'm a natural born killer," he said coughing, "and you're fucking Super Cop . . . And I should know, we've got police in our family."

"I'm going to take that rifle," Vilar said. "Don't move a muscle."

He moved a round into the chamber of his pistol, cocked it and stepped towards Sanz.

"Go ahead, I don't need it anymore. You're the one with the guns now. You see what you can do with them, whether they're any use."

He touched the side of his head and his fingers came away smeared with blood.

"Shit, it's bleeding again. That little fucker ripped my ear off."

He did not move as Vilar lifted the weapon onto his shoulder and took the cartridge pouch.

"Who ripped your ear off?"

"My fucking son."

"How do you know he's your son?"

"I just know. I can feel it in my balls."

"And when exactly did you start to give a shit? What about your daughter? You don't think about her much, from what I've heard."

Sanz was leaning back against the sofa, his eyes closed. His chest shook with something that might have been a chortle or a silent cough.

"You talked to that slut, that's how you know . . . how you traced it back to me . . . I don't give a fuck about her and her little brat. I never wanted a kid. She was the one who wanted to keep it when she found out she was pregnant. I warned her . . ."

338

Vilar stared at the man who, in the past four months, had murdered two women with his bare hands and slit a teenage boy's throat. He had desecrated the memory of Pablo, sullied his name, twisted a knife in old wounds. His duty was to knock him out, drag him back to Bordeaux and have him banged up for as long as possible. Instead of which, and without the least curiosity, he simply watched the man writhe with pain as blood seeped into the sofa.

And yet here before him was a human being capable of committing those crimes, motivated by such perversity. A human being with a face, an expression, one who could close his eyes, overcome by sleep, now so utterly drained and so helpless that any *gendarme* could probably come and slip the cuffs on him without waking him. He could hurt, he could suffer, even die. Perhaps Vilar believed in ghosts, but he did not believe in monsters. Neither monsters nor the heroes who hunt and kill them. But dealing with men like this, those who sow private chaos, falls to other men who must confront them with no assurance that they will defeat them. Vilar stared at the man. He had so badly wanted to make him suffer, to kill him. He had sometimes been woken in the night by terrible dreams in which he had the man at his mercy, but the blows he tried to rain down had no power, no effect, and his bullets bounced harmlessly off this body like paper pellets, and he would notice that the body had no face and realising it was a dream would wake with a start, his heart pounding with impotent rage.

Vilar vainly searched inside himself for some vestige of rage, of hatred. He wished that he felt overcome by a desire for revenge, because it would have been easier to lash out, to revel in each blow until the last, what they call the *coup de grâce*. But he felt nothing. There was nothing in him now but an expectation he no longer dared to name.

"Where are we supposed to go when we leave here?"

Sanz opened his eyes. He looked solemnly at Vilar, seeming to consider this question or perhaps the answer he might give.

"I already told you. You know where we're going. You know what we're going to find there. It's almost in the Dordogne. Two hours' drive. My brother is waiting for us. He's the one who figured it all out.

He just had to check to make sure. He called me yesterday, he was going to call you anyway. He said it was the least he owed you."

"Why did you kill him?"

"Who?"

"Morvan, the *gendarme*."

Sanz shrugged and sighed as though the question were of no interest.

"I don't really know . . . My brother thought he was dangerous. When we saw what was on the computers, he said we couldn't leave him alive. Apparently he had files on all the fuck-parties in the area and all the big shots who were at them, a bunch of rich arseholes, T.V. presenters, writers and singers off their tits on coke, a few politicians . . . Anyway my little bro didn't want all this coming back to bite him, given we were both involved back in the day, before I got banged up. He used to hang around to keep the paparazzi out, he did it as a favour to some colleague from Toulouse he used to work with. Anyway, we got the *gendarme* to talk a bit and then we wasted him. It was one less problem."

"Both of you?"

"Why? You surprised? Don't you get it? Your friend tried it once and he got a real taste for this shit. Once the rot sets in, it doesn't stop. You live by it and you fucking die by it. We might not be real brothers, but we're a lot like each other, him and me. You should know better than anyone what it's like, standing there like butter wouldn't melt, when if you didn't need me to drive you there, you'd be laying into me right now. You'd smash my face in and you'd get a fucking hard-on doing it . . ."

He trailed off, brought a hand up to the bandage that covered his ear and held it there for a moment, his eyes closed, breathing heavily through his mouth as the pain wrenched his face to one side. He clicked his tongue and waved his arm in a vague gesture.

"Fuck off, I'm done answering your questions. I'm thirsty."

He struggled to his feet and stood, swaying a little before he could take a step. Then he walked into the kitchen. Vilar followed him and

340

stood in the doorway. With a large glass of water Sanz washed down a couple of pills he had in the palm of his hand.

"He split my head open, that little fucker."

He splashed water on his face and drank some more straight from the tap.

"Where are the people who live here? What did you do to them?"

"They're in the garage, for fuck's sake. What, you think I butchered them and made a necklace out of their eyes? You watch too many movies."

Vilar hesitated about leaving Sanz alone for a minute, but seeing him, head bowed, leaning heavily against the sink he decided the man could not go very far.

Even before he turned on the light, he smelled the acrid whiff of urine and heard the muffled cries. When the bare bulb came on, he saw two little girls sitting in front of a large chest freezer, tied back to back with a length of electrical wire, their mouths gagged with duct tape. Their eyes widened in terror when they saw Vilar appear with the pistol in one hand and the rifle slung over his shoulder, they struggled as much as their bonds would allow them. They had pissed themselves. He reassured them, told them he was a policeman, that it was all over, that they didn't need to be scared anymore. From the opposite side of the garage the parents, who were similarly trussed up, grunted vehemently through their gags. He told them that there was nothing to fear and looked among the tools on a shelf above the workbench for something to cut them free with. He took a pair of wire cutters and walked over to the father, who looked at him, his eyes filled with fear or hatred. Just as he was about to cut him loose, he got to his feet again. The man stared at him in astonishment and grunted something, shaking his head wildly, while his wife tried to crane her neck to see what was going on. Her eyes were pleading, filled with tears, her face was red and swollen.

Vilar set the wire cutters down at his feet and explained that he had something urgent he needed to do before he set them free. He told them the *gendarmes* would be here soon. He found a Stanley knife and a couple of cable ties which he looped together so he would only have to pull them tight.

The man gave a strangled cry and the veins in his neck throbbed, the tendons bulged fit to burst. Vilar told him to calm down, said that he would send help and left the door ajar when he went out.

He went back to the kitchen, but Sanz was not there. He took out his pistol again, but there was no need to hunt in the dark for long: Sanz was lying on the sofa, one arm covering his eyes.

"Let's go."

When he did not react, Vilar jabbed the muzzle of the gun into his ribs. Sanz started and looked at him, his eyes wide and vacant.

"Let's go. Move it. We've got a long journey ahead of us."

Sanz did not move. His breathing returned to the regular cadence of imminent sleep. Vilar grabbed the collar of his polo shirt and lifted him up. Sanz cursed and struggled feebly as he was hauled off the sofa, collapsing onto all fours on the rug. Vilar grabbed him by the belt of his trousers and dragged him along. They bumped into the coffee table and the armchair, knocked over a plant stand and a potted plant. As he was being dragged through the door into the hall, Sanz yelled that that was enough, that he could manage by himself.

Vilar pitched him forward and he fell flat on his belly, then struggled to his feet.

Once they were outside and had closed the door behind them, they were swallowed by the night and for an instant Vilar was once again gripped by terror and had to breathe through his mouth so as not to suffocate. He ordered Sanz to walk on ahead and – inasmuch as it was possible to gauge in the darkness – stayed two or three metres behind, rifle aimed at his back, finger on the trigger. The bodywork of the car shimmered in the faint ambient glow. Vilar pressed Sanz back against the bonnet and shackled his wrists with one of the cable ties he had prepared. Sanz babbled incoherent curses and threats, clearly groggy from the pills he had taken, and Vilar hissed at him to shut his trap, told him he had nothing left to say. He pushed him onto the back seat and lashed his ankles together. Then, he unloaded the rifle and stowed it with the cartridge pouch in the boot.

Sliding behind the steering wheel, he asked which way they were headed. When Sanz did not answer, he repeated the question.

"Nowhere. Let me sleep."

Vilar turned off the engine and the headlights and sat in the shadows, his pupils dilating in the darkness. Blind. Nothing outside existed now. He listened to his heart hammering in his chest. Rage left him breathless.

"What did you say?"

Sanz muttered some obscenity, his voice slurred.

Vilar took a torch from the glove compartment, turned it on, then got out of the car and opened the back door. He lifted Sanz up, shone the beam into his drugged face and whacked his nose with the end of the torch.

"You fucking tell me where we're going – tell me where it is I've been wanting to go all these years, as you put it – or I'll skin you alive."

Lying on the back seat, Sanz blinked into the torchlight, grimacing, but then suddenly a smile disfigured his face.

"Tell me," Vilar growled, his fist gripping the man's polo shirt.

"You're looking for your son? Me too. Thing is, I found my son and he stabbed me in the thigh, the little queer, and then he smashed my face in. But that's O.K., I get it. What about you, what sort of state do you think your son will be in when you find him?"

Vilar lifted the bandage and gave a brutal tug. Sanz screamed and tried to struggle, but Vilar kept him on his back, his rigid arm pushing him into the seat. The gauze pad, which had been stuck in place with dried blood, made a ripping sound like Velcro as it came away, and in the torchlight Vilar could see the glistening wound: a deep, bloody gash that ran down along the scalp and through the outer ear, slashing half of it away.

"Talk, or I'll rip the rest of your face off."

Sanz was whimpering now, lashing out weakly with his bound legs,

343

feebly hurling himself against the car door. Vilar hit him just above the mangled ear. Sanz spluttered and then let out a piercing wail that sounded almost like a child. Vilar wanted to hit him again, suddenly overwhelmed by the rage he thought he had mastered. Now that he was standing over this man, now that he had him at his mercy, he wanted to make him suffer; wanted to see him die. Wanted to watch the faint spark in his eyes snuff out.

He grasped the bloody, scabbed ear and Sanz screamed "No!" and his teeth beginning to chatter. "Head for Castillon. After that, I'll explain how to get there. I can't take this any longer." He curled up and pressed the sodden remains of the bandage to his ear with his bound hands.

Vilar drove fast and, without passing another car or encountering any roadblocks, found himself on the road to Bordeaux. Once or twice on the dual carriageway he saw police lights in the distance, but they disappeared into the darkness like abstractions that might as well never have existed. He called the emergency services, alerted them to the people tied up in their garage. He would have liked to know what had become of Victor and the other kid that Sanz had mentioned. He asked but, knocked out by the tranquillisers, the man did not answer.

He convinced himself that Sanz could not have done them any harm, he had never attacked children. This whole time Sanz had been brooding about the discovery that he might have a son, and he seemed to have cast himself in the role of the misunderstood father. There was no end to his delusions. Vilar tried not to think about the boys, since there was nothing he could do. He gunned the engine, eager to get away from the Médoc as quickly as possible and leave all this behind him. He sped down the motorway, barrelled through the interchanges, crossed the suspension bridge over the river, oblivious to the city and its halo of light below.

I'm coming, little man, I'm coming, you don't have to be afraid anymore.

His eyes filled with tears. He felt again the hard, bitter lump in his throat. He felt exhausted with grief, with rage, with loneliness. Vainly he tried to imagine what he would find when he got there. He knew

344

only that he would get there at the darkest hour of night. Into the primordial abyss of all terrors.

Over and over he silently mouthed Pablo's name simply so that he could give some meaning to the journey, so he could keep on driving rather than pull over onto the verge to sleep, or to die after putting a bullet in the belly of the man who had been mutilated by a terrified boy, who now lay sleeping on the back seat. But sometimes his invocation produced no effect, no answer, stripped of its magic by the silence.

Driving at more than 150 k.p.h., the twinkling headlights of the cars he passed were reflected in the rear-view mirror which he checked every now and then to see whether Sanz had woken or was sitting up. He took the bypass around Libourne, stuck behind a Spanish truck he could not overtake on the narrow two-way road, sped past Saint-Émilion, his hands clutching the steering wheel. As he approached Castillon he shouted to Sanz to wake up because they were nearly there. When the man did not reply, he thought about stopping and knocking him about a bit, but then saw him sit up, framed in the headlights of the cars behind, rubbing his eyes, clicking his tongue and complaining that he was thirsty.

25

The tide drove him onward.

His panic subsided as the jetty retreated into the distance and the details blurred into a dark mess of shadows quivering against the light. Reeling from the pain, the man had staggered back in the water, thrashing his blood-drenched body and his arms, and for a long time the boy could hear his howls and his threats above the roar of the river. Then suddenly the figure disappeared, and Victor did not know if he had fallen into the water or made it back to the riverbank.

He tried to see if Julien had got to his feet again, but before long all he could make out was the silhouette of the dock jutting out into the water. The current had carried him into the middle of the estuary, and he was helpless against this power, this inexorable slowness. The banks were now no more than hazy lines weighed down by a sky that seemed about to push them underwater and drown them. Twisted leafless branches drifted alongside him, sometimes rolling so that their severed limbs ploughed the water like blind fingers trying to catch something in the rushing torrent.

Victor wondered which of the boat or the dead tree would better survive the whims of the raging current. He kept his mind busy with such thoughts, staving off the mounting panic that gripped him, adrift as he was on this roaring vastness that surged around him in its relentless power. Never had he felt so far from everything.

The sun was setting in swirls of dazzling flame and for a moment the boy was confused, lost in a blaze of phosphorus beyond which he could see nothing. He sat in the back of the boat clutching the bag to avoid this brightness that threatened to consume him, reduce him to ashes, to an inconsequential dust that would immediately be absorbed by the water. He laid a hand on the urn inside the bag and whispered to his mother, sharing his terrified thoughts.

"Manou."

Then the flames guttered out, leaving nothing but a fading golden glow, and the blue of the eastern sky grew gradually deeper. Two waves whipped past over the swell. They lifted the boat gently and he watched as these ripples moved away into the distance until all their energy was dissolved.

He was moving upstream. He passed the village, recognised the steeple of the church, tried to make out the details of the bank, hoping against hope that Rebecca or Marilou might be there, might see him pass and wave to him, but he was too far out, too small in this vastness for anyone to see him or even think to look for him out here. There was a rustle of trees, a slight backwash, as with every passing minute the river became dark, impenetrable even as the tide surged forward, causing the boat to lurch and roll at times, carving out hollows in the water in front of the bow.

He wondered what they were all doing now, trying to picture Marilou's dark eyes, trying to feel again Rebecca's kisses on his lips. He smiled in spite of everything. Then he thought about Julien and he felt a shudder in his chest that made him turn to look back into the gloom. He pictured again the brutal punch, heard once more the dull, blunt thud, saw the little body fall backwards like a lump of wood. Surely no-one could die from a single punch. Lots of punches, maybe. And besides, the kid had taken his fair share of beatings in the past, the kind of beatings that left him sprawled on the ground while he was punched and kicked anywhere it might hurt. He had told Victor about it one night when they were on the terrace staring at the stars, picking out the constellations that Julien could never seem to recognise. Staring up at the sky, Julien had talked about it in a neutral tone, pretending not to care about the thick leather strap, talking about his mother screaming, huddled under the table to avoid the blows, about his father laying into him, talked about the terrifying sight he had discovered coming home from school – his father's body lying in the bath, the head half blown away, brains splattered on the bathroom tiles.

The kid had said all this then suddenly fallen silent, heaving a sigh, bowing his head, and had stayed motionless for a long time while Victor tried to think of something to say – grisly images of blood and human remains flitting through his mind, corpses sprawled in impossible poses – wondering how he would have reacted had he seen his mother so horribly mutilated. He had tried to share in the horror that still terrified Julien, but his own horrors quickly engulfed him again, keeping him at a distance from the other boy's tragedy. They had sat in silence, each with their own ghosts.

Victor suddenly wanted to see them all again. He wanted to feel their presence. Wanted to hear their chatter and their laughter. He wanted to feel Marilou's furtive eyes on him, to see Julien's scrawny frame dangling precariously between two garden chairs. He tried to use his crude plank to steer towards the bank. He grunted with the effort, slashed at the water with his makeshift oar to subdue the rising tide, to break the back of this monster. He managed to turn the bow of the boat towards the bank, but now the swell lashed the side of the boat, threatening to capsize it. He struggled on for some minutes more, tossed on the current, then fell back into the boat and howled in frustration. He lapsed into a sort of tired stupor.

He could see the wharfs of the old Pauillac refinery coming towards him. The beacons were lit now. Further upriver, a red marker buoy bobbed on the water. He did not know what time it was, but he knew it was late. Nine o'clock possibly. A lighthouse appeared in front of him and he quickly made out the dark mass of the island, bristling with tall trees whose tops still flickered in the setting sun. The estuary was narrowing, and along the banks lights gradually appeared, some blinking, others steady. Victor watched the night draw in, expanding and settling into the crevices of the shore, then spreading to erase the contours of the landscape, obliterating colours until that instant when the blue in the west faded completely from the starless sky. He waited for the moment when everything is in darkness, when eyes grow wide to drink in the dense shadows to make out the faintest trace of light on things.

The boat moved so close to the island that he could hear the last of the birds chirrup as they went to sleep. He picked up his paddle again and steered towards a clump of trees that seemed to dip into the water. The current was clearly weaker now, because he was able to draw alongside, grasp a low branch and wedge the boat against a tree stump and tie it up.

Night had now enveloped everything. The river lapped and sang against the boat. From time to time, a light from the far bank trembled on the water. In the distance, he could see the wharfs at Pauillac, the lights of the marina. The headlights of passing cars. Other people going about their ordinary lives while he was so far from everything, so alone, happy perhaps, for the first time since she died. He knew that it would be possible to feel that wholeness again. There would be other moments like this, simple and mysterious. The darkness and the murmur of things. He felt strong and sure as though in some impregnable refuge.

He took the urn out of the bag and hugged it to him.

Manou. Look how beautiful it is, and here we are sitting peacefully. Look, over there. And sometimes the fish jump out of the water. Can you hear them?

He felt himself suffocating and, with something like a whimper, sucked air into his lungs.

I know you're here and I know I'll never see you again. I talk to you, but you don't answer anymore, but I know you're listening.

He ate in the darkness, groping, unable to see his hands. He let his fingers feel their way, taking the knife, opening a tin, scooping mouthfuls that he chewed slowly, solemnly, savouring the moment as much as the food.

Then he lay down in the bottom of the boat on the fisherman's blanket and studied the sky, waiting for a star to flicker on just for him, letting sleep wash over him, driving out his tiredness, and still he could see nothing in the heavens, no sign, nothing but that useless powdery light that was probably already dead.

26

They stopped in the car park of a hypermarket next to the petrol station outside Castillon. Vilar immediately got out of the car, slipped the pistol into his belt, stretched himself to shake off the stiffness in his shoulders. He opened the back door and cut Sanz free with the Stanley knife, but the man simply sat there, his head thrown back, his mouth half open. Vilar looked at him, realising he was in a bad way and wondered whether the blow to the head had been just too forceful. He found himself worrying that Sanz would die or lapse into a coma before all this was over. Always supposing it would soon be over, that it would ever be over. It seemed to him that Sanz's dying would be one last dirty trick on his part.

He took a few steps, desperate for a cigarette, looked across the wide expanse of tarmac dotted with little shelters filled with shopping trolleys. It was depressing and ugly. The heat soaked up by the earth now rose in steady waves carrying the unpleasant smell of tar and motor oil. Behind him he heard the sound of voices and laughing. He turned and saw a guy who was filling up at the petrol station chatting to some people sitting in the car. Two or three heads bobbed; the people inside were larking around and the car bounced on its shock absorbers. He could hear them laughing. It was Friday night. A group of mates heading for a nightclub, Vilar thought. An arm appeared through an open window, offering the man holding the petrol pump a square bottle, gin possibly. The guy refused, suggesting his mate stick his dick in it and stop drinking. The car rocked with a roar of laughter.

They shot off in a screech of tyres, and then there was silence. Vilar went back to Sanz who was looking around, dazed.

"Right," Vilar said, "what the hell do we do now? Are we supposed to wait until opening time? What time is your brother showing up?"

"He'll come when we phone him. You do it. The number's on a piece of paper in my right-hand trouser pocket."

Vilar dug into the bloodstained pocket, found the paper and dialled the number. Pradeau answered immediately.

"We're at the hypermarket car park. Next to the petrol station."

"I'll be there in three minutes."

"What exactly is it that you found?"

"As I said, I'll be right there. Is Éric with you?"

"Of course he's here. I was hardly going to leave him behind. Not alive at any rate."

"Yeah, I get it."

They hung up simultaneously. Vilar walked away from the car, sucked air into his lungs to get rid of the weight that was pressing on his chest, gazed at the hypermarket, all its lights out. He could not think straight, could not come up with any plan, any idea. He saw pits filled with water and bodies dumped in them. He saw a figure running away, unreachable. He retraced his steps, watching the road so he would see Pradeau arrive. Sanz was smoking.

"Give me a cigarette."

Sanz indicated the pack and the lighter on the seat next to him. The cigarette pack was smeared with blood.

"Don't worry, the ciggies are dry."

He coughed. The same cough he had as he choked and spluttered over his obscenities on the telephone.

The first puff made Vilar dizzy. He took another few steps. He could not picture the sort of place Pradeau would lead him to. He felt as though all his vital functions were suspended: his thoughts, his pulse, his breathing.

He scanned the car park beneath the useless glow of the street lights, and thought about Pablo appearing at the far end, his small frame, barely visible, caught between the darkness and the artificial light, still held back by the shadows, before suddenly breaking free and walking towards him, his footsteps slow and shaky. He focused every ounce of mental energy he could still muster on this vision, despite the breathless state he had been floating in since they arrived here, because sometimes he let himself go, sometimes he allowed himself to believe in the heart-rending illusion of a magical wish that might come true. He stared at a door and dreamed that it might open so that his son could step through; he listened to the hushed silence, expecting that his mobile would ring and he would hear his boy's voice. He dreamed impossible things, telling himself that for as long as was at all possible, he would stay alive.

The headlights glided towards him almost without a sound. He shuddered when he saw them. He slipped a hand into his pocket and touched the warm steel of the gun and felt miserable that simply touching the pistol reassured him.

Pradeau parked at a right angle to Vilar's car. He opened the door, seemed to hesitate for a second and then stepped out. He glanced at Vilar and then went over to Sanz, leaned into the car and asked him what had happened, how he felt.

"My son hit me with a fucking pickaxe or something, I don't know. Ripped my ear off, the little fucker."

"Your son? What son?"

"Victor. Nadia's kid."

"We have to get you to a hospital. Are you in pain?"

"Some. But don't worry about me, I've got painkillers. Anyway, I don't give a shit. You have to take this guy where he has to go. Do what you need to do."

Vilar stepped closer and listened.

"What the hell are we doing?" he said.

Pradeau waved at him vaguely, to wait or to shut up. He was still bent over his brother, trying to persuade him to let him take him to see a doctor. Sanz was swearing and telling Pradeau to leave him in peace. Their deep voices rumbled inside the car. Sanz was getting angry.

352

"Look, what does it matter, this is it. You said it yourself . . . I don't know if I can carry on much further . . ."

Pradeau stood up again. For the first time since he arrived he looked at Vilar, stared into his eyes, and Vilar could finally see him properly. He was thinner, the skin on his face looked like crêpe paper. His eyes were both too wide or veiled by drooping eyelids. Vilar thought he must have taken something, or that he had been taking so many pills recently that he no longer knew what it meant to sleep. He spoke in a monotone, betraying no emotion, as though talking to a squad before a police operation.

"It's ten minutes from here. I don't know what we'll find there. The guy who hangs out there is called Jean-Luc Lafon. It's his house in the country. He started out as a chartered accountant and compliance officer in the '70s. The sort of work that opens doors, means you've got files on everyone. He was well known in business circles in the area. Heavy industry, wine-making, everyone swore by him. I'm guessing he's still got a lot of dirty laundry he could wash in public. I did a bit of searching – it was easy, Morvan had done most of the groundwork. He gave up everything in '95 to do business with Eastern European countries. I don't know any more than that. Morvan had sent a memo requesting that a formal investigation be opened into Lafon's dealings. He suspected the guy was involved in human trafficking: illegal workers, prostitutes and kids."

"So, we contact Interpol, we send them Morvan's paper."

"I don't think you get it. He's the one who has photos of someone we think might be your son. We found more of them on Morvan's hard drive. Lafon swapped files with a ton of people. I've brought a couple if you want to see them. Morvan found them and managed to trace them back to this guy. My brother sent them to you without telling me, there was nothing I could do to stop him, to stop this."

Vilar felt his eyes fill with tears. He opened his mouth to suck in as much air as he could.

"Just as there was nothing you could do for Morvan, I suppose? Since you couldn't stop this bastard from killing him, you thought you'd give him a hand, is that it?"

Pradeau looked at him without reacting, seeming not to understand what had been said. Then Vilar strode over to the car, grabbed Sanz by his blood-soaked collar and dragged him out. Sanz whined and flailed his arms weakly, collapsing on all fours on the tarmac.

"Pick up your shit before I drive over it. He's getting blood everywhere. And anyway, I don't want him dying in my car. I think I'd rather go alone. Just tell me where it is."

Pradeau helped his brother to his feet and carried him to his own car where he had no alternative but to let him slump onto the back seat. He closed the car door carefully, as though not wanting to wake the injured man, before coming back to Vilar, standing closer to him than he had when he first arrived.

"I'll come with you. I owe you that at least. There's no knowing how they'll react if they know you're alone and working unofficially. Éric and I knew this guy back in the '90s. He used to throw orgies down at Cap-Ferrat or at Pyla with a whole crowd of filthy rich scum, Éric must have told you."

"Sandra de Melo already told me everything. And your fucking brother murdered her."

"I know."

"Yeah, you know. You've known everything from the start and here I am talking to you instead of putting a fucking bullet in your brain. I don't know what's happening anymore, what I'm doing standing around in the middle of the night with a couple of scumbags when my son might be somewhere nearby in God-knows-what state, Jesus fuck, I don't get it. Why didn't you stop him?"

"I couldn't control him anymore. I knew that if you were sniffing around Nadia's case you were bound to find out about the shit him and me had been mixed up in. And then he decided to fuck with your head with all that stuff about your son. He was crazy, he thought using Pablo was an way of pressuring you so you'd lose it altogether. There was nothing I could do."

"You could have talked to me. We were friends, weren't we? Isn't that what they call it?"

354

"I would have had to tell you all this, and there was no way I could do that. Besides, if I'd let you arrest Éric, he would have spilled the whole story. I was trapped . . . And then there was my mother . . . He's the only one she still recognises. The only person who still connects her to her past, who could give her back her sense of self – sometimes. I couldn't have taken that away from her, you have to understand . . ."

Vilar shook his head. He took a step back, drew this pistol from his pocket and pointed it at Pradeau's head.

"I don't understand anything. This is what I should do. And put a bullet in my own head after."

Tears streamed down his face. His voice trailed off in a dry cough.

Pradeau had not moved. He went on in the same monotone. "When they feel trapped, they're prepared to do anything to save their arses. They murdered two girls who tried to blackmail a magistrate. They'd recognised him because he'd banged up one of their friends for a drugs offence."

"How do you know that? Was it your brother? Is he the one who . . . ?"

Pradeau shrugged.

"He made the bodies disappear. He tossed them in the ocean off Hendaye. One of them washed up on Hossegor beach a month later. After that, I got myself out of that shit. I couldn't take it anymore."

"Of course not, because deep down you're a good man. When it comes down to it, you're just too nice, is that what you're saying? I'm betting it was you who drove the boat, yeah? What were you doing, talking to seagulls?"

"Don't be so fucking stupid. When the girls went missing a month apart I realised what had happened. That was when I got out. That's when Éric and I lost touch. I even stopped going to visit my parents so I wouldn't run into him."

Vilar glanced towards the car where Sanz lay asleep. He put the gun back in his pocket.

"I don't give a shit about your family problems. Take me to this place and keep your trap shut. I don't think there's anything else you can say in your defence."

Pradeau turned away and sighed. He climbed behind the steering wheel of his car and drove off.

Vilar followed him through the centre of Castillon and turned onto a road that had once been an old towpath along the Dordogne. Below them was the river, but they could not see it because it was so utterly black. After a couple of kilometres, Pradeau turned the car onto a dirt track and stopped almost immediately, switching off his headlights. Vilar did likewise and night once again closed over him. He got out of the car, allowed a breath of wind to wash over his face and forced himself to take deep breaths because once again the weight of the darkness was suffocating him. He tried to make something out in the murk, but not a glimmer, not a shadow could be seen. He was aware of the trees only from the rustle of the breeze through the leaves, of the river only from the sound of lapping against the bank.

"Pablo," he whispered, but this time the name found no echo, was engulfed by shadows, where before the air about him seemed to tremble at the mere mention of the name.

He heard Pradeau click the breech of a gun and slide it into a holster. He saw him shine a torch against his hand to check it was working.

"It's at the end of this path, about a hundred metres. Lafon and his wife will be there, and a younger guy. I've been keeping tabs on them for four days. I haven't spotted anyone else."

Vilar opened the boot of his car, took out the rifle, felt the weight of the cartridge pouch, then decided to leave them.

Pradeau walked on ahead. As he passed Pradeau's car, Vilar said, "What about him?"

"Are you going to miss him? I think he's asleep. I'll sort him out after. Come on, we don't need any light to follow the path, it's flat and it's not far. It's a big place, almost a mansion. We'll see the lights."

"No dog?"

"No. Not that I know of."

They walked on in silence. All that could be heard was their breathing and the crack of footsteps on pebbles. Above the trees to the left a blue halo indicated the lights of Castillon. The house appeared, tall and pale, dimly lit by two small lanterns flanking a flight of steps. Two of the ground-floor windows were clearly lit up. A little further off, on the edge of the circle of light, four cars were parked.

Pradeau stopped dead. Vilar, walking behind, almost bumped into him.

"What is it?"

"Gravel. They'll hear us."

Vilar carried on regardless. The sound of his footsteps echoed off the facade, a sort of muffled crackle that could probably be heard from the road. Inside the house a dog barked. Short high-pitched yelps. Vilar could already picture the breed of dog, the kind he could kill with a single kick. He climbed the flight of steps. Pradeau followed him. The dog went on yapping. Vilar drew his pistol and gently pushed the door, which was not bolted. He was no longer thinking about anything. He was aware only that the cruel sands of these minutes as they trickled through the hourglass with inexorable slowness weighed more than his whole life. He knew that he would live with this weight forever or be buried by it. His feet knew, as they walked on unstoppably in the darkness; his lungs knew, as they breathed evenly and deeply; his calm heart and his whole body knew, responding now with not a trace of tiredness or tension. He crossed a large hall and found himself at the foot of a staircase, turned and saw the shadowy figure of Pradeau join him. The dog suddenly fell silent.

On the right, they heard the muffled sound of a television. A burst of voices from some American movie.

Vilar headed in this direction, the pistol pressed against his thigh. When he opened the door, he saw only the vast television screen, shadows dancing around it. He stepped into the room and noticed a form lying across a low table but did not at first recognise what it was, so he moved closer and now saw that it was the body of a naked man whose head had been hacked off – or rather beaten to a pulp, since the

357

arcing sprays of blood and brain matter were streaked across the wall opposite, and the piece of modern art that hung there. Vilar crouched down and felt his stomach heave when he realised that the lower jaw, with its row of terrifyingly white teeth, was still attached to the base of the skull. He stood up, gasping as he tried to suck in as much air as he could, choking back the nausea that welled in his throat, shaking off the disorientating paralysis he could feel creeping through him. Pradeau, who had just stepped into the room, let out a cry of revulsion which was drowned out by the chatter of the television, but Vilar ignored him and turned to the wall looking for what he was certain he would find: the blast of buckshot that had embedded itself in the partition wall and ripped the canvas in two places. The wall was riddled with shot. Here and there the plaster had come away and there were small, irregular craters dotted amid the splattered human remains. Vilar guessed that two shots had been fired simultaneously, hence the damage to the body. It was already beginning to smell. Death must have taken placed about two days earlier.

He avoided looking at the corpse and turned to Pradeau, who had switched on two lamps on top of an antique chest. He had pulled on his latex gloves as though about to examine the crime scene.

"Can you explain this?"

"I've no fucking idea. It's not like I was sat outside all day and all night."

"Who is this guy?"

Pradeau moved forward a little, stepping around the sofa and glancing coldly at the body as he turned off the television.

"The young guy who lives with them."

"He was fucking both of them?"

Pradeau gave a crooked smile and shrugged.

"They didn't exactly invite me in to watch. But it would be their style."

"We have to find the other two."

Vilar went out into the hall, hesitating as to which door to open first. The wave of nausea had passed, but he could feel a migraine pounding dully against his temples. He felt as though he were in some parallel dimension. With every step he fell deeper into the nightmare, and he knew it would only end when he slipped, exhausted, into unconsciousness. In the kitchen he found dishes in the sink and the remains of a meal on the table. An electric coffee maker was plugged in and gave off a revolting smell of burnt coffee. He discovered a living room decked out in black leather and stainless steel and hung with garish paintings, a dining room lit by a crystal chandelier, filled with antique furniture. Pradeau followed behind him. Sometimes he could feel his breath on the back of his neck.

The dog began to bark again, a long, continuous howl. It was coming from the floor above. Vilar ran up the stairs, shouldered open the doors.

The smell of excrement and putrefaction hit him just as he was dazzled by a blaze of white light. Lit by three small, round spotlights, the bodies of a man and a woman lay entwined on the vast bed. The man was lying between the woman's thighs. Vilar could see his flabby back, his sagging arse around which one of the woman's legs had been crooked. The warm air and the pervading stench was unbreathable.

The dog had rushed ahead into the room, and his high-pitched yaps were now deafening. It was one of those small, shaggy dogs, beloved of elderly women, that look like mops, with hair hanging down from their bellies in dubious tassels. The dog managed to dodge two kicks, but the third lifted him off the ground, winding him and sending him flying to the far end of the room where he crouched by the wall, ears flattened.

There was blood everywhere. On the sheets, the carpets, the walls, the upturned bedside table.

Vilar stepped closer to the bodies and saw the gaping chest of the woman, her left breast and shoulder reduced to pulp by the force of the shot. The man no longer had a face and for a second Vilar could not understand how the whole front of his head – forehead, eyes, nose, jaws – could have been shot away. He assumed he must have been shot in the temple at point-blank range. Some of the contents of his skull had dripped onto the woman's face creating a glutinous, brownish mask. Vilar jerked back, suddenly bent double by a wave of nausea. Spasms wracked his stomach, he vomited bile, coughed, swallowed great mouthfuls of the warm fetid air.

Just then he noticed the video camera mounted on a tripod and behind it on a small table, a computer with a webcam. As he lifted his head, the migraine now pounding full force, he saw Pradeau standing in the doorway holding a pump-action shotgun.

"What's the hell's going on?" Vilar said. "What the fuck is this place?"

"The house belongs to a guy who knew too much. A bit like you. I'm just cleaning house, is all. What did you expect? You really think I give a fuck at this stage?"

Pradeau pumped the shotgun and Vilar threw himself to the floor just as the back of an armchair behind him exploded and toppled to the ground. He pulled his hand from under him, still gripping the pistol, and managed to blindly fire off two rounds and saw Pradeau leap back and disappear. The air was filled with plaster dust. An acrid cloud of smoke from the gunshots floated above the corpses. He stepped out of the room and immediately ducked, hearing the boom of the shotgun and seeing the flare coming from the stairwell just as the wall behind him splintered into shards of brick and plaster. Bent double, he scuttled over to the banister and lay on his belly, stunned, vaguely trying to convince himself that all this would stop, that reality would resume, that time would start up again from the moment he pushed open the front door and stepped onto the gravel. He stared into the darkness of the ground floor, all the more impenetrable after the glare of the bedroom, and could see nothing. He tried to calm his breathing the better to hear, but he could not make out even a faint rustle. Then he heard a clattering from the bedroom and, turning, saw the little dog appear. Seeing Vilar, it stopped in the doorway, then trotted towards him, wagging its head as though happy to have finally found someone. The animal moved closer, pressing its snout against his face, and viciously he shoved it away.

He noticed that the stench of death clung to the dog's shaggy coat. It came back, sitting about two metres from him like some baleful creature, a harbinger of calamity and pestilence. He waved at it to go away. Eventually, the animal trotted off on its thin paws and disappeared down the stairs. Vilar heard the faint scratching of its claws on the stairs and then a door creaking.

He got to his feet and walked to the stairs, moving slowly down them with his back pressed against the wall. As he reached ground level, he looked up at the luminous rectangle from which a livid light spilled only to be quickly swallowed by the darkness. He got his bearings and crept past the doors he had pushed opened earlier. There was nothing he could do when a hand grabbed his shoulder and dragged him into a pitch-dark room.

He stumbled down three steps, twisting his ankle, and found himself on all fours on the rough tiles, his pistol skittering across the floor. A bare bulb flickered on. Pradeau had the shotgun trained on him.

"It has to look convincing, don't you think?"

The room was some sort of scullery with whitewashed walls and a low, dark-panelled ceiling, with gaps between some of the beams. In one corner was a stone sink and a laundry basin. Under three small, rounded windows stood a workbench with a vice and a clutter of tools, and above it was a board on which hung some other tools and also coils of wire, electrical cables and string. Upended chairs stood on top of a wooden table. Pradeau stepped towards him. He was smiling, the shotgun resting against his shoulder.

"No point firing all over the place. Shit, we're not cowboys. And besides, it's really important that your death is a suicide . . . Important to me, I mean . . . Here you are, the desperate detective searching for his son, you've just killed that sad paedophile fuck. And here I am wiping out two witnesses who were becoming a real pain in the arse. That fucker upstairs was prepared to spill all my dirty little secrets just for the sake of bringing down a cop. Clever set-up, don't you think? I should have been a movie director. Besides, you make the perfect audience, you'll believe any shit, you dumb fuck."

His voice was slurred and he blinked against the bright light. His upper body was swaying back and forth almost imperceptibly.

Vilar tried to make sense of what was happening. Pradeau's words hung in the air between them and then finally the penny dropped.

"Pablo . . ." he said.

He was overcome by a wave of grief and rage. He would die without discovering anything, without knowing anything, without understanding anything. Here his son's name was meaningless; it was sucked into this sordid quagmire.

From the hall came the sound of a door slamming, glass shattering. They heard Sanz calling to his brother. The voice was frenzied, breathless. Pradeau seemed to hesitate. He did not take his eyes off Vilar, but it was clear that he was listening. Sanz's shuffling footsteps were coming towards them. They could hear him panting and moaning. He babbled incoherently, cursing his brother, shouting threats.

Pradeau came and stood behind Vilar, pumped the shotgun and raised it to his shoulder just as his brother appeared in the doorway. Vilar hurled himself backwards, anticipating that Pradeau was not in a firing position. He slammed into him, sending both of them sprawling onto their backs while Sanz hobbled towards them, a knife in his hand. Pradeau's head hit the tiles with a dull thud and Vilar had time to wriggle free and roll onto his side. He grabbed the barrel of the shotgun and was surprised to be able to take it from him with no resistance. One arm over his eyes, one knee raised, Pradeau struggled feebly.

Vilar managed to prop himself on one knee, but Sanz launched himself towards him, brandishing the knife. Vilar squeezed the trigger and saw Sanz's body spin, huge and black beneath the dazzling glare of the bulb. He reeled across the room, and then collapsed.

Vilar got to his feet and it took a few seconds for the white-hot intensity of the migraine burning his eyes and his brain to subside. He looked down at Sanz, sprawled on his belly, one shoulder almost completely blown away, leaving only shreds of skin and fabric. He lay in a pool of blood that streaked the floor. Pradeau seemed to be asleep, one arm shielding his eyes. Vilar nudged him in the ribs with his foot. Pradeau only groaned. Vilar saw the pistol under the table and went to get it. He unloaded the cartridges from the shotgun, dry fired the weapon and tossed it in the corner.

Pradeau allowed himself to be tied up, offering no resistance. As Vilar yanked his arms behind his back he could see the man was crying. He tried to think of something to say but found nothing, nothing that might make him suffer more than the present catastrophe. He bound his elbows with wire and his ankles with rope, then lashed the two together so that he could not move. He did the same with Sanz, who howled every time he was forced to move. It was not particularly his intention to hurt him, yet each moan brought a sense of satisfaction. He realised, in spite of the heat and his terrible thirst, his mouth was watering.

By the time he had finished and gone back to the kitchen, it was almost 3.00 a.m. He took a long drink from the tap, rinsed out his mouth and blew his nose, unable to get rid of the putrid stench. It was as though he himself had begun to rot. For a moment he sat down on a chair and stared at the remains of the meal, the familiar domestic chaos that could so easily be tidied away, but he was thinking about the irreparable chaos all around him, the decomposing bodies, the house that might well conceal yet more terrors.

He gripped the edge of the table and hoisted himself to his feet. A wave of dizziness forced him to lean against the workbench. The throbbing migraine plunged him into an anguished stupor. He wiped tears from his face though he had no sense that he was crying, and went out into the hall. He looked for the door to the wine cellar, since a house like this was bound to have one. He found it to the left of the staircase; it was padlocked. He went back into the scullery, took the shotgun and loaded it. The two men did not react to his presence. Sanz did not move at all, he might well have been dead, Pradeau, lying on his side, watched him, his eyes wide in fear or shock, his mouth open.

It took two shots to blast open the cellar locks. He pressed the light switch and went down the stone steps. The smell of damp stone and mildew pervaded the place, and it was cool. Set into the beaten-earth floor were two pillars that supported the vaulted ceiling. He followed the line of duckboards, moving between the crates filled with thousands of wine bottles. The cellar was organized by *château* and by vintage, marked out on labels or signs. The cellar was lit by spotlights which gave it a comfortable, convivial atmosphere. Vilar stood and contemplated the space. He could imagine people gathering here to sample fine or rare old vintages, trading pretentious chatter about the world of wine, revelling in this haven in the timeless pleasure of true privilege based on complicity and impeccable taste. He tried to imagine the couple rotting upstairs rhapsodising with their posh friends over the bouquet of a Médoc. He pictured the man whose face had been blown off roaming among these liquid assets, and as he did so the wine cellar was transformed suddenly into a macabre crypt.

Just then, he noticed a low, narrow door on the right. A couple of kicks put paid to the lock and the stout wooden door crashed open. There was a step down. The smell here was the same, though he thought he could make out something which he assumed was the musty odour of a room long unused. There was no light. Gradually, his eyes grew accustomed to the darkness, feebly illuminated by the glow from the wine cellar.

He could make out a mattress. A chair. His heart did not seem to know whether to stop or to hammer fit to burst. He went back to the cellar and, in the drawer of a cupboard stocked with glasses and decanters, he found a torch.

A blue washbasin. A chamber pot. The walls of the room were piled high with junk: suitcases, trunks, shelves lined with old books, their bindings blackened.

He stepped towards the mattress and realised he was trembling, he could not breath for the lump in his throat. The beam of the torch faded, but he could see a thin piece of rope lying on top of a pile of rags. He ran his fingertips over the bright colours and noticed that they were mostly strips of fabric cut crudely from bed sheets. He began to rummage through them and pulled out a T-shirt printed with a cartoon character, then a vest and a pair of shorts. There were other children's clothes.

He wiped away the sweat that was coursing down his face, his back like rain.

He turned when he heard a movement behind him. The torch bulb gave out just then and there was nothing but a faint, useless afterglow that made him think he could see shadows moving amid the piles of junk. He stared into the darkness, expecting to see a ghost.

"Pablo?"

Vilar did not see the dawn break. By the time he came back upstairs, the sun was streaming in through every window, causing colours to bloom everywhere he looked. He did not recognise the house he had entered the night before. Everything was suddenly beautiful, peaceful.

It was unbearable. He called Daras and told her the situation, groping to find the words and struggling to utter them. He heard the anger and the fear in his voice while on the other end of the line she struggled to remain calm. She told him she would call the *procureur* and the local police and send the emergency services. She asked him how he was feeling, but he did not know what to say, so he said he would be fine. After they hung up, he went out and sat on the steps in the sunshine to wait for them.

27

He woke because he felt eyes staring at him. At first he could see only the teeming stars, but the sound of water splashing brought him to his feet. There was a dark figure standing in the water some ten metres from him. Its head was covered by a large hood, it was faceless. Still groggy with sleep Victor's mind conjured fantastical visions. Death was standing before him, here on the riverbank. In its invisible hand it probably clutched the mooring rope of the boat and would stop him from leaving. Then the creature move and took shape.

Ears pricked. An eye glittered in the moonlight. A horse. It advanced soundlessly. Standing up to its belly in the water, it stretched its muzzle towards the boy. A white stripe ran from its forehead to its nose. It was black or possibly brown, the colour of night. It did not move.

And yet the power of the river was palpable, the murmur of the current lapping against the bank, the boat, tugging at the mooring line. The current wove its way between the horse's legs and the animal stood, impassive, or perhaps surprised, staring at this boy who had washed up here.

Victor leaned forward and the animal gave a quiet whinny that echoed in the boat. The boy clicked his tongue softly, reached out his hand, stretching his whole body, and petted the nose of the horse which bent its neck slightly, allowing itself to be stroked. Victor could feel hot breath against his fingers, could feel the nostrils flaring, the soft warm skin. "What are you doing here?"

He wanted to wrap his arms around its neck and press his face to this large, gentle head. The horse moved closer. Victor leaned his forehead against the animal's muzzle and the animal stood, motionless, and the boy could hear nothing but the muffled roar of its breath, all the power in a chest that cleaved the water and forced the river to flow on soundlessly.

The horse jerked imperceptibly then moved its head away. It sniffed the water and tapped its hoof. Victor could see it better now, could see the gleam in its eyes, the tuft of hair falling over its forehead. The sky had brightened and gradually everything became visible. The river became bluer. The horse half turned and heaved itself onto the bank. Once on dry land, it looked at the boy and then disappeared into the trees.

The river was once more flowing towards the ocean. Victor could now see the broad mass of water gliding slowly, peacefully, untroubled by the eddies of the rising tide. It seemed to be governed by a universal harmony. The boy untied the rope and used the plank of wood to propel himself into the current. He watched as the island disappeared into the distance, the mass of emerald trees framed against the brightening sky and the fading stars.

He saw the horse between two thickets. It was grazing in a field, black against the shifting brightness of the long grass. Victor kept his eyes on the animal for as long as it remained in sight, then he settled in the bow, staring straight ahead, making no attempt to work out where he was, but simply watching the landscape broaden as the sun rose. He waited, expecting at any moment to see the wall of spray where the river hurtled into the sea. He felt as though he were speeding towards rapids that would hurl him over a waterfall or into dangerous whirlpools. Instinctively, he clung to the sides of the boat. He felt the rush of air against his face.

He had drifted into the very middle of the estuary. The banks flashed past, and quickly disappeared, a single line underscoring the horizon while before him the sky was becoming infinite. He was not thinking about anything, utterly focused on this solitude. He reached behind him and touched the metal urn in his backpack and as he did so, a deafening wail rent the air making him jump in alarm.

Two hundred metres behind was the bow of an ocean liner, white, and sharp, that seemed to fall inexorably towards him like a giant sword. He picked up his plank and struggled to change tack, but the boat simply swung around without moving away from the path of the ship. The siren blared again. He could hear the keening of the water beneath the bow, could see the muddy swell it pushed before it, tall as a ridge carved out by a ploughshare. His arms began to cramp from rowing, the boat seemed locked in the current which dragged it onward and made it impossible to turn. Victor saw the white blade bearing down, now barely twenty metres from him. People leaned over the bulwark, screeching and waving like great dumb birds. A huge wave lifted the boat, tossing Victor sideways, and he barely had time to jump before the boat tipped over and capsized.

Muddy water filled his mouth. The churning of the motor was deafening, a terrifying racket that threatened to burst his eardrums. He surfaced, the sun's glare forcing his eyes closed, water coursing into his lungs until, coughing, he went under again, flailing wildly and in vain to find some purchase. He surfaced once more and saw the capsized boat some metres away. He tried to swim, thrashing around at random and managed to float despite the gobbets of mud that sprayed from his mouth or lodged in his throat until he could hack them up.

His hand slid over the curve of the hull as his head slipped under the water again, but he managed to grab the side and hang on, keeping his head above water, spewing out water and sucking in lungfuls of air. He coughed and spluttered and every time he did so his head banged against the wood.

Then he remember the backpack. The urn. "Manou!"

He plunged back into the water, forcing himself to keep his eyes open, his ears ringing, but very quickly found himself engulfed in a cold, murky heaviness where light itself died as he got deeper. He had to resurface, blinded by the mud, his mouth filled with dirty water. Grunting, he managed to hoist himself onto the upturned boat and lay on his belly, gasping for breath. He spat and breathed in between groans and sobs. The sun and wind dried his hair and his skin leaving him grey with dust, he kept his arms and legs outstretched so as not to fall back into the river, because suddenly this mass of water hurtling towards the ocean frightened him. Because he had been more frightened to die than to live.

When he had got his breath back and his eyes were clear of mud, he thought about his mother at the bottom of this filth and sobbed and asked her to forgive him. He was not sure that she heard him and he could not imagine what her answer would have been. She was gone. The absence stretched away before him across this immensity that dazzled in the sunlight.

He let himself be overwhelmed by exhaustion and grief.

He raised his head when he heard a voice calling his name and the roar of an engine. The sun was higher now. A man was leaning over the side of a patrol boat, reaching out a hand towards him. Another man was holding a red buoy. He felt hands and arms pressing around him and voices asking if he was alright. Faces and peaked caps. Uniforms.

He managed to explain that it was possible that his backpack was stuck under the boat. Two men used a grapnel to turn it over as he watched, holding his breath. There was nothing at the bottom of the boat but a little brownish water.

They offered him water and a sandwich. He reluctantly ate everything he was given and got some of his strength back. Sadness replaced tiredness.

Settled in a narrow cabin, he saw nothing of the return journey. One of the crew sat with him and gave him some chocolate. The boy said nothing. He was thinking of Her at the bottom of the estuary. He wept silently. His tears traced pale tracks through the drying layer of mud. He went up to the bridge as they came alongside in Pauillac. The quay was thronged with police and firemen. Once again he found himself surrounded, being asked if he was alright. Hands pressed against him.

He felt the dry river tug at his skin.

He walked through the crowd and then he saw them and he felt a twinge of happiness. First Nicole and Denis, hugging each other, their eyes red, their faces drawn. Then Marilou, who was smiling, the wind whipping her hair across her face. Julien was there, his face swollen, one eye black, a bandage on his chin. Victor waved and walked towards them.

Further off among the crowd of onlookers, Rebecca called to him. She waved her tanned arm and the gesture made her body sway. She was smiling as he had never seen her smile before.

The remains of three children have been found in a house in Castillon: two boys and a girl, all aged approximately nine or ten. They were buried in the grounds near derelict outbuildings in which a hiding place was discovered, where they may have been imprisoned. Two rings embedded in the wall were probably used to restrain someone, however the fittings were clearly old and no further evidence has been found. In the cellar discovered by Commandant Vilar, the beaten earth floor preserved considerably more evidence: a milk tooth, a small earring, some hair. Soil analysis leads us to believe that one corner of the cellar had been used as a toilet by at least one of the children. Probably over the course of several weeks.

D.N.A. tests have confirmed that the girl was Sonia, who disappeared, aged nine, from the Caen region in 1998. Nothing is known about the two boys. No match has been found in the records of missing children in metropolitan France in the past fifteen years. It is suspected that they were kidnapped abroad or perhaps even bought, potentially in Eastern Europe, which would make identification almost impossible. Forensic pathologists have confirmed that the most recent death dates from approximately five years ago.

Obviously, we have delved into the past of both Jean-Luc Lafon and of his partner Marie-Hélène Cassou. The dates and details of extravagant parties and orgies Vilar uncovered during his investigation have been confirmed and corroborated by a number of witnesses. We have in addition identified those who supplied the cocaine and the *petits-fours*. Various names have circulated, some of them famous. Entertainers, politicians, even a celebrated writer. Television stars. The respective roles of Commandant Pradeau and of Éric Sanz have been clarified and a former *commissaire divisionnaire* who had assigned them minor jobs at these parties has been called before the Police Disciplinary Body.

Little has been confirmed about the paedophile activities of the Lafon couple. An internet file-sharing network has been uncovered but it is impossible to interrogate dead bodies that, overnight, nobody will admit to having known. The identity of the young man whose head was blown off remains unknown. No identity papers. It is impossible, for obvious reasons, to create an e-fit. All of these leads are still being actively pursued.

Éric Sanz is dead; when the police arrived they assumed he had been shot by Commandant Pradeau during a violent altercation. Little was done to establish the facts and, since the case was complex and contained much surprising material, the *juge d'instruction* had been happy to accept the version given by the responding officers.

Laurent Pradeau has been found hanged in his cell at Gradignan prison after his second hearing before the magistrate at which, as before, he refused to answer any questions. He left no note. No explanation.

*

Vilar lets the November rain flow down his windscreen, remembering it all. Remembering the dead, specifically.

He is parked outside the school, sat behind the steering wheel. He is in no hurry. No-one is waiting for him now. He was firmly advised to take a long leave of absence to take stock and to give his superior officers time to think of some other position to which he might be allocated, within the police force or elsewhere. The world quivers and shatters into dozens of soft, shifting slivers as the rain courses down. From time to time the windscreen wiper resets the scene, then once again the world begins to dissolve.

He was there when the J.C.B. stopped digging and the forensic technicians from *l'Identité judiciaire* climbed down into the trench to finish the job. He ran towards them, slipping in the mud. He watched them working with silent, painstaking care, all eyes were focused on the trench and the white figures within it, brushing away the earth. A skull appeared and in that instant Vilar felt the ground slip from under him, hurling him into the pit. Apparently he screamed.

When he came around, a paramedic told him he had been unconscious for an hour but that he was fine.

"Are they finished?"

The paramedic shook his head. It would be a long job. They were trying not to mix up the various sets of bones.

Ten days later Vilar discovered that Pablo was not buried there. He called Ana to tell her. She said nothing. From her breathing, Vilar thought that she was crying. They hung up without another word.

The rain stops and he thinks that the children will be able to go home without getting wet. He sees the lights in the classroom, and children's drawings pinned up here and there. It is 11.23 a.m. The school gates are still closed and there are people waiting outside, always the same people; over time he has come to recognise them. He lays his hand on the gun which he has covered with a cloth. The sun appears from between two clouds, everything becomes dazzling. Behind the windscreen Vilar can see nothing but blinding light, so he gets out of the car and turns away from the sun so that he can see this little street where water gurgles in the gutters and young women chatter in front of the school gates.

He looks at his watch. Two minutes.

He cannot carry on. Pablo is dead, like the children buried in the pit. It was not him, but Vilar saw him. Across time and space. He knows. Over the past weeks, this thought has been slowly taking root in his mind. Now it sprouts in this damp sunshine.

And already the predator is lying in wait, or is on the prowl. For days now, perhaps for months. Somewhere other than here. Obviously.

Vilar bursts into tears and gets back into his car and drives off, turning on the windscreen wipers which cannot wipe away his tears.

He leaves the city and drives for almost an hour. He stops beneath some pine trees in the roar of the west wind. As he crosses the dunes, he screws up his face against the gusts of wind damp with sand and spray.

Finally, he runs towards the ocean that shimmers white-hot with rage.

HERVÉ LE CORRE was born in Paris and is currently teaching in the suburbs of Bordeaux, France, and is the author of several crime fiction novels. He also writes for the literary magazine *Le Passant Ordinaire*. *Talking to Ghosts* was awarded the Grand Prix de Littérature Policière and the Prix Mystère de la Critique.

FRANK WYNNE is a translator from French and Spanish. His translations include works by Michel Houellebecq, Marcelo Figueras' *Independent* Foreign Fiction Prize-shortlisted *Kamchatka*, and *Alex* by Pierre Lemaitre.